Shiloh

G.J. Walker-Smith

Star Promise

Print Edition

© 2015 G.J. Walker-Smith

Cover by Scarlett Rugers, http://www.scarlettrugers.com
Formatting by Polgarus Studio, http://www.polgarusstudio.com

Other Books by G.J Walker-Smith
Saving Wishes (Book One, The Wishes Series)
Second Hearts (Book Two, The Wishes Series)
Sand Jewels (Book 2.5, The Wishes Series)
Storm Shells (Book Three, The Wishes Series)
Secret North (Book Four, The Wishes Series)
Silver Dawn (Book 4.5, The Wishes Series)
Star Promise (Book Five, The Wishes Series)

Contact the author:
https://www.facebook.com/gjwalkersmith
gjwalkersmith@gmail.com
gjwalkersmith.com

For my mother-in-law, Beryl.
The one who enables me to get on with it.

CONTENTS

Prologue
Six years earlier

CHARLI

The stretch of beach in front of the cardboard village was a hotspot for local hawkers peddling their wares. Everything from handmade jewellery to knock-off designer bags were on offer, and one woman controlled the whole operation.

"Necklaces for you, Charli," called Mimi, waving a bunch of beads as she approached. "The best in Kaimte."

Pretending to take a closer look, I leaned over the railing of the veranda. "They're beautiful, Mimi."

Her smile was huge. "All for you."

I shook my head, hoping I looked regretful. Two days from now I'd be New York bound; travelling light was my plan. Being weighted down with beads I'd never wear was nonsensical. "I'm leaving in a few days," I told her. "My bags are full."

Kaimte is a transient place, but news of my departure didn't sit well with Mimi. She stomped onto the veranda and dumped her spoils on a deckchair. "Where are you going?" she asked, hands on hips. "Kaimte is your home now."

For nearly three months it had been. It took a year of travelling for Mitchell and I to finally settle, and the small town on the coast of West Africa was the perfect place for us. The weather was brilliant and life was laid back, but it wasn't enough to hold me.

Over time I'd come to the conclusion that above all else, your heart determines the course of your life, and mine was pulling me toward the French American boy I'd lost my grip on a year earlier.

"It's time to move on," I vaguely explained. "Mitch is staying, though."

She screwed up her face at the mention of his name, which didn't surprise me. Mimi and Mitchell had their differences. One of Mitchell's many part-time jobs was tending the bar at the local pub. When she wasn't flogging dodgy handbags, Mimi worked there too. She thought he was lazy and flaky, which he sometimes was. Mitchell thought that Mimi was crazy, and the mere fact that I agreed with him meant she truly was off kilter.

Faith in superstition was practically her religion. Her whole life was spent warding off invisible threats of karma and bad juju. Mitchell never bought into it, but I found it fascinating. Her every tale was dark and sinister, which probably explained why she was too afraid not to comply with the juju rules.

She once told us that thunderstorms only occur when the devil is beating his wife. "And if you leave your door open," the words hissed as she pointed at me, "he'll come for you too."

Mitchell scoffed at the notion. "Storms are pretty rare in these parts," he noted. "Does that mean he's friendly most of the time?"

Mimi might not have been fond of Mitchell, but I was. He'd spent the past year moulding my smooshed heart back into shape. Nothing fazed him – not even my recent admission that despite his best efforts I was still feeling crushed. I'd cut Adam loose long ago, but there was no getting over him. Most people would've demanded that I try harder and move on once and for all – but not Mitchell Tate. "Get brave, Charli," he demanded. "Toughen up and go after what you want."

It was the shove I needed; and now my bags were packed, much to Mimi's disappointment. She flopped into a chair. "Mitchell won't cope without you," she declared. "He's too dumb."

As harsh as her comment was, I couldn't help smiling. Mitchell was a quiet achiever – unassuming and irresponsible. But underneath the carefree façade was one of the most genuine and brilliant people I'd ever known.

"That wasn't kind, Mimi," I chided. "You know he's a good man."

She grabbed her bundle of beads and pulled them into her lap. "Even good men can be dumb," she argued. "But I will keep my eye on him."

As much as Mitchell insisted he'd be fine without me, I knew I'd still worry. Mimi's offer to watch out for him was comforting. The least I could do in return was buy a necklace or two. I pointed at the pile on her lap. "Can I see?"

Grinning, she rattled them wildly. "Plenty of good juju for you, Charli."

It was a bold claim, but everything about Mimi Traore was bold. A staunch traditionalist, she favoured exquisite West African fashion, and no one wore it better. Her boubous, the loose tunics worn over tightly wrapped skirts, were bright, loud and always teamed with a matching headwrap. Today's ensemble was bright yellow and perfectly pressed. No amount of colourful beads would make my simple pink sundress look that fancy, but Mimi was persistent. She draped a few necklaces around my neck and her dark eyes shone as she explained the power of the glass beads. "The green ones bring you luck," she exclaimed. "And the blue ones will bring you blessed babies."

I whipped the blue necklace off at warp speed. At nineteen, I was not in the market for a baby – blessed or not. I tangled my fingers in the string of green beads at my throat. "Perhaps I should get Mitch a few of these. I'd like to leave him with some good luck."

Mimi wagged her finger. "I have something more powerful for him." The sudden dark edge to her tone made me anxious. "Something very special." She reached into her bag of goodies and pulled out a small calico bag. "Hold out your hands."

She upended a small handful of cloudy white rocks into my cupped hands. Glass beads were a mystery to me, but rocks were my thing. I lifted my head, beaming. "White quartz," I announced knowingly.

"Trick rocks," she corrected. "The devil thinks they're diamonds."

I frowned, which was all the encouragement she needed to explain.

The land around Kaimte was rich in diamonds. They had lain relatively undisturbed for generations, but word eventually got out and people came from far and wide to mine them.

"The devil was on their backs," she hissed. "He made those with black hearts mine them day and night, then deliver them all to him."

According to Mimi people are never just rotten: the devil is the driving force behind every evil deed ever committed. Her faith in that was unshakable.

She picked one of the rocks out of my hand and held it to the light. "Angels filled the diamonds with all the good things," she explained in a much gentler tone. "Love, hope, good health and great wealth. That's why they are so valuable to him. The devil has none of those qualities." The stones clinked as she dropped it back onto the pile. "The angels were furious," she continued. "So they fooled him."

My imagination kicked in, trying to predict the rest of the story before she spoke again – and I was fairly close to the mark. The greedy miners scooped up every gem in sight and delivered them to the devil. But unlike them, he could spot a fake diamond a mile away. Thinking they were worthless, he rejected the quartz stones and cast them into the desert like rubbish.

"The angels started putting all the goodness in the quartz, not the diamonds." Mimi spoke smugly as if she'd hatched the ingenious plan herself. "He didn't know he was throwing away the good juju."

I dropped my head and studied the rocks. I'd never seen uncut diamonds, but some quartz was supposedly a dead ringer. No wonder the devil was confused.

Mimi held the small bag open and I carefully poured the rocks back in. "The trick rocks will look after Mitchell while you're gone," she claimed. "They only aid the pure of heart. He is dumb, but he is good." I laughed out loud at her almost-compliment. She secured the bag with the ribbon tie and handed it to me. "All the good juju he needs is in here. These will save him from harm."

If there was the slightest chance that her claims were true, I had to give it a shot. As capable as Mitchell was, he wasn't unbreakable. That had been proven a few weeks earlier when he was jumped in an alleyway and robbed of our rent money.

I held up the bag. "So what do I do with them?"

Probably thrilled that she'd made a believer out of me, she smiled brightly. "Write a note and put it in the bag. Tell the angels who you wish to protect," she instructed.

"Okay, that's easy enough."

"Then hide them close to where Mitchell sleeps." She wagged a finger. "But he must never find them."

That was decidedly trickier. Hiding anything in our barren shack was impossible. The last thing I'd tried to conceal was my diary, which Mitchell had found and unashamedly read from cover to cover.

"I'll try," I said unconvincingly.

Mimi lurched forward, grabbed my hand and held it much too tightly. "You must do it, Charli."

Her demand was as rough as the so-called trick rocks, but I understood the desperation. Superstition is a senseless fear. It requires no proof, just faith. And Mimi Traore had plenty.

I tried to put her worried mind at ease. "I'll hide them, Mimi," I promised, trying to wrestle my hand free. "Mitchell will never know."

She picked a pinch of sand off the deck and threw it into the wind, mumbling something in Afrikaans. Clearly it wasn't meant for my ears, but the performance was unsettling.

My soul held enough belief in superstition to follow her instructions. The day before I left Kaimte, I wrote my note to the angels and hid the trick rocks in a place Mitchell would never look.

The rest was up to the juju universe.

Meat Recovery

SHILOH

Gladys Evans was a sweet old lady – unless she had a skinful. Then she became a geriatric weapon of mass destruction. Today, she was creating havoc in the local supermarket.

We arrived to find her cornered in the meat section by a nervous deli manager wielding a broomstick. I couldn't blame him for being cautious. By all appearances, Gladys' bender had been ongoing for a while. Her snowy white hair was frizzy and wild, her clothes were dishevelled, and I could literally smell the booze wafting off her.

"Identify yourselves," she demanded as we approached.

We continued our cautious walk. "You know who we are, Mrs Evans," I calmly replied. "We're the police."

"Stay back!" Her slurred voice was hardly authoritative, but I stopped. My partner Allan wasn't as compliant.

"What are you doing, Gladys?" he asked, continuing toward her. "Other than making a fool of yourself again."

His blasé tone riled her even more. "Get back, copper!" The old woman staggered back and reached into her coat pocket. "I've got a gun!"

This wasn't our first rodeo. We dealt with Gladys' shenanigans at least once a week, but the threat of a gun was new. Erring on the side of caution, I moved my hand to my holster, which turned out to be pointless.

There was no gun. In an absurd move that completely summed up my policing career in the country town of Lawler, Gladys pulled out a lamb shank.

"Get back or I'll shoot!" she warned, thrusting it forward as if she was trying to pull a trigger.

Unfazed by the craziness, Allan made his move, hooking his arm around the wannabe assassin and gently leading her to the door. "Time to go, Gladys," he said simply.

Perhaps realising she'd reached the end of the line, Gladys dropped the meat. "You have to braise lamb slowly," she muttered. "That way it'll be lovely and tender."

Allan chuckled. "Are you telling an Irishman how to cook lamb?"

"I've never trusted the Irish," she said. "They're nothing but a nation of drunks."

***

Lawler had no claim to fame. That made the blink-and-you'll-miss-it bush town in Western Australia's southwest an ideal place for those seeking a quiet life.

I hadn't landed there seeking a quieter life. I was posted to Lawler straight out of the police academy. Non-stop action and adventure was my plan, but I'd since lowered my expectations. In the year I'd spent there, I'd dealt with nothing more exciting than drunken old ladies and speeding drivers.

Allan Kelly, the town's police sergeant, didn't share my disillusionment. The Dublin native relished the laid-back lifestyle Lawler afforded him. It was such a change of pace for him that he jokingly referred to his current position as semi-retirement. "Gardaí from Ballymun deserve early retirement," he reasoned.

After years of policing in the tough areas of Dublin, Sergeant Kelly's no-nonsense approach when dealing with those on the wrong side of the law was perfectly understandable. He dealt with me in exactly the same way, cutting me no slack whatsoever. That became apparent as he helped Gladys to the car. The old lady picked that moment to confess that she'd shoplifted more than a lamb shank.

Maintaining his firm grip on her arm, Allan opened the car door. "What else do you have?"

"A pack of sausages," she replied blithely.

"Where?"

Gladys dropped her head, telling us everything without speaking.

"Oh, sweet Jesus," said Allan, angling her toward me. "She's all yours, Shiloh."

Retrieving a tray of stolen meat from a tanked old lady's pants wasn't the most pleasant of tasks but I was nothing if not diligent. I grabbed the pack of sausages and dropped them on the pavement.

"Anything else?" I asked.

"No," she replied. "The cutlets wouldn't fit."

***

I learned a long time ago that not everyone can be helped. Gladys' career as a serial boozer was long and distinguished. The best we could do was hold her until she sobered up, which seemed to be taking forever. By late afternoon she'd belted out her full repertoire of favourite songs, including a rambling rendition of *Danny Boy* that she dedicated to her "favourite Irish copper".

In keeping with the rest of the town, the police station was tiny. The old stone building consisted of a couple of offices, a front reception area and a single holding cell at the end of the hall – perfectly adequate for a police force of two in a town with a ridiculously low crime rate. Unfortunately for us, it also meant that there was no escaping the noise.

Allan leaned back in his chair and tapped his pen on the desk. "Do you think she takes requests?"

"Please don't ask," I begged. "I couldn't stand it."

For a short moment my sergeant's hearty chuckle almost drowned out Gladys' crooning. "Make her some coffee," he suggested. "That might quieten her down."

Anything was worth a try. I headed for the kitchen and concocted a brew strong enough to sober up a small army and delivered it to the holding cell. When I opened the door, I realised we'd only been privy to half the show. Not only was Gladys singing, she was dancing – sashaying around the small cell as if she had an adoring audience looking on.

"How are you feeling, Mrs Evans?"

Gladys stopped singing and spun giddily to face me. "Fighting fit," she replied.

I smiled and handed her the mug. "That's good to hear."

She sat on the small steel bench and glanced around the cell. "I don't think much of the décor here."

There was nothing to like about stark grey walls and bare concrete floor. That was the point.

"Why are you such a menace?" I asked.

She brought her coffee to her lips and smiled. "Because I'm free, Shiloh."

"But you're not," I pointed out. "You're in the lockup."

Gladys set her mug down and put her shaky hand on her chest. "My heart is free," she clarified. "No one can tame a wild heart. I will sing and dance and kiss the sun forever."

It sounded like a romantic notion but wasn't. The whole situation was dreadfully sad. The raucous woman of a few hours earlier was gone. However free her heart might've been, she looked old, frail and beaten. Somewhere along the line, life had walloped her hard.

"You need to get out and kiss the sun once in a while too, girly," she added. "You're too young to be such a stick-in-the-mud."

It wasn't the first time she'd accused me of kyboshing all things fun and reckless. Every time Gladys ended up in custody she strongly voiced her opinion that the line I walked was far too straight and narrow.

"I'm a police officer," I reminded her. "We're notorious sticklers for rules."

"Oh, live a little," she grumbled. "Remind yourself that you're alive. I could teach you a thing or two."

Gladys Evans wasn't mentor material. I saw nothing more than a sad, old, drunken thief, but it wasn't my job to enlighten her. My job was to keep her safe and protected from herself.

I urged her to get some sleep, backed out of the room and pulled the door closed.

***

Being threatened with a lamb shank was the most excitement we saw that week – right up until Friday afternoon. Just before five a man strolled through the front door of the station, his intense frown hinting that the reason for his visit was either complicated or unpleasant. I didn't care to find out which. Hopeful of getting out on time, I continued shoving files into the filing cabinet.

The man thumped his hand on the service bell. "I'm looking for Constable Brannan."

We were both in plain view, which meant he was arrogant. Sergeant Kelly does not do arrogant. He pushed his chair away from his desk and rose to his feet. "We're all looking for someone," he replied, wandering to the counter. "I'm looking for a decent barber." He smoothed down the top of his hair. "My wife thinks I look like I've been in a fight with a lawnmower."

"Constable Brannan," he repeated. "Is she here?"

"I'll check." Allan turned to me. "Are you here, Constable Brannan?"

I bumped the drawer of the filing cabinet shut with my hip. "It depends on who's asking."

The man reached into his wallet and pulled out a business card. Allan snatched it from him as soon as it was within reach.

"Agent Dan Grace," he read aloud like a first grader. "Australian Federal Police."

His profile fit the bill: stiff suit, stiffer hair and a stiff expression. The curt detective might've been good looking if he smiled, but at that point it didn't seem possible.

"You and I need to talk," he rudely demanded.

My mind spun in a hundred directions. I had no idea what I'd done to deserve the attention of the AFP, but it couldn't have been anything good. I pointed toward the small office to my right. "We can talk in there," I said. "As long as you don't bite."

I think I almost saw him smile. *Almost.*

Agent Grace strolled into the office leaving me to follow his lead. By the time I closed the door behind me, he'd made himself at home. "Take a seat, Constable." He leaned back in the chair and undid the buttons on his suit jacket. "This might take a while."

I stood firm with my back against the door. "What's this about?"

I hadn't noticed the bulging manila folder he was carrying until he dropped it on the desk. Then all I could focus on was my name scrawled across the cover.

"Am I under investigation?" I asked, grasping at straws.

"Of sorts." He waved to a chair. "Sit."

I did as I was told, but didn't go quietly. "I've only been on the force for fourteen months," I said pointedly. "I haven't had a chance to do anything crooked, and if I was that way inclined it's hardly likely to go down in a backwater town like Lawler."

"Do you like working here?" he asked.

I shrugged. "It has its moments."

"Tell me about it," he urged.

I had no idea what he wanted to hear. With limited choices, I decided to share the highlight of my week. "Well, on Tuesday I wrestled a packet of sausages from a drunken old lady's pants."

He laughed, disproving my theory that his face was made of stone. It put me slightly at ease – until he picked up the folder. "The police force wasn't your first choice of career, was it?" he asked, thumbing through the loose pages.

I folded my arms tightly across my chest. "No, but I'm guessing you know that already."

"Four years in the Navy," he read from a page. "Tell me about that."

The constant demand for information was like an irritating catchphrase. "How about you tell me something," I suggested grumpily. "What do you want from me?"

Dan closed the folder and dropped it back on the desk. "You have to give a little to get a little, Constable."

I quickly realised I wasn't going to win. I was becoming more frustrated with every passing second. Dan just looked bored.

"I did my time and then got out," I vaguely explained. "It wasn't for me."

"Did you get a trade qualification?"

I motioned to the folder with an upward nod. "You tell me."

He looked me dead in the eyes, speaking with absolute surety. "Abel Seaman, Shiloh Brannan. Electronics Technician."

I shrugged, feigning apathy. "You've done your homework."

Now I just needed to figure out why. My stint in the Navy was uneventful for the most part. I signed up at eighteen and got out at twenty-two with a qualification I'd never used since.

"What came next?" he asked, moving the conversation along.

Agent Grace wasn't overly interested in hearing about the year I spent bumming around Europe after being discharged from the Navy. Nor did he care about my short gig as a telemarketer when I got home. I got the distinct impression that I wasn't going to be able to tell him anything he didn't already know. The folder on the desk led me to think he was well versed in all things Shiloh Brannan.

"Security work," I mumbled. "At a bank."

He frowned. "When?"

"Two years ago." I shrugged. "Maybe three."

He grabbed the folder and flicked through the contents.

I stared at him, enjoying the slight look of concern on his face as he pored over papers. "What's the matter, Dan?" I asked. "Did your research minions leave that part out?"

His eyes locked mine and the fleeting moment of triumph I'd felt was gone. "You never worked for a bank," he accused. "You did a nine month stint up north as a security officer at the Jorge Creek Diamond Mine."

"And hated every minute of it," I revealed.

Even telemarketing beat working for Jorge Creek. It was by far the most boring job I'd ever had, and for some reason I told him so.

"Why?" he asked curiously.

"Have you ever seen an uncut diamond?"

He shook his head.

"Very uninspiring," I told him. "Perhaps that's why no one bothered to steal any while I worked there."

"Is that what you were hoping for?"

"Absolutely," I replied. "That's the only reason I took the job."

There was no shame in admitting it. I naively expected that working security at a diamond mine would be hugely exciting. If I'd had my way, crooked employees would've been trying to make off with buckets of sparkly gems on a daily basis. The reality was much different. No one ever stole a thing, and diamonds in their raw form aren't remotely sparkly.

"So let me get this straight." He leaned back in his chair and flicked the end of his tie. "The military wasn't exciting enough, security work wasn't exciting enough, and then you tried your hand at the police force."

And a year down the track, that wasn't shaping up to be exciting enough either.

"Yep." I slapped both palms down on the table. "And here I am – fishing sausages out of old ladies' dacks."

It sounded extra pathetic when said out loud, but Dan didn't seem to notice. His focus was back on the folder as he neatened up the inside pages. "I'm glad I came here, Constable Brannan," he said. "I think you're exactly who we're looking for."

"Tell me about that," I suggested.

"Jorge Creek has several mining operations," he began. "One of them is in West Africa – a place called Kaimte."

"Never heard of it."

Dan stood and walked to the window, lifting a slat of the blind to peek outside. "It's not as large as their Australian mine, but they see a little more of the action you're seeking."

A laugh escaped me. "I'm not looking for action."

He turned to face me, frowning as if I'd just told the blackest kind of lie. "Over a million dollars' worth of diamonds go missing from the processing plant each month," he revealed. "We're almost certain it's an inside job."

Detectives are trained to unnerve people with their intimidating words but AFP agents play on a whole other level. They command attention with steely glares and long pauses. To escape his eyes, I dropped my head and began picking invisible lint off my pants. "What does that have to do with me?"

Agent Grace sat down, clasped his hands and finally offered an answer. "As a past employee, you're well versed in Jorge Creek operational procedures. We need someone on the inside – preferably a security officer."

The absurdity didn't end there.

"You tick all the boxes, Shiloh."

I jumped to my feet, gearing up to put an end to the nonsense. "I don't have a box to tick, Agent Grace."

Ignoring me, he calmly slid the folder in my direction. "I beg to differ."

"Look, Dan," I began. "Everything in that file is like a practice run." I drummed my finger on my handwritten name. "I don't even know if the police force is for me. I'm a year in and still undecided."

It was the absolute truth. At twenty-six I'd never stuck to anything because nothing ever held my interest. To date, everything from career choices to yoga classes had been a flash in the pan.

The steely agent glanced around the small office. "Being stuck in Lawler won't help your cause. It's hardly inspiring."

My shoulders dropped, which was the only hint of resignation I was prepared to show him. He was right and he knew it.

"Why me?" I asked. "What could I possibly have to offer?"

"Knowledge of company procedures. Police training." He ticked off each point on his fingers, "Security training. Meat recovery."

As much as I fought against it, his smile was contagious. "I'm still not exactly sure why you're here," I confessed. "What do you want?"

The cloak and dagger was gone. For the first time since walking into the station, AFP Agent Dan Grace made his intentions very clear. He hadn't come all the way to Lawler to interrogate me. He'd come to recruit me.

***

I was sworn to secrecy before he finally left. "There's not a person on earth you're free to discuss this with," Dan warned as he got to the door. "If you want to know more, you call me."

I took the business card he thrust at me and promised to at least think about the idea of an undercover stint with the AFP. Perhaps realising he wasn't going to get one, he abandoned his initial demand for an immediate answer and agreed to give me a day to think about it.

I probably wasn't cut out for the job he had in mind. I broke his first rule the instant his car pulled out of the car park by running next door to the Sergeant's house to tell Allan everything.

The police station and adjoining house were as old as the town. The heritage listed building was quaint and charming, with a garden to match. Sergeant Kelly couldn't take credit for any of it. His wife Lynette was the one with the magical green thumb. I slowed my walk as I made my way up to the house, distracted by the aroma of the jasmine hedge lining the path.

"Don't you be picking my flowers," warned a familiar Irish brogue. "I know how many are there."

I quickly scanned the yard searching for the tetchy Irish woman. Lynette finally appeared, walking across the immaculate lawn cradling a black rabbit like a baby.

"Dinner?" I teased.

"He should be," she grumbled, brushing her blonde her from her face with her free hand. "Furry little bastard has been digging up my carrots. He's a hopping cliché."

Her ire wasn't the least bit convincing. The Kelly household was a veritable menagerie. Lynette had a soft spot for all manner of stray animals, and almost all of them were permanent residents. Her promise of rehousing them hardly ever held, and Allan seemed to have given up nagging her about it.

"Come inside," she urged, walking us up the path. "I want to show you the joey."

My eyes widened. "You have a kangaroo now?"

"His mother got hit by a car," she replied. "But he'll be alright – unlike this rascal." The black rabbit scurried away as soon as she lowered him to the ground. "Watch yourself, bunny," she warned. "I've got a crockpot with your name on it."

Much like her husband, Lynette Kelly was all bark and absolutely no bite. She didn't suffer idiots – even those of the furry variety. I wasn't sure if it was an Irish trait or a Kelly one, but either way I appreciated it.

"Stay for dinner," Lynette demanded.

Before I could answer, Allan appeared on the porch. "You're in for a treat tonight, Shiloh," he taunted. "We're having lamb shanks."

***

As desperate as I was to tell them my news, I managed to hold off until after dinner. I expected tutting and disbelieving chuckles upon hearing of the job offer I'd received. It would've completely validated my opinion that the whole idea was ludicrous. What I wasn't expecting was stone cold silence and blank expressions.

"I haven't committed to anything yet," I added, desperate for a response. "He gave me until tomorrow to think about it."

Both of them continued the silent stare down from across the table. The only movement came from Jenson, the oversized brown Labrador. He slowly approached from the living room and unceremoniously dumped a couple of soggy jigsaw pieces on my lap, which I quickly knocked to the floor.

"Are they corner pieces?" asked Allan listlessly. "He only ever eats the corner pieces."

I didn't get a chance to answer. Lynette snatched our plates and loudly stacked them one on top of the other. "Talk some sense into her, Allan," she ordered. "I beg of you."

However confusing it might've been, that was her only input. Lynette stormed out of the room with the fat old Labrador in slow pursuit.

Allan managed a smile, but his handsome face was full of concern. "She worries," he said simply.

"There's no need to," I weakly replied.

"Working undercover isn't easy, Shiloh," he told me. "It's dangerous. You must realise that."

Until then, the notion of putting myself in harm's way hadn't even crossed my mind. I'd been concentrating on the thrill factor. Nabbing international diamond thieves seemed far more appealing than busting petty shoplifters.

The rose coloured glasses I wore were probably inherited from my mother. I'd only been out of high school a week when I sat my parents down and told them that I'd enlisted in the navy.

The parental concern was entirely my father's. "How will you cope if you're sent into combat, Shiloh?" he worriedly asked. "You could be killed."

My mother piped up. "She'll be fine, Steve," she assured him. "I'm sure they'll give her a gun."

Much to my father's relief I never did see much action, even after two deployments. What I did see were a few parts of the world that I would never have visited otherwise. I also gained a kick-arse appreciation for order and discipline. I like structure and rules, which is why the police force was the obvious choice when it came to changing careers. Apprehending crooks was supposed to be the icing on the cake – except Lawler had no cake.

"I can take care of myself," I pointlessly defended.

"You'll have to," Allan replied. "The minute you're thrown into the mix, you're on your own."

I downed the last of the wine in my glass, buying time while I thought things through. I still couldn't focus on the risk involved. I was more intent on deciding whether I had the nous and experience to do the job, and what would happen if I couldn't.

"Are you ready to give up your whole life?" Allan asked, still trying to tip the scale of reason. "If you take this on, Shiloh Brannan will be no more.

You'll be given a new identity, which is fine until you wake up one morning and realise that every single aspect of the life you're living is a lie."

I knew he was speaking from experience. Many quiet days on patrol were made brighter by my sergeant's tales of his time in the Gardaí. Four of those had been spent undercover in the Organised Crime Division. He'd seen the very best and the very worst that life had to offer, including the death of his partner during a botched bank robbery.

"Will you be mad if I go?" My voice was unreasonably small. He was my boss, not my father, but when I was first posted to Lawler, the Kellys took me under their wing – just like every other stray they selflessly adopted. In a sense, they *were* family, and their opinion mattered to me.

"Never." His brown eyes crinkled at the edges as he smiled. "I'll support you all the way."

The strength of his answer was hugely reassuring, but he wasn't my biggest obstacle. His wife probably had a Crockpot with my name on it.

"Do you think Lynette will come around to the idea?"

"Never in a million years," she interrupted, storming back into the room. "I'm not going to be the one to call your mother and tell her you've been murdered by drug dealers."

We were getting a little off track. I had no idea why drug dealers had rated a mention, but knew better than to question her. Lynette thumped down in her chair, tightly folding her arms across her chest while she scowled at me.

"Don't you worry, Shiloh," soothed Allan. "*I'll* call your mother and tell her you've been murdered."

"Thanks, I think."

He grinned. "No problem at all."

"You're both bloody fools." Lynette thumped both palms on the table and pushed her chair back. "I'm going to make coffee."

I was looking forward to the reprieve, but her exit was delayed. Jenson appeared in the doorway looking as guilty as a fat Labrador with a cupcake in his mouth could.

"Oh, sweet, Jesus," muttered Lynette, prising his jaw open. She waved what was left of the cupcake at him. "This is the end of the line," she chided. "It's doggy boot camp for you, fatso. First thing Monday morning."

His brown ears went back, he slowly wagged his tail and his epic look of shame intensified.

"I think you've hurt his feelings," suggested Allan. "You know he's sensitive about his weight."

Lynette turned back, looking ten times guiltier than the dog. I was doing all I could not to laugh, and a quick glance across the table showed that Allan was close to cracking too.

"I was harsh, wasn't I?" She turned back to Jenson and handed him the contraband cake. "I'm sorry, boy. You're not fat. You're just a little husky."

It was the gentlest tone I'd ever heard her use. It wasn't the least bit believable, but Jenson seemed to buy it. Cupcake in mouth, he waddled to his basket in the living room.

"Now," muttered Lynette, smoothing down her hair as she continued to the kitchen. "About that coffee."

As soon as she was gone, the giggle that had almost become painful tumbled out of my mouth.

"You could take a leaf out of his book," Allan said, motioning to the dog with an upward nod. "Jenson's the best undercover operative I've ever known. He could steal the crown jewels of England, blame it on the nearest Beefeater and make a clean getaway."

I frowned, confused. To me, Jenson's cupcake heist didn't exactly scream success. "He got busted."

"Being undercover is all about creating illusions," Allan explained. "You need to pretend and create to get the job done. Do you understand?"

I nodded but said no.

"Jenson just played Netty like a fiddle," he continued. "His mind was on the mission and his eyes were on the prize. He's a genius."

Unconvinced, I turned to study the crooked old dog who was now fast asleep. All that was left of the cupcake was the red paper wrapper on the carpet.

"Sorry, Sergeant," I replied. "I just don't see it."

Allan's wry smile broadened. He stood up and made his way over to the dog's basket. Jenson tumbled to the side as he lifted the ratty old cushion, but he barely opened his eyes before settling back into position. "Do you see this?"

I craned my neck, shocked by the sight of at least ten more red cupcake wrappers hiding under the cushion.

"He played the part and got the job done," Allan said proudly. "He let Netty think she caught him red handed. She'll never blame him for the rest of the haul because she thinks he's too dumb to get away with it. That was part one."

I'd never been more desperate to hear a part two in all my life. Mercifully, the intermission was brief. Probably wary of Lynette's impending arrival, he sat back down and continued.

"Part two." Allan held two fingers in the air. "He charmed her with pitiful looks and a wagging tail." He looked across at Jenson. "He's a handsome bastard and he knows how to use it to his advantage."

A bad case of the giggles overtook me again. "Who'll take the fall for him?" I asked, barely composing myself.

Allan leaned down and whispered, "Well, between you and me, he's never had much time for the cats."

My eyes widened. "Cats eat cake?"

Allan straightened up in his chair. "It doesn't matter either way," he replied. "Jenson did his homework. Those cats are done for." He swiped his hand across his neck in a cutthroat motion. "Stitched them up good and proper."

"Perhaps I should ask him for some tips," I joked.

"The formula is simple." Allan spoke quietly and seriously, sucking every ounce of humour out of the conversation. "Look like the innocent flower, but be the serpent under it, Shiloh," he instructed. "If you can manage that, you might just make it through."

***

Three days after agreeing to take Dan up on his job offer, I was gearing up to kiss life in Lawler goodbye. A temporary posting to the city was the official explanation for my quick exit, which meant my position at the Lawler station would be held until I returned.

"If you don't get murdered," grumbled Lynette when I told her.

Ignoring her gripe for obvious reasons, I pulled her into a tight hug. "I'm going to miss you, Netty."

However disgruntled she might've been, she held me tightly. "Protect your soul at all costs, my girl." Her Irish brogue made it sound like an especially important command. "It's the only truth you'll have for a while."

Leaving the Kellys behind was one of the hardest things I'd ever had to do. A drawn-out goodbye would've been impossible to endure so I was glad it happened quickly.

All boxes were checked. My bags were packed, my furniture was in storage and, for now, I'd let my adoptive family go.

Shiloh Brannan was officially off the grid.

***

Agent Grace wasn't the friendliest man I'd ever met, but I soon realised that his gruff demeanour during our first meeting was actually his sweet tone. My last day in the country was spent holed up in his office while he drilled me with information. There was no need for me to read the contents of the two files he'd thumped on the desk in front of me. He did it for me – several times over.

"How did you find out so much information?" I asked curiously.

He hesitated, perhaps unwilling to answer. "We have another operative in Kaimte," he finally replied. "All your contact with us will happen through him."

"So how do I find him?"

Dan shook his head. "You don't. He'll find you when the time is right."

The cloak and dagger frustrated me no end. Every last detail of the operation was on a need-to-know basis. The AFP needed to know everything, but apparently I didn't.

"Awesome," I muttered. "I look forward to meeting him."

"These are the only two men you need to focus on." He pressed a hand on each folder. "Do you understand?"

"Yes."

"They're not lightweights, Shiloh," he reminded me for the millionth time.

"Okay."

My one-word answers pissed him off. Dan exhaled a long breath and leaned so far back in his chair that I worried it might tip over. "Don't underestimate them."

That was never going to happen. The bulging files in front of me held a wealth of information, and it wasn't the stuff of fairy tales. I'd finally recognised that the strange sensation buzzing through my body was fear. I just wasn't prepared to show it to Agent Grace.

"I can do this," I said confidently. "One of these men has a diamond fetish, and I'm going to find out who it is."

Surprisingly, Dan laughed, a deep chuckle I'd never heard from him before. "I hope you do."

"Who's your money on?" I leaned forward and slapped my hand down on the file to my left. "Tweedledum?" My other hand hit the file on the right. "Or Tweedledee?"

He barely paused for thought. "Tweedledum," he replied, motioning to the file with a nod. "I just need you to get me the proof."

***

Two hours before I was due to leave for the airport, a highly-strung blonde woman stormed Dan's office. I probably should've questioned why she was dragging my luggage behind her, but I was too focused on her shoes. I'd never seen anyone team a pair of white sneakers with a tight black pencil skirt and blazer before – even in Lawler. It was such an odd match that I questioned her about it.

The woman looked down at her feet. "I cover more ground in these," she explained. "Heels slow me down."

Still perplexed, I nodded.

"I've been through your luggage," she added, pulling my suitcase forward. "It's good to go."

I must've looked as annoyed as I felt when I jumped to my feet because Dan moved quickly to explain. "We've taken out anything that might be detrimental to your cover."

My angry stance crumbled as my shoulders dropped. Even I had to concede that their scrutiny made sense. "Fine," I muttered.

Dan reached into his desk drawer, grabbed a large envelope and upended the contents onto his desk. One by one, he pointed out each item. "Phone, passport, credit cards."

I snatched the passport up and studied the details closely. The picture I'd posed for the day before wasn't any kinder than my real passport photo, but the name made me smile. Choosing a bogus surname had been the only part of the process that I'd had any say in.

"It has to be something simple," Dan instructed. "Something you'll remember."

I volunteered an answer at warp speed. "Jenson," I replied.

Agent Grace signed off on it without question. If he had asked the origin, I probably would've lied. Taking the name of a fat brown Labrador probably wasn't the done thing.

Ne'er-do-well

MITCHELL

The call of the sea had always been deafening, which is why Kaimte was the perfect place for me.

Perfect surf conditions conjured up by the South Atlantic Ocean is the drawcard for diehard beach lovers. Cheap rent and the low cost of living was a plus too, but village life isn't for everyone. Most people can't survive long without the mod cons of supermarkets, tarmac roads and a constant internet connection, but it was an adventure I'd been living for nearly seven years.

Being a beach bum had its obvious perks, but it was hardly productive. I spent the first few years doing the bare minimum to scrape by, working the odd labouring job during the day and bartending at night.

The bar owner at the time was a salty old bloke called Nelson. He had a filthy mouth and a low tolerance for fools. I'd seen him turf blokes out the door for looking at him the wrong way, which is no mean feat when you're seventy-six and crippled by arthritis.

As rough and tough as Nelson was, poor health eventually beat him. After thirty years of pouring warm beers, he was forced to return to his hometown of Durban – but not before tying up a few loose ends.

"I'll sell you this joint, Aussie," he offered out of the blue. "Ten thousand dollars and it's yours."

It sounded like a bargain, but wasn't. The Crown and Pav Bar wasn't exactly upmarket – two shipping containers welded together on the beach hardly screamed class. But there was an upside. It was the only pub in town, and everyone drank there.

Eking out enough of a living to pay rent and buy food is fine when you're twenty, but there comes a point when it transitions to being pathetic and lazy. For that reason alone, I agreed to buy it on the spot.

Predictably, I didn't have ten grand. At the time, I didn't have ten cents. Pushing pride aside, I phoned my father and asked him for a loan. He obliged, but not before sinking the boot in. "Hopefully it'll make a man out of my ne'er-do-well son."

My dad no longer has any financial interest in the Crown and Pav. After three years of hard slog, I managed to pay him back every cent that I owed him, plus interest. The ne'er-do-well had finally come good.

Cardboard Village

SHILOH

I stepped off the small charter plane and pulled in a long breath of pure desert heat. Lawler was isolated, but it had nothing on Kaimte. Lawler had roads and buildings and people. From what I could tell, all Kaimte had was sand, low-lying scrub and flies.

What the hell had I gotten myself into?

I stood on the edge of the dirt runway and watched the small Cessna take off, feeling utter relief when it was gone. Nerves had first kicked in when I boarded the plane in Cape Town. Being vigilant was not to my advantage. I would've fared much better had I not noticed that my seat wasn't actually bolted to the floor, and the constant flickering of the overhead reading light had me convinced that fire was about to break out in the cabin at any moment. The three-hour flight felt like ten, and I wasn't feeling any safer now that I was on the ground.

At least I wasn't alone.

I turned to see a man running toward me frantically waving a stack of papers. "Mrs Shiloh! Mrs Shiloh!"

I took a step back as he ground to a halt in front of me.

"I have your visa," he explained. "You need to come with me."

His voice held zero authority, and so did his presence. He couldn't have been more than five feet tall with a boyish face that perfectly matched his slight stature. My eyes drifted to the company emblem on the pocket of his khaki shirt. He was a Jorge Creek Diamond Mine employee.

"My name is Baako." His white smile was especially brilliant against the contrast of his dark skin. "Whatever you need, I will get."

"The company sent you?" I asked.

Baako made a grab for my suitcase. "Yes. I am the meet and greet man."

His job title was exactly as it implied. All I had to do while Baako quibbled with the customs officer over the validity of my paperwork was breathe, which wasn't easy. The heat in the windowless room was stifling, and the slow rotation of the ceiling fan didn't help one iota. By the time I got out of there, I was close to throwing up.

Baako looked worried. "Your car." He pointed to a white Toyota Prado parked on the verge. "Your boss will take you to your house. It will be cool in the car."

The car *was* much cooler, but so was the atmosphere. The man in the driver's seat made no attempt to greet me as I got in. If anything, he looked inconvenienced by my arrival.

Baako loaded my luggage and handed me his card. "You can call me," he offered. "Whatever, whenever."

My so-called boss didn't give me a chance to thank him. Without warning, he sped off leaving the poor bloke eating dust. My hands gripped the sides of my seat as we barrelled along the dirt road, but I refused to speak until he did.

"You won't last a week here," he finally predicted.

He was decidedly English, but the sexy accent did him no favours. His reflective aviator sunglasses and the Bluetooth earpiece stuck to his ear weren't advantageous either. He was a dick and looked the part.

"I'm looking forward to proving you wrong," I replied strongly.

He glanced across at me, almost cracking a smile. "I'm Glen Harris."

"Shiloh Jenson."

"I'm head of security," he explained.

I knew exactly who he was. He was Tweedledee.

Glen's position within the company made him an obvious person of interest. Few people on site had as much access as him, but suspicion wasn't enough. The AFP needed proof, and it was my job to get it.

"You report to me, and only me," he added.

"Aye, aye, captain."

Nothing about Glen Harris intimidated me. I was well aware of my role. Little did he know, I reported to someone far higher up the ladder than him.

***

Glen wasn't exactly helpful. After casually informing me that he hadn't bothered organising any company accommodation for me, he dropped me off on the outskirts of town at a place he referred to as the cardboard village.

"Most expats live here," he said through the gap in the window. "Talk to a man called Leroy. He might be able to rent you something."

Knowing he was about to speed away at any second, I took a step back.

"I'll pick you up here on Monday morning." The car was rolling forward as he spoke. "Five o'clock. If you're late, I'm not waiting."

***

Dragging a thirty-kilo suitcase along the beach is no mean feat but I somehow managed, passing the entire row of shacks before finally stumbling upon Leroy. The grey-haired old man was sitting on the veranda of the only house that looked habitable. "What do you want?" he roared.

"I'm looking for Leroy."

He smashed his cane down on the deck. "You've found him. Now what do you want?"

I purposefully kept the conversation short, which seemed to work in my favour. After minimal explanation, Leroy agreed to rent me one of the abominable shacks. "I've only got one available."

"I only need one," I replied.

"Just came vacant," he continued. "The last tenant took off in a hurry. Left all his belongings behind."

I was nodding before he even finished speaking. "I'll take it."

For some reason, Leroy threw his head back and laughed – a derisive cackle that made me nervous. "I need the first month in advance."

"Fine."

I would've agreed to anything at that point. I'd had less than two hours sleep in as many days. All I wanted was a shower and a decent bed. The irony was, I knew I wasn't going to get it.

I waited on the sand while Leroy fetched the keys, and then followed him at a snail's pace as he headed down the beach to shack number fifty-nine – an impossible address considering there were only fourteen shacks.

"Well, this is it," he finally announced, smashing his cane against the bottom step. "Home sweet home."

I studied the ramshackle cabin. The only thing that seemed to be holding the small timber structure together was the peeling paint, and when I straightened up, I realised the whole place was on a lean.

"Is it safe?" I asked incredulously.

"Do you have another option?" he asked.

"No."

"Exactly." Using his cane to steady himself, Leroy threw his head back and guffawed again.

"Do I need to sign a lease or something?"

"No," he replied, composing himself in an instant. "The rules are simple. Pay your rent or you're out. No parties or you're out. No fighting or you're out."

"An unlikely scenario," I interrupted.

Leroy pointed his cane at me and grinned. "Welcome to the cardboard village, Aussie."

***

Within ten minutes of being in the shack, I vowed to find myself somewhere else to live. I was all for integrating with the locals – it was necessary – but even I had limits.

The last tenant must've really been in a hurry when he took off. From what I could tell, he'd left empty handed. I had no idea what to do with his personal effects, but I sure as hell wasn't going to store some strange bloke's belongings.

In the only kitchen drawer that actually opened, I found a roll of garbage bags. I wasn't completely ruthless in my spring-cleaning, electing only to bag up his clothes. Considering the only possessions I had were wardrobe related, pots and pans would probably come in handy.

I dumped the bags on the veranda, flopped down on the beanbag and quickly fell asleep.

Compatriot

MITCHELL

I'm not exactly a monk. I've brought girls home before, but I'd never arrived home to find one already there waiting for me.

I had no idea who the woman sleeping in my house was, but I was curious to find out.

"Hey, Goldilocks." I nudged the beanbag with my foot. "What's the matter with the bed? Mattress too hard?"

She jumped to her feet quicker than I thought possible. "Who are you?" she demanded.

"I'm Mitchell. I live here," I replied, bemused. "Who are you?"

Whoever she was, she was a long way from home. Hearing an accent that matched my own was nothing short of awesome.

"I'm Shiloh. I just moved in," she replied. "Leroy said you'd done a runner."

"I've been gone for three hours." I almost laughed at the absurdity. "I was at the beach."

I didn't get the chance to ask her any more questions. The front door flew open and the landlord from hell appeared. Completely ignoring me, he spoke only to Shiloh. "Settled in okay?"

"Not really," she grumbled, frowning at me as if I was the enemy. "We have a problem with the sleeping arrangements."

Leroy maniacally laughed like only Leroy could. "You'll work it out," he told her.

Shiloh took a big step toward him. "How? He still lives here."

"You told her I'd done a bunk?" I asked angrily. "Seriously, Leroy?"

He pointed his wooden cane at me. "You piss me off," he grumbled.

"I've been pissing you off for seven years," I reminded him, "but I always pay my rent."

Leroy turned and hobbled back to the door. "And now I've found you a roommate. You're compatriots – it's a perfect arrangement."

The wiry old tyrant had pulled off an outrageous stunt, and the only place on earth he could get away with it was Kaimte. Arguing the point was hopeless. As soon as he was clear of the doorway, I slammed it shut.

"What now?" asked Shiloh.

I barely glanced at her as I passed. "We're roomies, I guess."

I was of the relaxed opinion that we would co-exist and just make do until she could make other arrangements. Shiloh wasn't quite so laid back. If anything, she looked close to detonating.

"You don't even know me," she snapped. "I might be a serial killer."

I turned back. "Are you?"

She took a long time to answer, which made me smile. "No," she finally replied. "I'm reasonably harmless."

"Good. So am I."

The brunette powder keg followed me into the bedroom. "As soon as I can find something else, I'll leave," she offered.

"Okay."

"My company offers employee housing," she added. "It shouldn't take long."

I knew of only one company that worked those kinds of deals. "You work at the mine?"

She nodded. "I start Monday."

I was surprised, and a little disappointed. I'd never been a fan of the work Jorge Creek Mining carried out. Ripping apart the countryside to dig up diamonds seemed awfully destructive, but what would I know? I was just a beach bum publican.

I pulled open the top drawer of my dresser. "I'm sure you'll love whooping it up with the fat cats on the hill."

The hill was more than metaphorical. A row of identical company-owned houses overlooked the beach that the cardboard village stood on. By western standards they were modest, but in Kaimte, they were considered palatial.

"I'm sure I won't," she replied.

I didn't care either way. At that point, all I was interested in was finding a shirt to wear. The top drawer was empty. *All* of the drawers were empty. There could only be one culprit.

"Where are my clothes?" I demanded.

Shiloh pointed to the front door. "I bagged them up and put them on the veranda," she explained. "I thought you'd moved out."

She wisely moved aside as I stormed past and threw open the front door. As expected, there were no bags on the deck. "Just perfect."

"They're gone?" she asked, eyes wide.

"Of course they're freaking gone!" I ranted. "We're in a third world country, Shiloh. People are poor and hungry. How long do you think a discarded bag of clothes is going to sit unattended?"

Her shoulders dropped. "I'm sorry."

"Me too." I held my arms wide. "My entire wardrobe now consists of a pair of shorts."

Desert K-Mart

SHILOH

Under different circumstances, his one-piece wardrobe would've been perfect. Mitchell was ridiculously good looking – a poster child for tanned and built surfer boys.

Vanity clearly wasn't a demon of his. His sun-bleached hair was short but messy, and the scruff on his face was days away from being reclassified as a beard. He stood a foot in front of me, waiting for me to speak. If he wanted a stronger apology, he was out of luck. I was too focused on staring at him.

"I'll go shopping," I eventually offered. "I'll replace everything."

He let out a hard laugh. "Where?" he asked. "Desert K-Mart?"

That snide comment was an unwelcome reminder that the big picture was depressing. In the past week I'd learned more about diamond classification, customs regulations and personal information about Jorge Creek employees than I'd ever hoped to, but no one had prepared me for life in Kaimte.

So far, I wasn't a fan.

The wooden floor creaked in pain as Mitchell strode off to the bathroom. So far, my compatriot wasn't a fan of me either.

I used the time he took in the shower to really check the place out. The picture grew bleaker by the second. I'm all for living simply, but Mitchell's shack brought new meaning to the word.

With the exception of the phone charging on the floor, nothing was modern or in good repair. The living room furniture consisted of two beanbags – one of which was held together by strips of duct tape. There might not have been a clothing shop in town, but there had to be a hardware store. A crack in the front window had also been repaired with tape, and the fridge door was held closed by a piece of rope.

The floor creaked and I turned around in time to see Mitchell cross from the bathroom to the bedroom – as naked as the day he was born.

He didn't close the door because there wasn't one. Out of politeness, I should've turned away, but didn't.

And my new roommate didn't care one bit.

"Didn't your mother ever tell you it's impolite to stare?" he asked.

"Neanderthal," I muttered under my breath.

Mitchell continued mussing his hair with the towel he should've been using to cover himself with. "What's a bloke to do, Shiloh?" he asked. "You gave away my clothes."

"So you're just going to parade around naked from now on?"

Finally, he wrapped the towel around his waist, grinning at me like he'd just won something. "No," he replied. "I'm going to go next door and beg my neighbour for donations."

I bit my lip to stop myself replying. I had no right to be snarky with him. As good as he looked naked, it wasn't a practical long term arrangement.

Feisty New Friend

MITCHELL

Melito and Vincent had been my neighbours since I first arrived. We were good mates, which is fortunate considering our houses are separated by less than fifteen feet of beach sand.

Despite the fact they were the most senior residents, they were the party animals of the cardboard village. I wasn't exactly sure how old they were – all I knew was that I'd attended Vincent's fiftieth birthday party three times in the past year.

Greek national holidays were another cause for celebration. In what seemed like weekly events, the whole neighbourhood was summoned to the beach to party to partake in festivities. It was impossible to believe that one country could have that many holidays, but no one ever questioned it. Once the ouzo and homemade Greek pastries made an appearance, no one really questioned anything.

Vincent opened the door when I knocked, but it was Melito who rushed to speak. "I have your clothes, my friend." He pointed to a pile of rubbish bags stacked neatly on the floor. "The girl tossed them out."

The sleek Greeks were the equivalent of the bush telegraph. Nothing got past them, least of all a pretty new face.

"Who is she?" asked Vincent.

I began rifling through my bags. "Her name is Shiloh," I replied. "She works at the mine."

"Doing what?" quizzed Melito.

"I'm not sure." I hadn't thought to ask. She didn't strike me as being a girly girl, but I couldn't picture her driving a dump truck full of ore either.

"Well, we'll find out tomorrow night," assured Vincent. "At the party."

The groan that escaped me was involuntary. "What's the occasion this time?"

"It's a welcome-to-the-neighbourhood bonfire." He grinned. "For your feisty new friend."

I dragged on a pair of jeans and threw on a shirt. "Can I leave these here for a while?" I asked, pointing at the bags.

Nodding, Melito frowned. "But why?"

"Because I'm an arsehole," I replied. "And I have a feisty new friend."

Crown and Pav

SHILOH

About four percent of people are accomplished liars and can do it very well. Mitchell isn't one of them. He tried hard to sell me the story that his neighbours had lent him clothes, but I didn't buy it for a second.

"So they're exactly the same size as you?" I asked looking him up and down. "That shirt's a perfect fit."

Mitchell grabbed his keys off a hook near the door. "At least now I have something to wear to work," he grumbled.

The beanbag crunched beneath me as I scrambled to my feet. "You're leaving?"

"How else am I going to keep you in the lap of luxury, Shiloh?" He threw his arms wide. "A man's got to work."

My eyes darted around the derelict room. "I appreciate the effort."

"Give me your phone," he demanded, palm outstretched.

I handed it over without question. "If you need anything, call me," he instructed, tapping his number onto my screen.

We were not off to a good start, but at least he was being a good sport about it.

"Don't you want my number?" I asked.

"No." He handed my phone back. "Why would I need to call you?"

Mitchell was half way out the door when I called out to him. "Where do you work?"

He didn't even slow his walk let alone turn around. "Get in the car and I'll show you."

***

Mitchell's jeep wasn't a pleasant ride. As soon as he turned the key, exhaust fumes filled the car. His solution to the sudden gassing was to lean across and wind my window down. It made no difference. A hacking cough overtook me.

"Toughen up, princess," he taunted. "You're in Africa now."

I was under no misconception whatsoever. I'd somehow wound up at the arse-end of the earth. Kaimte wasn't lush jungle. The sub-Saharan terrain was harsh, dry and hot. The only redeeming feature was the ocean, which looked like a blue oasis against the desert backdrop.

The jeep ground to a halt on a stretch of beach not too far from the cardboard village. I saw no hint of what Mitchell did for a living until we walked down the short steep trail and onto the open beach.

"Welcome to the Crown and Pav," he announced with reverence. "Impressive, right?"

I wasn't sure. All I could see was a rusted shipping container and a handful of weathered wooden picnic tables.

"A tool shed?" I guessed.

"Plenty of tools frequent this place," he said, huffing out a sharp laugh. "But, no. Not a tool shed."

He kept me guessing until it became obvious. In a huge display of strength, he hoisted open the side of the container, propping open the makeshift awning with heavy steel poles. The Crown and Pav came to life.

The polished wooden bar looked out of place against the rest of the rusted structure, and the meticulously organised shelves behind it were lined with bottles and glasses.

"A pub," I announced.

Mitchell disappeared through a side door, returning a moment later with a barstool. "The best in town," he boasted. "Mainly because it's the only one in town."

The stool sank into the sand as I sat. "It's popular then?"

"You'll see," he hinted. "It all kicks off when the sun goes down."

It was never going to be Club Med, but after a few minor adjustments to the décor the Crown and Pav became the most inviting place I'd come across since leaving home. Mitchell set up bar stools, speared big umbrellas through the centre of each table, and, when the sun finally began to fade, lit up the leafless tree near the bar with the flick of a switch.

We stood side by side, admiring the twinkling display.

"Did you buy the fairy lights at Desert K-Mart?" I teased.

"My sister sent them to me." He briefly glanced at me. "She has a good eye for sparkly things."

New Talent

MITCHELL

Setting up for opening took less time than I expected. With half an hour to kill before things got rowdy, I offered to buy Shiloh a beer. For now, we were roommates. The least I could do was make an effort to get to know her.

I headed through the side door and Shiloh took up residence at the bar. "What else do you serve?" she asked.

"Anything you want." I motioned toward the shelf behind me with an upward nod. "As long as it's beer or whiskey."

Her eyes narrowed as she studied the bottles on display. "All those bottles are whiskey?"

The bottles rattled as I plucked one from the centre. "Except this one. This one is a mystery." The clear liquid sloshed around as I shook it. "It's not labelled and no one is game enough to try it."

It was the first time I'd heard her laugh, and it sounded sweeter than I expected it would. She was looking a little less caustic too. The frown that had been permanently etched on her face all day was gone. She was a very pretty girl – minus the mayhem.

I cracked the lid off a bottle of beer and slid it toward her. "You don't seem too happy to be here, Shiloh."

She took a sip before replying. "I'm sure I'll get used to it," she mumbled dejectedly. "I'll have to."

Africa is not for sissies. Even on the best day, life here is hard. I couldn't fathom why someone would pack up and move to Kaimte unless they were seeking adventure or a simpler way of life.

"What brought *you* here?" I asked. "Did you lose a bet or something?"

She shook her head. "No, I got a job transfer."

I still didn't even know what she did at the mine and when I asked, her answer surprised me. Shiloh was a security officer, which shot down my theory that she was a sissy. Protecting Jorge Creek's stash of diamonds had to be a pretty serious posting.

"Sounds hardcore."

Her line of sight dropped to her beer and she began absently peeling the label. "Not really," she replied. "It's quite boring at times – just people watching – like a glorified store detective."

I dipped my head, chasing her eyes. "At desert K-Mart?"

"Yes." She softly laughed. "Exactly like that."

It didn't take me long to realise that my initial impression of Shiloh was wrong. I had her pegged as a drama queen who'd unashamedly busted her way into my life and home without permission. It wasn't an honest assessment. Leroy had been the driving force behind the drama that day. Shiloh was merely along for the ride.

"You'll settle in." That probably wasn't honest either, but it was the most encouragement I could offer.

Shiloh set her beer down. "I'm just going to do my job and then I'm out of here," she replied, straightening up on the stool. "Kaimte is temporary."

"I said the same thing years ago." I grinned across at her, arms spread wide. "And yet here I am."

"What brought you here?" Her eyes darted around the bar. "This place?"

I explained that my life as a publican didn't come into play until Nelson's departure a few years earlier. "My friend and I were partway through a surfing holiday when we stumbled across Kaimte. The waves were the initial pull."

"Is your friend still here?" asked Shiloh.

I almost sounded sad when I told her no. "She gave the cardboard village up for the bright lights of New York."

"A girlfriend?"

I grimaced as I pondered the question. I wasn't sure how to define my relationship with Charli, but girlfriend wasn't it. "No, nothing like that," I finally replied. "Just good friends – purely platonic."

It was a notion that Shiloh seemed to struggle with. She frowned and began picking at the last of her label. "In my experience, platonic relationships never work, especially when you live together."

"Awesome news." I wiggled my eyebrows at her. "Based on that theory, you'll be in my bed by the end of the week."

She laughed but didn't get a chance to hit me with a comeback. We were interrupted by the arrival of the first customer of the night, and it wasn't one I could be bothered being particularly polite to.

"What do we have here?" he asked, sidling up behind Shiloh. "New talent?"

I thought Louis Osei was a dick, and as hard as he might try, it was unlikely he'd endear himself to Shiloh either. He stood so close to her that she shuffled forward on her stool.

"What can I get you, Louis?" I asked, trying to divert his attention.

He spoke to me, but only had eyes for the nervous brunette he had pinned against the bar. "This beautiful woman."

I reached for a beer and slammed it on the counter. "You'll have to settle for a drink," I replied sternly. "She's with me."

Louis straightened up, throwing both hands out in surrender – a gesture that didn't match the sly look on his face. "Forgive me. I didn't realise."

"Well, now you do."

Caveman isn't usually a role I play, but in this case, it was necessary. Shiloh already had adjustment issues. The last thing she needed was a night spent rebuffing the advances of Louis.

What he lacked in charm, he made up for in muscle. I had no idea why he needed the protection of the two henchmen who followed him like a shadow, but while he schmoozed at the bar, they stood six feet behind him like loyal guard dogs.

I craned my neck, looking past Louis. "Alright, fellas?" I asked sarcastically.

One nodded. The other continued his pointless stare-down, and Louis continued working on Shiloh. Her skin must've crawled when he put his hand on her back. "When you tire of him, come and see me," he murmured in her ear.

Either frightened or disgusted, she didn't say a word.

I slammed another two beers down on the bar, inadvertently splashing Shiloh in the process. "For your friends," I offered. "On the house."

Smirking, Louis straightened up and with a click of his fingers called his goons forward to collect their drinks. "I'll take your beer," he told me. "The rest will come in time."

I understood his cryptic comment perfectly. Shiloh, however, did not. As soon as Louis and his goons left, she leaned across the bar and whispered a desperate question. "Was he talking about me?"

I watched the group of men take up residence at the table furthest from the bar. "No," I promised, handing her a napkin. "He's talking about my pub."

Louis Osei had been trying to buy me out for years, and the more I refused, the more determined he became. The last offer I rejected came with the threat of him burning the place to the ground, and I didn't doubt for a second that he was capable of doing it. I'd heard whispered tales of everything from gun running to drug smuggling where Louis was concerned. None of it had ever been proven, but it was fair to assume that the import–export company he ran was far from legitimate.

"He wants to buy the Crown and Pav but I'm not interested."

Shiloh dabbed at her beer-stained shirt with the napkin. "He's a little on the creepy side, isn't he?"

"Nothing to worry about." I smiled, mainly to put her at ease. "Just steer clear of him."

Groundwork

SHILOH

Sheltered and slightly nervous was the picture I'd painted of myself to Mitchell, which meant I'd already descended into the shady world of lies and illusions.

I couldn't dwell. My alter ego might've been creeped out by Louis, but steering clear of him was never going to happen.

Louis Osei was Tweedledum.

A lot of groundwork had been done where Louis was concerned. Studying his file had been as compelling as any good novel. No tangible link had been made between him and Jorge Creek Mining Company. It was the dealings of his shady shipping company that made for good reading.

Corruption was rife throughout Kaimte, and it extended all the way up to the government. Friends in high places come in handy, and Louis had many. In exchange for hefty bribes, port officials happily turned a blind eye while he held incoming shipments for ransom on the wharf. Nothing got through without Louis' say-so, and the only way to get it was to cough up exorbitant amounts of cash. The simple but lucrative scheme had worked without a hitch for years, and it was up to me to find out whether any of the proceeds were being used to buy stolen diamonds.

I turned my head, covertly studying the crooked party at the far table. Louis might've built an empire based on fear and intimidation, but he wasn't fearless. He was smarmy and suave, but the edginess to his demeanour was undeniable. His eyes constantly darted as he scoped out his surroundings, and his goons were just as vigilant. It took only seconds before one noticed me, and it wasn't a pleasant exchange. His vacant stare and menacing scowl were so unnerving that I had to look away.

My heart nearly thumped out of my chest as the gravity of the situation set in. Surveilling Glen Harris would be relatively simple because we worked together, but there was no way I could get that close to Louis.

All I could do was wait for the other agent to make contact. The best I could hope for was that he had some semblance of a plan.

***

The Crown and Pav really fired up after dark. All the tables on the beach were occupied and a loud blend of laughter and chatter filled the air. Mitchell was run off his feet, and the most help I could offer was to stay out of his way. I perched at the end of the bar for the whole night, sneaking quick conversations when he had the time.

"Sorry about the spilled drink," he said. "Can I make it up to you with another beer?"

I folded my arms, trying to hide the stain on my once-white top. "No thanks," I replied. "I already smell like a brewery."

A roguish grin swept his face. "You've sat on one drink all night," he teased. "You're not good for business, Shiloh."

I twisted on the stool, checking out the merry crowd behind me. "It looks like a full house to me," I replied. "Do you work every night?"

He swiped a cloth along the length of the glossy bar. "Except the weekends." The corner of his mouth lifted. "Crazy Mimi works those shifts."

If the detailed description he followed through with was even half true, her nickname was well deserved. He described Mimi as a moody and volatile woman with a fascination for the macabre.

"She's petrified of the devil," he told me. "She spends her whole life trying to stay out of his way."

I leaned across the bar, following his hand as he motioned to a posy of dried leaves hanging above the door.

"Bay leaves," he explained. "Apparently they keep demons out."

His smile led me to think he wasn't completely sold on the idea.

"You're not a believer?"

He flicked the cap off a bottle of beer and set it in front of me. "I'm more afraid of Mimi than the devil," he confessed. "She's much easier to deal with when I let her have her way. If she wants to hang bunches of leaves in the bar, so be it."

***

Last call was at eleven. Mitchell spent the next hour trying to clear the beach in front of his pub of stragglers, which was akin to rounding up wayward livestock. No one was in a hurry to leave, even once the awning was lowered and the outside lights were turned off.

I would've given up and left them to it, but Mitchell stood watching until the last bloke staggered up the hill to the car park and stumbled at the top of the trail. The police officer in me kicked in.

"He's too drunk to drive," I muttered.

"He's tanked," agreed Mitchell unconcerned. "Chances are, he doesn't have a driver's license either."

"Seriously?"

Mitchell collapsed the last of the umbrellas and hoisted it over his shoulder. "The rules don't apply here, Shiloh," he explained with a grin. "Welcome to Kaimte, baby."

Adonis

MITCHELL

Leroy's ridiculous meddling hadn't had the desired effect. Presumably he was hoping for a turf war that ended with me being overthrown and evicted, but it wasn't to be.

There *was* tension when we arrived back at the shack that night, but it was the good kind brought on by the dilemma of only having one bed. Shiloh's solution was that we share.

"We're both adults, right?"

Her optimism proved how little she knew me, but I agreed to the dangerous plan and set about making the bedroom as girl-friendly as I could.

It was a confusing shift because I hadn't given a damn about making her feel welcome when she first arrived.

"It's probably a good thing that you chucked my clothes out," I teased. "It's less mess for me to clean up."

Rehashing the not-so-stolen clothes debacle was a mistake. She hadn't bought my story for a second, and I'd just given her reason to call me out on it. "Your neighbours picked them up, didn't they?"

I glanced at her, trying not to look too sheepish. "Melito took them for safekeeping." I swiped a flattened pillow off the bed and thumped it back into shape. "But you know that already, don't you?"

A smile swept her face. "Leaving them there was a terrible strategy, Mitchell. I knew they hadn't been pinched the second I saw your shirt."

I took a few slow steps forward, using the pillow as a buffer between us as I pressed her body against the wall. "It was a fine plan," I murmured in a low tone.

Her brown eyes locked mine. "Amateur at best."

Chuckling blackly, I released my hold on her and dropped the pillow on the bed. "Which side do you want?"

She gazed at the bed. "The safe side."

I folded my arms, eyeing her with mock suspicion. "How do I know you're not a threat to *my* safety and virtue?"

"Because I'm tired," she said simply. "I need at least two days of sleep before I can even consider robbing you of your virtue."

I grabbed the collar of my T-shirt and dragged it over my head. "Two days, eh?" I muttered, mainly to myself. "I can hardly wait."

***

I had no idea how long it would take for Shiloh to sort out company housing, but for now it didn't matter.

I can't tolerate high-maintenance women for long – even my own sisters – but Shiloh was down to earth and held no airs and graces. Instead of screaming when she spotted a nasty black spider in the bathroom the next morning, she picked up a shoe and walloped it.

"Impressive technique," I praised from the doorway.

"Thanks." She dropped the shoe and brushed past me. "I killed the last one with your toothbrush."

***

The shack didn't have many redeeming features, but the location was world class. If anything could help Shiloh adjust to life in Kaimte, the view from the front deck was it.

We sat outside for a long time that morning, enjoying the sun before the heat took hold. The water was calm and so was the mood.

Shiloh leaned on the railing of the veranda, staring out to sea. "This really is beautiful." She breathed out the words in a long sigh.

"You're welcome to stay as long as you need to."

She glanced over her shoulder. "I'll sort something out as quick as I can."

I nodded in support of her plan, but didn't mean it. I might've tried harder to make her stay, but I was distracted. Vincent wandered out onto the deck next door wearing nothing but a pair of purple board shorts.

He spotted us too, calling out to remind me that we had plans that evening. "An extravaganza," he boldly claimed. "Melito is already baking."

I couldn't smell anything cooking, but I had no problem catching a whiff of coconut oil as Vincent greased himself up in preparation for a day in the sun.

"There will be plenty of food and drink for everyone," he promised, rubbing his big belly like a lucky Buddha.

He set his sights on Shiloh. "How are you settling in, beautiful lady?"

"Fine thanks," she politely replied.

"And what do you think of our Adonis?" Vincent motioned toward me with a nod. "Are you as smitten as we are?"

Shiloh giggled as if the notion was absurd. "Not yet," she replied. "I'm pacing myself."

Unknown Element

SHILOH

I began to worry that I was becoming distracted. The cardboard village was a haven of sunshine and good vibes, and hanging out with Mitchell tended to throw me into holiday mode. I'd spent a lot of time getting to know him in the past day, and it was completely without motive. He was funny, interesting and unashamedly flirty, which left me with a feeling of hopelessness that wouldn't have existed if I were solely focused on the job I'd been sent to do.

I had two days to get my act together. When Monday morning rolled around, I vowed to be on my game.

***

The party started at dusk, and the guest list was huge. People milled around on the beach in front of the shacks, making the most of Vincent and Melito's extraordinary hospitality. True to their word, they'd been cooking up a storm all day. Melito passed trays of Greek pastries around and Vincent kept the ouzo flowing like water. After being introduced to more people than I'd ever remember, I stole a minute away by wandering further down the beach.

I mistakenly thought I was invisible out of the glow of the roaring bonfire, but Vincent soon appeared. Before I could protest, he upended a bottle of ouzo into the plastic cup in my hand.

"Drink until you see stars," he recklessly urged before disappearing again.

I couldn't take another sip. The powerful taste of anise wasn't remotely pleasant.

"Not a fan?" asked Mitchell, sidling up beside me.

"I can't drink any more of this," I complained. "It's poison."

He took the cup and poured it onto the sand. "What *is* your drink of choice?" he asked, cocking one eyebrow. "We've established that it's not beer or ouzo."

Before I could speak, his hand flew up. "Think carefully," he warned. "If you tell me you have a thing for champagne or fruity cocktails, this romance is over."

"Idiot," I mumbled, dropping my head to hide my laugh. "What romance?"

He took a step forward and whispered in my ear. "This one."

I had a vague game plan when it came to dealing with the likes of Tweedledum and Tweedledee, but no idea how I'd handle Mitchell. He was the unknown element I'd been warned to look out for – far more dangerous than any crook.

"Red wine," I replied, getting back on task. "I'd take merlot over champagne any day of the week."

"I'll keep that in mind and add it to my list."

"What list?"

Even in the low light, his smile was bright. "The list of things I know about Shiloh Jenson."

His words hit me hard, in a place that was supposed to be off limits. Shiloh Jenson was a work of fiction, and it was a book that was never meant for him.

Team Demon

MITCHELL

If I had been planning to ramp up the flirty exchanges with Shiloh, my posse would've been entirely responsible for keeping me in the friend zone. Vincent and Melito were eccentric nutters, but Mimi's calibre of crazy was out of this world.

She came barrelling down the beach a little after midnight, moving so fast that sand flew in her wake. She must've spotted us sitting on the sand because she made a beeline for me.

"Mitchell! Mitchell!"

I ignored her at first, but she yelled louder. "I'm talking to you, dumb boy."

Shiloh leaned closer. "A friend of yours?" she asked.

"Brace yourself," I muttered from the corner of my mouth. "It's mad Mimi."

The crazed woman ground to a halt in front of us. "I've been calling you all night," she snapped, hands on hips. "Answer your phone."

"And miss out on the pleasure of having you yell at me in person? Never."

Shiloh directed her laugh at the sand but being discreet was pointless. Mimi's sights were firmly set on her. "Who are you, girl?"

"I'm Shiloh," she replied, politely extending her hand.

Unimpressed, Mimi rudely left her hanging. "Where are you from?"

"Australia."

"You know him?" Mimi pointed at me.

Shiloh withdrew her hand. "I do now."

"He has the protection of a thousand angels," she told her. "The devil can't have him."

The random comment should've sent her running for the hills, but it didn't. "I'll be sure to let him know he's off the list," Shiloh replied.

As far as first impressions go, Shiloh had made the worst one possible. Her remark didn't go down well. Mimi's faith was the simplest of religions to understand. Angels are good and the devil is bad. As far as she's concerned, you're friends with one or the other. Unfortunately for Shiloh, she'd just implied that she was on Team Demon.

Mimi picked up a handful of sand and threw it into the still night air. A slew of Afrikaans words followed – possibly a prayer or two, but more likely a vicious round of insults.

I tried diffusing the situation, with minimal success. "What did you come all this way down here for?" I asked.

"I want you to pay me," she snapped, refusing to release Shiloh from her glower.

"Fine," I replied, already reaching for my wallet.

"I need next week's pay too," she added.

"Mimi, you realise that most people actually have to work before they get paid, right?"

"I need it," she muttered. "Bills to pay."

Shiloh was still trapped by her intense stare down, but nothing in her demeanour hinted toward fear. I wasn't frightened either. I was just embarrassed, and powerless to stop it. I waved a small wad of notes at Mimi. "Is there anything else I can help you with tonight?"

She snatched the money and stuffed it down the front of her dress. "No," she huffed, backing away. "But I will help you." She pointed her finger at Shiloh. "By all means necessary."

I knew better than to ask what that meant. Shiloh, however, was curious. As soon as the crazy woman was out of earshot, she asked me.

"I'm not sure," I replied vaguely. "But it's bound to involve bay leaves and chanting."

Shiloh laughed. "You have an interesting group of friends, Mitchell."

"I do," I agreed. "Where do you fit into the mix?"

"I'm not sure yet," she replied. "I'm still trying to find my place."

Eye On The Prize

SHILOH

I was dreading my first day at my fake job, which made dragging myself out of bed at four o'clock on Monday morning dreadful. I tried not to wake Mitchell when I got up, but sneaking around the rickety wooden shack was impossible. The whole building moved with every step I took.

"How are you getting to work?" he sleepily mumbled.

"My boss is picking me up," I whispered. "Go back to sleep."

He threw back the covers. "I'll walk you up to the road."

"You don't have to do that."

"It's dark, Shiloh," he taunted in a creepy voice. "Witching hour."

The biggest ghoul I was likely to come up against was Glen, but I kept that thought to myself. "I feel like I'm headed to the first day of school," I said glumly.

Mitchell picked up his clothes from the night before and dragged on his jeans. "You don't look much like a naughty schoolgirl," he teased.

"That's not quite what I meant."

He grabbed me by the shoulders. "It'll be a good day for you," he encouraged, shaking me. "Just be yourself and do your thing."

There was no way I could take his advice. In order to do my thing, I needed to spend the day pretending to be someone else. It was a tangled mess before it had even begun.

"Thank you," I mumbled. "You've been really kind to me."

The corner of his mouth lifted. "I try."

***

Nothing was ever too much trouble for Mitchell, even trekking up the beach in the dark and waiting on the side of the road for my idiot boss to pick me up. I was glad he was so gallant. The dead of night in Kaimte really did feel like witching hour.

"Why are there no street lights?" I asked glancing in every direction.

"Because there are no streets," he replied. "Very little infrastructure."

"This is a road." I stamped my foot on the tarmac. "A pretty decent one, actually."

"Yeah, and look where it goes." I squinted into the darkness, following his pointed hand. "There are three tarmac roads in this town," he explained. "One leads to the port, one to the mine and this one heads up to the fat cat's camp on the hill."

Me eyes widened. "Jorge Creek owns the roads?"

"Not exactly. It was officially called a community donation. The good ol' company builds a few roads to make their life easier and then claim they're improving the town." Mitchell gazed at the row of identical stucco company houses. "Self-serving environmental terrorism at its finest."

Mitchell's disdain for the mine had been evident from the minute I met him, and it wasn't hard to understand his mindset. He'd settled in Kaimte two years before the mine broke ground, which meant he'd seen the changes first-hand.

"Obviously, the diamonds have always been here," he continued. "But the locals were digging them out with their hands, not blowing the countryside apart with explosives and heavy machinery."

I felt the sudden urge to confess that we were both on the same side, but of course it was impossible. I volunteered a very censored show of unity instead. "I'm not a fat cat," I declared, pointing at myself. "I just work there."

"Settle down, kitty," he teased. "I never said you were."

From the corner of my eye, I noticed a porch light come on. "Well, someone's awake," I muttered.

The screen on Mitchell's phone lit up as he checked the time. "What time did he say he'd be here?"

"Five," I replied. "He should be here any minute."

Mitchell waved his phone at me. "It's already quarter past."

At that moment ire was simmering, but when we were still standing on the side of the road nearly half an hour later, I was ready to explode.

"I guess day shift starts at six," said Mitchell.

All the porch lights were on now, and a steady stream of employees in mine vehicles began passing us – except Tweedledee, who was obviously content to stay in bed and leave me stranded on the roadside.

"My boss is a jerk," I muttered. "He told me to be here by five."

Mitchell smiled wryly. "There are plenty of jerks in this town, Shiloh. Just keep your eye on the prize."

I hoped that the flash of panic that accompanied statements like that would eventually stop. It wasn't logical to assume his words were anything other than innocent. I'd told Mitchell nothing. "What's the prize?" I asked calmly.

He grabbed my shoulders and turned me toward the ocean. "That's the prize." His voice was low in my ear. "You're living in paradise. Don't waste your energy on jerks."

***

Glen finally made an appearance, almost an hour late. He wound the passenger window down, leaned across and demanded that I get in the car.

Obviously Mitchell was as offended as I was. When he took a step forward, I grabbed a fistful of his T-shirt and pulled him back. "Leave it," I whispered. "I'll see you tonight." Somehow, he managed to keep quiet.

"Get in," repeated Glen.

Mitchell finally snapped. He stooped down and growled through the open window, "Grow some manners, jerk."

A horrid smirk crossed Glen's face, and at that moment I determined to nail him. He'd already exposed himself as a self-important arse. Nothing would bring me greater joy than proving that he was a dirty low-down thief as well.

***

Jorge Creek Diamond Mine was situated twelve kilometres from the township, and the short journey was made seriously uncomfortable purely because of the company I was in.

"I see you've settled into the cardboard slum," Glen goaded. "Found a boyfriend and everything."

Defending myself would've been a waste of breath. It wasn't a one-off. Glen had a plan of tormenting me until I broke, and I refused to let that happen.

I pulled in a settling breath and gazed out the window.

"How's a pretty little thing like you going to cope in a place like this?" he continued.

The condescension was wasted on me. I was almost flattered. I'd been a lanky five-feet-ten since my teens. No one ever referred to me as little.

The snide comments continued all the way to work, and I ignored every one of them. By the time we pulled up at the security gate, I was daydreaming about ripping the Bluetooth earpiece from his ear and ramming it down his throat.

Glen got out and slammed the door. "Wait here," he ordered, leaning down to bark the command through the window.

I happily complied, using the time alone to have a good look around.

The perimeter of the mine was secured by nothing more impressive than chain link fencing and a boom gate that barricaded the road. Two men dressed in company uniform sat in a small air-conditioned guard hut, and another stood outside talking to Glen. When one of them poked his head out of the door and waved at me, I recognised him in an instant. It was Baako, the meet-and-greet man.

I smiled and waved back, and that's where the pleasantries ended. Glen jumped back in the car, the boom gate lifted, and we sped off leaving Baako eating dust for a second time.

***

The car screeched to a halt outside an office building, so violently that my head whipped forward before smashing against the headrest.

"Go to the Site Services office," ordered Glen, slamming the door as he exited. "Tell them you need uniforms and a security pass."

Clearly, orientation day was over. He was in the door and out of sight before I'd even undone my seatbelt.

The AFP had gathered a huge amount of intelligence on Glen Harris. The notes in his file described him as difficult and belligerent. If I ever saw that file again, I vowed to add a few notes of my own. He was an arsehole, plain and simple.

***

The staff in the Site Services office were far more accommodating than my so-called boss. Once I'd been measured for uniforms and had completed the security access paperwork, a man called Reyo offered to give me a tour of the site. I liked him immediately. He was enthusiastic and friendly, and had a constant grin on his face.

The first place he showed me was the processing plant. The massive shed was a tangled maze of conveyor belts, machinery and tumbling rocks. I feigned interest for as long as I could, but after just a few minutes I was desperate to get out of there.

"Can we move on?" I yelled, fighting to be heard over the noisy machines. "It's really warm in here."

When Reyo pointed toward the door, I almost ran to get to it. Despite the fact it was over forty degrees outside, I instantly felt better. "You don't like the Kaimte heat?" Reyo asked, jogging to catch up with me.

"I'll get used to it," I replied, flapping the collar of my shirt to cool myself down.

"I thought Australia was hot." He seemed confused. "My cousin went there once. He said it was hot."

"He wasn't lying." I smiled at him. "Some parts are hot, but it's not like this."

Nothing compared to this.

"No," he agreed. "We don't have koalas here." Reyo slapped his hand on his thigh and burst out laughing as if he'd just told the world's funniest joke.

When he finally regained his composure, he offered to show me another place. "The diamond building," he said, pointing to a small building a few hundred metres away.

I shrugged. "Sounds good."

My indifference was a crock. I was elated by the prospect of scoping it out. The diamond building housed the sorting room, which was the Holy Grail. Jewellers sorted the gems there, separating the industrial-grade stones from the valuable high-quality diamonds.

I was eying off the unassuming building long before we reached it. From the outside there was absolutely no hint of what went on inside. And from a security perspective, that was a good thing. Like the admin building, it was a generic stucco structure painted the same shade of beige as its desert surroundings, and as soon as we walked through the door I was hit by a strange sense of déjà vu.

Agent Grace had maintained that my short stint at Jorge Creek's Western Australian mine would be an advantage. At that moment, I believed him. The inside layout of the diamond building was exactly the same as the one I'd worked at four years earlier. Even the rigmarole to get in was the same. After passing through a security gate and a turnstile, Reyo swiped his access card, which got us as far as the foyer.

"I can't take you any further until you get security clearance," he said regretfully.

I didn't need to go any further to know what was beyond the big steel door behind him. There would be another foyer, a few small offices, and a big viewing window. And if my memory served me correctly, behind thick bulletproof glass were a couple of jewellers sifting through masses of diamonds.

"Is everything alright?" asked Reyo.

It was an odd moment for me. Perhaps I looked strange because of it. "Fine," I muttered.

He stooped down to quietly murmur, "Bad juju in here for you?"

I fought against rolling my eyes. The juju nonsense seemed to hold half the town to moral ransom. On the plus side, it probably kept a great deal of people honest too. Ignoring his question, I asked one of my own. "You don't like diamonds?"

His ebony lips formed a straight line as he shook his head. "They are rocks from the devil's garden."

It was a slightly different take on it than the one Mimi ran with, but clearly the devil was a common theme.

"Why do you work here then?"

"The pay is good," he replied. "Why do you work here?"

I shrugged. "I've been dancing with the devil for a while now, Reyo."

Zen Personified

MITCHELL

My uptight roomie arrived home from work a little after six, looking no less strung out than usual.

"How was work?" I asked, meeting her at the door.

Shiloh walked past me and dumped an armful of clothes on the beanbag. "Long," she replied. "But I survived."

"Did you stop by Desert K-Mart on the way home?"

Finally she smiled. "No, they're my uniforms," she explained. "I'm officially a Jorge Creek minion now."

I held up my hand. "Nice one, lady."

Shiloh completed the juvenile high-five by slapping my hand. "Are you going out?" she asked, looking me up and down.

"I have to go to work."

"Oh." She frowned. "I guess pizza and a movie are off the agenda then?"

I grabbed my keys, chuckling my way out the door. "Pizza and movies have been off the agenda since you left home."

***

As a rule, Monday nights at the Crown and Pav were quiet. It paved the way for vermin to crawl out of the woodwork, and tonight's pest was Louis Osei. He took his usual position at the bar while his goons stood guard three feet behind him.

"What can I get you?" I asked, barely looking at him.

"I have a shipment for you," he replied. "It's waiting in my warehouse."

Only Louis could make six cases of booze sound like a shady drug deal.

"Excellent." I flipped the lid off a bottle of beer and slid it toward him. "I'll pick it up tomorrow."

"I want you to do something for me first," he replied.

My glower must've looked fierce because the henchmen took a step forward.

"I don't have to do anything for you," I said, drumming my finger on the bar. "That shipment was bought and paid for. All I need to do is collect it."

Keeping his eyes firmly on me, Louis beckoned one of his men with a click of his fingers. He dutifully stepped forward and handed him a roughly gift wrapped parcel.

"You shouldn't have."

"It is not for you." Louis dropped the package on the bar. "I want you to give it to Shiloh."

It wasn't surprising that he'd set his sights on her. A pretty white girl was always going to be noticed in Kaimte, but the angle he was working was hopeless and I took great delight in telling him so. I pushed the parcel back toward him. "She's not interested."

Louis leaned back on the stool. "Three thousand dollars," he demanded, slamming his hand down on the bar. "If you want your beer to clear customs, that's what it will cost you."

All goods enter Kaimte via sea, and Louis' crooked mates were the gatekeepers. As government-appointed customs officers they controlled the port, demanding huge payments in exchange for the release of goods. But even blatant corruption needs to be done on the sly, which is why Louis was the enforcer. He wasn't a crooked government official. He was just crooked and well connected.

Most business owners paid up without question – but I wasn't one of them.

"I'm not giving you a cent, Louis." I turned around and tossed the bottle cap into the bin. "I've made that mistake before."

He threw his arms wide. "A bar with no beer will eventually close," he taunted. "Perhaps then I will buy it for a cheap price."

My eyes shifted to the two men standing obediently behind him. Neither of them struck me as being particularly quick thinkers. It made me wonder how much damage I could inflict on their boss before they jumped in to rescue him.

Thankfully, a cooler head prevailed. "My pub is not for sale," I said for the millionth time. "And I'm not paying for goods I already own."

Louis slid the parcel toward me. "We can forget about the money," he offered. "All you have to do is give this present to pretty Shiloh."

"And if I don't?"

He straightened up and motioned toward his goons. "My friends will change your mind."

I wasn't concerned by what might happen at that moment, but the thought of looking over my shoulder wherever I went wasn't appealing. They weren't the sharpest tools in the shed, but they were persistent.

I looked down at the parcel, deliberating. "What is it?"

He grinned – a triumphant expression that I wanted to punch. "Just a small gift to welcome her to Kaimte."

"She's not interested in you, Osei." I snatched up the package and tossed it under the counter. "Make sure my shipment is cleared and ready for collection tomorrow."

Louis picked up his beer and tilted it toward me. "It's a pleasure doing business with you."

***

I expected Shiloh to be asleep when I got home. Not only was she awake, she was busy. In the five hours since I'd left home, she'd turned my shack into a working sweatshop. Clothes hung from every surface and an ironing board was set up in the centre of the room.

I must've looked confused because Shiloh's explanation came at warp speed. "Melito lent me an iron." She pressed something, making it shoot a puff of steam into the air. "I needed to sort my work clothes out."

None of the shirts hanging on the curtain rail above the window remotely resembled Jorge Creek uniforms. I picked up the hem of a perfectly pressed T-shirt and shot her a quizzical look. "You ironed my clothes too?"

She suddenly looked worried. "I've overstepped the line, haven't I?"

"You sleep in my bed." I shot her a grin. "I think the line blurred days ago."

Shiloh motioned at a shirt with an outstretched arm. "Want me to mess them up again?"

I shook my head. "No, don't take it out on the defenceless shirts. Channel your frustrations elsewhere."

"I have no frustrations, Mitchell," she replied, putting her hand to her heart. "I am Zen personified."

That was a lie. Even on her best day, Shiloh Jenson was wound tighter than a drum.

"You're the most uptight person I've ever met," I accused. "Even when you're asleep." I stiffened, doing my best impression of a rigid sleeping Shiloh.

"Do I really look like that?" The look that crossed her face was one of sheer horror.

"Absolutely." I laughed. "But I like it."

I might've even loved it, but that remained to be seen.

Shiloh bunched up a shirt and waved it at me. "You can iron your own bloody shirts from now on," she snapped. "Ingrate."

"Here." Still chuckling, I thrust Louis' parcel at her. "I brought you something."

"A present?" Her brown eyes widened. "You bought me a present?"

I felt ridiculous explaining so I stuck to the basics. "No," I replied. "It's from Louis Osei. A welcome gift, apparently."

Her excitement quickly gave way to a frown as she studied the poorly wrapped present. "What do you think he wants from me?"

I spoke without thinking, which was a mistake. I told the truth. "I think he wants the opportunity to welcome you to town properly."

Poor Shiloh looked horrified. "And you're okay with that?" she gasped. "You're doing Louis' bidding now?"

I was appalled, mainly with myself. I ripped the package from her grasp and tossed it onto a nearby beanbag. "I wouldn't do a bloody thing for Louis Osei."

Prettiest Goat Herder

SHILOH

I wanted to tell Mitchell that I didn't give a damn about receiving a try-hard present from Louis, but I didn't. I stuck to the script and continued pretending to feel terrorised by the unwanted attention.

Mitchell grabbed a beer from the fridge and retreated to the front deck. I should've left him alone and given him space, but I couldn't. I needed more information. I followed him outside into the warm night air, taking a few seconds at the door to glance around. I couldn't see a thing beyond the edge of the porch light, but there was no mistaking where we were. The Atlantic Ocean was so close I could taste the salt in the air.

Three waves crashed to shore before I managed to find my voice. "Are you upset with me?"

"Just leave it, Shiloh." Mitchell threw back his head and took a long sip of beer. "It's been a long day."

I pulled up a chair and sat beside him. "I'm just confused," I mumbled after a long pause. "You told me to steer clear of Louis and now you're passing on gifts from him."

Mitchell let out a low, pissed off groan. "You have no idea how this place works."

"Explain it to me."

"Kaimte is not all sand and sun." He stretched out in the deckchair, folded his arms and crossed his feet. "There are some bad people in this town."

My restive alter ego kicked in and asked a nervous question. "Louis is bad?"

He grimaced as I said his name, but an explanation followed. "The only way to get goods in is by sea or by air," he told me. "I buy stock for the Crown and Pav from a distributor in South Africa. It's shipped up here by sea."

I didn't need to hear another word to know how the story ended but kept my eyes fixed on his as he laid out the whole sorry tale. As expected, Tweedledum was holding his shipment to ransom.

"The quickest solution was to meet his demands," he muttered, sounding royally pissed off.

"You paid him?" I choked out the question, unable to suppress my disappointment, which wasn't a fair reaction.

"Never," he scoffed. "I went with option two and agreed to deliver his parcel to you. The imaginary debt was quashed and the Crown and Pav lives to trade for another week."

Trying to keep his business afloat with obstacles like Louis Osei must've been exhausting. I couldn't fathom why he was so intent on sticking it out. "Why do you do it?" My voice was barely there.

Mitchell flashed me a weary smile. "Because he doesn't always win, Shiloh," he replied. "Sometimes I am the spider, and sometimes I am the fly."

Tonight he was the fly, and there was nothing I could do about it. My focus was on Louis' suspected involvement in the illegal diamond trade. Corruption at the port wasn't an AFP problem. Therefore, much as it pained me, it wasn't my problem either.

"I opened the parcel," I confessed.

"I knew you would," he replied with a chuckle. "What was in it?"

"I'm not sure, but it needs ironing." I shrugged. "I'll show you."

I wandered inside, returning with the mystery gift. I draped the length of flowy batik cloth over his shoulder as I passed.

"It's called a mulafa," said Mitchell bunching it up in his hand. "Some of the local women wear them."

I flopped back onto the deck chair. "Like a sarong?"

Mitchell leaned across and dropped it on my lap. "It's worn a little differently."

More intrigued than I expected to be, I stood up and wrapped the brightly patterned fabric around my body, securing it with a tuck at my waist. "Like this?" I asked, showing it off with a swing of my hips.

"No." Mitchell laughed, a dark low sound that always made me smile. "Not quite." He stood and took it from me. "It's worn much more conservatively here." A cool waft of air drifted over me as he fanned the fabric over my shoulders. "We're in Africa, not Bali."

"You're very well travelled, aren't you?"

His blue eyes locked mine – so intently that I couldn't look away.

"Yes," he quietly replied. "Are you?"

It was the first time he'd ever asked me a direct question about my past, and having to answer with a lie chipped at my heart. "No," I mumbled. "I've never been anywhere."

Still keeping his eyes on mine, he tucked one end of the fabric underneath my right arm. "Well, Kaimte is a good place to start."

"You just got through telling me how this place is overrun with bad guys," I reminded him.

He half-smiled. "Like I told you, keep the eye on the prize."

I was almost certain that under different circumstances, my prize would've been him. Nabbing diamond thieves and living on the beach was only ever going to be the consolation prize – and it was a dangerous line of thinking that I needed to get out of my head, for both our sakes.

Mitchell draped the remaining fabric over my head and across my shoulder. "It's not perfect," he said, tucking my hair under the cloth. "But you get the gist."

I dropped my head and fussed with the fabric. "It's not sexy, is it?" I asked, making him laugh. "I feel like a goat herder."

"Prettiest goat herder I've ever seen," he mumbled.

My cheeks flushed with heat that I hoped he couldn't see. "I bet you say that to all the herders."

"Perhaps," he agreed with a smile. "But you're the only one I sleep with."

Fat Cat Rules

MITCHELL

I have two sisters, one of whom is my twin. They're messy, complicated and whiny, and living with them scarred me for life.

Shacking up with Shiloh was nowhere near as damaging. She was far from messy; if anything, she was a neat freak. For the first time since Charli left there was a fruit bowl in the kitchen – and it actually had fruit in it. Towels hung neatly in the bathroom, the curtains were open during the day and a faint whiff of perfume constantly hung in the air.

I could've done without some of her quirks, but those were the ones that made me wish she'd reconsider her decision to join the fat cats on the hill in company housing.

In the three weeks since she arrived, I'd never once brought up the subject of her moving out. In time, I hoped, she'd forget about it. As far as I was concerned, my arguments for keeping her around were solid – I liked her, and she smelled good.

My neighbours were also of the opinion that it should be a permanent arrangement, and they'd obviously put some thought into how to make that happen. Vincent and Melito were on their veranda when I returned from my morning surf, lying in wait to ambush me with misguided words of wisdom.

"You should be wooing Shiloh," called Vincent out of the blue. "Make her happy and you'll be happy."

I slung my wetsuit over the railing and grabbed the garden hose to rinse it off. "I am happy," I insisted.

"You need a good woman," Melito argued. "No man is an island."

I frowned at them. "What does that even mean?"

The blank looks on their faces led me to think they had no idea either. Vincent quickly moved on. "Eros is the Greek god of love," he said. "Matchmaking is in our blood."

Despite the fact that it was nine in the morning, ouzo was also in their blood, which meant there was no reasoning with them. I made them both promise to stay out of my non-existent love life and followed up with a not-so menacing wave of the trickling garden hose. "I don't need drama."

I'd spent my whole life avoiding it, and after twenty-seven years I almost had the skill mastered.

"All women are drama," complained Melito. "It's part of their charm."

Shiloh had plenty of charm, and I wasn't immune to it. She'd rocked up on my doorstep with a wicked sense of humour, legs that went on for days, and no aversion to killing spiders. I liked her. Common sense told me there was no need to ruin that by falling in love with her.

***

The Crown and Pav usually did a roaring trade on Fridays. On nights when I was feeling brave enough, I'd call on Mimi to help out behind the bar.

"It should be double pay tonight, Mitchell." That was her greeting as she stormed through the side door. "I have extra cleansing to do."

Mimi wasn't talking about washing glasses and dusting shelves. Her cleansing routine involved burning sage and any other weird acts of hocus pocus she deemed necessary to keep demons out of my pub. I'd been roped into being her assistant enough times to know that if I didn't make a quick retreat, I'd be stuck waving bunches of smoking sage through the air until opening time. "I'll leave you to it," I said, heading for the door.

Setting up the outside tables was my plan, but I got distracted by the sunset. Dusk in Kaimte is spectacular. After long hot days, the bright sun sinks below the line of the ocean, casting an eerie yellow glow that lingers until darkness sets in. It's pure magic, and I never got tired of seeing it.

"Those umbrellas aren't going to put themselves up you know, slacker."

I didn't need to turn around. "Shiloh Jenson." I breathed her name. "There's no escaping you, is there?"

"It's Friday night," she replied, sidling up beside me. "I figured the pub would be the place to be."

"You figured right." I speared the last umbrella through the table. "Did you walk here?"

"No," she replied, pulling a face. "Glen dropped me off on the way home. I caught him at a weak moment."

"You wore that to work?" I looked her up and down. "Doesn't looking like a girl break fat cat rules?"

It was a fair question. Her work uniform was a hideous combination of tradie's pants and steel capped boots. She glanced down and fanned out the bottom of her skirt. "I got changed at work."

It was a change that suited her. The blue dress was a huge improvement, and almost as distracting as the sunset, so I changed the subject. "I'm glad you're here, actually." I took her hand and began leading her to the bar. "I have something for you."

"No offence, Mitchell, but your presents usually suck."

I thought back to the mulafa debacle. "Not this one," I assured her. "This one's actually from me."

I had momentarily forgotten about the madwoman smoking out the joint with burning herbs when I ushered her through the door. Shiloh flapped her hand in a bid to clear the choking fog, which was a rookie mistake.

"Never hurry the process," barked Mimi from somewhere in the haze.

"I'm sorry," Shiloh apologised. "I didn't know."

With a huff, Mimi brushed past and tossed the burning posy onto the sand outside. "The candles will have to finish the job."

My eyes drifted to four candles lined along the bar. I wanted to chide her for dripping wax but thought better of it. "Are you nearly done?" I asked, remarkably calm. "We're opening in a few minutes."

"You should be thanking me, dumb boy," Mimi grumbled. "As long as those flames burn, you're protected."

"Fine," I yielded, throwing up my hands. "Just let us get past so we can get to the store room."

Mimi squashed herself against the bar, but it didn't make much difference. A shipping container was never going to be big enough for three people. We squeezed past and headed for the tiny storeroom, leaving her muttering under her breath.

"I don't think she likes me," whispered Shiloh.

"Don't worry about it," I replied. "Mimi doesn't like anybody."

Except Charli, I silently added.

Charli had never had a problem taming Mimi. I suspect that was because they both lived on the same cosmic cloud. Mimi was devastated when she left, and never really recovered. In her eyes, no one would ever measure up to Charli Blake. Poor Shiloh never stood a chance.

The tiny storeroom was a cluttered pile of boxes, but I found what I was looking for. I grabbed the bottle of red wine and handed it to Shiloh. She looked so genuinely excited by it that I thought she might cry. She turned the bottle, studying the label. "Tate Estate," she read aloud. "You have your own wine?"

My smile felt awkward. "My family own a vineyard in Tassie."

"Impressive."

"There's nothing impressive about picking grapes."

She waved the bottle at me. "There is when they're squashed into a bottle of Shiraz."

I directed my laugh at the floor. "I'm glad you like it."

"I love it," she clarified. "Thank you."

A weird moment of awkwardness set in, made doubly worse by the fact we were standing in the close confines of the storeroom. I motioned to the bottle in her hand. "Do you want a glass or a straw?"

"I'm going to save it," she replied. "It could be a while between drinks."

I didn't confess that I had another half dozen bottles stashed away for a rainy day. "Let's get out of here," I suggested. "I'll buy you a beer."

Mimi was standing at the open door when we walked out of the storeroom, graciously giving us space to escape the container without having to squeeze past. Shiloh went first, slowly heading for the door. Neither of us could've anticipated what was about to happen, or what Mimi's reaction would be.

One by one, the candles on the bar extinguished as Shiloh passed.

I couldn't explain why, but Mimi could – with wild eyes and wilder shrieks. It was like a horror movie. "Get out!" she screamed at her. "Heks! Heks! Heks!"

Shiloh froze, probably due to a mix of terror and confusion. I pushed in front of her, putting a barrier between her and the raving woman. "Stop it, Mimi," I demanded. "Right now."

"What's going on?" Shiloh whispered the question to me, but her eyes never left Mimi.

"You are a witch," Mimi accused. "You will get nothing from us."

I turned to the wannabe witch hunter and ordered her outside. For once Mimi did as she was told, but the denigration continued. "Heks girl must go!" she yelled.

Ignoring her as best I could, I turned back to Shiloh.

"What does heks mean?" Her voice shook. "What does she think I've done?"

Explaining it to her probably wasn't a good idea but I did it anyway. "It's Afrikaans," I mumbled. "It means witch."

Shiloh's eyes followed mine as I glanced at Mimi's wax spook detectors on the bar. "The candles went out when you walked past them," I explained. "It's supposedly a sign that evil spirits are nearby."

Her eyes widened. "I didn't do anything."

"I know." I gave her hands a reassuring squeeze. "Come on, I'll take you home."

Expecting Mimi to keep her mouth shut was beyond ambitious. We stepped outside and the production began. Mimi picked up a handful of beach sand and threw it into the air, chanting to herself in Afrikaans.

"Will you shut up?" I growled.

"If you keep the witch girl around, she will be the death of you," she warned. "No one escapes the devil alive."

I shook my head, incredulous. The woman couldn't even get her story straight. "Is she the devil or a witch?" Shiloh's grip on my hand tightened. "Make up your mind."

Mimi took a step forward, her eyes fixed on Shiloh. "She is all things evil," she purred in a creepy voice. "And I won't let her kill you."

Perhaps I should've thanked her. Instead I told her to get on with the job she was being paid to do and hold the fort until I got back.

Greek Celine

SHILOH

Mitchell apologised a hundred times on the short drive home, and at least another fifty once we got there. "It's not your fault," I told him. I didn't sound the least bit convincing. "Let's just forget it ever happened."

Forgetting it was going to be easier said than done. The memory of being called out as a witch who'd been sent to kill him would probably stick with both of us for a while.

"Tradition and customs are very important here." He sounded calm, but his demeanour gave him away. He bounced his keys in his hand, proving he was just as rattled as I was. "Stories have been passed down from generation to generation. Those who believe are fanatical about it."

I nodded as if I understood, but inside I was struggling. "You should go back to work," I urged. "I'll be fine here."

The key jingling stopped. "But you came all that way to see me." Half smiling, his eyes drifted, looking me up and down. "Dressed up like a girl and everything."

The flirty angle was welcome. Anything that deflected from talk of crazy Mimi was fine by me at that point. I dropped my bottle of wine on the beanbag. "I really went to the pub to talk to you," I explained. "I have some news."

"You're a witch?"

I scowled. "Not funny."

"No," Mitchell agreed. "Far too soon."

"They approved me for a company house," I said, getting back on topic. "I'll be out of your hair tomorrow."

At first I thought the look that flashed across his face was disappointment. When he spoke I realised that was just wishful thinking on my part. "About time," he muttered. "I thought I was never going to be rid of you."

This was a defining moment for me. I wanted him to be disappointed. I wanted him to ask me to stay, and I felt hurt when he didn't. It was proof positive that Mitchell Tate meant something to me, and that wasn't in my job description.

I couldn't really take all the blame for becoming distracted. At best, Agent Grace's decision to recruit an underqualified second year police constable was risky. Clearly it hadn't paid off.

My ineptness when it came to staving off the mini crush I harboured for my roommate wasn't my only act of incompetence. I'd been working at the mine for three weeks and hadn't uncovered a single useful piece of information. Catching Glen doing anything underhanded was impossible.

Tweedledee was stonewalling me.

I couldn't even get close enough to surveil him. He picked me up in the mornings and ditched me as soon as we arrived at work. Most days, I didn't see him again until we clocked off.

I had no idea how to turn things around, and no one to turn to for guidance. The promise of support from another agent hadn't panned out. No contact had been made, which led me to think that he was probably as useless as I was.

I figured it was a waiting game now. Sooner or later the AFP would realise what a lousy operative I was and pull me from the country – and the prospect of that happening didn't faze me in the least. I'd gladly return to Lawler, pick up where I left off, and be thankful for drunken old ladies and speeding drivers.

***

Mitchell reluctantly went back to work. I made use of the time alone to gather my belongings in preparation for my defection to the fat cat camp. I knew I wouldn't enjoy living there, but in a last-ditch effort to get my operation on track, I'd relentlessly pushed the issue with management. Glen avoided me like the plague at work, but it would be a harder to do if we were neighbours – at least, I hoped it would be.

Packing was a chore that took far longer than I expected. After stuffing my suitcase full of clothes, I dragged it to the door. I then decided to perform one last neighbourly deed and return the iron I'd borrowed to Melito and Vincent.

I wasn't sure they'd heard me knock. The warbling music coming from inside could only have been described as a power ballad. I had no idea what she was singing about, but the Greek version of Celine Dion sounded seriously narked about something.

As I prepared to knock one last time, the door swung open. The red silk robe Vincent wore didn't quite meet in the middle, and the view of his bronze potbelly was positively disturbing. Something in my expression must've conveyed horror.

"Don't be scared." He grinned. "I have pants on."

I was too terrified to check. "I brought your iron back." I thrust it forward. "Thank you for lending it to me."

Vincent shook his head, refusing to take it. "Keep it for a while," he urged.

I dropped my arm, lowering the iron to my side. "I'm moving out tomorrow."

"Mitchell won't let you go." He sounded absolutely sure of it. "He enjoys having pressed clothes."

It was hardly a romantic notion, but it made me giggle. And when Melito appeared at the doorway and joined in on Greek Celine's chorus, I laughed harder. Vincent beamed in approval, swiping his fingers through the air and swinging his head as if he was conducting the whole production. "Beautiful song, don't you think?" he asked.

"Lovely," I agreed, stepping back from the door.

"Don't leave," begged Melito. "Come inside and have a drink."

I smiled politely but continued edging toward the steps. "Thank you, but I have packing to do."

The door began closing. "Goodnight, Shiloh darling," called Vincent, dipping his head.

Declining their invitation hardly caused offence. As I stepped off the veranda, the music cranked up and both men started singing at the top of their lungs.

***

Occasionally, the dim porch light on the shack flickered. I'd never put much thought into it before, but tonight it unnerved me. Steely composure was hard to maintain in the presence of a faltering light, after Mimi's rant.

Something didn't feel right, and it didn't take long to work out why. As I got to the door, a rough hand wrapped around my mouth and pulled me backward. A man's forceful murmur scratched against my ear. "Stay quiet and open the door."

Adrenalin overruled fear. There was no telling what would happen if he got me inside the shack, so I stood still, which only seemed to aggravate him.

"I'll tell you again." His voice got rougher and so did his hold on me. "Open the door."

There was little chance of anyone coming to my rescue. The place was deserted. The cardboard villagers were all whooping it up at the pub – except Melito and Vincent, who were busy with Greek Celine. My only hope of escape was to cause this bloke some damage, and it came in the form of an upward punch to the head with the iron I was gripping.

When he staggered back and dropped to his knees, I thought I'd killed him. The iron thudded like a tonne weight as I dropped it, reminding me just how lethal my weapon of choice was. The gaping wound on my assailant's forehead was also a good indicator.

He groaned, which was a good sign, but I had no desire to rush to his aid. I stood cemented to the spot, filled with a confusing mix of anger and fear. "Get up!" I yelled.

Holding his hand to his face, the man lifted his head to look at me. I recognised him, and that's when true panic set in.

I'd just half-killed one of Louis Osei's henchmen.

The last time I'd seen him was at the Crown and Pav. He'd spent half the night staring me down from across the bar. It was a creepy exchange, but nothing compared to this.

Confident that he posed no further threat, I grabbed Mitchell's beach towel off the railing and tossed it at him. "Hold it to your head," I coolly instructed. "If you're lucky, it'll stop the bleeding."

I felt little sympathy for the man dripping blood on our deck. If I hadn't been wearing flip-flops I might've given him a kick for good measure.

"What do you want from me?" I demanded.

Still pressing the towel to his head, he looked up at me. "It never snows here on Tuesdays."

Delirium hadn't taken hold. I'd been waiting three weeks to hear that obscure phrase, and he was the last person I expected to hear it from. My mind worked quickly, breaking down the last few minutes: I'd half killed an AFP operative with an iron, and it had all gone down under a flickering porch light with Greek Celine crooning in the background.

Everything changed at that moment, including my desire to leave him bleeding to death on my deck. "I'm sorry," I mumbled. "I didn't know."

"Say it, Shiloh," he demanded.

I knew exactly what 'it' was. The cryptic cloak-and-dagger phrase was a two-part deal, and according to one of the many lectures Agent Grace had given me, mystery man couldn't deal with me until he heard me say mine.

"I prefer the snow on Wednesdays," I replied.

He leaned to the side, grabbed a bunch of keys and slid them across the deck. "You can drive."

***

It was the night of the eerie and strange, and getting weirder by the minute. After trekking up the steep track to the car park, I got into the driver's seat of a beaten up old Range Rover that belonged to a man who scared the hell out of me. It was a stupid act, any way I looked at it.

Still holding the towel to his head, my injured ally let out a pained groan and levered himself into the passenger seat. He probably wasn't in the mood for small talk, but I had a million questions for him. By the time I pulled out onto the road, I'd asked three quarters of them – and he hadn't uttered a word.

"Will you at least tell me your name?" I asked.

He glanced across at me for the first time. "Mike."

It didn't seem like the most opportune time to be cracking jokes, but I tried. "Can I call you Iron Mike?"

"No."

Evidently he had no sense of humour – understandable given his current state. It might also have been a prerequisite for Australian Federal Police Agents. Dan Grace had no sense of humour either.

I decided it was in my best interests to keep my mouth shut, which I managed to do until we got the T-junction at the end of the road. "Which way?" I asked.

"Go right."

It wasn't a course I felt comfortable with. Turning right meant we were heading out of town, nowhere near the Kaimte nursing post. I asked Mike where we were going, and when he didn't answer me, I threatened to pull the car over and get out until I got an answer.

"How on earth did you get this job?" He sounded thoroughly pissed off. "You're like a schoolgirl with a badge."

"For your information, they didn't give me a badge," I snapped. "They gave me a vague list of instructions, an impossible objective and a ticket to this hellhole."

Frustration had been building for weeks, and I'd finally come across someone I could unload on. Injured or not, Iron Mike was going to hear it.

"My boss is a pig." I smashed the heel of my hand down on the steering wheel. "I've tried a hundred different ways to get close to him and he shuts me down every time. After three weeks, I've got nothing," I ranted. "Why did you wait so long to contact me?"

"I had no use for you," he replied, adjusting his beach towel bandage.

The motionless car roughly idled as I stared at the T-junction sign, letting his words sink in.

Building rapport with Mike was never going to happen. He wasn't going to guide me like Allan did. That part of my life was gone. I was now a girl who didn't exist, living in a country with no rules.

Dispensing with the idea that I had any backup or support, I put myself back in charge. I wrenched the steering wheel, turned left and headed toward the Crown and Pav.

Mike didn't argue. In fact, Mike didn't say a word. I wondered if that was because he was losing consciousness, but didn't care enough to ask. My focus was on saving my own skin. There was no reasonable explanation I could give Mitchell for being AWOL at night. All I could do was slow him down and make sure I got back to the shack before he did. Temporarily breaking his car would definitely do the job.

"If Mitchell gets home and I'm not there, he's going to panic," I said, thinking out loud. "I need to buy some time."

The car park of the Crown and Pav was full of cars but absent of any people. Erring on the side of caution, I parked a good distance away.

I turned off the ignition. "I need a light."

Mike reached into the glove box and pulled out a small torch. "Do you even know what you're doing?"

The sarcasm in his tone was completely warranted. So far, I'd given him no indication that I was anything more than a bungling beat cop from Lawler.

"Watch and learn, Iron Mike."

Before he could cut me down, I jumped out of the car and made a beeline for Mitchell's jeep. As expected, it was unlocked. Car theft wasn't prevalent in Kaimte, and even if it were, the jeep wouldn't have topped any thief's wish list. I popped the hood, making sure the coast was clear before lifting it.

Mitchell was nobody's fool. Doing something obvious like pulling sparkplugs wasn't going to slow him down for long, so I decided on something more complicated. After flashing the small light around the engine bay, I finally located the fuse box, popped the lid, and pulled out the fuse to the fuel pump.

The hood made a hell of a clang when I dropped it, but I didn't hang around to see if anyone noticed the commotion. I bolted back to the car mumbling an apology to Mitchell, who was totally oblivious to the fact that I'd shamelessly ruined his night.

Mumbo Jumbo

MITCHELL

For years my mother used to call me once a week and beg me to come home. Her tearful argument was always the same. "Sooner or later you need to grow up and rejoin the real world," she'd wail.

She still calls weekly but never asks me to come home. At first I was grateful that she'd given up hassling me, but as time went on I began to wonder if I'd opted out of my own family.

I had nephews and a niece I'd never met. I'd missed weddings, birthdays and everything in between. I liked the life I'd built, but even I had to concede that my mother was right – somewhere along the line I'd stepped out of the real world.

Life in Kaimte was about as obscure as it gets, and dealing with the likes of Mimi Traore proved it. Mimi was a nutter and I was beginning to think that turning a blind eye to her antics was detrimental to my own sanity.

I returned to the pub with a firm plan of taking control. As soon as I walked in the door, I tossed every candle I could find out onto the beach.

Mimi squealed as if I'd just stabbed her. "We need the good juju in here," she protested.

"No more juju, mumbo jumbo, hocus pocus or talk of the devil," I demanded. "If you want to work here, those are the rules."

Furious, she narrowed her dark eyes and pointed a finger at me. "The witch girl got to you," she accused.

Shiloh *had* gotten to me, but not in the witchy sense. She provided a little slice of home that I realised I might've been missing. And I wasn't prepared to risk losing that because I indulged Mimi's nonsense.

"Shiloh is good," I told her. "And I won't have you saying otherwise. Got it?"

Mimi Traore was never one to back down. She had six children and usually pulled me into line by treating me like her seventh. I endured her indignant glare for as long as I could before finally breaking eye contact to serve a customer. I took his money, handed him two bottles of beer and turned around to find that Mimi hadn't moved.

"Don't you have something else to do?"

She threw her cloth on the bar. "She's not to be trusted, dumb boy." Her hands moved to my shoulders and shook me hard. "She will kiss you to death with lies."

Mimi was determined to make a believer out of me, but the notion was ridiculous. "I'll take my chances," I replied. "It doesn't sound like a bad way to go."

Asset

SHILOH

Taking on a job that involved doing bad things for good reasons was downright damaging, and I'd caused my fair share of damage that night.

Mike didn't say a word as we drove away, and I'd lost all desire to talk to him. I kept my eyes on the road, occasionally glancing in the rear vision mirror to see the lights of Kaimte slip further away. After a few minutes there was nothing but darkness surrounding the car.

There wasn't a whole lot of sunshine and light on the inside either.

"You don't trust me," Mike said unexpectedly.

"No, I don't." I wasn't in the mood for lying. I had more than enough of that to come when or if I ever made it back to the shack.

Mike unwrapped his towel bandage and tossed it onto the back seat. "Why not?"

"A few reasons." I shrugged. "You won't talk. That's not a good sign."

"Some might say you talk too much," he countered.

He was probably right. My list of professional shortcomings was glaringly long. "I don't think you're AFP," I said gruffly.

If he was shocked by the accusation, I couldn't tell. His voice gave nothing away. "I don't work for your government," he replied. "I work for mine."

My fingers tightened around the steering wheel, and my heart started thumping, overwhelmed by the predicament I'd found myself in.

In addition to the hundreds of other rookie mistakes I'd made lately, I hadn't asked him enough questions. I knew he wasn't Australian. The only thing Western about him was his name, and that was probably bogus. Mike looked and spoke like a Kaimte local, and no matter how deft his undercover skills were, those traits can't easily be faked to fit a profile. What I didn't know was how he'd become tangled up in my operation, or why.

"What do you want from me?" Keeping my voice strong took effort, but I managed.

"I want you to do your job," he coolly replied. "Our objective is the same."

The car slowed as I concentrated more on him than the road ahead. "You'll get nothing from me until you start giving me information," I said strongly. "It's a two-way street."

"Finally." His white smile transcended the darkness. "Now you're sounding like an asset worthy of information."

His choice of words only added to my mistrust. In our line of work, assets are intrinsically disposable and tradable. Sacrificing me to move his operation forward was a highly probable scenario at that point. Determined to keep my wits about me, I repeated my demand for information.

"Your government cares about stolen diamonds," he told me. "Mine is more interested in how the proceeds are spent."

I was grateful when he elaborated. It saved me from asking anything stupid. "If the funds are being used to finance insurgents, it could literally mean war for this country," he explained, "which is why we need to find out who is profiting from this." Louis Osei was his number one guess, but after months of surveilling him, he was still chasing proof. Louis' standover tactics at the port and his many other shady dealings weren't of concern to the Kaimte government. Their only interest was finding out if he was plotting a coup. "Diamonds buy a lot of guns," he said ominously.

Mike didn't explain how the AFP had become involved in the operation, but it didn't take a genius to work out why they'd taken it on. Jorge Creek was an Australian-owned company. If their diamonds were being used to fund an impending war, it was in their interest to put a stop to it. No amount of tarmac roads and community donations would make up for that.

I spent the next few minutes building a cache of questions in my head but didn't bother asking any of them. For now, my concentration needed to be focused on where we were heading.

The further we drove from the coast, the bleaker the landscape became. Despite the darkness I could tell the terrain was flat, uninhabitable desert. I didn't protest when Mike instructed me to turn left onto a crude dirt track. I glanced at the odometer, covertly noting that we'd driven just seven miles from the Crown and Pav. If it came down to it, the walk home would be long but manageable.

"Fear jeopardises your operation, Shiloh," he told me. "I can tell you're frightened. Replace it with another emotion."

"I'm not afraid of you." I snapped out the lie. "I was just thinking how I wish I'd worn more sensible shoes."

Mike laughed – a seemingly genuine chuckle that infinitesimally put me at ease, and when lights came into view in the distance a few moments later I felt even better.

As we approached the camp, I realised it looked very similar to the cardboard village, but without the great view. There were three small shacks made of tin and concrete bricks. Goats, chickens and dogs ran free, and when a couple of small children saw the Range Rover pull in, they ran free too.

"This is my home," he declared, somehow managing to ignore the two little boys knocking on the passenger side window. "You'll be safe here."

"I wasn't feeling unsafe until you approached me from behind like a thug," I snapped.

With one hand on the door handle, he turned to face me. "You're not as weak as I expected you to be."

I nodded and waited until he was out of the car. "Kicked your arse, pal," I muttered.

***

The woman who tended Mike's wounds was obviously used to patching him up. As soon as we walked through the door, she grabbed a basket of medical supplies and wordlessly went to work.

Being there felt intrusive and uncomfortable, but as I sat on one of the brightly coloured cushions scattering the tiled floor, I reminded myself that I'd had little choice in the matter – and I still wasn't sure whether I was free to leave.

Mike's home didn't appear to be part of any cover story, and if it was, his family certainly weren't. Thrilled that their father was home, the two little boys ran amok, bouncing off cushions and chasing each other around until Mike ordered them out of the room.

An elderly lady shuffled in, carefully balancing a tray of tea. Mike made no attempt to help her out by taking it, nor did he thank her when she set it down on the mat in front of him.

"Tea?" he asked me.

My answer was unimportant. The lady was already pouring it. The glass she handed me was no bigger than a shot glass, and when I brought it to my lips I realised the tiny portion was necessary. The minty black tea was sweetened beyond belief.

"Your first taste of Kaimte tea?" asked Mike, raising his glass to his lips.

"It's very sweet."

"Mostly sugar," he replied. "An acquired taste."

I made of a point of thanking the old lady as she left the room, mainly because Mike hadn't. She smiled, which was the most friendliness I'd been shown in hours.

The lady wielding the medicals supplies snipped at the end of the gauze with a pair of scissors and gathered up her basket. I didn't understand a word of the rant she directed at Mike, but knew it was harsh.

He put his hand up to the bandage, let out a chuckle and dismissed her, adding weight to my theory that Iron Mike was an arse.

As soon as we were alone in the room, he got straight down to business. He'd claimed that he hadn't made contact before that night because he had no use for me. As soon as he started speaking, I realised that had changed.

"You have expertise with electronics." I wondered what else he knew. The whole notion of him having intel on me pissed me off. "I have a job for you," he added.

Nothing about being his errand girl appealed, but I sipped my tea and let him talk.

"Another quantity of stones went missing from the mine two days ago," he explained. "Intel suggests they're being shipped out of the country within the next few weeks."

A pocket full of diamonds was no good to anyone in their raw form. The only option the thieves had was to send them out of the country to be cut and sold, which is why Louis Osei was a sure bet.

The sticking point was that it was far bigger than a one-man operation. Louis had the means to get them out of Kaimte, but not the mine. Presumably that's where Glen Harris came into the equation.

I really had nothing to add to the conversation. Every bit of my information had come from a file in Dan Grace's office. It was embarrassing that another theft had occurred right under my nose, and humiliating that Mike was the one to tell me about it.

"What do you want me to do?" I asked.

"I can't be with Louis twenty-four hours a day." He refilled my glass and held it out to me. "I want to know where he goes and who he sees when I'm not there. I want you to put a GPS in his car."

Risking the onset of a diabetic coma, I took the glass from him. "Tracking his phone would be easier," I suggested.

Mike frowned. "I'm not seeking the easiest solution," he replied. "I want a permanent, hardwired device concealed in his vehicle. Can you do it or not?"

Almost every word out of his mouth was offensive in one way or another, and whether I was being over-sensitive or not, I figured I'd put up with enough. "I can definitely do it," I told him, placing my tea glass down on the tray. "The bigger question is what can you do for me?"

The grin that slowly crossed his face was positively sinister. "What do you want?"

"You have a source working at the mine," I said pointedly. "Someone there is giving you information."

Mike chuckled at the floor. "I have sources all over town."

"Do you know Glen Harris?" I asked. "He's head of security. He's also my boss."

"I know he's the mule who's getting the diamonds out – a small but vital player."

"I want you to get me closer to him," I continued. "I can't do my job if I can't get near him."

He nodded, just once. "I can do that," he replied. "Do you have any other demands?"

He was humouring me, but I didn't care. "Yes," I replied strongly. "I want some lock-picking tools – titanium so I can get them through the metal detectors at the mine."

Mike's bandage began to slip, much like my tenacity. Obviously I had no locks to pick, but I was determined to pretend otherwise.

He pushed the dressing clear of his eye and stared at me. "Do you know how to breach a lock?"

"Better than most criminals," I retorted.

That much was true, and for a quick moment I allowed myself to marvel at the fact that my skill set was actually quite diverse.

"Fine," he replied, seemingly satisfied. "Give me two days, three at the most."

"Okay." I nodded stiffly. "Get me the GPS and some tools too."

"What else will you need?"

I chewed my bottom lip, pondering the massive task ahead. "Time to work," I replied. "It's going to take a while if you want it hardwired."

Mike promised to work out the details and get back to me. I hoped for both our sakes he was a meticulous planner. Getting caught screwing with Louis Osei's car didn't bear thinking about.

"How will you contact me?" I asked, moving the conversation along.

He turned his head and shouted to someone in Afrikaans. A minute later the old lady shuffled back into the room with a zip lock bag. Mike grabbed it from her and tossed it into my lap. "With this."

The bag held a mobile phone and charger, both of which looked at least ten years out of date.

"It's untraceable," he explained, once she'd gone. "You and I shouldn't need to meet in person again."

I nodded in relief. Never seeing him again suited me perfectly fine.

Mike's instructions regarding the phone were very clear. Contact would only be made via text. I was to hide the phone and let no one know of its existence.

"Keep it turned off at all times," he added.

"How will I know if you're trying to contact me?"

I hoped it was a reasonable question, but it was impossible to tell. Iron Mike had a knack for making me feel foolish.

He frowned, momentarily deliberating. "I will signal you," he eventually replied. "The T-junction sign in town – you pass it often, yes?"

I shrugged. "A couple of times a day, at least."

"If I need to contact you, I will put a chalk mark on the signpost." He almost smiled, perhaps impressed by his own ingenuity.

"And if I need to contact you?"

"You won't," he replied. "I would be of no use to you."

***

I made it back to civilisation without being murdered or dumped in the desert, and was almost proud of the accomplishment. At my insistence, Mike dropped me off on the corner and, like a kid afraid of breaking curfew, I ran home along the beach.

There was some housekeeping to do when I got there, and when I glanced at my watch and realised it was after midnight, I wasn't sure if I was going to be able to get it done before Mitchell got home.

I started with the blood on the deck. Iron Mike wasn't much of a talker, but he was definitely a bleeder. Small crimson spots peppered the weathered wood. The slow trickling garden hose proved useless at removing them, but I persevered because I had no other choice. Mitchell could never know what had gone on that night, and as I carried out the task of scrubbing a man's blood off the floor, I realised he'd be better for it.

Fire And Brimstone

MITCHELL

My car was a twenty-five-year-old piece of junk, but usually reliable. When it refused to start, I took it as a sign from above that I needed to slow my roll. I didn't even try to fix it. I threw my shoes on the back seat, locked up and began the long walk home along the beach.

Midnight strolls are usually reserved for lovers and the lonely. I'd been both in my lifetime, but tonight I was stuck somewhere in between.

The cloudless night was warm and still, and the bright sky cast a silver glow for as far as I could see. It was a scene that should've been shared, and only one person came to mind when I thought of who I'd share it with. Shiloh Jenson seemed to be invading my thoughts a lot lately, which bugged me because I knew I'd never act on them.

A job transfer had brought her to Kaimte, not a burning sense of adventure or a desire to explore somewhere new – and that's how I knew she wasn't the girl for me. Pursuing her was pointless, no matter how strong the attraction was.

I felt guilty that Shiloh's time here had been so rough. The antics of creepy Louis and mad Mimi kept her in a constant state of unease, which had to be nothing less than exhausting. Living in the shack was no picnic for her either. It was creaky, dilapidated and seriously under-furnished. Not once had she complained, but the luggage standing by the door when I arrived home was a stark reminder of how desperate she was to get out of there. Right or wrong, my plan was to let her go.

Shiloh sat bolt upright in bed as I walked into the room.

"You're awake?" I asked, stripping off my shirt.

"I was getting worried about you," she replied. "It's late."

The small gesture of caring whether I was alive or dead made cool detachment impossible. I smiled at her. "My car wouldn't start so I had to walk home."

"Oh," she mumbled into her lap. "I'm sorry."

"Why are you sorry?" I asked. "It's an inconvenience, not a tragedy."

She lifted her head. "Nothing ever fazes you, does it?"

I silently answered her question by dropping my pants to the floor and walking buck naked to the bathroom. "Life's too short to spend it stressing," I called.

If she replied, I didn't hear. I stepped under the flow of the shower and spent the next few minutes washing the day away.

***

Considering she was only moving five hundred metres up the hill, waking up beside Shiloh the next morning felt remarkably final. I crept out of bed and left her sleeping, opting for a few hours in the water so I didn't have to deal with the tinge of loss I was feeling.

The clear night had paved the way for a brilliantly bright morning. A quick check of the weather gauge on the deck showed that the temperature was already pushing thirty degrees.

"It's going to be hot, hot, hot," called Melito from a distance. I turned to see him and Vincent strolling up the beach after their morning swim.

"How's the water?" I asked.

"Calm and warm," he replied. "Not ideal for you."

"No," I agreed, grinning. "I like it cold and rough."

"Like your women?" teased Vincent, awkwardly staggering through the sand as he towelled himself dry.

"If that's the case, he needs to rethink his affection for the lovely Shiloh," suggested Melito. "An ice cube and a hard slap on the butt couldn't make that girl cold and rough."

Their infectious guffaws stopped dead the second Shiloh stepped outside. I hoped she hadn't heard the tactless comment, but one look at her face told me she probably had.

"Hey," I quickly greeted her.

"Hey," she returned, drawing out the word. "My ears were burning."

"Not surprising," I replied. "It's hot out here."

Having thrown me under the bus, the sleek Greeks made a hasty exit into their shack. A change of subject was my only hope.

"I was going to go for a surf, but I can't find my towel," I told her. "Have you seen it?"

"No." Her expression was filled with worry as she glanced around the deck. "I haven't."

"I left it on the railing," I explained. "Somebody probably swiped it during the night."

True to form, Shiloh looked much too concerned – a side effect of over-thinking things. I slung my arm around her and gave her a quick shake. "It's just a towel," I reminded her. "No worries, okay?"

"None." She nodded stiffly. "Just a towel."

For the second time in less than a minute, I found myself trying to divert her attention. I turned her to face me. "I should probably go down and fix my jeep before it gets too hot to work on it. You should come."

"I'm supposed to be moving today."

I dropped my hold on her and put forward a deal designed purely to keep her around a bit longer. "Help me fix my car and then I'll help you move. Deal?"

Granting me a tiny smile, she nodded.

"Excellent," I replied, heading for the door. "I'll get my keys."

Shiloh called my name at the last moment, and like a fool, I turned back.

"Just for the record," she began, "ice cubes would probably cool the core temperature of all girls."

Maintaining eye contact was difficult, but being a smart arse came easily. "Even witches?" I teased.

The cheeky question elicited a wicked smile befitting any witch in town.

"Mitchell Tate," she huffed in mock annoyance. "We're not entirely made of fire and brimstone, you know."

***

It wasn't the best day to be trekking a long way on foot, even along the beach. The weather was scorching.

Shiloh strolled at the water's edge, trying to stay cool by keeping her feet wet. It was effective, but slow going. I wasn't in any hurry, but that didn't stop me teasing her. "Could you move any slower?" I asked, stopping for the umpteenth time to let her catch up.

"Yeah." Like a petulant child, she stopped dead in her tracks and threw her arms wide. "I could just stand here for a while. How do you like them apples?"

I stalked toward her. "Fighting words, lady."

With her hands up in a stay back motion, Shiloh edged away. "You won't win, Mitchell," she warned.

I was prepared to take my chances. Without warning, I lurched forward with the intention of throwing her over my shoulder, but it was a move that quickly went bad. Shiloh countered by turning sharply, twisting my arm behind my back and kicking my legs out from underneath me. Before I knew what was happening, I was face down, eating sand.

I groaned, mainly to prove I was still alive.

"Mitchell!" She rolled me onto my back. "I'm so sorry."

"Where did you learn a move like that?" I choked.

"Self-defence class," she replied, brushing sand off my face. "But I've never had to use it before."

I put my hands to my chest and laughed, ignoring the pain it caused me. It was easy to forget what she did for a living because until that moment I didn't know she had an assertive bone in her body.

"You've never had to throw anyone to the ground at work?"

Shiloh lay down beside me. "No," she replied, looking at the sky. "Bouncers at nightclubs would see more action than me. My job involves a lot of standing around and looking important."

Shiloh Jenson suddenly made a whole lot more sense to me. Despite her vocation, the majority of her bravado was on paper. The company transfer hadn't altered her job description – she was still spending her days standing around trying to look important. The difference was, it was playing out in a third world country where crooks are brazenly crooked – and it was fair to assume that a few of them were working at the mine.

Her résumé probably implied she had the experience to handle it, but nothing could be further from the truth. A lack of street smarts is a difficult shortcoming to hide, and Shiloh was clearly struggling.

"Are you worried that you can't do your job?" I asked gently.

"Every single day." Her voice was quiet and serious. "I'm a fraud, and sooner or later, the powers that be will notice."

Mechanic

SHILOH

The most convincing lies are always laced with an element of truth. That's what makes them believable. The trick is knowing when to stop talking. The minute I felt in danger of giving Mitchell too much information, I put an end to the conversation.

I levered myself up and grabbed his hands, trying to pull him to his feet. "If we stay here much longer we're going to cook."

The day was brutally hot. I was uncomfortable, sweaty and now covered in sand, but I didn't dare complain. It felt a lot like karma.

Mitchell's jeep was stranded in the car park of the Crown and Pav because I broke it. The least I could do was make the trip down there with him to fix it. Mitchell stood and brushed the sand off his clothes. "When we get there, I'll buy you a beer," he offered.

I put my hand to my heart. "So bloody generous."

"If you're a really good girl, I'll make it a cold one."

I was probably going to need it. The temperature seemed to rise a few degrees as we left the beach. By the time my feet hit the gravel road I felt ready to drop at any second.

The jeep was right where he'd left it, looking as lonely and abandoned as a car could. Mitchell wasted no time. While I stood idly by, he popped the hood and set about diagnosing the problem.

All he had to do to get the car started was push a fuse back into place. In theory, we could've been sipping beer on the beach ten seconds after that. But it soon occurred to me that it might not be that simple.

"How much do you know about cars, Mitchell?" I asked curiously.

He gave the battery cable a wiggle. "Enough," he replied. "It's probably the battery."

He was clueless, which killed me.

I pointed to a large rock near the edge of the trail. "I'm just going to sit over there," I muttered. "It's hot."

Mitchell took off his T-shirt and draped it over my head, gifting me a tiny bit of shade. "It won't take long, I promise."

It was a promise he couldn't keep. As enjoyable as it was watching a shirtless Mitchell hunched over and tinkering with an engine, aggravation soon set in. He didn't seem the least bit bothered that he was getting nowhere with it, even after half an hour of trying. When he started talking about pulling the engine apart, I knew I had to intervene.

Shiloh Jenson's knowledge of cars was non-existent, but Shiloh Brannan was at the end of her rope. I jumped to my feet and made my way to him, gearing up to point out the fuse box he'd so far managed to ignore.

Then his phone rang.

It wasn't difficult to work out who his caller was. Mimi's bark echoed around the car park. Holding his phone to his ear, Mitchell absently wandered away, occasionally grunting into the phone in reply.

As soon his back was turned I made my move, pushing the fuel pump fuse back into place and snapping the box shut. I was sitting in the driver's seat when Mitchell returned. Now he looked pissed off, but it had nothing to do with the car. "Mimi's called in sick," he told me. "I'm going to have to work tonight."

Clearly she was punishing him for the telling off he'd given her the night before, but I wasn't willing to say it out loud.

"I'll still help you move," he offered, ducking back under the hood. "This shouldn't take much longer."

Before he had a chance to inflict any more damage on the engine, I turned the key. The old jeep rumbled to life as if there had never been a problem.

Mitchell straightened up, staring at me through the dirty windscreen, looking shocked and bewildered.

"You fixed it!" I said excitedly. "What was the problem?"

He shook his head, frowning. "I'm not entirely sure."

I turned off the ignition, got out of the car and slammed the door. "Good juju, Mitchell." I tossed his shirt at him as I passed. "Now you owe me a beer."

***

Our leisurely beers on the beach outside the closed pub were limited to one. Mitchell was determined to leave enough time to help me move before work.

It was a thoughtful gesture that my mind managed to twist. Was he desperate to be rid of me or just trying to be helpful? I didn't know, and it was ridiculously juvenile to even ponder the question.

***

The amount of luggage I had to move wasn't what made it a two-person job; I only had one suitcase. The problem was, there was no way I could get it up there by myself. Mitchell made it look easy, carving a line in the sand as he dragged it up the steep hill.

"I really appreciate your help," I said, trudging along behind him.

"No worries. I appreciate you giving me my bed back." There wasn't a hint of humour in his tone, which stung enough to make me bite back.

"Just having a bathroom with a door will be a treat," I told him. "I can't wait to move in."

Of all the lies I'd told him lately, that one felt like the worst. I didn't want to leave the shack and I didn't want to leave him – but the feeling wasn't mutual.

Mitchell dragged my luggage the last few metres and dumped it at the edge of the road. "I have to get to work," he muttered. "You can take it from here, right?"

Both of us looked up at the small row of houses across the street. The only thing uglier than its dull beige facade was the sight of Glen Harris staring us down from his front porch. I suspect the rigid posture, folded arms and scowl were supposed to be intimidating, but I paid him little attention. I was more focused on Mitchell, and his sudden determination to make a quick getaway.

"You don't want to see inside?" My voice was pathetically small.

He wiped the sweat off his forehead with the sleeve of his T-shirt. "No," he replied flatly. "Believe it or not, I've seen bathroom doors before."

"Wait," I grabbed his arm as he turned away, "Are you mad at me?"

"Of course not," he replied. "Enjoy your time in the fat cat camp, kitty." He shrugged me away and glanced back at Glen. "But watch out for the lions," he warned. "I hear they bite."

***

I had no trouble pulling my suitcase across the tarmac road, but the five steps up to the porch nearly did me in. Glen stood and watched me struggle, uttering his first word when I finally cleared the top step. "Trouble in paradise?"

I had to be nice to him at work, but we were off the clock now so I replied accordingly. "If you're going to be a smartarse, first you have to be smart." I twisted my key in the lock and pushed open the door. "Otherwise you're just an arse."

***

No matter how hard I tried over the next few hours, I couldn't settle. I wandered aimlessly from room to room, growing more dejected by the second. It was a nice house – if beige is your thing. The walls, furniture and floor tiles were all the same monochromatic, depressing shade. It was functional but uninspiring – and I hated it.

The only redeeming feature was the bathroom, and the door wasn't even the best part. It had a bath – something I hadn't seen in weeks.

Not much thought went into my plan for whittling away the rest of the afternoon. I grabbed my bottle of Shiraz out of my suitcase, drew a bath, and spent the next two hours pretending I was living a perfectly normal life.

***

It was after midnight when I finally decided that being normal isn't all it's cracked up to be. After three hours of tossing and turning in my huge beige bed, I concluded that sleep just wasn't going to happen.

I lay flat on my back, staring up at the ceiling while I tried reasoning with myself. Mitchell didn't want me, and I sure as hell wasn't supposed to want him. And that's exactly what I kept telling myself as I stepped out of my beige house and quietly pulled the door closed. I paused at the edge of the steps for a moment, allowing my eyes to adjust to the darkness. Common sense was still screaming in my ear, only now its voice sounded a lot like Dan Grace's.

My life in Kaimte was built on a foundation of secrets and lies. Staying away from Mitchell would be doing both of us a favour.

That notion stayed with me as I strolled across the road. But when the warm asphalt under my bare feet turned to the cool sand of the beach, another thought took over, and they were the tough Irish words of Lynette Kelly. "Protect your soul at all costs, my girl," she'd told me. "It's the only truth you'll have for a while."

I was finally beginning to realise what that meant. More than my fair share of time was spent doing shady things for people I didn't trust. I didn't get to choose who I did business with, but the tiny amount of downtime I was afforded should've been spent hanging out with the one person who was good for my soul.

My plan was vague, but so were my intentions. All I could do was put it all out there and tell Mitchell how I felt. If he told me to take a hike and slammed the door in my face, I would take solace in the fact that I'd finally shown him some honesty.

And that was the thought that kept me going as I ran down the sandy trail to the ramshackle little house on the beach.

Torment

MITCHELL

No one ever knocked on my door, least of all after midnight. It was such an alien sound that it took me a long moment to realise what it was. It was a few seconds too long for Shiloh. She was almost at the edge of the deck when I opened the door.

"Hey," I quietly called. "Where are you going?"

She slowly turned around, looking one part mortified, one part confused and all parts lovely. "It's late," she mumbled. "Were you sleeping?"

"No, I just got home." She knew my schedule better than anyone. "Is everything okay?"

"Not really." She shook her head. "We need to talk before I completely lose my nerve."

"Wow. That doesn't sound good."

"Can I come in?"

I stepped aside and motioned with a swing of my arm. "Be my guest."

The trail of her familiar perfume lingered as she passed, and for a moment things were how they were meant to be. I didn't want to ruin it with words so I waited for her to speak, which seemed to take forever.

"Why didn't you ask me to stay?" she finally blurted, her brown eyes challenging mine.

For such a simple question, it was mighty confusing. I had no idea how to answer her, so like an idiot I said nothing.

"I would've stayed if you'd asked me to," she elaborated. "Why didn't you?"

I slowly shook my head. "Why would I?"

Shiloh flopped down in the nearest beanbag looking absolutely crushed. "I really did read this all wrong, didn't I?"

I crouched in front of her and held her hand. "I've spent weeks being tormented by you," I told her. "You're not my type."

I was a publican, not a scholar. Perhaps that's why I'd just thumped her in the chest with a bungled run of words that came out sounding awful.

Her free hand flew over my mouth. "Stop talking now," she demanded. "You're just not good at it."

I muffled my next words against her palm. "Let me finish, please."

After a long moment, she withdrew her hand.

"I like you, Shiloh. I do."

"But?"

"But, the girls in my past are shady as heck," I explained. It wasn't exactly the winning formula for a long lasting relationship, but it had always worked for me. "I'm not sure I deserve a good girl."

She huffed out a sharp breath, widening her eyes in surprise. "You think I'm good?"

I half smiled. "You iron your clothes for fun."

"I like things neat," she defended in a tiny voice.

I steadied myself by putting both hands on her knees. "And there's nothing wrong with that," I replied. "But it confuses me."

The next words out of my mouth were going to determine everything. The bottom line was, I felt guilty for being attracted to her. Never before had I been so fascinated by someone so naïve and green. I wasn't the bloke who enjoyed playing the part of protector. I liked girls who start fires and raise a little hell. Shiloh couldn't start a fire with a box of matches and a set of instructions, and yet I still fought the urge to kiss her half to death whenever she was in reach. I also felt a driving need to stand up for her and look after her when she needed it, which was often. It was downright confusing and I had no idea how to deal with it.

"I think you're too good for me." It wasn't exactly a full confession, but it was the best I could come up with. "I didn't ask you to stay because you don't belong in a shabby old shack." I glanced around the pitiful room. "And this is all I have."

She closed her eyes for a few seconds as if trying to make sense of my words. "You're scared," she said finally.

I wasn't sure if it was a question or an accusation. Either way, I agreed with her. "Terrified," I admitted. "I'm scared of disappointing you, hurting you and messing up your ironing routine."

She finally let her amusement show. Both of her hands moved to my face. "Maybe you should get out of your comfort zone and try something new."

My something new came in the form of a compliment – something she couldn't put down to flirty innuendo or a joke. "I think you're beautiful." My eyes were focused entirely on her mouth. "And I want you to stay."

"Really?" The uncharacteristically high pitch in her voice made me smile.

"Yeah," I replied. "What do you want?"

"I want you to kiss me," she murmured. "And make it good. Then I'll decide whether I'm staying or not."

Her smartarse comment threw us right back to a place I was comfortable with. The beanbag crunched beneath her as I lurched forward, urgently pressing my lips against hers as if there was a chance she'd come to her senses and change her mind.

She didn't. And within three seconds, I knew I was hers to keep.

Good Girls

SHILOH

Mitchell was under the impression that Shiloh Jenson was good. That meant I was playing the role well, but the performance wasn't flawless. Good, meek girls weren't his type – and yet here I was, pinned beneath him on a beanbag, lip-locked and breathless.

The reason for his confusion was simple, but not one I could ever share with him. Underneath the cover of lies, he'd managed to find a glimpse of Shiloh Brannan – and she was exactly his type.

I turned my head, momentarily breaking our embrace. "I want to stay," I whispered, "for a really long time."

I felt his smile against the skin of my throat. "That's fortunate," he replied. "Because I wasn't going to let you go."

***

I'd slept beside Mitchell every night for weeks. His bed felt like the safest place in Kaimte, but tonight was different. After spending twenty-two nights deflecting the sparks that came with accidental touches, I was finally able to give in to them.

I refused to think about what might happen after that night, and when he peeled off his T-shirt, lay beside me and pulled me close, I lost the ability to think of anything. My breath hitched as his hand wrapped around the curve of my calf.

"You have the most gorgeous legs," he whispered in my ear.

"You have gorgeous everything," I softly replied.

It was impossible to be more specific. There was a reason his neighbours had nicknamed him Adonis. His perfect body was a hard combination of ridges and hollows, but his touch was sublimely gentle. Mitchell slowly trailed a long line from my shin to my hip that left me tingling from head to toe.

Be it by chance or design, it was pure artistry.

"Do that again," I whimpered, barely holding myself together. "*Please* do that again."

"No, I don't think so." Far from regretful, his whole face lit as he smiled. "I've already moved on."

And he had.

My eyes fluttered closed, reacting as his hands deftly changed course. The tingling suddenly turned to surging volts that pinned me to the bed. I couldn't have moved if the room was on fire, and at that moment I was almost certain that it was.

My whole body burned in the best possible way, and I had to know if he felt it too. In a move that took huge effort, I shifted my hand to his chest, flattening my palm over his heart.

"It's there, Shiloh," he assured me, breathing the words against my shoulder. "Every part of me is here."

Even Witches Need To Eat

MITCHELL

If Shiloh had woken with a single ounce of regret that morning, everything would've gone to hell, which probably explained why I woke at the crack of dawn feeling weighed down by a sense of impending doom.

I decided to hit the water because salt water cures everything. And if I came back to find out that she'd hightailed it back up to the fat cat camp, I'd hit the water again.

I already knew the day would be cooler, and the light easterly wind made for perfect surfing conditions – something I hadn't seen in days. The slow rolling waves practically called my name as I stood ankle deep in the cool water, but for the first time ever I couldn't commit to them.

I didn't profess to be in love with Shiloh, but I wasn't too dumb to recognise that I might've been on the edge of something special. Without putting too much thought into the reason why, I hitched my board under my arm and headed back to the shack.

Once inside, I crept into the bedroom, leaned across the bed and planted a soft kiss on her back. "No surf this morning?" she lazily mumbled.

"It's not bad." I swept her hair off her shoulder. "But the conditions in here are better."

She turned over, granting me a smile that made me want to do wicked things. "Do you have plans for the day?"

I dropped my head, pressing my lips against her warm chest. "Just you."

I felt her soft laugh. "If you alter that plan to include food, I'm in," she replied. "Bacon and eggs and fruit and toast and coffee and –"

I cut her wishful rambling short with a kiss. "I'll see what I can do," I murmured against her lips. "Meanwhile, don't leave this bed until I get back."

Her arms wrapped around me. "I'm not going anywhere until I get food," she joked. "And don't forget the bacon."

Living in a third world country forces you to become resourceful, but even my epic hunting and gathering skills didn't stretch as far as bacon. Kaimte didn't have the luxury of supermarkets and restaurants. We shopped at the mid-week markets, spending half the morning sourcing the freshest produce we could find from the limited wares on offer. I'd become accustomed to scrubbing dirt off vegetables and washing the occasional feather off eggs, but it was one of the many reasons why life in Kaimte was reserved for hardcore travellers.

It wasn't all culinary doom and gloom. My sisters often sent me care packages – usually boxes of biscuits and chocolates – but nothing that could be conjured into a meal. Convenience foods were highly lacking. Cooking took time and even the most basic meals required major preparation, but I had a plan that morning. It was Sunday, and that meant the regular rules didn't apply.

***

Mimi Traore and her family lived on the northern edge of town, quite a distance from the scenic coast. Their aversion to living on the beach confounded me, but for some reason most locals preferred desert living.

Like most homes in Kaimte, the Traore home was a rough mesh of tin and cinderblocks that had been haphazardly extended throughout the years to accommodate her growing family. Mimi's brood was large – three boys and three girls. In stark contrast to their mother the girls were quiet and shy, so I didn't know them well. The boys, however, were a different story. The boisterous little blokes were the Kaimte equivalent of the English Premier League. The wannabe soccer superstars spent a ridiculous amount of time kicking a ball around their dust bowl of a yard, and that's where I spotted the oldest one when I pulled up to the house.

As soon as I got out of the car Francis ran over to greet me.

"How are you, mate?" I put my hand on the top of his head. "You're getting so tall. How old are you now? Seventeen?"

With a firm grip on his ball, he threw his head back and cackled as if my joke was hilarious. "I'm eleven," he answered.

"Oh, right." I grinned. "Where's your mum?"

Francis pointed to a long line of laundry running between the house and an outbuilding. Mimi stood at the end of it, adding more clothes to the already perilously low hanging structure.

"What are you doing here, Mitchell?" She sounded annoyed, but I knew her well enough to know that she wasn't. "Sunday is market day. You know that."

I did know that, which was the sole reason for my visit.

Mimi didn't frequent the sub-par mid-week markets in town – none of the local villagers did. They attended the mysterious markets that cropped up out of nowhere on the edge of the desert every Sunday morning. Expats weren't welcome there, and despite my connections, that included me. The only way I could access the treasure trove of goodies on offer was by convincing Mimi to be my personal shopper, which rarely worked.

Attempting to weasel into her good books, I grabbed the basket of laundry off the ground and held it for her. "I was hoping you could pick up a few things for me," I said optimistically. "I have a list."

Mimi snatched a shirt out of the basket and gave it a violent shake. "No."

"Please," I begged. "Just a few things to make a nice breakfast."

Her large brown eyes narrowed. "To impress the heks girl?" she asked sourly.

"Come on, Mimi." My smile was wry. "Even witches need to eat."

She roughly slung the shirt over the line, making the whole thing wobble. "Feed her sour milk and mouldy bread," she replied. "She deserves nothing better."

"Mimi Traore," I scolded. "Show some heart."

She turned to face me, looking downright furious. "I show you heart every day, dumb boy," she barked. "I look after you every day."

I took a large step back, worried that she might thump me. "I know you do, and I appreciate it."

"But you don't listen," she replied . "The girl is no good."

Absolutely nothing I said was going to change her mind about Shiloh so defending her was pointless. Nothing Mimi said was going to convert me into a juju believer either, so it was best to let it go.

I set the laundry basket on the ground and reached into my pocket. "Just some nice fruit and fresh eggs," I begged, holding a small roll of banknotes out to her. "Please, Mimi. For me?"

Finally, the toughest woman I had ever known took pity on me. She snatched the money out of my hand, which was the closest I was going to get to an answer.

"And some of those little cakes too," I cheekily added as she walked away. "I love those things."

"Fine," she grumbled. "You can watch the boys while I'm gone."

***

Keeping the boys occupied while their mother was away was a no-brainer. All I had to do was play soccer.

"It's not called soccer," insisted Francis. "It's football."

"Not where I come from, mate," I told him. "Where are your brothers?"

He motioned to the house with an upward nod. "Packing beads."

In addition to working part time at the Crown and Pav, Mimi ran a small jewellery business. Handmade powder glass beads were her specialty, and the small but steady influx of tourists kept her in trade.

I stepped onto the porch, pausing to check out the works in progress that were laid out on a table.

"You like them, Mitchell?" asked a small voice from behind.

I turned around to see Kenny, Mimi's middle son. He was little for an eight-year-old, but what he lacked in stature was made up for in cheek.

"I think they're awesome," I replied honestly.

"Buy some for your girl." He made it sound like a dare and considering she'd only been my girl for a few hours, buying Shiloh jewellery probably was a brave act.

I pointed to a long string of turquoise beads. "How much for these?"

Kenny flashed me a bright white smile. "Six hundred American dollars."

"Bloody hell," I choked. "Are they diamonds?"

"Glass," interjected Francis, rebuking his brother with a hard bump of his shoulder. "And they're ten American dollars."

Kenny still had the nerve to look smug as he hitched up his ridiculously long shorts. The T-shirt he wore was massive too – at least six sizes too big for his tiny frame. "Are you buying or not?"

"I tell you what," I replied. "We'll settle this on the field. If your team wins, I'll buy a necklace."

"You don't have a team," said Francis.

Picking his moment well, the smallest Traore boy wandered out of the house. I picked the toddler up under the armpits and waved him in front of his brothers.

"I do now," I replied triumphantly. "You and Kenny versus me and Ronaldo."

"He can't play," Kenny jeered. "He's too little."

"Mate," I drawled. "His name is Ronaldo. He was born to play football."

Ronaldo Traore didn't look much like a pro, and at just two years old his skill set was probably limited, but I wasn't exactly spoiled for choice when it came to picking a teammate.

I looked out at the makeshift sandy field, weighing up my options. "If Ronaldo doesn't live up to his namesake, I'll sub him for one of the goats," I suggested.

Both boys dissolved into a fit of giggles. "Goats can't play either," said Francis.

"Maybe not," I agreed lowering Ronaldo to his feet. "But that chicken over there looks like he has some serious kicking skills."

Concealment

SHILOH

The last thing I wanted to do was get out of bed. I was enjoying the feeling of excitement and optimism that comes with new romance – except this didn't feel new. After three weeks of living together, there was plenty of familiarity and zero awkwardness. I'd seen Mitchell naked a hundred times. Nothing had changed. He was still gorgeous and looking at him still made me blush – just for different reasons now. But the feeling of contentment only stretched so far. The niggling complication of being too far away from the phone that I'd been ordered to hide was at the forefront of my thoughts that morning – ahead of bed and bacon.

I needed to get it out of my suitcase and into the shack, and I needed to get it done before Mitchell got home.

*****

It wasn't overly early, but there wasn't a soul in sight as I made my way up to the fat cat camp, for which I was grateful. Doing shady things is always easier without an audience.

I unlocked the door, crept into the house and headed straight for my half-packed suitcase in the bedroom. Hit by an overload of boring beige, I had the sudden urge to pack everything up and drag it back to the shack where it belonged, but that wasn't the objective. The only thing I grabbed was the phone. Everything else could wait.

I knew finding a suitable hiding place in the tiny four-room shack wasn't going to be easy, and after considering every room, I concluded that it was downright impossible. Hopelessness quickly set in. Yet again, I couldn't get the job done. Burying the phone in my ironing pile was the best temporary solution I could come up with, which is where I was headed right up until a loose floorboard creaked under my foot.

Moments of ingenuity don't hit me often, but this one hit with full force. Using my house key, I levered the board off the floor and peered through the hole, seeing nothing but white beach sand.

The crawl space under the shack was the perfect hiding spot. Mitchell wasn't keen on spiders so he wasn't likely to venture under there without reason, but crawling under the house to check my phone for messages didn't bother me.

I picked my spot well, sliding the fridge forward to make use of the spare power socket behind it. I plugged the charger into the wall, prised the board off the floor underneath it and dropped the charging phone onto the sand below. The thin cord easily fitted through the gap when I pushed the floorboard back into place, and once the fridge was back in position the charger was hidden.

Excitement got the better of me as I gave into a short but epic victory dance that made the whole house wobble. Somehow I'd pulled it off. However fleeting the moment might've been, for now, Federal Agent Shiloh Brannan was playing the game to perfection.

Nine Goals

MITCHELL

I heard Mimi's beaten-up jalopy long before I saw it. The small hatchback's state of repair was on par with my jeep, but her exhaust was much worse. It sounded like a keening animal, but after an hour of having my arse kicked on the soccer field I was relieved to hear it.

"Last kick, fellas," I called. "Your mum is home."

It was going to take Team Ronaldo nine goals to win the game. To save my ego, we only needed one. I'd stuck to the rules until that point, but in the dying seconds, play got dirty. I scooped Ronaldo into my arms as I made a mad dash for the ball. With Francis and Kenny hot on our heels, I bent down, grabbed the ball and handed it to Ronaldo.

Perhaps realising the game had lost all integrity, both boys quickly gave up the chase and stopped dead, giving me a clear run to the goal. I lowered my toddler teammate to his feet and lined up the ball. "It's yours, Ronaldo," I encouraged. "Kick it!"

The tiny bloke's grin was much stronger than his coordination. He finally connected with the ball on the third swing of his foot and we stood watching as it rolled through the makeshift goal in slow motion.

I cheered with the enthusiasm of a man who'd actually won the game, much to the boys' amusement. All three cackled, which made me smile.

"How do you like that, fellas?" I gloated.

"You lost," Kenny reminded me. "Eight-one."

"I know, right?" I grinned. "Close game."

***

Mimi came through in a big way. She sent me home with a huge basket of the finest food Kaimte had on offer, and a stern warning not to share any of it with my witch girlfriend.

"You're a wonderful woman, Mimi." I tried to hug her but she pushed me away. "It's your sunny and gentle nature that I like best."

She laughed, half-heartedly rebuking me with a swat of her hand on my chest. "Go home and eat your food," she demanded. "And I want my basket back."

"I'll bring it to work tonight," I offered.

"I won't be there tonight." Her grin was wide and troubling. "You gave me the night off."

"I did?"

"Yes." She pointed to the basket in my hands. "And in exchange, I gave you cakes and fresh fruit."

"I knew you loved me." I smiled triumphantly. "You got me cakes."

Six of them," she replied, already walking away. "And some mouldy bread for the girl."

Secret Places

SHILOH

According to Mitchell, sourcing the perfect breakfast could only be a romantic gesture if it was served to me in bed. "And you have to be naked too," he added as an afterthought.

"Should I shower first?" I asked. "Maybe wash my hair and put on a bit of lippy?"

Mitchell set the basket of mystery goodies down on the bed. "You couldn't begin to imagine the delicacies that I brought home for you." His voice was low and gorgeous. "Or what I had to do to get them."

"I'm a little worried about that, actually." My hands linked around his neck. "You left to go shopping and came home two hours later shirtless and sweaty. What *did* you have to do to get them?"

"You wouldn't believe me if I told you." I felt his laugh against my mouth and when it morphed into a mind-scrambling kiss, I didn't care where he'd been or what he'd been up to.

I moaned out his name.

"Shiloh," he replied.

"Did you bring bacon?"

Chuckling, he pulled away and headed for the shower, ordering me not to peek in the basket before he got back. I was more interested in peeking at him, and then I realised I no longer needed to be sly about it.

"You're a perfect looking man, Mitchell Tate," I complimented from the bathroom door.

The smile he gave as he glanced over his shoulder was uncharacteristically coy. "Flattery will get you everywhere, Miss Jenson."

I hated it when he called me that. It was the biggest reminder that our budding romance was one truth away from falling in a heap.

Mitchell stepped under the shower and I flopped down on the bed, quickly saving the basket from tumbling to the floor by stopping it with my foot.

"What did you get up to while I was gone?" he called.

It was an innocent question that depressed me. The pat on the back I'd awarded myself after successfully concealing my phone now felt unwarranted. No one deserves praise for being shady.

"You wouldn't believe me if I told you," I replied.

"I'd believe anything," Mitchell replied, appearing in the doorway. "I spent the morning playing soccer with Ronaldo."

***

Breakfast definitely lived up to expectation. After weeks of eating floury apples and bruised bananas, I was treated to some of the best fruit I'd ever eaten. Mitchell was more interested in the baked goods – a homemade selection of little friands.

"Where did you really get all this from?" I was too curious not to know. As far as I was aware the markets only traded on Wednesdays, and compared to what we were eating, their produce sucked.

"I can show you if you want," he offered.

"Really?"

"Sure," he replied indifferently. "It's not a secret place."

I dropped the mango I was holding and unceremoniously lunged, pinning him beneath me on the bed.

"Pity," I murmured. "I like secret places."

Mitchell groaned as if I'd hurt him, but his wandering hands suggested otherwise. His hand slipped beneath the waistband of my shorts. "Do you have any secret places, Shiloh?"

I relaxed my body and dropped my head to his chest. "A few, but I think you've found most of them."

Mitchell trailed a long line up my back with his fingertips, taking my shirt with him. He tossed it across the room and I lay back down, enjoying the wonderful feeling of my bare skin pressing against his. I let out a breathy sigh. "It doesn't get better than this."

"Yes it does." He leaned, kissing the top of my head. "We're going to fall hopelessly in love, and then things are really going to get good."

***

If we were living in the real world, half a day in bed would've been topped off with a late lunch at a quiet restaurant somewhere, but we were on the edge of the desert in remote Africa so we needed to be more resourceful. When Mitchell suggested we go for a drive, I didn't question where we were headed. Talking only exacerbated the problem of dealing with the exhaust fumes that filled the car.

Mitchell leaned across and wound my window down, just as he always did. "Don't die on me, lady," he teased. "I'm not done with you yet."

We'd barely made it to the end of the road before I was hanging my head out the window like a dog, sucking in the hot but clean air. "You have to get that fixed," I demanded.

"I will," he promised. "But it needs a new exhaust and parts are really hard to find."

"You found cake, Mitchell," I pointed out.

"Yes I did," he slyly agreed. "It's all about prioritising."

***

We headed north on a road I was vaguely familiar with. It was the same route I'd unwillingly taken a few nights earlier, but this journey was nowhere near as frightening. Unlike Mike, the man beside me didn't have an intimidating bone in his body. He was sweet and kind and loving – all the traits I wasn't sure I deserved.

"Can I tell you something?" I asked out of the blue.

The corner of his mouth lifted. "You can tell me anything."

I wished that was true, but it wasn't. There was very little I could tell him, so I spent a long moment preparing my words before I said them out loud. "There's an old lady I know," I began. "Her name is Gladys."

Mitchell glanced across at me, silently prompting me to continue.

"She's a hopeless drunk." I shook my head. "Embarrassing at times, but sometimes quite insightful."

Without explaining the circumstances, I told Mitchell about Gladys' constant encouragement to change my ways and lighten up. "She said I should get out and kiss the sun once in a while." My voice was barely there, constricted by embarrassment. "Do you know what that means?"

Mitchell dropped the car down as gear as his focus shifted to me. Too chagrined to look at him, I gazed out the window. "Don't worry about it," I mumbled, trying to save face. "It's silly."

"You've never kissed the sun, Shiloh Jenson?" He dragged out the question, making me smile.

"Never," I admitted, finally turning to look at him.

"Well, that won't do," he replied. "I'll have to teach you."

I didn't doubt for a second that he could do it. If kissing the sun had anything to do with living freely, Mitchell Tate had it down pat.

"But I have something else in mind for us today," he added. "How good are your skills in espionage?"

I almost choked on his question. "I don't know," I replied, swallowing away the panic. "Who are we spying on?"

Mitchell's grin was shifty but bright. "The whole village of Kaimte."

Stupid Shoes

MITCHELL

The narrow row of steep hills on the outskirts of town acts as a buffer between the desert and sea. From the coast there's no hint of what lies beyond the rocky outcrop, but as soon as you get up high it's inhospitable desert for as far as the eye can see.

Shiloh didn't seem overly impressed by my suggestion that we climb to the top, but when I grabbed my backpack and got out of the car, she was left with little choice. "Put those dangerously long legs to use, lady," I told her, stopping to let her catch up. "Climb."

"I'm trying to bloody climb," she growled, battling to keep her footing as the loose rocks slipped under her feet. "Help me."

Women are not the weaker sex; they just wear stupid shoes. My usual MO would've been to stay put and lecture her about hiking in flip-flops, but none of my regular rules applied where Shiloh was concerned. I staggered a few metres down the steep incline and reached for her hand, practically pulling her the rest of the way.

"We should've stayed in bed," she muttered breathlessly.

Knowing she'd change her mind once we reached the top, I tightened my hold on her hand and offered some words of encouragement. "The harder the access, the sweeter the find." I turned back in time to catch her puzzled expression. "That's the first lesson in learning to kiss the sun," I elaborated. "Do you want to stop and write it down?"

She huffed out a breathless laugh. "No, I'm good."

"Didn't bring a pen, huh?"

Even when hot and bothered, Shiloh was a good sport. She was still giggling when we reached the top, but the second we caught sight of the view she fell silent.

I pulled a beach towel out of my backpack and fanned it out over the hot sand. "Sit," I ordered, gently pulling her down beside me. "We're supposed to be spying."

Shiloh propped herself up on her elbows, never once tearing her eyes from the spectacle playing out in the distance. Brightly coloured Bedouin tents were grouped together on the sand. People wandered from stall to stall, stocking up on groceries to get them through the week. Small puffs of smoke from the hot food vendors billowed into the desert sky, and everywhere we looked, children ran amok.

"You weren't kidding," Shiloh finally said. "The whole village is down there." She turned her head, shooting me a quizzical look. "Why aren't we there?"

My eyes drifted down to the festivities below. "Because it's by invitation only," I explained. "Expats never go there. It's strictly for the locals."

"Is that where breakfast came from?"

"I asked Mimi to pick me up a few things," I replied with a smile. "She usually says no, but I caught her at a weak moment."

Shiloh thought for a moment. "You've been here for years," she said. "You've never been there?"

"Never."

"What would happen if you just turned up?"

"I don't intend to find out," I replied. "I'm not that arrogant, Shiloh. We're visitors in their country. The least we can do is be respectful of the local beliefs and customs."

She let out a sigh. "It's hard to respect some beliefs."

I gently kneaded the nape of her neck. "But you're doing a good job," I praised. "Kaimte people are wary of newcomers, probably because so many of them have hidden agendas."

Shiloh turned on her side, locking her brown eyes with mine. "I have no agenda."

"I know." I gently kissed her lips. "And over time, people like Mimi will realise that."

She rolled onto her back, shielding her face from the sun with her forearm. "I'm never going to win that woman over."

"Don't be too sure," I hinted. I rummaged through the backpack, pulled out the long string of turquoise beads and draped them across her chest. "Mimi made these."

Shiloh tangled the beads around her fingers. "For me?" she asked in a tiny voice.

"Yeah," I confirmed. "She sells them at the midweek markets, but she gave me the pick of the lot this morning."

It was a tiny white lie designed to lift her spirits. Shiloh didn't need to know that I'd paid Kenny Traore twice what they were worth because I'd lost a football game. All she needed to know was that Mimi wasn't a crazy witch hunter all of the time. "She has a good heart, Shiloh," I assured her. "Even when it's hidden."

Slumming It

SHILOH

I spent most of the asphyxiating car ride home studying the long necklace hanging around my neck. In different angles of light, the green glass beads took on a blue hue. I thought it was apt. Very little in Kaimte was what it appeared to be, including me.

"I was worried that you might think it was a weird gift," said Mitchell, speaking for the first time.

"Why?"

"I don't know." The car seat squeaked as he shifted. "Maybe you'd think it was too soon or something."

I tangled the string of beads around my fingers, really thinking things through. For the first time in my life I was prepared to let myself fall hard and fast, because time was not on our side. I could be pulled out of the country on an hour's notice. My heart seized just thinking about it, which testified to the fact that I was already in deeper than I should've been.

I gave Mitchell a very condensed version of the worst-case scenario. "If I get another job transfer, I could be gone in a week."

His head whipped in my direction. "That soon?"

I nodded, probably looking doleful. "It's possible."

His focus returned to the road. "I guess we should hold off on the falling in love part then," he mumbled. "It might not end well."

I didn't want him to put the brakes on. I also didn't want to turn a blissfully easy day together into a downer by allowing the conversation to get serious.

"Stop being so good in bed then," I told him.

Finally he smiled, and it was as perfect as the rest of him. "You're unlike anyone I've ever met before, lady," he told me. "Maybe I'll just fall in love with you a little bit."

I laughed, welcoming the light turn. "And how long will you love me, Mitchell Tate?"

His eyes left the road for much longer than they should've while he stared at me. "Until I can't," he finally replied.

***

A well-timed sideward glance out the window as we turned into our street blew the whole afternoon to pieces.

Iron Mike had no concept of the theory that Sunday was supposed to be a day of rest. The T-junction sign had a chalk X scrawled on it, which meant I had work to do.

I didn't know what Mike would consider to be an acceptable response time to the message he'd left me, but I did know that scrambling under the house while Mitchell was around would be impossible. Every precaution I'd taken to make the secret phone secure had also made it less accessible.

The car pulled to a stop at the edge of the trail to the cardboard village. "I have to work tonight," Mitchell said randomly, dragging on the hand brake. "That was the price I paid for breakfast."

For once I was glad that Mimi's kindness was conditional. I let out a breath of relief that I hoped he didn't notice. "I'll try and wait up for you," I offered.

His hand slipped under the fall of my hair as he drew me in for a kiss. "You could come with me."

"I can't," I whispered. "I have to be up for work at five."

The regret in my tone wasn't an act. Spending time with Mitchell was becoming more important to me with each passing day, but for both of us work still took precedence – even if said work was crawling around under the shack.

Mitchell released me, groaning as his head lolled back against the headrest. "Listen to us." He sounded disgusted. "Making plans around work like a couple of responsible adults."

"I could write up a schedule if you like," I offered. "An equal roster of work, sex and ironing."

"I don't know if you could handle it." He turned to look at me. "That's a lot of ironing."

***

The first opportunity I got to retrieve the phone came while Mitchell was in the shower. I snuck outside and after checking that the coast was clear, leaned down and tore a section of lattice siding off the shack. It came off with such ease that it made me nervous enough to take a step back and wait for the shack to crumple into a heap – but thankfully, it held fast.

There was no need for the torch I'd brought. Plenty of light filtered through the holes of the lattice, allowing me a clear view of the entire crawl space. I half expected to see a stash of empty ouzo bottles or the corpses of Leroy's past tenants, but there was nothing except a few rusted pipes, white sand, and my phone dangling from its cord under the kitchen. Crawling on my belly to reach it was the best I could do, and as my undies filled with sand I wished there was an easier way.

Once switched on the damned phone took forever to fire up, which gave me too much thinking time. I had no idea what Mike had in store for me, but it was safe to say he wasn't making contact just to say hi.

I was put out of my misery when the screen finally lit up. I opened the message, carefully reading each word as if it was written in code.

It wasn't. Mike's instructions were short and predictably, not-so sweet.

- Lock pick set under table at pub

Considering there were fifteen tables at the Crown and Pav, retrieving the tools that I had no use for wasn't going to be easy. Nothing in this country was bloody easy.

I attempted to write a reply but struggled for something to say. And when the trickling sound of water draining through the pipe under the shower stopped, I gave up trying. I switched off the phone and backed out of the tight space as awkwardly as I'd crawled in.

After shaking as much sand as I could from my clothes, I pushed the lattice siding back into place and strolled back into the shack as if nothing was out of the ordinary. Mitchell was in the bedroom, almost ready to leave for work.

"Is it too late to change my mind about coming with you?" I asked .

"No," he replied, smiling at me. "I would love that."

He didn't ask the reason behind my sudden change of heart. Mitchell's tendency to take things at face value worked in my favour more than he'd ever know. The less I had to lie to him, the better I felt.

***

Very occasionally, things go exactly according to plan. The lock pick set was exactly where it was supposed to be – taped to the underside of one of the picnic tables at the Crown and Pav.

Retrieving it while Mitchell's back was turned was simple, but concealing it was a little trickier. Trying to appear normal with a small pouch of six sharp tools stuffed into my waistband wasn't easy.

"Beer?" asked Mitchell as I pulled up a stool at the bar. It wasn't really a question. He'd flipped the lid off a bottle and placed it in front of me before I'd even replied.

Even though he didn't know it, this was Mitchell at his best. The self-proclaimed lazy beach bum was anything but as he tended his beloved bar. I got a kick out of watching him prepare for the night ahead: double-checking that the fridge was stocked, straightening the bottles on the shelves, and polishing the bar to within an inch of its life.

"What did this place look like before you bought it?" I asked, peeling the label off my beer.

"Pretty rough," he replied. "But functional."

It was still rough, but it seemed to possess the same roguish charm as the proprietor, which probably explained why it was such a popular haunt. The atmosphere was always friendly – despite the somewhat shady clientele. Once the tables began filling up and the beer began flowing, the little pub on the beach was as rocking as any I'd ever been to.

I seemed to be the only Jorge Creek employee who realised it. Glen and his cronies never frequented the Crown and Pav, choosing to stay under their rocks and socialise in their beige houses, which suited me fine. The less I had to deal with them, the better.

Mitchell clearly felt the same way. "There's a hierarchy," he explained, swiping a cloth along the already shining bar. "According to your mates at Jorge Creek, they reign supreme. Expats like me are dirt under their shoes, and the locals rate even lower than that." He sounded disgusted, and rightfully so. "Very few of them embrace the Kaimte culture or way of life. They'd never drink here."

"Well, I drink here." I straightened up on my stool and slapped my hand down on the counter. "I like slumming it occasionally."

Mitchell laughed. "Quite the little barfly, aren't you?"

"I only come here for one reason."

"Which is?"

I leaned forward to whisper. "I have a crush on the bartender."

Mitchell sucked in a sharp breath and shook his head. "That's a recipe for disaster, lady," he sighed. "Didn't your mother ever warn you against falling for no-hopers?"

I flashed him my wickedest grin. "She did, but I have a good feeling about this one."

✳✳✳

I hadn't considered the probability of running into Louis Osei that night, or that Iron Mike would be with him. If I had, I might've prepared better. I was completely caught by surprise when he sidled up to me at the bar.

"My beautiful friend," he crooned in my ear. "How are you this evening?"

I locked eyes with Mitchell across the bar. "Fine, thank you," I answered.

It was becoming difficult to keep up the charade of being skittish and uneasy around Louis. It was a convenient front purely because I didn't like him, but ultimately it was making my job harder. As much as he irked me, the only way to garner information was to play nice. Without putting much thought into it, I spun the stool around to face him. "And how are you, Louis?"

Looking utterly shocked by my sudden shift in demeanour, he took a step back. "I'm fine."

Conversation quickly stalled after that, proving that at best, Louis' suave disposition was hit and miss. Trying to engage him again, I thanked him for the mulafa he'd gifted me. "It's really lovely." His triumphant grin was directed solely at Mitchell. "Let me buy you a drink," he murmured in my ear.

"She has a drink," snapped Mitchell.

I turned and picked my bottle up, struggling to look Mitchell in the eye. "I'll be back soon, okay?" I knew what his answer would be so I didn't wait to hear it. I followed Louis and his goon squad to a nearby table.

Having Mike in attendance brought no comfort. He sat beside Louis, glaring at me as maniacally as he always did – only now he looked even meaner thanks to a nasty wound on his forehead.

I had no idea if the other thug was an asset or a foe, so I paid him little attention. My focus was on Louis, but he was preoccupied, constantly glancing past me to smirk at Mitchell.

"Why are you trying to aggravate him?" I asked, calling him out on it. "I don't think we can be friends if you're going to behave badly."

Mike and his sidekick chuckled, perhaps amused by the childlike rebuke. Louis didn't see the funny side. He leaned across the table, speaking slowly and quietly. "You're scared of me."

At that moment, staring into his dark eyes, I realised that he wanted me to be. It was a persona he worked hard to maintain, and it made me wonder how he'd react if I challenged it.

"I'm not," I replied strongly. "I think we could be friends – on some level."

"I'm delighted to hear that."

My skin began to crawl. Clearly, the inch of friendliness I'd shown him had already been stretched a mile.

"I'm not going to sleep with you, Louis." My flat tone belied the revulsion I felt. "You'll have to find another use for me."

The ability to read between the lines is a talent that not everyone possesses. Fortunately, Louis Osei was talented. With a click of his fingers and a few foreign words, he dismissed his men from the table.

I glanced back at Mitchell, more relieved than ever that he was too far away to hear the conversation. The brief smile I gave was designed to reassure him, but all I got in return was a worried frown.

I couldn't dwell. I'd piqued Tweedledum's interest, and now I had to hold it.

"What makes you think I have a use for you?" asked Louis.

"I think you have a use for everybody you deal with." I motioned toward his hired heavies with a stiff upward nod. "Those men aren't your friends," I accused. "They work for you."

The corner of his mouth lifted. "Are you looking for a job too, Shiloh?"

"No," I replied. "The one I've got will do for now."

He knew I worked at the mine. Hopefully that made me valuable to him.

"So why are you here then?" He picked up his beer and tilted it toward me. "Drinking with me for free."

"I like useful people too," I casually replied. "You might be useful."

He brought his beer to his lips with a smirk. "What do you want?"

Apart from the opportunity to nail him, I could think of only one other thing. If anyone could get it, Louis could. "An exhaust for a 1991 jeep."

Clearly it wasn't a request he was expecting. After a long moment of silence, he threw back his head and roared with laughter. "That's it?" he asked incredulously. "You're prepared to be indebted to me for a car part?"

"No." I frowned. "I'm more than willing to pay for it."

Louis' face changed as his smile slipped away. "Car parts come cheap, but you're in Kaimte now, Shiloh." The menacing low tone was back with a vengeance. "Favours are very costly."

I looked him dead in the eye, ignoring the unpleasant feeling of having my heart in my throat. "I'm prepared to return the favour, Louis."

The carrot I was dangling was both foolish and dangerous. I had no idea what he had in mind, but I couldn't deny that I'd made serious headway that night. The best I could hope for was that he'd exploit my position at the mine and ask me to do something crooked. The worst didn't bear thinking about.

With another click of his fingers, Louis summoned his men. As soon as they appeared, he set his beer down and rose to his feet. "I'll be in touch," he said with a predatory smile. "I hope you're a woman of your word."

I replied with a stiff nod, absolutely convinced that Mimi was right. Kaimte was rife with devils.

MacGyver

MITCHELL

The girl who couldn't start a fire had inadvertently become an arsonist. Befriending Louis was a dumb move, and after everything I'd told her about him Shiloh had no excuse for stupidity. It wasn't my place to reprimand her so I kept my mouth shut, refusing to let it rate a mention.

It didn't take long for me to realise that it probably wasn't the best plan. By closing time, the silent lecture I'd been holding back all night was starting to cause me pain.

All I wanted to do was get home, but as it turned out, that was a tall order. Somehow, I'd managed to lock my keys in the car.

Shiloh rattled the handle. "I didn't even know you could lock it." She sounded remarkably upbeat for someone who had to be at work in less than five hours.

I wasn't feeling upbeat. I was frustrated, and more than willing to do some damage with the rock I picked up off the ground.

Shiloh was less than impressed. "That's your solution?" she asked. "Just smash out the window?"

"Unless you have a spare key or a coat hanger in your pocket, I can't think of another way."

She emphatically shook her head. "Nope. No lock pick set either," she joked.

I drew my hand back ready to strike the glass.

"Mitchell, wait!" Shiloh yelled at the last moment. "You'll undo all my good work." She didn't pause long enough for me to ponder what that meant. "We need to get that exhaust fixed," she explained. "I asked Louis to track down the part. If you bust out that window, we'll have another problem to fix."

"*We* don't need to fix anything." I tossed the heavy rock aside. "*My* jeep works perfectly well." And even if it didn't, I'd sooner choke to death on exhaust fumes than have Louis Osei supply the part needed to repair it.

"I was trying to help you." I could barely see her in the night light, but I didn't need the visual to know she was as pissed off as I was. "It wasn't easy asking that jerk for a favour."

I applaud bravery, but Shiloh hadn't picked her moment well. Dealing with Louis was a fool's errand. "I hope it was worth it," I told her. "He practically owns you now."

She took a step closer to me, giving me a perfect view of her gorgeous angry face. "I made it very clear that –"

I cut her short. "God, you're so naïve," I complained. "I don't want to have to look after you all the time, but you make it a full time job."

"I never asked you to babysit me," she snapped. "I'm not some delicate little kid."

I dropped my head and muttered at the ground, "More like a defiant little kid."

"Excuse me?" The rise in her voice dulled none of her rage. Things were getting serious. Her hands were on her hips.

"I told you more than once to stay away from Louis." I spoke quietly, acutely aware that I sounded like a jealous rock ape. "But you didn't listen." I turned around and picked up another rock.

"Put that down!"

"What's your problem, lady?" I snapped, dropping it with a thud. "I'll smash the window, and then you can ask your mate Louis to order us a new one. Win-bloody-win."

There comes a point during a bout of bad behaviour when you realise you've gone too far to back down. I was there – in all my juvenile, hissyfitting glory. I'd twisted the sweet gesture of organising a long overdue car repair into the heinous crime of crossing enemy lines. Shiloh had done nothing wrong. Even Louis had clean hands at this point. Very uncharacteristically, I was the one creating drama.

The best I could hope for was an opportunity to apologise later, but at that moment it didn't seem likely. Shiloh wasn't in a forgiving mood. She threw out her arms, calling me a slew of names that I completely deserved.

"Finished?" I asked when she paused for breath.

"No," she growled. "You're an arsehole."

I foolishly grinned. "You said that already."

"Well you are." She pointed at my feet. "Give me your shoelace."

Perhaps she was planning to hang me with it. If so, I probably deserved it. Maybe that's why I took off my sneaker without question. She snatched it from me. "Sometimes you have to think outside the box," she said, unthreading the lace. "As opposed to smashing your way through it."

Guided by the light of my phone, she expertly tied a slipknot in the centre of the lace. "Shine your phone through the window," she ordered. "I need some light."

Curious to see where thinking outside the box would take us, I did as I was told. My angry compatriot went to work, sliding the lace through the corner of the door and pulling back and forth as if she was flossing the window. Just a few seconds later, she'd worked the loop of the knot over the lock. In a show of pure MacGyver-like genius, she yanked the knot tight, pulled it upward and unlocked the door.

"How does a nice girl like you know a trick like that?" I asked, astonished.

Shiloh opened the car door. "I know a lot of tricks, Mitchell," she replied, returning my shoelace. "You just need to shut up and let me do my thing once in a while."

Subtle Offers

SHILOH

I felt like I was juggling a million balls in the air. Taking a step back and letting a few drop to the ground would've been the sensible solution, but I couldn't bring myself to do it.

From a professional standpoint, the ball I needed to drop was Mitchell. The mere mention of Louis sent surfer boy into a rage, and the chewing-broken-glass look didn't suit him.

Under different circumstances I would've respected his feelings and steered clear, but as things stood I needed Louis. Despite Mitchell's protests, I had no choice but to continue shaking the tree to see what fell out.

***

For the first time ever, Glen didn't keep me waiting the next morning. When I got to the top of the hill he was sitting in his parked car. It was the first hint that changes were on the way. The second came when he gruffly informed me that I'd be working with him from now on, and that wasn't the only adjustment to the programme. The mine operated twenty-four hours a day, and we'd been relegated to nightshift. I didn't know whether management had changed the roster or if Mike had pulled strings, but it didn't matter either way. I was finally where I needed to be – smack bang in the middle of the lion's den.

After weeks of doing his best to keep me at a distance, Glen was understandably miffed. Sticking to the script, I pretended to be less than pleased too. "Night shift?" I asked sourly. "That sucks."

"The pay is better," he muttered.

"They don't pay me enough to work all night." I dragged my seatbelt across my body and clicked it into place. "Nicking a few diamonds at the end of each shift might make it worthwhile, though."

The glint of mischief in his eyes as he glanced at me was unmistakable. "You'd do that?" he asked.

I shrugged. "If I thought I could get away with it."

Glen didn't utter another word for the rest of the journey, which was perfect.

The time for standing meekly in the background was over, and I could hardly believe how simple it had been to turn things around. By tweaking the persona of Shiloh Jenson, I'd given him pause for thought. A few well-placed comments was all it took to make Louis and Glen believe that I was corruptible. I'd made silent and subtle offers to both of them. All I could do now was wait and see who took me up on it first.

***

Shadowing Glen as he went about his working day afforded me the opportunity to check out the highly secretive sorting room. As head of security, it was his job to keep an eye on the grading process.

Tweedledee had no choice but to let me tag along, which I did with the enthusiasm of an excited puppy. "I've never been in there before," I beamed, following him along the narrow corridor.

Glen swiped his access card through the slot on the door. "You're still not going in. You can watch from the viewing room."

He'd been marginally pleasant until that point, but the shift in mood didn't bother me. I thought back to my short stint at Jorge Creek's Australian mine. Even then, I'd considered the diamond building to be a strange place. It had the depressing atmosphere of a morgue. It was clinical, quiet and no one seemed to speak. I used to think it was because of the serious nature of the business, but I was now considering another possibility. Maybe the locals were right. Perhaps diamond mining *was* the evil work of the devil.

After passing through two more security points, we finally made it to our destination. As instructed, I stayed on the admin side of the plexiglass. Glen swiped his card for the umpteenth time, waited for the beep that signalled the release of the door, and headed into the sorting room.

For a long moment I studied the every move of the two jewellers working inside. Both seemed unfazed by the changing of the guard. The outgoing security officer didn't say a word as he exited, and there was no greeting for Tweedledee. They simply kept working, sifting through piles of ugly cloudy stones with oversized tweezers.

Despite the high tech room, the grading process was relatively simple. The initial segregation was done by machine. The gems were weighed, sized and separated according to quality. They were also logged, which is how Jorge Creek first became aware that their precious gems were going walkabout. It was up to the jewellers to double-check the results and keep the machinery operating properly, and it was up to Glen to make sure they didn't pocket any rocks while doing it.

My eyes darted in every direction, taking note of the multitude of surveillance cameras that were in plain sight. They were there to keep an eye on everybody – including the security staff – and the feeling of being watched was inescapable.

For hours, I tried channelling my inner crook, trying to figure out how someone would get diamonds out of that room. Concealing them wouldn't have been a problem. Realistically, two or three diamonds the size of match heads could potentially be worth thousands. Swiping them while under the scrutiny of other employees and security cameras was the impossible part. No matter how hard I tried, I couldn't come up with a plausible scenario.

I forced my mind to slow down, reminding myself that for now it didn't matter. Moving forward was a slow process, but at least I was moving.

***

The first opportunity Glen had to ditch me came at lunchtime. I wasn't invited to sit with him, and as I sat down at a vacant table in the staff dining hall I realised I was relieved to escape him for a while. Even as we ate he was eying me from across the room, perhaps wondering if I'd make good on my earlier threat of stealing a few rocks.

I didn't have to avoid the uncomfortable glances for long. After just a few minutes, Reyo sat down opposite me.

"Good day to you, Shiloh." His wide grin was infectious. "Are you enjoying your meal?"

I looked down at the plate of curried rice in front of me. "It's great, thank you." Even if it wasn't, it would still beat whatever Mitchell and I could manage to rustle up for dinner. It was the best meal of the day by default. "Are you going to join me?"

"No, I just wanted to give you something." He reached into the plastic bag he was holding on his lap. "Do you like music?"

I'd given up being surprised by Reyo's random choices of conversation. Just a few days earlier he'd cornered me in the Site Services office to talk about cold and flu medicine. "All you need is sweet tea," he'd insisted. "Next time you are poorly, drink more sweet tea."

I spent the rest of that day wondering whether I'd somehow incited the advice by looking bedraggled, but when we spoke again and his chosen topic was monkeys and space travel, I refused to take it personally.

"I do like music," I confirmed.

With a broad white smile, Reyo set a Discman down on the table.

A strange squeak of delight escaped me. I couldn't help it. The last time I'd seen one I was barely a teenager. I pressed the button and checked out the CD inside. "The Backstreet Boys?"

"It's wonderful," he insisted quite seriously. "I want you to listen to it."

That wasn't going to happen for a few reasons. First, it was the Backstreet Boys. Second, I knew Reyo well enough to know that there would probably be some sort of pop quiz to follow.

"Thanks, but it's not really my style of music." I closed the lid and slid it toward him. "I appreciate the offer though."

Reyo pushed it straight back. "Take it, Shiloh." His tone was deadly serious. "You might learn something."

Either Reyo had a thing for boy bands or he was trying to covertly pass me information. On the off chance it was the latter I picked up the ancient Discman and thanked him. "I'll listen to it later," I promised.

His trademark smile swept his face. In an instant, the conversation was light again. "Tomorrow you must try the maafe," he instructed, pointing to my plate. "It's made with tomatoes and peanuts and meat."

Of all the thoughts I had at that moment, none of them were food related. I managed a stiff nod in reply.

Still smiling, Reyo pushed his chair back. "Enjoy the rest of your day, Shiloh," he said.

That was going to be easier said than done. I had another six hours of work left, and I was in the unenviable position of having my one-track mind focused on the Backstreet Boys.

Tom Tom Cookies

MITCHELL

Nothing compares to the feeling of knowing you've wrecked something good. The only reasonable conclusion Shiloh could draw after my ridiculous rant the previous night was that I was a controlling hothead, and I was ninety-nine percent sure we were over because of it.

I spent a long day trying to figure out a plan for making amends, and the minute she walked through the door that night, I launched into a bumbling apology. I started by assuring her that I wasn't a controlling jerk, and ended two minutes later by reiterating that I still wasn't a controlling jerk.

It hardly dazzled her. Shiloh flopped down on the beanbag, concentrating more on unlacing her boots than on my heartfelt ramble. I'd been silent for almost a minute before she finally looked at me. "I know Louis is a cretin, Mitchell." Her voice sounded flat and tired. "I don't need you playing the part of protective big brother to keep me away from him."

Her choice of words was horrifying. If that's how she regarded me, we'd stumbled way off track. "Is that how you see me?"

Her heavy boots thudded on the floor as she kicked them off. "No," she replied. "You're far more important than that."

When she reached out, I pulled her to her feet. Her hands slipped around my middle. Things suddenly didn't seem so hopeless any more, but I wasn't distracted. We had unfinished business.

I broke our hold, took her by the hand and led her to the bedroom. "I have something to show you."

I didn't need to elaborate. The instant she walked in, she spotted the DIY project I'd spent the afternoon working on. "You built us a bathroom door?" she asked, her eyes darting between the newly private bathroom and me.

My reply got caught in a laugh. "I didn't build the door." I swung it open and closed a few times – just to prove that it worked. "I just hung it."

If I had been remotely capable of stringing a decent sentence together I would've told her why.

For years, I'd held the blasé attitude that relationships always work out if they're meant to. Mine never did – usually due to an acute lack of effort on my part. I'd happily stand by and watch things fall apart without any care or consequence.

I didn't feel like standing by was an option where Shiloh was concerned. The only thing more confusing than the invisible pull I felt toward a girl I had nothing in common with was the desire I felt to make her happy and safe. Her view of the world was far too idealistic, considering she was living in a third world country, but I wasn't going to push the issue any more. From now on my focus was going to be on making her happy, and the gesture of fitting a door to the bathroom was bound to make a first-world girl ecstatic.

"Flowers are hard to come by here." I ran my hand down the edge of the door. "I thought this might be a nice alternative."

"And doors are easy to find?" she asked.

I shrugged. "If you know the right people."

The right people in this case were my neighbours. Until a few hours ago, Melito and Vincent had a functioning bedroom door. After a bit of pleading and lots of negotiating, they finally agreed to let me permanently borrow it. The price was three bottles of Tate Estate merlot and their pick of loot from Lily's next care package.

"We adore those Tom Tom cookies that your sister sends," said Vincent, rubbing his hands in glee.

"Biscuits," I corrected. "And they're called Tim Tams."

It was a small price to pay. The object of my affection seemed truly thrilled. "I knew you were a keeper," she said taking a slow step toward me. "Even before the bathroom door."

I couldn't quite believe her. She'd left for work that morning without uttering a single word to me.

"You're a terrible liar, lady."

The look that flashed across her pretty face could only be described as pained. "I'm not, you know," she mumbled. "I'm an excellent liar. I handed my house key back to the fat cat camp manager today," she explained. "I told him I couldn't possibly live in such a hovel."

"I see."

"It's not a hovel, Mitchell," she continued. "It has a bath and a coffee machine."

I looked her dead in the eyes. "So why give it up?"

Shiloh edged closer. "Because you don't live there, stupid."

At least we were both prepared to compromise to make it work. She'd go without good coffee and I'd forgo major parts of my sanity.

As soon as she was in reach, I grabbed her. "You make me crazy."

There was no other way of describing the effect she had on me. I was confused, enamoured and bewitched, sometimes simultaneously. Nice girls weren't supposed to have that kind of power, but I didn't even have to touch Shiloh to feel the sting. Just being close to her felt like a cross between a kiss and a hard slap.

Keen to rid her of the Jorge Creek uniform, I unbuttoned her shirt and pushed it off her shoulders. As it fell to the floor, Shiloh leaned in, pressing her soft lips against the hollow at the base of my throat. I pushed her backward, bailing her up against the wall with a little too much fervour. The whole shack shook.

"Careful, Adonis," she murmured. "You'll make the house fall apart."

"No." I wedged my legs between hers, keeping her feet off the floor as I pressed my lips to her ear. "I'm going to make *you* fall apart."

Shiloh's whole body responded to the wicked threat. Her breath hitched and the tight hold she had on me lost all strength. "No," she whispered against my cheek. "You're the one who keeps me together."

Boy Band Warbling

SHILOH

Guilt is a soul eating emotion, which is why I refused to let it have me. I was being punished enough by the stress of living a double life. I never got any peace – even while lying in bed watching the most perfect man I'd ever known sleep.

The only sound I could hear were the waves steadily crashing to shore just outside our door. I rolled onto my back, gazing up at the gauzy mosquito net billowing in the soft breeze. It was a perfect fairy-tale moment that was about to be ruined by opportunity.

Easing out of bed, I tiptoed around the room, pausing to check that Mitchell was still asleep every time the floor creaked under my feet. He was sleeping like the dead and beautifully naked, but in the cruellest of blows, my mind was back on the Backstreet Boys.

I sat on the floor at the foot of the bed and pulled the CD player out of my work bag. The first thing I noticed was that it had no batteries, which meant I'd be saved from a long session of painful boy band warbling. It also meant Reyo's reason for giving it to me probably had nothing to do with music.

Cracking it open was my next mission. Tools were usually in short supply in the shack, but I was in luck that night. Thanks to Mitchell's DIY efforts on the new door, his toolbox sat two feet away. Using the smallest screwdriver I could find, I took the back off the CD player, quickly realising that there was no need to be so delicate. Batteries or not, it wasn't likely to ever work again. All working parts had been removed to make way for the GPS tracking device that had been concealed inside. The accompanying note was all the explanation I needed: make, model and registration number of Louis Osei's car.

Once again the game had changed. Reyo was Iron Mike's contact at the mine.

My alliance with Mike was impossibly one-sided. He'd supplied me with a lock pick set. In return I was expected to break into a known criminal's car and fit an illegal tracking device – with zero backup or assistance. It was hardly a fair trade, but I got the impression that playing fair wasn't high on his agenda.

I hadn't been provided with a safe place and time to get the job done, or even the tools to do it. It was an oversight that troubled me, but I wasn't afraid of Iron Mike.

It's not the enemy you see that gets you. It's the one you don't.

A Gangster Or Three

MITCHELL

I wished I could tell Shiloh otherwise, but my decision not to open the Crown and Pav the night before had nothing to do with her. A pub can't trade without beer, and as things stood I had none. I vaguely explained the dilemma over breakfast on the front deck.

"Because of Louis?" she guessed.

I grimaced at the mention of his name. Just twelve hours earlier we'd made a pact to never discuss him again.

"I'm meeting with him at the port this afternoon," I told her. "With a bit of luck I can talk him into releasing my shipment."

Even if I could, it would only be a Band-Aid solution. The stranglehold he had on my business was getting worse with every passing week, and although I'd never admit it to Shiloh, she was more than likely the reason he'd tightened his grip. The play he'd made for her was unreciprocated, and I was paying for it.

"Can I come with you?" she asked .

"I'm not sure that's a good idea," I mumbled. "There's not much to see there. Maybe a ship or two…"

A gangster or three.

"I'll stay in the car," she offered, popping the last segment of her orange into her mouth.

I raised one eyebrow.

"Scout's honour," she added with a three finger salute.

I turned away, directing my long sigh at the ocean. "We really have the whole day together?" I asked dubiously.

"Yep." Shiloh levered herself out of her deckchair and tumbled onto my lap, resting her long legs on the railing. "First night shift starts tomorrow at six."

The change to her roster was a good one. I welcomed anything that gave us more time together.

My hand slipped beneath the waistband of her skirt as I pulled her closer. "Think of all the sex we can have in that time," I murmured.

"I'm not sure there's enough time for those kind of shenanigans, Mitchell," she teased. "My ironing pile is out of control."

The only thing out of control was my desire to get her back in the shack and naked. I was just about to share the plan when Melito appeared, calling out to Shiloh from the deck next door.

"I have something for you, darling," he crowed.

I leaned closer and whispered in her ear, "I have something for you too, darling."

Untangling herself from my arms, she delivered a sharp elbow to my ribs before venturing to the edge of the deck. Melito tossed something across to her.

"Cowry shells," he explained as she caught it. "I saw it in town yesterday and immediately thought of you."

Shiloh dangled the shell bracelet in the air. "Thank you," she replied. "I love it."

"You're welcome," he beamed. "Perhaps it might inspire Adonis to rain a few treasures upon you."

"He already did." She grabbed the end of her bead necklace and shook it at him.

Melito clutched his belly, unashamedly chortling. "Maybe he should've also told you how to wear it."

Shiloh glanced at me and frowned. I shrugged, as confused as she was. As far as I knew, necklaces are worn around the neck. I might've asked him to explain, but Vincent interrupted the conversation with an urgent request. "Get the broom, Melito!" he yelled. "That damned mouse is back."

The mouse problem took precedence over beaded jewellery conversation. Armed for battle, Melito disappeared back into his shack, an empty ouzo bottle raised above his head. We stayed put, even when he followed up with an unsettling war cry.

Shiloh sat down beside me, waiting patiently with her arm extended while I fumbled with the clasp on her bracelet. "Pretty, isn't it?" she asked.

"Pretty valuable too, once upon a time," I replied, finally managing to secure it. "Cowry shells were legal tender here until a couple of hundred years ago."

Shiloh slowly turned the bracelet on her wrist, checking out each shell. "I wonder if they caused as much trouble as the diamonds do," she mused.

"Probably," I agreed. "Greed is a terrible thing."

***

Louis Osei ran his dodgy importing business from a large warehouse at the port facility. On any given day the place was bedlam. Forklifts buzzed around the wharf in all directions, reminding me of out of control dodgem cars. A long convoy of trucks lined the road waiting to collect their deliveries, and workers wearing fluorescent vests were trying to control the chaos.

In stark contrast, Louis' warehouse looked like an oversized abandoned tool shed, and I'd never seen it look any different. It was located at the very back of the complex, almost too far from the wharf to be functional. It was quiet and isolated, which was probably the way he liked it.

When someone calls for a meeting at a deserted location, they want control. Louis liked to play the heavy-handed thug, and sadly, he was pretty good at it. Bringing Shiloh to the meeting was nonsensical, but I didn't want to frighten her by explaining why. Instead, I asked her to wait in the car.

"I promise I'll be quick," I assured her.

I expected an argument, but she hardly seemed to be listening. Her entire focus was on the souped-up Black Range Rover I'd parked behind. "Nice car," she muttered, staring through the windscreen.

'Nice' isn't how I would've described it. The black paint job, dark tinted windows and kitsch alloy rims were as thuggish as Louis.

"If you like that kind of thing," I replied.

"I don't." Finally Shiloh turned to look at me. "I've never liked that kind of thing."

I couldn't quite place the expression on her face, but she would've seen nothing but relief on mine. I'd grown up with materialistic sisters. At best, they were strange. When attracted by the lure of shiny things, they were downright dangerous.

I got out and walked to the passenger side, and spoke through the open window. "What if I never have anything more than this?" I waved my arms, showcasing the tired old jeep she was sitting in. "How long will you love me?"

The tiny smile that crossed her lips almost looked regretful. "Until I can't," she said.

I reached through the window and cupped her cheek. "I'll be back soon, okay?"

"Yeah." Shiloh tilted her head, leaning into my palm. "Go and get your beer."

She'd made it sound simple but I knew it wouldn't be. My alcohol shipment was bought and paid for in full, just as it always was. I didn't owe Louis or anyone else a penny, but he was going to try and screw me out of money for no other reason than he could.

The steel door slid open before I got to it, which was a sure-fire sign that the place was nowhere near as deserted as it looked. Exchanging pleasantries with the goon who greeted me would've been a waste of breath so I didn't bother. "Where's Louis?" I practically grunted out the question.

After checking that the coast was clear with a quick glance left and right, he replied with an upward nod.

My casual walk belied the unease I felt, and the further I ventured into the warehouse, the more convinced I became that the whole setting had been staged.

Two hundred cases of beer look remarkably small in an empty warehouse, especially when they're stacked neatly on the middle of the floor.

"Are these mine?" I asked, pointing at them.

The answer was obvious but the hired heavy shrugged as if he didn't know, which made me want to punch him.

"They could be yours," announced Louis, appearing from the shadows like a rat. "For a price."

Since Shiloh had been added to the equation, I couldn't be sure he was talking about money. Just thinking about it made my heart beat faster.

"I already own them," I curtly reminded him. "I have the receipts and shipping papers to prove it."

I would've produced them if he asked, but of course he didn't. They counted for nothing.

Louis slowly wandered toward me. "This is a large shipment," he said, kicking the bottom box with his foot. "Why so much?"

"I'm having issues with the importer," I replied dryly. "I'd rather order more beer less often. That way, I don't have to deal with him."

Louis raised his eyebrows, nodding as if he was sympathetic to my plight. "Makes sense."

"Just cut to the chase," I roughly demanded. "What do you want?"

"The list is long, my friend," he sighed. "But for now we'll start with the commission you owe me. A thousand dollars should cover it."

A long groan escaped me, which was the only reply I offered.

Louis put his hand on his chest, right where his heart would've been if he'd had one. "I have a sick mother," he shamelessly claimed. "Medicine is expensive."

"You really have perfected your craft, haven't you?" I asked bitterly. "You're a thief *and* a liar."

The only thing louder than Louis' condescending laugh was the snicker of the two men flanking him. They were paid to find me amusing. Louis just did it for kicks.

I was getting nowhere, and when his goon squad left his side to guard the door, I got the impression that calling it a day and walking out wasn't an option.

"Just give me my money, friend." He'd made it sound like a casual request, but nothing could've masked the fact that things were about to take a turn for the worse.

My eyes darted in every direction as I tried to keep track of where each of his henchmen was located. It made no difference. I didn't even notice the third man lurking behind me in the shadows, which was unfortunate because he was the one to make the first move.

Respect

SHILOH

Cargo shorts were functional long before they were fashionable, and despite the fact that they now held a style score of less than zero, I still wore them. Mine had six pockets, and every one of them was full.

As soon as Mitchell mentioned meeting Louis at the port, I started making plans. On the off-chance that I'd have the opportunity to offload the GPS tracker, I needed to be ready. While he stole an hour in the surf that morning, I raided his toolbox. Iron Mike had left me horribly ill prepared, but I managed to find a few basic tools that would allow me to get the job done.

The only thing missing was courage. There was no telling what might happen if I was caught messing with Louis' car, and considering I had nothing to gain by going through with it, the whole idea seemed ridiculous.

There were four cars were parked in front of the warehouse, but I was only interested in one. Even without Reyo's helpful note, I would've guessed that the kitted out Range Rover belonged to Louis. The car was obnoxious as he was, and the more I thought about it, the more I realised that there was a tiny part of me that might enjoy ripping the ignition to pieces.

"Just get it done and get out," I muttered, stealthily exiting the jeep.

Creeping wasn't necessary. There wasn't a soul around to stop me as I made my way to the Range Rover. No one saw me lift the door handle, and no one came running when the unlocked door opened with ease.

After a few steadying breaths, I slipped into the driver's seat and geared up to do some invisible damage.

Apart from tinkering with the odd dodgy toaster, I hadn't picked up a pair of wire cutters in years, but as I jemmied the steering column apart with a sharp shove of the screwdriver, all my naval training came flooding back to me. The tangle of wires that spilled out weren't daunting in the least. I knew exactly what to do. I needed a constant 12-volt power source. Following the wiring that led to the ignition, I found the one belonging to the interior clock.

Absolute control kicked in, which is something I hadn't felt in weeks.

Using the pick from my lock pick set, I gently pushed a hole through the plastic coating before poking my head up to take a look outside.

Still confident that I was on my own, I went back to work, carefully feeding the wires of the GPS through the hole I'd made before splicing it together. I gave the ignition wire the same treatment, bandaged the wounded electrics with some tape and secured the tracker deep under the dashboard.

The whole wicked deed had taken less than three minutes, but holding off on the victory celebrations turned out to be a wise move.

The steel door of the warehouse slid open, and the situation changed in an instant. The man who'd exited the warehouse couldn't see me through the tinted windows, but I had the perfect view of him casually strolling toward me.

Trying to keep a cool head as I forced the steering column back into place wasn't working out. Desperate to finish up and get out, I raised my knees, smashing the plastic column back into place. I ignored the crack it made. I was more interested in getting the hell out of the car.

Backtracking, I gave everything I'd touched a quick wipe with the hem of my T-shirt, opened the door and dropped to the ground.

Staying hidden isn't always about sticking to the shadows. Sometimes the best place to hide is in the brightest light you can find, and in order to do that, I needed to make some noise.

Showing a complete lack of care and consideration for the gift Melito had given me, I snapped the bracelet off my wrist. Cowry shells tumbled all over the sandy ground, and in a move designed purely to save my own skin, the theatrics began.

"I can't believe it broke!" My loud wail was pathetic but effective. It masked the thud of the car door closing, but drew the attention I needed. I crawled around on my hands and knees pretending to pick up the shells.

The patrolling goon made his way over. "What are you doing here?" he growled. "No one is supposed to be here."

Pretending to be caught by surprise, I jumped at the sound of his voice.

"Help me find my shells," I snivelled. "My bracelet broke."

He hardly looked sympathetic. He didn't look familiar either. Obviously Louis' army of henchmen extended further than Iron Mike and his simple mate.

This man was tall – huge, in fact – but kind of gangly, thanks to the oversized jersey he was wearing. I realised it was a common fashion trend amongst Kaimte thugs, despite the forty-degree weather.

"Get up," he ordered.

I looked him up and down as best I could. Unable to spot any weapons, I decided to protest a bit louder. "I need to find my shells."

Unmoved by my plight, he grabbed me under my arms and hoisted me to my feet. "You're with the white boy," he speculated.

Something about his tone troubled me. The shells were forgotten, and so was the crying act. "Yes," I replied. "Where is he?"

"He's having a bad day."

I couldn't decide if it was his choice of words or his sickening grin that brought on my sudden bout of nausea. Either way, it didn't matter. I was no longer in control of the situation. With a firm hand on my shoulder I was marched across to the warehouse. I held my breath the whole time, dreading to think what might be waiting for me inside.

The worst scenario I came up with wasn't nearly as bad as the reality.

I saw Mitchell before I'd even made it through the door, sitting on the floor slouched against a stack of boxes. The front of his grey T-shirt was saturated in blood, and when his head lolled back, it wasn't hard to work out why. In the fifteen minutes since I'd last seen him, his perfect face had been pulverised.

"Why did you bring her here?" Louis' furious voice echoed throughout the vast space. "Get her out."

Rough fingers dug into my shoulder as the man behind me tried to obey his boss. I refused to move, cementing my spot by shoving him away. Lashing out with a backhanded slap was his plan, but Louis intervened before he could follow through. "Leave her," he yelled.

I turned, looking at him for the first time. "What have you done?" I hissed through gritted teeth.

He dared to smile at me. "There are rules in Kaimte, Shiloh," he explained. "Men of my standing command respect."

If that was his justification for thrashing Mitchell to within an inch of his life he truly was a monster, and I had to tread very carefully because of it.

In any desperate situation the temptation is to act fast, but running to Mitchell's side wouldn't have been the wisest move. My first step was to assess the situation and figure out how bad things really were, which proved that there was no longer a line between who I was and what I did for a living. I couldn't be loving and compassionate. I had to be effective.

"Respect is earned where we come from," I bitterly replied.

Louis ambled toward me. I used the time it took him to reach me to scope out the surroundings. Compared to the bright light outside, the warehouse was dangerously dark. I could see two men lurking in the shadows, but it was the ones I couldn't see that worried me.

"Mitchell had a debt to settle," he casually explained. "He disrespected me by showing up to our meeting with empty pockets."

"There's more to it than that," I insisted, shaking my head.

In a move I wasn't expecting, Louis reached out and gently brushed the back of his hand down my cheek. As revolted as I was, I held fast and didn't move. Whether he realised it or not, he'd explained everything without uttering a word.

"This has nothing to do with money or respect," I accused. "You're jealous. That's why you hurt him."

"I have much to offer a woman like you, my beautiful friend." He reached again, tucking a wayward piece of hair behind my ear – and I let him.

"Friend?" The word was like acid on my tongue. "How can we be friends after this?"

Louis exhaled heavily as if the whole dreadful saga was nothing more than an inconvenient interruption to his day. "How can I make it up to you?"

Such a ridiculous question didn't deserve an answer, but it didn't get that far anyway. Mitchell coughed, a wretched choked sound that caught everyone's attention. The second cough was worse. His head jerked forward and a spray of blood splattered across the cement floor.

"See to him," said Louis, taking a step back and waving me forward.

I didn't waste another second; barely letting my feet touch the ground as I rushed over to Mitchell. I dropped to my knees, taking his face in my hands. "Can you stand?" I asked in a tiny voice.

"Shiloh," he mumbled, grabbing my wrist. I doubt he could see me. His eyes were so swollen that he probably couldn't see anything. "I knew you wouldn't wait in the car."

I might've laughed if I wasn't so appalled by his appearance. He was a mess, and I wasn't sure where to begin when it came to fixing him. I quickly checked his face, concluding that most of the blood was coming from his nose.

"I'm going to get you out of here," I quietly promised.

He managed a nod.

At that moment, Iron Mike decided to make an appearance, wandering in from somewhere behind us. Ordinarily his presence wouldn't have bothered me, but Mitchell's reaction turned my indifference to horror. In a move that looked painful, he shuffled to the side as if he was gearing up to defend himself.

I grabbed his hand in a feeble attempt at keeping him still. "Did he do this?" I whispered, giving a tiny nod in Mike's direction.

Mike didn't notice the nod Mitchell gave. No one did. Louis and his cronies stood a few metres away casually chatting amongst themselves as if we weren't even there.

As far as I was concerned, my alliance with Iron Mike was over. He was a brute, and no less dangerous than Louis. Perhaps he was worse, which was a troubling notion that I refused to deal with. For now, my focus needed to be on Mitchell.

"I'm going to get you out of here," I promised for a second time.

"Ready when you are, lady," he mumbled.

Protector

MITCHELL

It wasn't my first run-in with Louis' brand of cruelty, but it was certainly the most vicious. If not for the fact that I'd been completely blindsided, I might've been disappointed in the low number of punches I got in.

It wasn't merely a fist that flew at me, it was a fist wrapped in a length of chain, served up by Louis' number one henchman. Considering he regularly drank at my pub – for free on more than one occasion – I could only assume he was completely without conscience.

The objective hadn't been to kill me. If it had been, I would've been dead. The malicious beat down had nothing to do with money or beer either. It was about Shiloh – more specifically, the fact that she was spending time in my bed rather than Louis'. Calling him out on it earned me the hardest blow of the lot, and as I lay on the floor in a heap, I was fairly sure the damage I'd suffered because of my smart mouth was permanent.

By the time Shiloh appeared, I was out of it. I could barely breathe, let alone speak, but if I had been capable of words I would've told her to run as far and fast as she could.

And she would've ignored me.

Strangely, she was less afraid of Louis now than she'd ever been. The meek girl who'd sat quaking at the end of my bar was now a distant memory. The woman crouched beside me was playing on a whole new level.

Despite the hostile situation, she wasn't interested in peacekeeping. She wasn't in the mood for negotiating, either. After surveying the damage to my face, she rose to her feet and made a beeline straight for Louis. "Are you satisfied?" she yelled. "Has his debt been settled?"

As expected, the goon squad rushed to their boss' side, eager to protect him from the angry girl. With a click of his fingers, Louis stood them down. I tried to stand Shiloh down too, but the words came out in a jumbled groan that she paid no attention to.

"It's about respect," Louis replied in the smooth tone he reserved only for her.

"I have no respect for you," she shot back.

Ignoring the pain it caused, I squinted, trying to get a clearer view of the massive shift in power that was taking place in front of me.

Like a love-struck teenager, Louis worked hard to placate her. "I'm prepared to make it up to you."

Shiloh glanced around the warehouse, perhaps pondering her next move. "I want our beer delivered to the Crown and Pav before opening time tonight," she finally demanded.

"Very well," he agreed.

"All of it," she clarified.

"Of course." Louis threw his arms out wide. "See? No real harm done."

That was a lie. I was bleeding like a stuck pig and seemed to have lost the ability to swallow. I'm no doctor, but I was pretty sure it would take more than a few Band-Aids and an aspirin to get me back on my feet.

Louis wasn't the least bit pissed by the stand Shiloh was taking. If anything, he seemed even more enchanted. "Be on your way, my lovely friend," he quietly permitted.

Shiloh leaned closer to him, unfortunately looking more seductive than menacing. "We were leaving anyway." Her voice was soft and slow. "Whether you allowed it or not."

The least I could do for her was try and make our exit a smooth one. When she grabbed my hands, I tried my best to lever myself up. That's when the real agony hit. Excruciating pain filled my chest, stealing the last of the air in my lungs. I fell forward onto my knees, unable to move.

Shiloh put a gentle hand on my side. "Your ribs are probably broken," she said quietly. "Just be still for a minute."

I didn't see the gesture, but I heard the familiar click of Louis fingers as he beckoned his men. "Help him up," he ordered.

Shiloh released her hold on me and jumped to her feet. "Not him!" she yelled.

I lifted my head in time to see the heavy who'd viciously beaten me stop dead in his tracks.

"Fine," agreed Louis, shoving another candidate forward.

Shiloh's eyes never left the first man. "You stay away from us," she warned. "If I ever see you again, it won't end well for you."

I believed her, and judging by the solemn expression on the man's face, he did too.

Someone else had the privilege of helping me to my feet, and then my protector took over. With my arm around her shoulder, Shiloh managed to get me out of the warehouse and into the car.

We were safe, but I didn't feel out of danger. One look at the front of my shirt led me to think I was in absolute dire straits.

"It's not that bad," she assured me with a quick sideward glance. "Your nose is broken. Noses bleed a lot."

"Be straight with me," I mumbled. "My modelling days are over, right?"

She huffed out a small laugh that sounded more like relief than amusement. "No," she replied. "You're still beautiful, darling."

Brute

SHILOH

The best way of keeping Mitchell awake on the short drive home was to crunch the gears. Every time I did it, he groaned as if I'd somehow worsened his injuries.

"Ease off the clutch," he spluttered.

"Stop bleeding on the upholstery," I countered, trying to raise a smile from him.

His head lolled against the headrest. "I have blood in my mouth." The tinge of fear in his tone was understandable. I was worried too, but didn't dare let it show. "That's not good," he added.

"I'm going to fix you up," I assured him. "By the time I'm done, you'll be even prettier than before."

It was going to take a while before he was pretty again. Once I got him home and really checked him over, I realised I was seriously underequipped when it came to patching him up.

Antiseptic and gauze took care of the cuts and scrapes, but his nose was still bleeding profusely. I knelt in front of him at the foot of the bed and geared up to tell him that phase two of operation patch-up was going to be a little unorthodox. "Do you want the good news or the bad news?" I asked.

"Good," he replied. "Start with the good."

I rested my elbows on his knees, holding a cloth to his face. "I'm almost certain that your nose is broken," I revealed. "But at least it's straight."

"Peachy. What's the bad news?"

"It's still bleeding and I can only think of one way to stop it."

The poor man was so spent that he didn't even ask how. "Just do what you have to do."

I disappeared into the bathroom, returning a moment later holding the only solution I could come up with. Mitchell had two sisters. I didn't have to explain a thing.

"You are not shoving tampons up my nose." The cloth he held to his face did nothing to mask his horror. "I'll bleed to death first."

"Don't be such a baby." I sat beside him and dropped the box onto his lap. "We're not exactly spoiled for choice when it comes to medical supplies."

His shoulders slumped and I knew I'd won. "Promise me one thing," he demanded.

"Anything."

"What happens in this room stays in this room."

I leaned across and whispered in his ear, "I'll bet you say that to all the girls."

"No, Shiloh," he mumbled. "Just you."

***

Once his wounds were sorted, the most important thing on my agenda was ridding him of his bloodied clothes. It wasn't an easy job. His body was stiff, reacting to the brutal pain of being kicked in the ribs. I ended up cutting his T-shirt off, purely to save him from the ordeal of having to raise his arms.

"You should probably get some sleep," I suggested, gently smoothing down the gauze taped to his forehead.

"I have half a tampon wedged up each nostril," he reminded me. "How am I supposed to sleep?"

I pulled back the covers and patted the mattress. Every move he made as he struggled to lie down must've been excruciating. His face twisted in pain.

"What can I do?" I asked. "More pillows?"

"No," he groaned. "You've done enough."

It was a telling statement. I wondered if he thought I was to blame for the attack. I'd been taking advantage of the crush Louis had on me to push my operation forward. If it had come at the expense of Mitchell's safety, Mimi Traore had been right all along. I was little more than a witch who'd been sent to kill him.

***

I'd always had a tumultuous relationship with Kaimte, even before the events of that day. I didn't share Mitchell's view that we were living in paradise. As laid back as it seemed on the surface, it had a vicious underbelly that pulled me further under every day.

I was completely losing sight of myself, which is exactly what Allan predicted would happen. The bigger problem was that Mitchell was beginning to wonder who I was too.

Long after I thought he'd fallen asleep beside me, he asked a difficult question. "Why weren't you scared?" he whispered. "I wasn't expecting you to stand up to Louis like that."

If I answered with a lie, chances are I'd have to follow up with ten more lies down the track just to keep my story straight – a tiresome prospect. For once the truth won out. I turned my head, mumbling my reply against his bare shoulder. "Because I knew he wouldn't hurt me. He's still trying to win me over."

"Having me beaten up is pretty poor form then, isn't it?" he suggested.

"A bit of a misstep, yes," I agreed.

"It's not the first time," he mumbled weakly. "I doubt it will be the last."

"He's done this before?"

"Once."

Considering his current state it probably wasn't fair to press for more information, but I found myself doing it anyway.

"It was years ago," he replied with a careful sigh. It was impossible to tell if his lax tone was incited by fatigue or disinterest. Either way, he kept talking. "Back in the day he was just a petty thief."

Even thugs have to start at the bottom. According to Mitchell, Louis got his start on the streets, running a shady little pawnshop at the mid-week markets. Jumping people for the change in their pockets was a side venture.

"A few months after we got here, I was roughed up and robbed of our rent money," he explained.

"By Louis?"

He shrugged, which was a mistake. He sucked in a sharp breath. I gently laid my hand on his chest as if I could make the pain stop.

"Louis never lays a hand on anybody," he groaned. "His dogs do his dirty work." He placed his hand on mine, holding it in place. "It was the last straw for Charli. She started making plans to leave after that," he explained.

Mitchell often talked about Charli, always with reverence, but often describing her as errant and crazy. I got the distinct impression that his over-protective streak stemmed from the year he'd spent trying to keep her out of trouble.

"We were totally broke," he continued. "But she had a very expensive opal necklace that her boyfriend had given her. One day she came across Louis' pawnshop. He offered to buy it, and she was so desperate to get to New York that she agreed to sell it. She had no idea who he was."

"He ripped her off?" I guessed.

"No," he replied. "He paid her fair and square."

If the tale had ended there Louis would've come out smelling of roses, but of course, it didn't. The road to debauchery is long and winding.

"I knew it killed her to part with it," said Mitchell. "I felt responsible, and I wanted to get it back for her."

After months of saving up, he ventured down to Louis' store and offered to buy it back. It was a textbook Mitchell Tate gesture that made me want to kiss him all over – even at the risk of causing him immense pain. Fortunately for him, I kept my lips to myself.

"That was our first official meeting," he said sardonically. "Louis pretended not to know me."

"Was the necklace still there?" I asked.

"Sure was," he confirmed. "He even agreed to sell it to me for what he'd paid. I handed him three grand and he handed me the necklace."

I lightly kissed his shoulder. "A happy ending, then?"

"Not exactly," he mumbled. "When I got to the end of the street, his thugs were waiting for me."

I guessed the rest of the story before he uttered a word, but hearing him say it out loud was still horrendous. Louis' men robbed him a second time, stealing the necklace and giving him another thrashing for good measure.

"I just couldn't win a trick." There was a tiny hint of humour in his voice, but the story wasn't remotely funny. "It's been that way ever since."

As Louis' reputation for being a brute grew, so did his businesses. His whole empire was built on fear and intimidation, and the only way to stay off his radar was to turn a blind eye to his thuggish ways. Mitchell tolerated Louis Osei because he had to.

"The Crown and Pav is my livelihood, Shiloh," he said. "If I have to close the doors because he makes it too difficult to trade, I'll have nothing."

If Louis ramped up his game he'd have no choice but to call it quits. Trying to stick it out wasn't worth losing his life over.

"Do you ever think about going home?" If I thought he'd get on the plane, I would've offered to drive him to the airport there and then. "Your family would be thrilled to have you back."

"And what would I do when I get there?" he asked. "Living life off the grid is costly, Shiloh. After a while, you become so lost that finding your way home becomes impossible."

Femme Fetale

MITCHELL

If Louis decided to make good on delivering my shipment to the Crown and Pav before opening time, I wasn't going to be there to see it. I woke after two hours of sleep feeling like I'd been hit by a train. I imagine I looked worse. Nostrils packed with tampons is a hard look to pull off.

"Can I take these out?" I put my hand to the cotton under my nose. "I'm good now."

"No." Shiloh pulled my hand away. "If it's still bleeding we'll have to start all over again. You need to give it a few more hours."

Perhaps confident that I'd do as I was told, she lay back down, gently resting her head on my shoulder.

I kissed her forehead. "Thank you."

"For what?" she whispered.

"For being here."

A strange choked groan escaped her. "Me being here is the reason this happened in the first place."

I didn't blame her, but I couldn't deny that what she said was true. The problem was, I couldn't articulate it – and staying silent was as good as accusing her of being a deadly femme fatale.

Moving carefully so she didn't bump me, Shiloh slipped out of bed. "I'll work your shift at the pub tonight," she volunteered.

Considering the only drinks on offer were beer and whiskey, bartending at the Crown and Pav was hardly a specialised position. I didn't doubt she'd be able to handle it, but nothing about her flat tone suggested she wanted to. "You don't have to do that."

"It's fine, Mitchell," she replied. "Someone needs to be there when the beer arrives."

She wasn't going to take no for an answer, and I couldn't muster the energy to argue with her. "If Louis turns up, close the bar and leave," I instructed.

"I will."

"Promise me, Shiloh."

She leaned across the bed and lightly kissed me. "I promise."

I wasn't buying it. Despite her sweet smile and butter-wouldn't-t-melt demeanour, I'd seen enough that day to know she had no fear of rocking the boat. My concern was that if she ended up overboard, I wouldn't be there to keep her afloat.

Messenger

SHILOH

If a promise is broken before it's even made, it's nothing more than a dirty lie. I'd told my fair share lately, and it wasn't getting any easier.

I was banking on Louis showing up at the Crown and Pav that night. In a normal world I would've been staying well out of his way, but my world wasn't normal.

At least Louis was a diligent thug. Half an hour before opening time, he and his band of misfits arrived laden with two hundred cases of beer. His smug look suggested that I should've been impressed by the gesture. I wasn't. As far as I was concerned, hand delivering it was the least he could do.

I unlocked the storeroom and ordered the men to stack them neatly. "And don't touch anything."

Louis waited just outside the open door, trying to look important. "I expect this will go some way to making amends with you, Shiloh," he said.

"You expect too much, Louis."

He smiled. "You are a tough woman to impress."

I stepped aside, allowing the men balancing cases of beer on their shoulders to pass. "Did you think hurting Mitchell would impress me?" I asked sarcastically. "Call me crazy, but beating him to a pulp isn't exactly endearing behaviour."

"He's not a good match for you," he replied.

Unfortunately he was right. Mitchell Tate was good to the core. He deserved a million times better than the wickedness I'd brought to his doorstep, but I'd never admit it to Tweedledum. Trying hard to ignore him, I picked up a cloth and began wiping down the already spotless counter.

"You have a fire in your eyes that he doesn't see," continued Louis in a sly tone that sent a shiver down my back. "I see it, Shiloh."

"How observant of you." I was furiously scrubbing the bar now, unable to stop. "What a pity you didn't make better use of it while you had the chance."

Louis casually leaned against the door. When the last of his men filed outside to collect more boxes, he spoke. "All is not lost," he stated.

Acutely aware that I might've finally broken some serious ground, my heart began thumping at an alarming rate. "Speak," I demanded.

Louis looked from left to right, double-checking that the conversation was still private. "I have some upcoming business at the mine," he quietly explained. "Perhaps you could be of assistance."

Yes! Yes! Yes!

I shrugged. "What is it?"

"Not your concern, beautiful friend." He let out a condescending chuckle. "You mustn't ask questions."

I let the fact that he'd admonished me like a naughty child slide. My whole career operated on a need-to-know basis. If the good guys weren't prepared to keep me up to speed on vital information, it made sense that that bad guys would take the same approach.

"Tell me what you want me to do."

Louis reached into his pocket and grabbed a small but bulky envelope that could only have contained money. "I need you to deliver this to one of your co-workers," he replied. "Will you do that for me?"

I had only seconds to decide. Once my hand touched that envelope, there would be no going back. "Who do I need to give it to?" I asked, still hesitating.

"A man called Glen Harris," replied Louis, thrusting the envelope at me. "Do you know him?"

The prospect of nailing two birds with one stone was almost more excitement than I could bear. It meant the end was in sight, and I could go home.

In an attempt at keeping my expression straight, I bit my bottom lip. "I'll pass it on to him," I offered, snatching it from his grasp.

Louis' grin was triumphant. "Your good deed will be rewarded, Shiloh."

I shoved the envelope into my back pocket. "It had better be," I replied. "Favours are costly, Louis."

***

Somehow, word must've gotten out that I was running the Crown and Pav alone that night. It was busier than I'd ever seen it, and by nine o'clock my feet were killing me. Everyone was curious to know the reason behind Mitchell's absence. Some people asked me, and others stood at the bar and speculated.

"He's dead," one bloke suggested. "He never misses work."

His mate stood beside him, overzealously nodding in agreement. "The big waves got him."

"What big waves?" I scoffed, reaching for the bottle opener. "There haven't been any big waves lately."

"She's right," he agreed after a long moment of thinking things through. "Maybe she killed him."

I slammed the bottle of beer down in front of him. "He's not dead," I snapped.

"So where is he?"

"Taking some time off," I replied. "Any more questions?"

The two bozos actually took a step back, put their heads together and discussed it. No matter how far I leaned across the bar, I couldn't quite catch the whispered conversation, which frustrated me no end. Hands on hips, I stared straight at them, waiting for the two-man huddle to break apart.

The man on the left finally spoke. "We have one question, Miss."

"Yes, one question," his mate assented.

I threw both hands out. "Hit me with it."

Both men put a closed fist to their mouths, trying to conceal their schoolboy chuckles. After a long wait, one of them finally pulled himself together enough to ask the question. "Why do you wear your beads on your neck?"

I self-consciously grabbed the long necklace, winding the glass beads around my fingers. Melito had already hinted that I was wearing it incorrectly. If I'd been smart enough to ask him what I was doing wrong, I might've saved myself the awkwardness of dealing with the giggling twits in front of me.

"Where else am I supposed to wear them?"

The cackling got louder and neither offered an answer. Instead, they picked up their beers and wandered away.

***

It had been a long day full of nothing but drama, and I was desperate to put an end to it. Two hours early, I stepped outside and dropped the awning. It wasn't quite how Mitchell announced that the pub was closing, but it was effective.

The merry crowd slowly made their way up to the car park, following each other like a wayward flock of drunken sheep. Within minutes I was alone, picking up discarded beer bottles off the beach under the light of a bright moon.

It was too much to hope that I'd be left in peace to clean up. I'd barely filled the first rubbish bag when the two giggly men from earlier reappeared, and this time they weren't alone.

The young woman stumbled in the sand as one of the men shoved her forward. "This is Hiatte," he announced. "My sister."

I had no idea why she was there, but said hello.

Gifting me the brightest smile I'd ever seen, Hiatte nodded. "I can help you," she offered.

I glanced around at the mammoth job ahead before politely declining her offer. "Thanks anyway." I waved the half full rubbish bag. "It won't take me long to clean up."

Her dickhead brothers began chortling again, but Hiatte was having none of it. Whatever she snapped at them in Afrikaans shut them up in an instant.

"Please," she said, speaking in a much gentler tone, "can we go inside?"

Perhaps I was curious, or just too tired to protest. I dropped the bag of empty bottles on the sand and pointed toward the door of the pub. "Be my guest."

Raincheck

MITCHELL

No matter how hard I tried, I couldn't sleep knowing that Shiloh had been left alone to run the pub. When I finally heard the key in the door, I felt utter relief – despite the fact she was an hour earlier than expected.

"You're home," I muttered, trying to sit up.

She barely slowed her walk as she rushed through the bathroom. "Lie down," she ordered. "You're still broken."

For once, I welcomed her bossiness. Dealing with the unbearable wave of pain that ripped through my chest whenever I moved couldn't be done sitting up. "How was it?" I called.

"Very informative," came a distant reply.

I dreaded to think what that meant. After the day we'd had, the possibilities were endless. Deciding against questioning her, I stared up at the slow moving ceiling fan and waited for her to speak again.

"How long did you say you'd been here, Adonis?" she asked. "Seven years?"

"Yeah," I confirmed with a heavy sigh. "Seven years."

"As it turns out, you've learned nothing about women in that time," she replied. "But lucky for you, I'm prepared to teach you what I know." The newly fitted door to the bathroom swung open and Shiloh sauntered in – practically floating to the edge of the bed wearing nothing but a pair of skimpy undies. I had no idea what the lesson plan was, nor did I care. I was too busy drinking in the view. "Am I dead?" It was a fair question, all things considered.

"No," she replied, edging closer. "I'm pretty sure you're still with me."

She was just inches away from me when I finally noticed that her turquoise necklace was hanging around her waist. I reached, slipping my fingers beneath the beads at her hip. "New fashion trend?" I asked.

"No, a very, very old one, as it happens." Her voice was pure silk. "It's not a necklace, Mitchell. I met a lady at the Crown and Pav who was good enough to set me straight. They're called bin bin beads," she explained. "They're worn around the waist, beneath the clothing. It's basically pretty African gift-wrapping that a woman shares only with her lover, like lingerie."

I was very familiar with the Kaimte brand of mumbo jumbo, but I'd never heard of bin bin beads. The notion of improving her perfect body with decoration was redundant – like gift-wrapping a sunrise – but I couldn't take my eyes off her. "So this is just for me?" I ran my fingertips along the beads, making her flinch.

"Yep," she confirmed. "And I've been walking around displaying my bin bin goodies to the whole neighbourhood."

The poor girl went on to explain that she'd been copping strange looks and sly comments all night until a couple of complete strangers enlisted the expertise of their sister to sit her down and explain the ins and outs of African jewellery. "Like a pubescent school girl being given the birds and bees lecture," she complained.

In one of the few moves that didn't hurt, I grinned at her.

"It's not funny," she scolded.

"It's a little bit funny," I replied.

"You're supposed to be putty in my hands at this point." A smile swept her beautiful face. "Bin bin bling is supposed to be highly seductive. It's a look that's been making African men happy for hundreds of years."

"You can make me happy any time you like," I offered.

Shiloh shimmied her hips, making her beads rattle. "I'll take you up on that when you're a little less fragile," she replied. "And when you don't have feminine hygiene products wedged up your nose."

I was so distracted by her appearance that I'd almost managed to forget how horrendous mine was. "Raincheck?" I asked.

Shiloh gently pressed her warm lips against my chest. "Oh, the irony," she mumbled against my skin. "The fools finally learn the game, and the players have dispersed."

***

My body was far too banged up to take advantage of the gorgeous leggy brunette in my bed, but having her sound asleep beside me was a decent consolation prize.

When I lightly grazed my fingertips across her bare stomach she flinched, as I expected her to. I knew Shiloh's body well. It was her mind that was a mystery. She didn't wake, but shifted just enough to free my arm.

I was under strict instructions not to touch the dressings on my face until morning, but unless I cleared my nose sleep was never going to happen. I awkwardly rolled off the bed and slipped into the bathroom to check myself out in the mirror.

Seeing the extent of the damage wasn't good for morale. It also proved that Shiloh's advice of leaving the dressings alone was probably sound. From what could see, gauze was the only thing holding my face together. Removing it wasn't a brilliant idea, but I was determined.

Shiloh's mysterious pink toiletry bag had been a permanent fixture on the bathroom counter for weeks. Ordinarily, I'd never consider rifling through it but just in case my nose started bleeding again, I needed backup cotton.

Absolutely nothing in that bag should've fazed me. My sisters were the queens of girly junk and I truly believed I'd seen it all – right up until I reached into Shiloh's bag and pulled out an envelope packed with money.

I was so taken aback that I stood there stupidly shuffling two thousand US dollars from hand to hand. I couldn't think of a logical reason why Shiloh would be in possession of that kind of loot, or why she'd keep it hidden in the bathroom. While I racked my brain trying to think harder, I counted it again.

"What are you doing?" Despite her soft tone, Shiloh's voice ripped through the silence, making me jump.

I turned to see her standing in the doorway, looking so betrayed that I wished I'd made use of the new bathroom door when I came in. I'd been caught red-handed, and my kneejerk reaction was to snap at her because of it.

"What are *you* doing?" I waved the wad of cash at her. "What's this for?"

I was more alarmed than angry, but Shiloh couldn't have known that. "What do you think it's for?" she asked.

I dropped the envelope back in her pink bag. "A large amount of US currency can't be for anything good – not in this town."

She folded her arms tightly across her chest, clearly offended. "So what's your theory, Mitchell?"

"I don't have a theory, Shiloh," I said sourly. "All I have is a broken nose and some busted ribs."

And that was the sole reason my mind had jumped to such wild conclusions. I couldn't rule anything out any more. The only time big chunks of cash exchanged hands in this town was when someone was being extorted or bribed. In a few short minutes, I'd all but convinced myself that someone was trying to drag her to the dark side. "If you're in trouble, you can tell me," I urged, calming my tone.

Shiloh shook her head. "You've been here too long, Mitchell," she said pityingly. "It's making you crazy."

As she turned to walk away, I grabbed her arm. "You work at a diamond mine in one of the most corrupt places on earth," I reminded her. "It's not crazy to think someone would take advantage of that."

Shiloh gently took my face in her hands. "No one is taking advantage of me," she insisted. "That money is to pay for the new exhaust on the jeep."

I felt like a complete moron for a few reasons. First, Shiloh had taken it upon herself to pay for the stupid car repair that I needed but didn't want, and second, I *was* acting crazy.

"Maybe I have been here too long," I conceded.

She stretched up on tiptoes and whispered in my ear. "Maybe you should let me take you home – back to the real world."

Years after leaving, I'd met a girl who actually made the possibility of going home one worth considering. Shiloh was special – frustratingly confusing at times, but uniquely special. On some level I already loved her, but it was much too soon to admit to it – even to myself.

"Maybe I'll take *you* home instead," I countered.

"Really?" she asked grinning.

"Sure," I replied, sweeping my hand through her hair. "But we'll need a good contingency plan first, otherwise my sisters will eat you alive."

Witch's Brew

SHILOH

It was hard to decide what was more troubling: the carelessness I'd shown when it came to hiding the money Louis had given me, or the ease with which I'd lied to cover it up. I couldn't dwell on which was the bigger failing. Both were less than righteous acts.

Louis hadn't mentioned the jeep exhaust since I first asked him to find me one, but Mitchell didn't need to know that. What he did need was some major first aid to making sleep a little easier. I just wasn't sure if I could be the one to administer it.

"Taking the cotton out of your nose is really going to hurt," I warned him. "I wish you'd just wait until morning."

"It's still going to hurt in the morning." He sounded exhausted. "I can't sleep like this."

I swept my thumb along the bruise under his eye. I was a police officer. I'd seen the very best and worst of human behaviour in my time, but it was still unfathomable to think one man could willingly inflict that kind of pain on another.

I loathed the air that Iron Mike and Louis Osei breathed, which made me even more determined to cut ties with Mike and shut Louis down. I pushed the wild and vengeful thoughts as far away as possible, concentrating on Mitchell as I picked up our paltry first aid kit, took him by the hand and led him back to the bedroom.

"Sit," I ordered.

Mitchell sat on the edge of the bed. Knowing I'd probably need to hold him still, I wedged myself between his knees.

His hands moved to my hips. "Just do it quickly."

"I'm not sure that's going to help."

"Please, Shiloh." The only thing worse than the tired desperation in his voice was the pitiful look in his blue eyes. "Just get it done."

I cupped his cheeks in my hands and gently tilted his head back. "Breathe," I whispered.

Mitchell closed his eyes and pulled in a slow steadying breath through his mouth. "You always smell amazing," he mumbled. "I don't think I've told you that before."

"I'm sure you can't smell a thing at the moment," I replied smiling down at him."

"No, but I remember."

"What do I smell like?" It was a strange question but I was too curious not to know.

"Crisp and fresh and amazing." His eyes remained closed as I gently peeled a strip of tape off his cheek. "Like rainwater hitting the ocean," he added. "Maybe that's why you remind me of home."

Mitchell wasn't exactly renowned for being sweet and sentimental. The unexpected words trickled through my chest like heat, making a reply impossible.

I gently pulled at another piece of tape, uncovering a graze that wasn't nearly as horrific as I remembered. Deciding against re-dressing it, I dabbed it with some antiseptic-soaked cotton. Perhaps I should've warned Mitchell it was coming. He winced, letting out a low groan.

"Stay with me," I whispered.

"You can see it coming, you know," he mumbled.

"See what?"

"The rain," he replied. "And if you lie down flat on your board, you can feel it before it even hits. I miss the rain."

Vulnerability sounds a lot like truth. Mitchell's tough but perfect exterior had been cracked, but he was far from broken. I enjoyed the unguarded, candid man I was seeing, regardless of how brief the glimpse had been.

Taking advantage of his moment of distraction, I quickly tugged the wads of cotton from his nose, which felt like ripping him apart all over again. With a woeful groan of agony, he threw his head forward, trying to ride out the wave of pain by pressing his forehead against my stomach. His fingers dug into the flesh of my hips. It wasn't the most comfortable position I'd ever been in, but I didn't move. "You're okay," I told him. "It's over."

When Mitchell finally lifted his head, I checked him over as best I could. Mercifully the bleeding had stopped, but that was little consolation. Tears streamed down his face, and his breathing was hard and laboured.

I wasn't breathing at all. "Now you can sleep," I said in a shaky voice.

When I was sure he'd cope with moving, I gracelessly scrambled across the bed and pulled back the covers. Mitchell lay back, huffing another pained groan as his head sank into the pillow.

I lay beside him, splaying my hand across his middle. "Are you okay?" I asked.

He didn't reply but after a long minute, the tempo of his breathing changed. The rise and fall of his chest slowed, and I felt his body relax against mine.

With the exception of the Atlantic Ocean rolling in, the whole world was quiet. If I could be certain he wouldn't hear me, I would've used that moment to empty my head of all the words I was desperate to tell him — starting with an apology for every lie I'd ever told him.

At that moment, the risk of compromising my cover wasn't the driving force for keeping quiet. It was the fear of not being forgiven.

Trailing my finger across his bare chest, I absently traced the most important word I'd never told him over and over again – sorry.

Taking me completely by surprise, his quiet murmur broke the silence. "Nothing to be sorry for, lady. Go to sleep."

***

Even if Mitchell was the forgiving type, Mimi Traore was not. It was just after dawn when she turned up at our door, pounding on it with the strength of a lumberjack swinging an axe.

"Let me in, witch!" she yelled.

I could only assume that she'd heard the news that Mitchell was missing in action, and it wasn't too much of a stretch to assume that she thought I had something to do with it.

"She's not going to go away, is she?"

"Not a chance," came Mitchell's groggy reply. "She'll huff and puff until she blows the house down."

Of all the people I'd met in Kaimte, Mimi terrified me the most. Getting out of bed and answering the door was an act of bravery.

I'd barely turned the handle before she pushed her way in.

"Good morning, Mimi," I greeted her. "Do come in."

"Where is the dumb boy?" she barked.

Mimi was Mitchell's self-appointed scary fairy godmother. She was fiercely protective, which meant I was going to be in a whole world of trouble when she laid eyes on him.

"He's still in bed," I replied. "It's very early."

As expected, an apology for waking us wasn't forthcoming. Mimi dumped the wicker basket she was carrying on the beanbag and stomped through to the bedroom. I followed at a safe distance, hanging back near the doorway.

She didn't say a word as she checked him over, but the pissed-off tutting was constant.

"It's not that bad, Mimi," insisted Mitchell. "I'm okay."

She reached behind his head, thumping his pillow back into shape. "The heks girl did this."

It wasn't a question. The crazy woman spoke as if she was stating fact. Despite his best efforts, nothing Mitchell said was going to convince her otherwise. Even after hearing the whole story, she lumped the blame on me.

"Witches are sent by the devil," she hissed, glaring at me. "He wants you to believe that you've found an angel." Mimi sat on the edge of the bed and roughly tugged a piece of gauze on his cheek. "She makes you fall in love with her and then she strikes."

Mitchell's groan wasn't brought on by pain. He was frustrated and fast losing patience with her.

"Why, Mimi?" he grumbled. "Why would the devil bother with me?"

She cupped his face in her hands, showing him the most tenderness I'd ever seen from her. "Because you are good, my boy," she said quietly. "And he always tries to steal the good souls."

Despite her claims, I hadn't come here to steal souls. Stolen diamonds were my thing, but it was becoming impossible to stay on task because Kaimte was crazy town. I'd altered course so many times because of it that I no longer had a clue which direction I was heading in.

I was never going to beat Mimi. The only option I had at that point was to join her. When she finally stopped fussing with Mitchell's face and walked out of the room, I was hot on her heels.

She reached into her wicker basket and pulled out a large pot. "Boil some water," she demanded, thrusting it at me.

"We have a kettle," I replied.

Even with her elaborate head-wrap, I had to be at least a foot taller than her but Mimi had no problem fronting up to me. She looked so menacing that when she stepped closer I stumbled backward.

"Do you want him to heal?" Her voice was as angry as her expression. "Or would you rather see him in pain?"

Until she arrived, Mitchell wasn't in any pain. He'd slept through the night quite comfortably, only waking because of her incessant pounding on the door – but I was much too cowardly to point that out.

"Of course I do," I mumbled, snatching the pot from her grasp.

Lighting the antiquated gas stove was a process. In the five minutes it took me to get a flame happening, Mimi went to work.

The kitchen table was one of the few pieces of furniture in the shack, and by the time she was done every spare inch of it was covered with bunches of herbs, small bags of coloured powder and bundles of sticks. I had no idea what she was up to and didn't dare ask.

"I'm scared of you, Mimi Traore," I told her. Despite the weak admission, my tone was strong. "Maybe you're the witch."

"No." The corner of her mouth lifted but she didn't look at me. "Heks are bad women."

If I had to wear the title of witch, it only seemed fair that I was given a thorough job description. I demanded to know more.

"A witch is wicked," she explained. "Mysterious and charming at first – then deadly." Mimi picked up a bunch of twigs and began stripping the leaves. "Men are easy prey for her. She seduces them with lies and beauty, and then causes them much trouble and unhappiness."

Her definition described my recent behaviour to a T, but I refused to be affected by it. I'd attended enough domestic disputes during my career to know that she was describing any woman who treated men badly. They were the traits of a bitch, not a witch.

I waved at the pile of junk on the table. "What's all this for? If you're planning some weird ceremony to drive the devil out of him, you might as well stop right now." There was no way I was going to let her put Mitchell through that. He didn't have the strength to push her out the door but I was prepared to give it a crack if need be.

Mimi glared at me, her chocolate eyes hard as flint. "The devil isn't in Mitchell," she said. "He's creeping up behind you."

The woman unnerved me so much that it took effort not to turn around and check. "I am not a witch," I angrily replied. "Tell me what I have to do to prove it to you."

The basket she'd brought with her was huge. I didn't doubt for a second that she had some sort of witch detector in there. As long as it didn't involve drawing blood or setting me on fire, I was prepared to let her use it.

Mimi didn't take me up on the offer. Instead, she dropped a handful of herbs into the stone mortar she'd brought and began grinding. "You're not that brave," she told me.

She was probably right, but I was too stubborn to back down. "Try me."

Abandoning the herb crushing, she walked to her basket and pulled out a bottle of clear liquid. I recognised it immediately – it was the mystery bottle from the Crown and Pav.

"Witch's brew," she announced, waving it at me.

"Mitchell said that bottle's been on the shelf for years," I replied, sounding far more frightened than I'd hoped. "No one knows what it is."

"I know what it is," she replied, edging closer. "It's witch's brew – and if you're a witch, one sip will kill you."

Putting any sort of faith in Mimi was nonsensical. For all I knew, the bottle contained drain cleaner. I was stupidly stubborn, but I had no death wish. "I'm not going to drink that," I declared.

Mimi slammed the bottle on the table. "Because you are a heks girl."

Where I come from, the justice system requires evidence before a conviction. All crazy Mimi needed was a hunch. On the plus side, acquittal was a simple process, too. All I had to do was take a sip of drain cleaner.

As I stared at the bottle, something deep inside me snapped, possibly the last thread of my common sense. Desperate to put an end to the madness and clear my witchy name, I picked it up. "I must be out of my freaking mind," I muttered unscrewing the lid.

Without putting an ounce more thought into it, I threw my head back and took a swig. The clear liquid burned my throat and the flavour was vile, but within seconds I knew I'd live to see another day.

"It's gin," I spluttered, wiping my chin with the back of my hand. "Gin kills witches?"

Mimi shrugged "I have no idea." She smiled, perhaps for the first time ever. "No witch in her right mind would've agreed to drink it in the first place."

The laugh that tumbled out of my mouth was involuntary. I should've been furious with her. "You're a crazy woman, Mimi," I told her. "Are you happy now?"

"You're not a witch," she finally conceded. "But you are trouble." She took a step closer to me and whispered a harsh warning. "And as long as you're in this town, the devil will be right behind you."

Rules

MITCHELL

Mimi Traore sometimes reminds me of my mother. Both women are hard and share the same style of tough-love parenting, but it's a method that's always worked for me.

It had taken Shiloh hours to patch me up the day before, but it was all for nothing. As soon as Mimi arrived she ripped every bit of gauze off my face, all the while muttering under her breath about what a terrible job the heks girl had done.

Shiloh didn't take it to heart. In fact, she put a lot of effort into winning Mimi over that morning, which was extraordinary considering Mimi had gone to great lengths to terrorise her.

Forging the peace treaty seemed to be going well. I couldn't hear any screaming or yelling from the kitchen, but I could hear calm chatter. I could also smell something cooking, and it wasn't remotely pleasant. When Shiloh appeared, I asked her what it was.

"Marigold, cayenne and a few other bits and pieces," she replied, crawling across the bed. "It smells foul, doesn't it?" She lay down and gently rested her head on my shoulder. "I think she's going to make you drink it."

"No she won't." I smoothed my hand through her hair. "She's making a poultice."

Having a wound plastered with a pungent mix of bread soaked in herbs is only scary the first time. Mimi had used this method to patch me up a million times over the years, usually after I'd been shredded by low-lying reef in the surf, and once when I stood on a rusty nail. "It's pretty gross," I conceded. "But it works like magic."

"It *is* magic," boomed Mimi, marching into the room. "Two days from now he'll be back to his old dumb self." She knelt beside me, stirring a bowl of gloop with her bare hand.

"Be warned, lady," I mumbled. "Sleeping beside me for the next few nights will be hell. A few hours from now I'm going to stink like a wet dog."

"You won't be my problem," she replied. "I'm on night shift, remember?"

"You have to come home some time."

Without warning, Mimi slopped a handful of goo on my face. From the corner of my eye I saw Shiloh wince. I didn't move. It wasn't painful, just warm and unpleasant.

"Hang in there, soldier," she encouraged.

"He is not a soldier," snapped Mimi. "He's a dumb boy who doesn't know how to play by the rules."

"Whose rules?" asked Shiloh.

Mimi shot her a filthy look but didn't reply. I had no problem spelling it out for her. "Louis' rules. Mimi thinks the best way to keep the peace is to meet his demands and pay him off."

"It is the only way," she grumbled. "He is a very bad man."

Considering my current state, it was hard to argue the point. I stayed quiet and Mimi continued painting my face with slop, but Shiloh had a few burning questions.

"Have you had any dealings with him, Mimi?"

"Not even Louis could get blood from a stone," she scoffed. "I am a poor woman." She pressed a warm cloth to my cheek, holding her mushy concoction in place. "I have no money for him."

Poor locals weren't of any interest to Louis Osei. It was predominantly the businesspeople of Kaimte who kept his crooked rackets going. As long as Mimi stayed out of his way she had nothing to fear.

"Just steer clear of him," I suggested. "He's a loose cannon."

Mimi let out a choked growl. "I am not afraid of him," she spat. "Man is far less dangerous when obnoxious and throwing his weight around."

"Why?" asked Shiloh.

Mimi turned around to look at her. "Because the roaring lion catches no prey."

Bad Attitude

SHILOH

African medicine is not for the faint of heart. By the time Mimi left late that afternoon, the shack smelt like a fridge full of rotting food. Strangely, the bedroom didn't stink, which meant Mitchell was still totally kissable – he just wasn't cute any more.

"You look like a giant bowl of porridge."

"Come here and say that, lady." His voice was low and gorgeous, totally making up for his disgusting appearance. "I dare you."

I stood firm by the doorway. "I'm not coming anywhere near you," I replied, brushing my hands down the front of my shirt. "I'm already dressed for work."

"So I see," he replied. "You're looking as lovely and crispy as always."

The ribbing was warranted. My strange penchant for ironing wasn't a Shiloh Jenson trait; the quirk was entirely Shiloh Brannan's. Perhaps that's why I was happy to own it.

"Trust me, Adonis," I told him, "you're in no position to be teasing me about looking crispy."

"It'll all be worth it." He put his hand to his face. "Tomorrow I'll be good to go."

I kissed him gently. "I'm looking forward to it," I whispered.

"Me too," he mumbled. "Be sure to iron your bin bin beads."

***

Every time I walked out of the shack, I left one life and walked into another. I was getting good at starting over, but that didn't mean my job was getting easier.

My heart pounded as I made my way up to the road to meet Glen. I trudged through the sand as if my shoes were made of cement, but it was the wad of money in my back pocket that was really weighing me down.

I had no strategy when it came to dealing with Glen Harris, unless playing dumb was a strategy.

As soon as I got into the waiting car, I handed him the envelope.

"What's this?"

Clearly he was good at playing dumb too.

"Money." My flat tone implied disinterest but inside I was jelly. "Your mate Louis asked me to give it to you."

Without bothering to count it, Glen slipped the envelope into his back pocket. When he started the car and pulled away from the curb I feared the conversation was over.

That's when my plan of playing it dumb started to fall apart. Dumb girls don't ask questions, which meant I had no choice but to keep quiet. Fortunately, Glen was curious. After just a few minutes, his subtle but obvious interrogation began.

"How do you know Louis?"

"I'm not sure that I do," I replied vaguely. "He's an odd bloke."

I glanced across just long enough to notice the sly smirk forming on his face. "So he just gave you a bunch of money and you took it?"

I leaned my head back on the headrest and sighed, adding to the illusion of apathy. "Running errands is easier than stealing diamonds."

"You were serious about that?" The surprise in his voice was unmistakable. It sounded a lot like victory.

I lazily turned to look at him. "As long as he pays me for my services, I'm up for anything."

"You have a bad attitude, Shiloh," he told me.

"And you have a big fat wad of money in your pocket," I reminded him. "So I guess that makes two of us."

***

In a dizzying shift, Glen barely left my side that night. I doubt I'd risen in his estimation. It was more likely that he was keeping an eye on me. The newfound chumminess even extended as far as eating together. When our dinner break came at midnight, Glen joined me at a table in the corner.

After hours of avoiding the subject, I finally mentioned Louis' payoff over a plate of curried fish and rice. "So what did you do to earn that kind of money?"

I tried not to predict his answer, but my mind was already in overdrive. I suspected Glen was stealing diamonds and on-selling them to Louis. I just needed him to confirm it.

He glanced at his watch. "In half an hour from now you'll find out."

Playing it cool was getting harder to do, but I tried. "Excellent," I replied. "Enough time to finish dinner."

When he checked his watch again I realised it was a nervous gesture. And when his foot started bouncing under the table, I wondered what the hell I was in for.

***

Now more than ever, I was convinced that the change to our roster was deliberate. The mine ran completely differently at night. The process was the same, but dark corners appeared that weren't there in the daytime.

There wasn't a soul around to see us get into Glen's car in the dead of night. Considering my trust for the man was at an all-time low, I wasn't sure if that was a good or bad thing.

He drove for quite a while, following the dirt road that lined the perimeter fence. I knew better than to ask where we were going. If ever there was a wait-and-see moment, this was it.

Glen finally spoke. "Have you been to the maintenance workshop before?"

I nodded. "Once or twice." I'd never seen the workshop at the Kaimte mine, but presumably it was the same as the Australian operation. From what I remembered, it housed the massive assortment of mining equipment and tools used for the day-to-day running of the mine. "Are we meeting someone there?" I asked.

Glen didn't answer. In fact, he didn't say another word until we pulled up outside the massive steel maintenance shed. "Get out," he ordered.

I did as I was told, mainly because there was nothing remotely threatening about the scene we'd driven up to.

Unlike the rest of the processing plant, the workshop was a hive of activity. Everywhere I looked, there were people working on trucks and other heavy machinery. It was noisy and busy – and it was the last place I expected a diamond trade to go down.

When Glen walked over to the perimeter fence, I followed. The desert beyond the fence line was pitch black, but when he gazed into the distance as if he could see for miles, I did too.

"What are you looking at?" For some reason I whispered the question.

"Nothing," he replied. "I'm more interested in what's looking at us."

Glen took a small torch out of his pocket and pointed it at the fence, flashing it on and off three times.

"How cliché," I mocked.

"But effective," he replied, returning the torch to his pocket.

He was right. Not more than two seconds later, all hell broke loose.

Three sets of blinding headlights lit the darkness on the other side of the fence. As the vehicles drew closer a group of men came running out of the workshop and cut the chain link fence apart with the precision of a crack SWAT team.

Before I realised what was happening, the police officer in me kicked in. My hand instinctively shifted to my side, reaching for a gun I didn't have. Thankfully, Glen didn't pick up on the move, but he must've sensed my nervousness. "Don't look so worried," he teased. "You're amongst friends."

A ute pulled up first, closely followed by a large flatbed truck. The last vehicle to join the party was very familiar to me. It was Louis' thuggish black Range Rover.

Six men jumped off the tray of the ute and made a beeline for the workshop. Louis moved more slowly. He got out of his car and stalked toward me, his sly smile cutting through the darkness.

"Welcome, Shiloh," he drawled, arms spread wide. "How wonderful of you to join us."

"Wouldn't have missed it for the world," I replied, trying to sound upbeat.

At first, I wasn't sure what "it" was, but when Louis' men began hauling goods out of the workshop, things became a whole lot clearer.

It was a robbery, and it had nothing to do with diamonds. Louis had paid Glen thousands of dollars to turn a blind eye while his men robbed the joint.

Everything from generators to fuel tanks was loaded onto the back of the ute. Standing by and watching it happen went against everything I've ever stood for, but my moral compass was so askew that it barely even registered as a crime.

Too preoccupied to make small talk, Louis wandered away. Glen and I watched from the sidelines as he played the part of project manager, barking orders at his men and yelling at them to hurry up.

Glen leaned his back against the car and lit up a cigarette, unfazed by the criminal chaos in front of us. It made me wonder if shenanigans like this were commonplace.

"Not quite what you were expecting, eh?" he asked.

I glanced at him only briefly. "No," I conceded. "I was hoping for something a little less in-your-face."

Glen chuckled, a rumbly noise that sounded as crooked as he was. "It's a decent little earner," he explained. "Osei scratches my back, I scratch his. If you're a good girl, maybe he'll let you in on a little more action."

There's an art to letting someone think they're corrupting you. I couldn't appear too eager or too reluctant. I had to sell my story carefully, and I did it with a hint of reluctance and a small dose of arrogance. "This is a diamond mine," I reminded him. "Why would I bother with small-time schemes like this when there are diamonds here for the taking?"

His cigarette sparked through the air as he flicked it onto the ground. "This isn't a small scheme," he replied.

At that moment an engine fired up noisily from somewhere close by. A minute later, a massive bulldozer slowly backed out of the workshop. I watched in absolute disbelief as it was loaded onto the back of the flatbed truck.

"They're stealing a freaking bulldozer?" I asked incredulously. "Surely management will notice it gone."

"Nope," replied Glen, pulling another smoke out of the packet. "It'll be back before anyone misses it."

I wasn't expecting him to elaborate, but then I remembered what a bigheaded jerk he was. Tweedledee was a bragger, and by the time he'd taken the last drag on his cigarette, he'd laid out the whole story.

Along with his many other dodgy ventures, Louis was in the construction game. It didn't matter that he had no heavy machinery to carry out the work. Every time he landed a job, he'd steal what he needed from the mine and return it when the work was complete.

"Unbelievable," I muttered.

"I don't look at it as stealing," Glen explained. "It's more like borrowing."

The look of disgust I directed at him wasn't appropriate. I was supposed to be on board with the stupidity. "So nothing to do with diamonds?"

He shook his head, grinning. "You backed the wrong horse this time."

It's always strange to hear insightful words coming from a fool's mouth. Glen was oblivious, but the gravity of the situation hit me hard. I was effectively back at square one – no closer to getting to the bottom of the diamond thefts than the first day I stepped off the plane.

***

An hour later, the stolen cargo was loaded up and good to go. Louis made a point of approaching us before leaving. In a strange display of respect and good manners, he shook Glen's hand. "Until next time, friend," he said. I wanted to retch, but held it together. Louis turned to me. "I want you to come to my shop on market day." His tone was quiet but demanding. "I will pay you then."

It was a less than ideal arrangement. From what Mitchell had told me, Louis' pawnshop at the markets wasn't the safest of places.

"I expected payment tonight." Trying to sound outraged, I snapped out the words.

Louis grabbed my hand, dipped his head and kissed it. "All good things come to those who wait, beautiful friend."

It was another insightful statement out of the mouth of a different fool. For now the waiting game would continue, but good things were coming. Sooner or later I was going to nail these men to the wall.

Angst

MITCHELL

I spent nearly a week laid up in bed, which was almost as excruciating as my injuries. Thanks to Mimi's unorthodox nursing methods, my face healed quickly. There was no quick fix for broken ribs, but at least I was on my feet by then.

Despite the fact that surfing was off the agenda, morning was still my favourite time of day. I always woke early, stealing a wasteful hour or two lazing on the deck before Shiloh got home. Mother Nature had been serving up dismal waves to the Kaimte coastline all week. Perhaps she was taking pity on me. After a few days of useless chop, the ocean was as calm as a millpond, which is more than could be said for my neighbours.

Vincent and Melito were men of excess. Everything was over the top – from the parties they hosted to the amount of booze they consumed. Living in Kaimte should've curbed their frivolous ways, but it didn't. They just shopped accordingly. Every few months they'd make a three-day bus journey south to Cape Town, stock up on ouzo and baking supplies, and then make the long trek home. They were leaving later that day, and excitement was getting the better of them.

"You should come," encouraged Melito, dragging a suitcase out onto the porch. "Bring your darling girl."

My Jeep was a chariot compared to the Cape Town bus. How they endured it was beyond me, but they loved ouzo enough to put up with the overcrowding and livestock roaming free in the aisle.

"Maybe next time."

Vincent stepped out and threw an empty suitcase onto the beach. "Pack this one too."

Melito leaned over the railing to look at it. "How am I supposed to pack a suitcase?"

"Very carefully," he replied making me chuckle. "I don't want it damaged."

"You just hurled it onto the sand!" Melito complained. "You, my good man, are a fool." Both men retreated inside, but it made little difference. Their conversation could've been heard a mile away.

Blocking it out wasn't difficult. Shiloh wandered into view, giving me something far more pleasant to focus on. "Hey." She stepped onto the deck. "How's the patient?"

"Patience is gone, lady," I replied. "It's all angst and frustration here." As soon as she was within reach, I pulled her into my lap.

"It looks good on you." She moved her mouth to my ear. "All that angst."

"*You* look good on me," I corrected, undoing the top button on her stiff work shirt. "Even when you're dressed like a bloke."

I'd rather she was buck naked, but it wouldn't have been a polite scenario considering we were in plain view of the neighbours. For now, I had to settle for a bit of cleavage.

"You are so beautiful." I leaned forward and kissed her collarbone. "I think you should let me take you to bed."

"I think you should take her to Cape Town instead," interrupted a voice from next door. "The bus leaves at two."

"Oh, my God," muttered Shiloh, quickly rebuttoning her shirt.

The embarrassment should've been all Melito's, but he leaned against the railing as if he'd just started a casual conversation.

"Show the lady some proper romance," he continued. "It'll keep the flame alive."

Shiloh scrambled off my lap, nowhere near as gently as she'd sat down. "I'm going inside," she muttered. "To die in private."

"Enjoy your day, darling Shiloh!" called Melito, following up with a friendly wave that she didn't see. The man was incorrigible.

I levered myself out of the deckchair as the front door slammed. "How long did you say you were going to be out of town for?" I asked.

Melito grinned. "Two weeks."

"Good." I nodded. "That's good news."

"Why?"

"Because you're damaging to my love life," I replied heading for the door. "That's why."

***

I expected that my bin bin plans had gone up in smoke, but Shiloh wasn't one to give in easily. By the time I got inside she'd already changed out of her work uniform and was plotting our escape.

"There's just no privacy, Mitchell," she grumbled. "We need to get out of here for a while."

"Okay." I slipped my arm around her middle and hauled her in close. "Where do you want to go?"

"A hotel."

"There are no hotels here," I pointed out. "You know that."

Perhaps she had plans for making the two o'clock bus to Cape Town with the sleek Greeks and the caged chickens. After spending the longest week of my life in bed for non-recreational purposes, I would've been on board with that outlandish plan, but Shiloh doesn't do outlandish.

"I know of one," she said quietly. "The Fat Cat Four Seasons. The service is terrible, but the rates are cheap."

"Great." I leaned, kissing her beautiful mouth. "Let's do it."

***

Making use of the Fat Cat facilities should've been simple. The problem was, the small house was locked up tighter than a drum. Both front windows had security screens and the front door was dead-bolted. If Shiloh was counting on me to get us in, she was sorely out of luck.

"I could kick the door in," I joked, glancing at her, "but someone might notice."

Shiloh stepped up. "I can get us in."

"Do you want to borrow my shoelace again?"

She flashed me a sly smile that probably matched my own. "Not this time," she replied, reaching into her pocket. "We're going to take a more professional approach."

I had no idea what the two small tools in her hand were for, but I didn't have to wait long for an explanation. "They're lock picks." She waved them at me. "Sexy, right?"

I shook my head. "They're not doing it for me so far."

That was a lie. Every now and then, the good girl turned rogue – and it was hotter than hell.

Shiloh took a step closer to me. "This is a tension wrench," she murmured, holding it out to me. "It's used to apply pressure to turn the lock cylinder."

I didn't even look at it. The hard press of her body against mine was all I could focus on, and when she turned to push the wrench into the lock, I moved with her.

"Apply a little bit of torque to the cylinder, and it turns just a little bit," she explained.

My arm closed around her as I undid a few buttons on her shirt and slipped my hand inside. "Then what?" I whispered in her ear.

"Then it stops." Her calm, breathy tone was a crock. I could feel her heart hammering. "You have to feel the firmness of the stop. If you turn it the wrong way, it'll feel firm and stiff. If you turn it the right way, there's a little more give."

With my free hand, I swept her hair off her shoulder. "Stiff and firm," I murmured against her neck. "Got it."

She managed to hold the small wrench in place while she pushed the pick into the lock. Clearly the lesson in breaking and entering was over. The commentary ceased too, and after a few sharp moves with the pick, the door opened.

Shiloh hesitated a fraction too long so I stepped inside, pulling her with me before kicking the door shut with my foot. Impatient to feel her skin on mine, I dragged my T-shirt over my head and threw it on the couch behind her.

And then I slowed my roll, taking a long moment to study her beautiful face.

"What do you see?" The shakiness in her voice led me to think it was a deadly serious question that deserved an honest answer.

"Different things, depending on the day." Her breath quickened at my touch as I combed a wisp of hair from her face. "Sometimes I see vulnerability and little flashes of fear."

I undid the last few buttons of her shirt and pushed it off her shoulders, closing my eyes for a second as my lips brushed across the warm skin of her chest. "And then you do something fearless and show me kick-arse determination and spark," I added. "What do you want me to see?"

I wondered if she knew. Shiloh Jenson was by far the most confusing, mystifying woman I had ever known, and I'd never been more intrigued in all my life.

"I want you to see everything," she softly replied. "Even when I steer you wrong."

I understood her perfectly. We lived in a dog-eat-dog land, and whether we liked it or not, we all put up barriers to survive.

I raked my fingers through her hair, settling my hand on the back of her neck. "Everything in Kaimte is to the extreme," I gently explained. "I can't just pull beers for a living. I have to negotiate with thugs to get the beer – and we both know that doesn't always end well." The corner of my mouth lifted, fighting a smile. "I don't usually have a confrontational bone in my body," I continued. "But I'm who I have to be to get through the day."

Her shoulders slumped. "My job is awful, Mitchell." The words came out in a rush; as if it was a confession she was glad to be rid of. "I don't belong there."

From the minute I met her I'd thought she seemed like an odd fit for Jorge Creek Diamond Company, but I'd never questioned it. Now I felt like an utter jerk for not taking more interest. "Do you want to talk about it?" I dipped my head, chasing her eyes. "You can tell me anything."

"No." She shook her head. "I can't tell you a single thing about my job."

I took no offence. She handled the security of diamonds for a living. It was fair to assume that there were strict policies in place when it came to sharing information with others.

"Just stick it out until your transfer comes through," I urged, leaning to kiss her forehead.

"Then what?" Her voice was tiny. "What will happen with us?"

"We'll go home," I replied matter-of-factly. "And start again in the real world."

It was an idea I'd been toying with all week. Since my run-in with Louis at the port, paradise was well and truly lost, and the only good thing I had left was a plan to jump ship as soon as her job transfer came through.

Shiloh didn't look convinced. "You'd really leave this place?"

"Yes." I focused only on her mouth. "Without you here, I have no reason to stay."

The bruising kiss that followed was spectacular – fierce yet gentle, and just as confusing as the rest of her.

Determined to have every square inch of her body, I gathered her in my arms and pulled her to the floor. As her body melted against mine, she turned her head and whispered, "I love falling in love with you, Mitchell Tate." The words floated from her lips like a sigh, touching on my cheek like a soft kiss.

But falling implied that we'd eventually bottom out, and I was going to do everything I could to stop that from happening.

Chez Fat Cat

SHILOH

As the crooked circles that I moved in began to widen, I started to crave some level of normality. Spending the day at Chez Fat Cat helped immensely.

After a blissful few hours on the living room floor, Mitchell and I moved to higher ground, making the most of the wonderfully deep bathtub. My whole body felt like jelly – boneless and weak, which was the exact opposite of the way Mitchell looked. The pent-up tension was gone, but no part of that man's body could ever have been described as soft.

A few tiny grazes and a slightly swollen nose were the only visual reminders of the horrible state he'd been in a week ago, but I knew he was still sore, and having my legs wedged by his side probably wasn't helping.

"Thirty-three inches," I said randomly.

"Huh?"

"That's my inseam measurement," I replied. "I am quite literally all legs so no bath can hold me."

His dark chuckle echoed around the bathroom. "I think this is the perfect position for you." Starting at my ankle, he slowly trailed a line up my shin. "And your beautiful legs."

I clamped my knees together, trapping his hand. "Tell me something random that I don't know about you."

I didn't think it was a difficult question, but he frowned as if coming up with something took effort. "Well," he began. "I have a twin sister."

"I know that already."

"We're not identical." He grinned at me. "Random enough?"

Releasing my grip on his hand, I settled back into the water. "I'm sure you're much prettier."

He laughed. "Don't tell Jasmine that."

My thoughts drifted to a faraway place, imagining how different his life in Tasmania would be compared to the hard-knock life he'd built in Kaimte. Mitchell always spoke fondly of his sisters, but I got the impression that they weren't particularly close. He once told me that Mimi was a pussycat by comparison, and if that was true he had good reason to keep his distance.

"When you go home, what will you do?" My voice was small, possibly because it was none of my business.

"I'm not sure yet," he replied. "I have a bit of money saved so I'll be okay for a while." His hand wrapped around my foot. "I'm looking forward to reconnecting with my family, but I'm worried that I don't have a place there any more. I might get lost."

"I'm sure that's not true," I said confidently. "You'll be fine."

He smiled, looking more self-assured. "Home is where the heart is, right? And you'll be with me."

I tried picturing myself by his side, but couldn't. Even closing my eyes didn't help. Our happy ending had been ripped to shreds by the very first lie I'd told him. He just didn't realise it yet.

"We have a lot to work out," I mumbled, raising my knees to my chest.

Mitchell hunched forward, showcasing every sculpted muscle on his side. It looked good, but it was a move that hurt. He rested his forehead on my knees and exhaled a long breath before speaking. "I have a confession to make."

That makes two of us, I didn't reply.

"I find myself daydreaming about times we've never had." He lifted his head to look at me. "Proper dates – dinners in fancy restaurants and other grown-up things. I've never done that before."

I put my hands on the side of his face, gently swiping my thumb along the faded bruise under his eye. "I can't believe I found you now – in this place." The frustrated edge to my tone was lost on him.

"I know, right?" He flashed me a killer smile. "Of all the rotten luck."

"I hate this town, Mitchell."

"I know you do," he murmured.

The conversation had taken an unexpectedly serious turn. My eyes welled with tears that just couldn't be blinked away. "I never get any peace here."

The bad guys kept me in a constant state of unease, and the good guys were just as tiring. Living on a knife's edge was taking a severe toll. The pure exhaustion I felt couldn't even be cured by sleep any more.

A strong arm wrapped around me, dripping warm water down my back. "I'll take you somewhere quiet," he offered, breathing the words against my cheek. "Tonight, after the pub closes."

"Away from this place?" I sniffled.

He kissed the top of my head. "Away from the whole world."

Dumb Boy

MITCHELL

Shiloh's mini-meltdown had been on the cards for a while. No matter how boring and monotonous her desert store detective job might've been, a week of working nightshifts had wrecked her. Thankfully she had the next four days off to recover, and I was determined to make it a decent break for her.

With Melito and Vincent whooping it up in Cape Town, life in the cardboard village was bound to be quieter. The only drama I foresaw was Mimi, who was proving even harder to deal now that she'd called off her witch-hunt.

When we arrived at the Crown and Pav that afternoon, she was already hard at work smoking the place out with burning sage.

"At least she's not waving it at me any more," mumbled Shiloh from the corner of her mouth.

Considering she'd been covering my shifts all week, I should've been bowing at Mimi's feet, but as soon as Shiloh wandered out of earshot I pulled her aside and read her the riot act. "No craziness tonight, please."

Mimi shot me a look of pure acid. "My craziness healed your face, dumb boy," she snapped. "I can break it again."

"I know you can," I replied. "Just be nice, okay?"

She answered with a stiff nod and ordered me out of the bar. "Make yourself useful," she demanded. "Set up the umbrellas."

Refusing to let her have the win, I mumbled my way out of the door as if I was pissed. Truthfully, my mood bordered on epic. Nothing was going to bring me down – even the realisation that six of the outdoor umbrellas had been nicked while I was away.

Shiloh looked outraged. "Are you going to report them as stolen?"

My reply got caught in a laugh. "Who to?"

Perhaps remembering where we were, she shook her head. "Never mind."

I looped my arm around her waist. "You're beautiful when you're being righteous and civic-minded."

Finally, she broke a smile. "Suits me, right?"

"Absolutely," I murmured, dipping her backwards. "You should've been a copper."

***

Now that I was back at work, there wasn't any need for Mimi to hang around, but just like the burnt sage smell, I couldn't get rid of her.

"It might get busier," she claimed. "Then you'll need me."

Shiloh pulled up a stool and sat at the end of the bar, which pleased Mimi no end. She leaned across the counter and attempted to whisper to her, which was pointless. The woman couldn't whisper in a silent room. "I have something for you, girl."

Looking far too excited by the prospect, Shiloh straightened up on the stool. "You do?"

"Not here." Mimi glanced at me. "It's secret business."

"Go somewhere else then," I suggested, shooing her away with the cloth in my hand.

For once she didn't argue. The side door slammed and seconds later, Shiloh was being led away by the elbow.

"Bring her back in one piece," I called. "I mean it, Mimi."

Keeping a watchful eye on them as they disappeared on to the dark beach was impossible, but I wasn't overly worried. Mad Mimi had given up trying to exorcise Shiloh, and Shiloh was more than capable of kicking her arse if she tried.

I had no time to worry anyway. Just as Mimi predicted, business did pick up. Being busy reminded me that I actually missed the place, and for a short while everything was golden.

From what I could tell, the usual crew of locals was happy to have me back – especially those who'd thought I was dead.

"You bring us good juju, Mitchell," crowed one bloke.

I handed him a bottle. "No, I bring you beer."

"Same thing," he replied.

I stood watching as he weaved his way through the tables in a bid to reach his mates, and then the bigger picture caught my attention.

My beloved pub on the beach was rocking, and now that I'd made the decision to leave, that realisation was hugely important.

I had no idea what I was going to do with my life when I got home, but suddenly I realised it didn't matter. Seven years ago I took on a floundering, rundown business and turned it around. That meant I could do it again.

Secret Business

SHILOH

There were no shades of grey where Mimi Traore was concerned. If she hated you she wished you were dead, but if she liked you she took you under her wing like a fierce mama hen. For the time being I was on her list of beloved.

As soon as we were clear of the bustle of the pub, she marched me out onto the open beach.

When Mitchell talked about Kaimte being paradise, this was surely what he meant. The bright moon lit the ocean, giving us a perfect view of lazy waves that were barely crawling to shore.

"What a lovely night," I wistfully declared.

Mimi wasn't as entranced. "Hold out your hand," she demanded.

Digging my heels into the cool sand, I did as she asked. Mimi pulled string after string of beads from the front pocket of her dress and dropped them into my palm.

"Bin bin beads?"

A flash of surprise glinted in her eyes. "Who told you?" she barked, snatching them back. "It's secret business."

Unwilling to throw Hiatte to the wolves, I kept my answer vague. "A lady at the pub."

Mimi rattled a fistful of beads at me. "You must never tell."

I threw both hands up. "I won't, I swear."

Seemingly satisfied with the level of terror in my voice, she released me from her iron glare – and then things got weird. "Take off your pants."

"No!"

Despite my loud protest, the crazy woman lurched forward and tugged at my shorts, managing to drag them only as low as my hips. "That will do."

"I'm bloody pleased to hear it," I snapped. "Now what are you doing?"

Showing slightly more consideration for my modesty, she dropped to her knees and draped a string of glass beads around my waist. "These will keep him enchanted," she assured me. "Purple beads combine the energy of red and the stability of blue."

I couldn't see how she fastened it, but within mere seconds she'd moved on to the next string. "White beads for faith and purity."

As she squinted at the pile in her hand looking for her next string of choice, I asked an important question. "How many will I be wearing?"

"That depends." Mimi looked up at me. "How long do you want him to love you?"

The answer effortlessly tumbled from my mouth. "Until he can't."

She deliberated for a short moment before plucking a yellow string from the pile. "Forgiveness," she said, draping it around my middle. "Yellow brings the power of mercy and forgiveness, and I think you need plenty."

On some level, Mimi was on to me, and the next words out of her mouth proved it. "When you love someone you protect them from pain," she said, rising to her feet. "You don't become the cause of it."

"I know that."

With a stilted nod, she motioned behind me. "Then stop bringing the devil to his doorstep."

I slowly turned, squinting through the darkness at the lone figure wandering toward us. I knew who it was even before I could see his face. The devil has a very distinctive swagger.

I spun back to Mimi. "This was all a ruse to get me down here?" I asked incredulously. "You set me up?"

"I had no choice."

"He's the man who hurt Mitchell," I bitterly reminded her. "And you brought him here?"

"I had no choice," she repeated.

There wasn't time to speak again. When I turned back, Iron Mike was standing there, audaciously greeting me with a smile. He wasn't as sociable when it came to the traitor beside me. All Mimi got was a rude dismissal. "Go," he snapped.

I could hear her remaining stash of beads rattling in her pocket as she scurried away. I couldn't blame her for the cowardly escape, but running wasn't an option for me. I had no choice but to stay put and make it look like I had the confidence to be there.

"How did you get her to set this up?" I asked sourly. "Threats or bribes?"

"I threatened to burn her house down."

"You are the most despicable person I've ever met." The words raged out of me. "And you need to stay the hell away from me."

"That's not going to happen, Shiloh." His voice was as dark as his heart. "I want information."

"I'm giving you nothing."

Mike cocked his head to the side. "That wouldn't be the wisest decision."

"What are you going to do?" I scoffed. "Burn my house down too?"

Giving him cheek wasn't smart. If anything, it was probably a prelude to a smack in the mouth, but I stood firm. "I did everything you asked of me," I said pointedly. "And while I was installing your GPS into Louis' car, you were beating Mitchell half to death."

"Stupid girl," he muttered. "What do you want? An apology?"

"I want you to leave me alone," I replied through gritted teeth.

"Perhaps you've forgotten the objective."

"How can I?" I was reminded of it every waking minute and was sure I was slowly dying because of it. "I am completely on task."

"If that were true, you'd realise you're sleeping with the wrong man," he replied. "You should be focusing on Louis. The bartender is nothing more than a hindrance."

There was nothing I could say to adequately defend Mitchell. The man was my gravity. When the lies I had to tell were pulling me out of reality, he kept my feet touching the ground.

"Mitchell has nothing to do with any of this," I snapped. "He didn't deserve the hiding you dished out."

Iron Mike dropped his head, chuckling down at the sand. "I was following orders," he said. "I also followed the order to spare him. If I'd had my way, I would've finished the job properly."

A strange strangled growl tumbled from my mouth. "You have no soul."

"You can question my morality later," he shrugged. "But for now, there's work to be done."

"I'm not doing a thing for you."

As far as luck went, I'd pushed mine to the limit. Mike lurched forward and grabbed my arm. "When people are no longer useful, they become expendable." His grip tightened, painfully biting into my flesh. "Much like your boyfriend."

No amount of acting was going to convey indifference. I was so scared I could feel my heart thrashing against my ribcage. "What do you want from me?"

Mike loosened his grip but didn't let go. "Some tools and heavy machinery were removed from the mine last week."

"I know, I was there," I replied. "It was all returned two nights ago."

As it turns out, Louis' crew were as deft at returning goods as they were at stealing them. Just like the initial theft, the dead-of-night operation had gone off quickly, quietly and without a hitch.

"Louis secured the contract for a construction project," he explained, still gripping my arm. "His men spent four nights building a road."

I shrugged, managing to free myself in the process. "Nothing of interest to me, then."

"It's not just a road, Shiloh," he replied ominously. "It's an airstrip."

Now I was interested. "You think he's going to use it to transport the diamonds out?"

"It's possible," he replied. "But there's still nothing linking him to any diamonds."

I abhorred him, but I couldn't deny that Mike was a strong source of information. As much as it pained me I had no choice but to ride his coattails to stay in the game.

"He has to be involved," I insisted, taking a much-needed step back. "He's in it up to his neck."

"Prove it."

"What do you want me to do?"

"Make yourself available," he told me. "Let it be known that you want in on the deal."

I nodded. "I'll try."

"Trying isn't good enough any more." As if a switch had been flicked, his vile, menacing tone was back. "You need tangible results. Don't allow yourself to become expendable."

Spending another minute in Iron Mike's company would've been an exercise in futility. All information had been exchanged, which meant all I was going to get from here on in was more threats and nastiness. I began walking away.

"One more thing," he said, calling me back. "I have a message from your aunt."

I turned. "Excuse me?"

Mike took a few slow steps toward me. "A message from your aunt Grace."

Speaking in riddles was both annoying and redundant. The conversation had been quite candid until that point, and I had no desire to protect Agent Grace's position when he wasn't doing a thing to protect mine.

"What is it?"

His smug smile was borderline cruel, and I knew something terrible was on the way. "She said to make sure that you're in bed with the right people," he recited. "And if you're not, change beds."

I refused to give credence to his words. I didn't trust Mike as far as I could throw him. To think that the AFP had any measure of faith in the man was unfathomable.

"Thanks all the same, but you can let my aunt know that I'm quite happy with the current sleeping arrangements," I replied.

"Your government trusts me," he reminded me. "Perhaps you should too." He leaned closer, lowering his tone. "Of course, if you manage to come across intelligence that you deem more reliable than mine, feel free to act on it."

He'd done nothing to allay my fears, and the fifty new seeds of suspicion he'd just planted in my head seemed mighty intentional.

"You're just one big mind wrench, aren't you?"

"It's a delicate game, Shiloh," he replied. "I hope you live through it."

Killer Bees

MITCHELL

Shiloh returned from the beach looking a little worse for wear. Mimi didn't return at all, and for a short moment I wondered if Shiloh had done away with her. "Where's Mimi?"

She shrugged, and that was close as she came to replying. She pulled up a stool and sat at the end of the bar, a slight frown etched on her face.

"Is everything okay?"

"Perfect." Her small smile was only half believable. "Can we get out of here soon?"

"Had enough excitement for one night, huh?"

Again she didn't reply, and I decided not to press the issue. Chances were, Mimi had said something to upset her, and I valued my life too much to get involved. "Another hour and we're out of here, okay?"

Shiloh leaned across the bar. "Are you going to take me away from this place, Mitchell?" Her voice was pure silk. "That was the deal if I remember correctly."

I flipped the lid off a bottle and slid it toward her. "I'm going to take you away from the whole world, baby."

***

When you're cursed with the mischievous streak of a twelve-year-old boy, a country with little to no rules is a good place to be. Showing Shiloh absolute peace and quiet was only half my plan. The other half involved blowing it to smithereens, and to do that I needed the help of someone shadier than me.

Kenny Traore fitted the bill. The miniature entrepreneur would do almost anything for a buck, which was worrying for his mother but handy for me. It only took a few phone calls to organise the late night entertainment I wanted, and when the pub closed at midnight, we drove out to Mimi's house to collect it.

Kenny didn't even try hiding it from his mother. As soon as I stepped onto the rickety porch he handed me a large box. Mimi stood behind him, looking unconcerned by the exchange. Her focus was on Shiloh, who'd elected to wait in the car.

"Is the girl alright?"

"She's fine." I glanced back at the Jeep. "Why? Did you say something to upset her?"

Mimi stiffly shook her head. "No."

Questioning her would be a waste of time, so I turned my attention back to Kenny. "Is everything in here?"

"Yes. Even the killer bees." His grin was huge. "Your girl will be impressed."

I gave the box a shake. "You're a champion, Kenny."

"But I don't come cheap," he replied, holding out his hand.

The boy had more brass than most men, but I could help being impressed by his tenacity. I slapped a wad of small bills into his palm. "You're going to go far, kid."

With a blinding smile, he motioned to the box. "So are those killer bees."

***

It was the perfect night for a little orchestrated magic. Not even the choking exhaust fumes that wafted into the Jeep could put a dampener on things. We drove for miles. Every passing minute took us further away from town and closer to nowhere. When the last of the lights disappeared in the rear vision mirror, life off the grid took on new meaning. We were now invisible.

Shiloh had already checked out. She hadn't said a word since we left Mimi's place, so I felt compelled to ask if she was still conscious.

"Of course." She softly laughed. "I think I'm immune to the fumes now."

"You haven't asked where we're going." I reached for her hand and brought it to my lap. "Aren't you curious?"

"I trust you," she replied, turning her attention back to the window. "As long as you know where we're going, we're good."

"Any guesses?"

"The desert?"

Considering we were surrounded by endless sand, it wasn't a very imaginative guess. "Let's hope I don't get us lost," I teased. "I'd hate to have to rely on you to get us home."

"I could do it," she blithely replied. "I'm an excellent navigator."

I looked at the star-shot sky through the windscreen. "Guided by the light of the moon or the stars?"

A smartarse question usually calls for a smartarse answer, but in true Shiloh style, she schooled me instead. "If the situation were life or death, I'd probably look to the stars," she began. "But sand can be just as telling."

I slowed the car, giving her my full attention.

"Sand dunes form at ninety degrees to the prevailing wind," she explained. "So if the winds prevail from the east, the dunes will run north to south. It's a simple way of getting your bearings."

I didn't find it simple. It sounded like a theory straight out of the MacGyver handbook – and it wasn't the first time she'd dazzled me with her knowledge of random lifehacks.

"I'm beginning to think you're some kind of rebel survivalist or something."

"No, I just paid attention in school."

"Well, I turned up to school every single day, and not once did someone teach me how to pick a lock or decipher sand patterns."

After a long silence, she volunteered a different answer. "My dad's a locksmith."

I talked about my sisters all the time – mainly because it's hard to keep quiet about a pair of divas who eat glitter for breakfast. Shiloh wasn't as forthcoming. Until then she'd never mentioned her family.

I winked at her. "Well, I guess picking locks trumps growing grapes."

It should've been a light topic of conversation but judging by her tight expression, it was causing her some measure of grief.

We hadn't driven as far as I would've liked, but a diversion was in order. I pulled the car to a stop, steering clear of the loose sandy edge.

Shiloh straightened up, taking a long look in all directions. "This is it?" she asked. "We're here?"

I opened the car door. "If I drive any further we'll end up in Portugal."

"Not likely," she replied, grinning. "You drove east."

I leaned across and undid her seatbelt. "Get out of the car, MacGyver."

***

I couldn't have set a better scene if I'd called the heavens and tailored my order. There wasn't a wisp of wind, which meant the sands were completely still, and a full moon made the night exceptionally bright.

Leaving our shoes at the roadside, we trudged through the dunes until the car was just out of sight.

"Here will do," I said, lowering my box of Kenny contraband to the ground. I grabbed the blanket off the top, fanned it out over the sand and ordered Shiloh to sit.

"What's in the box?" she asked, peering across. It was the first spark of curiosity she'd shown since we left Mimi's. Mercifully, whatever had been troubling her had been left in the car.

I sat beside her, gently pushing her on to her back by covering her body with mine. "Killer bees," I murmured against her mouth. "But they're the grand finale, not the main event."

Her long leg wrapped around my waist, pulling me in impossibly closer. "Is this the main event?"

Resolve was crumbling, but I somehow managed to untangle myself and roll onto my back. "Close your eyes," I instructed, reaching for her hand.

Letting out a long sigh, Shiloh shuffled closer until her shoulder pressed against mine.

"What do you hear?" I whispered.

After a long moment of deliberation, she gave my hand a gentle squeeze. "Nothing," she whispered back.

Absolute silence is something that most people never get to experience. With no breaking waves, no traffic and no people, all that's left is peace. And no one needed it more than Shiloh.

I raised her hand to my mouth and kissed her fingers. "Total peace and quiet," I murmured. "That's the main event."

Last Defence

SHILOH

Life in Kaimte was constantly set on fast forward. Everything was ramped-up and amplified, tonight more than ever.

Hanging out in the desert at two in the morning brought a solace that I'd never felt before. Just as Mitchell had promised, the whole world was gone.

We lay side by side on the blanket for hours, speaking only when something important needed to be said.

"I love it out here," I whispered.

"You can be anyone you want to in the desert." He kissed my cheek. "Even yourself."

I allowed the tiniest hint of panic to trickle through my mind before abruptly putting a stop to it. It wasn't a veiled dig at me. It was innocent words from a man who recognised that I needed a break from myself.

"I couldn't live here without you," I told him.

"Well, that's a coincidence." I could hear the smile in his voice. "Because I don't think I could live at home without you."

If not for me, moving back to Australia would never have even crossed Mitchell's mind. Just thinking about it made me feel wretched. No matter which direction the story went, I already knew the ending.

"We have so much to work out, Mitchell." Namely, how I was going to avoid smashing him to pieces when I disappeared from his life without warning. "It's all so complicated."

"No it's not," he replied. "You go home and sort out whatever you need to, and then come and live with me on the beach."

My body shook with silent chuckles. "You think it's that simple?"

"It has to play out that way," he explained. "How else are we supposed to fall madly in love?"

But we were already half way there. Historically, strong love isn't built on the foundations of a six-week long relationship. In the real world we would've both been baulking, but we were on fast forward mode in the desert – in a place where love was our last defence.

"You might feel different once you get home," I hinted.

"About you?" He traced a finger down my cheek. "I doubt it."

A kinder woman would've been working toward letting him go, but I was too selfish to even try.

"Whatever happens, I just want you to be happy," I whispered. "Whether I fit into your world or not."

He laughed hard, once. "No one fits into small town life in Tasmania. That's why we all spend our childhoods plotting to escape. We don't have to stay there. We can go anywhere you want."

I propped myself up on my elbow. "I want you to promise that you'll stay for a while. Spend some time with your family."

It wasn't my place to demand anything of him, but I knew the disconnection he felt had been troubling him for a long time. He wanted to be closer to them and had told me so a hundred times. I also had the foresight to see that his family were probably going to be the ones picking up the pieces after I was through smashing him up.

His eyes shone in the night. "Do you like kids?" he asked randomly.

"Why?" I asked. "Are you offering to give me a few?"

"No." He laughed. "It's just that my sister has a whole bunch of them, and I suspect that they're terrors. I'm not sure how I'll handle them."

"And you thought I'd have a few ideas?"

He reached, tucking my hair behind my ear. "Maybe."

"I don't know anything about kids," I replied. "But I'm going to get a dog one day."

"You've never had a dog?"

"Never. I promised myself I'd get one when I was grown up and responsible. I reckon I'm almost there."

Mitchell put his hand on his chest, probably protecting his injured ribs as he laughed. "I can picture you with a big slobbering Saint Bernard."

"You picture wrong then, Adonis." I lay back down, looking at the star-filled sky. "I want a French bulldog," I announced. "And I'm going to give her a fancy regal name to match the glittery pink collar she'll wear."

His laugh got louder and seemingly more painful, as he clutched his middle. "Obviously you've put some thought into this."

"I have. I've narrowed it down to two names." The poncy accent I adopted came out of nowhere. "She'll either be called Katherine or Peppermint."

I turned my head to look at him and was met by a blinding grin. "You're going to get on famously with my sisters. They'll see your Peppermint and raise you a Nancy."

"What's a Nancy?"

"A bald Pomeranian," he replied making me laugh. "We're all class in Tassie."

***

Streaks of daylight began creeping across the horizon, which meant it was time for the grand finale.

"Don't move," instructed Mitchell, pointing at me as he backed away. "And no peeking."

I promised I wouldn't, but couldn't help stealing a look as he scurried around in the distance, placing items from the box in the sand.

After a long few minutes, he called out. "Remember how I told you that there weren't any rules here?"

"Yeah." How could I forget? That's what made the place so damned dangerous.

"Well, it's not always a bad thing," he replied. "It means we get to do things here that would never fly at home."

With that, he lit a series of fuses and sprinted back to me. Before I was really sure what was happening, the sky exploded in wild streaks of gold and red.

"Fireworks?" I asked incredulously. "You got us fireworks?"

"Yep," he triumphantly replied. "Like a boss."

"You're bad arse, Mitchell Tate."

"Not as bad as Kenny Traore," he replied. "God only knows who he rolled to get hold of these bad boys."

I hooked my arm through his and shuffled closer, resting my head on his shoulder. "They're buzzing," I noted, listening to the rogue sparks that shot away and exploded in all directions.

"Well, of course they are, darling," he drawled. "That's why they're called killer bees."

Complex Attraction

MITCHELL

After a few weeks of serving up useless chop, Mother Nature finally got her act together. The waves were magnificent that morning – slow rolling and perfectly formed – much like my roommate.

Shiloh appeared a little after nine, wearing nothing but one of my T-shirts and a lazy smile.

"How did you sleep?" I already knew the answer. She looked more relaxed than I'd seen her in weeks.

"Great," she replied, wandering toward me. "A little bit of alone time in the desert works wonders."

I reached for her hand and pulled her onto my lap. "We're alone here too." I chased her lips. "No commentary from the sleek Greeks this morning."

I couldn't admit that I missed them, even though I did, but the absence of the stench of coconut oil was a welcome treat.

"Think of all the trouble we could get up to on this deck in two weeks with no adult supervision," she whispered in my ear.

My hand slipped under her shirt, settling on the thin strings of beads at her hips. I dropped my head to her shoulder, breathing her in. "I don't think we should put too much thought into it at all," I suggested. "We should just go with the flow."

There was no denying it. Our flow was spectacular. I'd never connected with anyone like I had with Shiloh. If I'd had the skill to put it into words, I would've told her so. Instead, I kissed her – hard, because I meant it.

"You're beautiful," I said, finally breaking free.

Her wide grin was as lovely as the rest of her. "It's the beads, isn't it?" she asked. "You only love me for my bin bins."

My fingers tangled around the beads in question. "Among other things," I teased. "It's a complex attraction."

Her smile slipped, and I wasn't sure why. "It won't always be," she said quietly. "Eventually, you'll have me all worked out."

"You're not that much of a mystery, Shiloh." I rested my forehead on hers. "I like what I know and I know what I like."

"Do you think you'll be different when you get home?"

"Do you want me to be?"

"No." She laughed quietly. "I'm just curious."

"I'm a creature of habit," I told her. "I sleep, eat and surf no matter what part of the world I'm in. The only difference will be my employment status."

She linked her arms around my neck. "Have you put any thought into what you might do?"

"Not really." I said it mildly as if I didn't care either way, but it wasn't true. Returning home as an unemployed beach bum is fine when you're twenty, but at twenty-seven it's pathetic.

"Something will come up," she encouraged.

"Of course it will," I agreed. "And if it doesn't, I'll join the family business and squash grapes into bottles for a living."

***

After being out of action for a week, the only plan I had for the day involved taking advantage of the perfect surf conditions. But as Shiloh reminded me, it was market day and our cupboards were bare.

I looked out to sea, groaning as if I was on the verge of giving up a kidney. "But I don't want to go shopping," I whined.

"You're in luck then, you big baby," she replied, swatting my upper arm. "I want to go shopping."

The offer she laid out was a good one. She'd head to the markets to stock up on dirty potatoes and I'd play in the clean surf.

"Are you sure you'll be okay by yourself?" I asked.

She nodded, looking nowhere near as apprehensive as I thought she should. The markets weren't a dangerous place, but every man and his dog converged there, which made them crowded and tricky to negotiate.

"Stick to the main stalls," I instructed. "And don't let anyone rip you off."

"Got it." She leaned forward and chastely kissed me. "No one will get the better of me today."

Catwoman

SHILOH

Kaimte's midweek markets made the main street of Lawler seem like Rodeo Drive. It was crowded, stiflingly hot and the air smelled like dirt.

Sourcing food for the week wasn't my only objective that day. I had business to attend to. In a strange reversal of roles, I was headed to Louis' pawnshop to collect money – namely my payoff for the small part I played in the bulldozer heist.

A lone white girl wandering around a market might as well be wearing a neon sign. Although I felt completely out of my comfort zone, I tried to walk with the poise of someone who belonged. The crowd eventually began to thin as the temporary stalls gave way to a row of rundown permanent shopfronts, but I couldn't shake the feeling of being watched.

A big woman wearing a flowy red mulafa and a gold headwrap called out as I passed her shop. "Come inside, lovely girl," she coaxed. "I have fabric for you." I wasn't interested in her wares, but I did need a minute to gather my thoughts and calm myself. With the brightest smile I could muster, I stepped through the curtain shielding the door and wandered to the back of the store. As expected, she followed me. "Batik, silk, satin or hemp," she crowed. "Whatever the lady likes."

I'd never seen so many bolts of fabric in all my life, and strongly suspected that they were the only things stopping the walls from collapsing. "What do you recommend?"

The woman threw her head back and let out a laugh. I was clueless, and she knew it.

"The girl doesn't want fabric," came a voice from somewhere near the door.

It was no surprise to see Mimi appear when the front curtain swung open. I would've recognised that caustic tone anywhere.

"You've been following me, Mimi Traore." My angry tone was a crock. I was actually relieved to see her. "Why?"

She pointed a finger at me. "Because you're doing bad things," she hissed. "Heks girl."

The mere mention of witches was enough to make any local recoil in fear, and the shopkeeper was no exception. She threw open the front curtain and pointed to the bright light of the outside street. "Go now!" she demanded. "There's nothing for you in here."

Embarrassed and pissed off, I did as I was told – and like a dog with a bone, Mimi followed. "What are you doing down here?" she asked, almost running to keep up with my fast strides. "This is no place for you."

I could feel the weight of a hundred eyes on me as curious onlookers took in the show. I stopped walking and spun back to face her. "You're making a scene," I growled.

Her hands moved to her hips. "You don't like that, do you, heks girl?"

It was foolish to think the witch nonsense was behind us. As long as I was committing shady acts, Mimi was always going to be suspicious of me.

"You listen to me," I ordered exasperatedly. "I *am* a witch."

She stumbled back; clutching her chest as if I'd just punched her. "I knew it," she hissed.

"But I am a *good* witch, Mimi," I claimed. "I am trying to do good work."

Expecting it to be fast and painful, I braced for her reaction, but Mimi surprised me by taking a gentle approach. "You are watching over the diamonds," she said knowingly.

The proverbial rock and a hard place had never been harder. I couldn't give her an honest answer even if I wanted to, which I didn't.

"You need to stop interfering, Mimi." She probably missed the force in my tone, but there would've been no escaping my pissed-off expression. "This is none of your business."

As soon as I began walking away, she called me back – using my actual name. For that reason alone, I turned around.

"I can help you," she offered.

"No, you can't." I shook my head. "Nobody can."

***

Mimi Traore has a knack for getting her own way. In a move I didn't see coming, she coaxed me into a café over the road from the fabric shop. The building was in a terrible state of repair, but apart from a group of old men arguing over a card game in the corner, the vibe was good.

A boy approached and set a pot of tea on the table. When he returned a minute later with a plate of scones we hadn't ordered, I knew that I was in for a long morning.

Mimi swung her head in every direction, making no secret of the fact that she was checking the place out. I was busy marvelling at the tablecloth. The table underneath was probably as grimy as the plastic chairs, but the white cloth covering it was pristine.

"Her name is Verda," said Mimi, motioning to a woman behind her. "She killed her husband with the poison of three vipers."

I glanced over at the murderess. Verda stood at the counter, filling a jar with scoops of sugar from a large hessian sack. The kindly looking woman in her mid-fifties didn't look like a killer – and considering that her shaky hands were dumping more sugar on the counter than in the jar, she didn't strike me as someone who'd be overly skilled at handling snakes either.

I turned back to Mimi, narrowing my eyes with suspicion. "Where did you hear that?"

"Everybody knows it's true," she muttered with a mouthful of scone.

"So why isn't she in jail?"

Her shoulders lifted. "She apologised to the snakes, and nobody liked her husband anyway."

Her serious expression lasted mere seconds. Perhaps amused by my horror-struck stare, she burst into a fit of raucous laughter.

"You're lying, Mimi Traore." I held up a serviette to stem the flow of scone crumbs that flew at me as she laughed. "That was a wicked thing to say."

Finally composing herself, she dropped her scone and dusted off her hands. "This place is not all that it seems," she replied. "You think it's bad because you only deal with bad people."

"I deal with you," I reminded her.

Mimi picked up the teapot and filled the two small shot glasses. "I am one of the good," she told me.

I wasn't convinced, but couldn't be bothered arguing. "Can we just hurry this along, please?" I glanced at my watch. "I have somewhere to be."

"Who are you meeting?" she asked.

I didn't reply, leaving Mimi to jump to her own conclusion, which she did at warp speed.

"That man on the beach last night – he works for Louis Osei." Her grim expression probably matched my own. "Louis Osei is a very bad man, but not interested in diamonds. You're wasting your time with him."

I hadn't given Mimi a skerrick of information, which meant she was far better at putting two and two together than I'd given her credit for.

"Someone is stealing diamonds from the mine, Mimi." My words were barely clearer than a mumble, probably because I knew that confiding in her was a monumental mistake.

"Not Louis," she insisted, looking me dead in the eye.

I leaned close. "How can you be so sure?"

"Juju," she replied.

Belief in juju was the be-all and end-all. If Louis was a believer, there was no way he'd ever run the devil's errand of stealing diamonds – but that was the only line he wouldn't cross.

"He's done some terrible things, Mimi," I reminded her. "Including robbing people."

She emphatically shook her head. "But not diamonds," she replied. "He'd never steal diamonds."

I pushed my glass to the centre of the table and tried to make a desperate question sound casual. "Do you have any idea who would?"

"No," she replied. "But I can help you find out."

I was shaking my head before she even finished, which only made her more determined to sell her absurd plan.

"People talk to me," she said, drumming her finger on the table. "And I have a cousin who works at the mine."

I groaned. Half the town worked at the mine, and the half who didn't had relatives who did. "I won't involve you, Mimi."

I made it sound like I was concerned for her welfare, but in truth I was protecting my own skin. Mimi Traore was the most inquisitive and demanding woman I'd ever met – and not once had she asked what my agenda was. That troubled me.

"I can help you," she said for the umpteenth time.

"How do you know you can trust me?" I asked.

She shrugged. "The dumb boy trusts you – even after all that's happened."

I hated the fact that Mitchell had rated a mention. It was nothing more than an unwanted reminder of the constant drama I'd brought to his life, and my inability to keep him out of harm's way. Mimi, on the other hand, had always protected him. And that might've been reason enough to trust her.

"My work here is dangerous," I told her, "and I don't know how bad things are going to get."

It was a depressing statement that should've sent her running for the hills, but Mimi wasn't fazed. She took a sip of tea and set the glass down. "What's going to happen to the bad men?"

"Well, hopefully they'll be punished."

She nodded thoughtfully. "And what's going to happen to the good men?"

I could only think of one, and there was only one possible outcome I could live with. "He's going to go home and reconnect with his family," I said resolutely. "Agreed?"

"Yes," she replied. "But I will miss him."

***

The desire to ditch Mimi waned by the third cup of tea. By that stage I was so late for my meeting with Louis that when she insisted on tagging along, I didn't argue.

"Do you know where the pawnshop is?" I asked.

Mimi pointed directly across the street. "Right there."

I couldn't believe I'd missed it, but in fairness the only hint that the dilapidated tin shed was a pawnshop was a crappy hand-painted dollar sign above the door.

As we crossed the dirt road, I rattled off my short but precise list of instructions. "Don't ask questions," I demanded. "And don't give him any lip." Mimi's lack of response was not reassuring, but it was too late to send her away. Before heading inside I muttered one final warning. "Behave, Mimi."

She beamed at me. "My boy, Francis, likes Batman comics," she said randomly. "I've read a few."

"Wonderful. Let's go."

Grabbing me by the elbow, she held me back. "Catwoman helps Batman sometimes," she explained. "Today I am your Catwoman."

She followed up with a few animated kung fu chops that did little more than stir up the hot air between us.

"You think I'm Batman?" I asked, stifling a laugh.

"Yes," she confirmed, grinning. "You are Good Witch Batman."

***

Louis' pawnshop was a dark, dingy hovel. Like the fabric shop next door, it was packed to the rafters with all manner of junk, and the most pleasant thing in it was him.

He stepped from behind the counter, arms wide. "My beautiful friend," he beamed with his usual insincerity. "You're late." He turned to Mimi. "What are you doing here, Mrs Traore?"

She motioned to me with a stiff nod. "Keeping the dumb girl out of trouble."

Louis guffawed. "She will find no trouble here, woman."

"I will decide that," she snapped.

My hopes for a smooth meeting were dwindling fast. We'd been there less than a minute and Catwoman was already getting mouthy. Doing my best to scold her with a harsh frown, I turned to Louis. "Where's my money?"

He reached into his back pocket and pulled out an envelope. "You did good work, Shiloh," he praised. "It impressed me."

I hadn't done anything other than deliver money to Glen and keep my mouth shut. Perhaps crime really did pay. When I made a grab for the envelope, he pulled it away. "I might have more work for you soon."

"I'm only interested in diamonds from now on," I said, snatching the envelope from his grasp. "I've heard that's where the big money is."

I couldn't work out if the look on Louis' face was one of horror or revulsion. Maybe it was both. "I do not deal in diamonds." He turned to Mimi and barked a few sharp words in Afrikaans.

"I told her you would never cross the devil." She threw both hands up. "The dumb girl wouldn't listen."

Louis' angry expression slipped as his focus returned to me. "Shiloh, diamonds are bad juju," he warned. "Terrible trouble for a nice girl like you."

The hypocrisy was dizzying, but I forged ahead. I waved the envelope at him. "This is not enough," I said strongly. "I came to Kaimte for the diamonds."

Louis returned to the business side of the counter, and I was hot on his heels. "You can help me," I insisted. "I just need to know who's dealing."

"A very bad man steals the diamonds for the devil," he replied, pointing a finger at me. "I want no part of that white man juju." There was a hint of fear in his voice that I'd never heard before. "Talk to your boss at the mine. He will entertain your foolishness."

"He's dirty?" I asked.

The look in Louis' eyes was one of absolute contempt. "As the devil himself."

I could've jumped up and punched the air – I was that elated. Louis' word was worth nothing, but there was no arguing with the law of juju.

Keen to get out of there, I thanked Louis for the lead. "I won't mention your name," I promised him.

He jumped on the defence as if there was hidden meaning to my words. "Are you threatening me?" His raised voice alerted his goons, and three men came rushing in from the back room.

I ignored them as best I could. "I would never threaten you, Louis." My sultry tone was shameful but instantly got him back on side. "I know how powerful you are."

His chest seemed to puff at the compliment, but the result was fleeting. He quickly changed the subject. "The car part you ordered has arrived," he said. "You can collect it from my warehouse at the port tomorrow."

"Thank you, but I don't want it any more."

Mitchell would sooner die of carbon monoxide poisoning than repair his jeep with a part supplied by Louis, and the only way to get him to revisit the warehouse again would be at gunpoint. Still, Louis seemed surprised that I'd cancelled the order. "Why not?" he asked, eyebrows raised.

"Mitchell would never allow it."

His lips formed a thin line. "I trust that he's recovered from his injuries?"

I forced a polite reply. "He's doing well."

"The boy is as strong as an ox," declared Mimi. "You can beat him down, but he will get straight back up."

I winced at the sound of her voice. She'd been good until that point.

Louis grinned at her, which was too much smugness for Mimi to bear. Goons or no goons, all hell was about to break loose. When she took a step toward the counter, I grabbed her and pulled her back.

"Take Mrs Traore home, Shiloh," Louis instructed. "And perhaps teach her some manners before someone else does."

Without uttering a word I bustled Mimi out the door, and that's when her rambling apology began. "I couldn't help myself," she told me. "He is a nasty man."

I hooked my arm through hers as we wandered down the street. "You did perfectly, Mimi," I assured her. "I got the information I wanted." Pulling her to a stop, I handed her the envelope of cash. "Buy your boys something nice," I said.

Her eyes were the size of saucers as she flicked through the cash. "There are hundreds in here," she said gleefully.

At that moment I felt more like Robin Hood than Batman. It was probably more money that she'd ever been in possession of before, and it felt wonderful to give it to her.

"I'm a good witch, Mimi," I reminded her. "Don't ever forget that."

***

I wanted to strike while the iron was hot. After quickly buying enough food to get us through the week, I headed home – but not before making one last stop at the Fat Cat camp to stir some trouble with Glen.

Not surprisingly, he wasn't pleased to see me.

"What do you want?" He snapped as soon as the door swung open. "Go home."

I wedged my shoulder against the door to stop him pushing it shut. "Are you drunk?" I could smell the booze wafting off him. "It's barely midday."

"That's why days off are called R and R," he muttered. "Rest and rum." He held up a half-empty bottle. "Go home."

"Wait," I pleaded, bumping the door again. "I want to talk to you."

After a few choice words he motioned me in with a wave of the bottle. "You have five minutes."

Considering the state he was in I was pretty sure I could take him out if necessary, but there was no way I was going to set foot in his house. I pointed to the small table and chairs on the veranda. "We can talk out here," I suggested. "It's cooler."

Glen grabbed the essential supplies –cigarettes and rum – and followed me. "What's this all about?" he grumbled.

"I went to see Louis Osei today," I began. "He paid me for the job we did last week."

Glen shrugged. "I don't know what you're talking about."

"That's how you're going to play this?" The rise of incredulity in my voice was intentional. "Pretend that you don't know anything?"

He picked up the cigarette packet and tapped a smoke straight into his mouth. If it wasn't such a filthy habit, I would've been impressed by the trick.

"What do you want, Shiloh?" he asked wearily.

I leaned across the small glass table that separated us. "I didn't come to Kaimte to faff around with petty equipment heists," I said. "I want to earn some serious money."

He lit his cigarette. "How?" Glen's decision to feign obliviousness was frustrating but not unexpected. He had every right to be wary of me. All I could do was hope that he was dumb enough to be swayed otherwise.

"I want in on the diamond job."

He puffed a foul plume of smoke in my direction. "You have a diamond job."

As far as defining moments went, this was the most pivotal one I'd faced since the operation began. "Look, I know you're lifting gems."

The accusation sobered him in an instant. His dopey look gave way to pure thunder. "Now, why would you say something like that?" Even his voice was mean. "Spreading rumours like that could get a girl in serious trouble."

Everything hinged on the next words out of my mouth, and one way or the other I needed to make them sound spectacularly convincing. "I asked Louis if there were any big jobs going," I explained. "He told me to come and see you." I had no misgivings whatsoever when it came to throwing Tweedledum under the bus, even after assuring him I wouldn't. "He's very impressed by the scale of your operation," I continued. "It's a pity he hasn't got the balls to get on board."

"He was never invited." The words seemed to tumble out of his mouth unintentionally – probably a side effect of too much R and R.

"I could be a huge asset to you, Glen," I insisted. "You could double the number of stones that leave the mine – and all it would cost you is twenty percent of the takings."

What started as a deep chuckle morphed into a hacking pack-a-day cough. Finally, he recovered. "Twenty percent is ambitious," he said, taking another drag of his smoke. "You'd be looking at closer to five."

I stared out to sea, pretending to think things through. In reality I was trying to calm myself down. The end was so damned close I could feel it. "I'd do it for five," I conceded. "It means I'll have to get more rocks out the door."

Glen opened the bottle of rum and slid it toward me. "You've got some balls, Shiloh."

I would rather have taken a hundred swigs of Mimi's witches brew than touch his rum. I declined with a wave of my hand. "Do we have a deal?"

He picked up the bottle and chugged at least a quarter of it. The look on his face when he turned back to me was straight out of a horror movie. "Do you know how easily people can disappear around here?" His voice was low and menacing. "The desert is a big place – get lost out there and no one would ever find you."

I swallowed hard – a nervous move I hope he didn't notice. "I hate this godforsaken place," I replied, looking straight into his soulless eyes. "All I'm trying to do is make a bit of money to ease the pain of being here." I pushed back my chair and stood up. "If you can't help me do that, I'll start my own venture. That way, my profit margin will be a hundred percent."

Fearlessness in the face of adversity is the most appealing trait a crook can possess. Despite the fact that it was artificial, at some point in the last five minutes Glen Harris had seen that in me.

"I'll let you know in a few days," he muttered. "In the meantime, keep your mouth shut."

"You only have a few days," I replied, already walking away. "And then I'm going it alone."

Home

MITCHELL

Shiloh was already home when I arrived back from the beach, standing at the kitchen table sorting vegetables. Sidling behind her, I kissed her neck.

"Those are the bad ones," she said, pointing to the pile on the left. "And those are worse."

Resting my chin on her shoulder, I looked at the table. "Excellent. We live to eat for another week."

She twisted in my arms. "How was the water?"

I grimaced. "Above anything I'm capable of at the moment."

Two minutes after paddling out I knew I was punching above my weight. I wasn't anywhere near healed enough to be out there.

"Did you hurt yourself?"

"I came to my senses before it got that far." I tightened my hold on her. "I lay on my board like a girl while the best waves I've seen in weeks rolled underneath me."

"That was very mature of you," she teased, patting my chest.

"I'm all about maturity lately," I replied. "While I floated around like a cork, I put a bit of thought into our plans of leaving town."

"Really?" Her eyebrows lifted.

When I suggested that we sit and talk, Shiloh jumped to the conclusion that something bad was on its way. "Don't back out on me now, Mitchell," she muttered, flopping on a beanbag. "Nothing good can come from staying here."

"I'm not backing out of anything," I assured her. "But leaving isn't going to be as easy as I thought."

A lifetime of procrastinating is a hard habit to break, but there were decisions to be made – and none of them seemed particularly simple. The fate of the Crown and Pav was foremost in my thoughts. As run-down and two-bit as the place was, it was a legitimate business that had worth. The problem was the only other person who realised it was Louis Osei. Taking him up on his offer of buying the place was never going to happen. I'd take to it with a sledgehammer first, which was a righteous pose but not very profitable.

The prospect of saying goodbye to old friends was also gnawing at me. Vincent and Melito had been my neighbours for seven years. Whether I wanted to admit it or not, I was going to miss the inane banter brought on by their ouzo binges. And leaving Mimi behind would be hard on my heart. The woman had picked me up and dusted me off a hundred times over the years – for no other reason than she loved me like her own.

It took forever for me to explain it to Shiloh, and to her credit she didn't interrupt until every thought I had was laid bare.

"I can't tell you how to deal with closing those chapters," she said, reaching for my hand. "All I can do is remind you of the new ones that are opening."

A rambling monologue about reconnecting with my family and settling back into life at home followed. The picture she painted was one of sunshine and light, but not once did she mention herself.

"And what about us?" I tried not to sound bothered by the oversight but failed.

She dropped my hand. "What do you mean?"

"Well, where do you see us headed?"

"Home," she replied simply. "And if you still want me when we get there, I'm yours."

Larceny

SHILOH

The next few days were some of the best I've ever had. We stayed up late, slept in late, and generally made the most of the peace and quiet while Melito and Vincent were out of town.

It was radio silence all round. I hadn't heard a peep from Glen, which led me to think that throwing my hat into the ring might've been a misstep. I tried not to dwell on it, but when Friday afternoon rolled around I was less enthused than ever to pull on the steel-capped boots and head to work. I declined Mitchell's offer to walk me up to the road.

I had no idea what sort of reception I'd receive from Glen, but as it turned out, I had nothing to worry about. There was no reception. He didn't pay me so much as a sideways glance as I got into the car.

Keeping my mouth shut and making the most of the silence would've been the smart thing to do, but I broke after just a few seconds. "Hello." I spoke as if calling out in an empty room. "How are you?"

Nothing.

"Nice weather lately, huh?"

Nothing.

I gazed out the window, still talking. "Yep. It looks like the perfect night to pocket a few rocks."

Finally, he bit. "Do you really think it's that simple?" He didn't pause long enough to let me answer. "Just grab a few gems that take your fancy and stick them in your pocket?"

No, I didn't think it was that simple. I'd spent weeks trying to catch him doing exactly that, without any success. To this day I had no idea how he was pulling it off.

"I'm sure there's more to it," I replied. "That's why I want you to teach me."

I was finally wearing him down. I could see it. His grip on the steering wheel tightened and his face contorted into a pained frown. "You've got no idea what you're getting yourself into."

"So you'll do it?"

Glen glanced across. "You do exactly what I tell you to do," he growled. "I'm not going down because of some greedy little upstart with a big sense of adventure."

I turned my head, reserving my triumphant smile for the outside view. I was in. All I needed to do now was stay there.

***

My lesson in larceny took place in Glen's office. I'd only been in there a handful of times, and had never been made to feel welcome. Tonight the atmosphere was a little different.

"Sit." He pointed to the empty chair opposite his desk.

Gearing up to take as many mental notes as I could, I did as I was told.

"There's a jeweller in the sorting room," he began. "His name is Joseph."

I couldn't put a face to the name, probably because my focus was always on Glen. "I don't know him."

"Get to know him," he snapped. "He's your new personal shopper."

To untrained eyes, all diamonds look the same. Industrial diamonds are practically worthless, and certainly not worth stealing. Having a jeweller to preselect the valuable rocks made total sense.

Glen managed to smoke three cigarettes in the time it took for him to lay out the blueprint of his wicked deeds – and I was amazed by his ingenuity.

First, after selecting a few choice diamonds, Joseph the crooked jeweller accidentally knocks three of them onto the floor. I'd seen it happen a few times, and apart from the short interruption to the process it barely raised an eyebrow. The jewellers used a twelve-inch long tool called operating tweezers to pick through the stones. They were big and clunky, and it wasn't much of a stretch to think that occasional slips could be made.

"He bends down and picks two up." Glen leaned forward and stubbed out his cigarette in the overflowing ashtray on his desk. "I pick up the third."

I frowned. "You're not permitted to touch the rocks." That was a steadfast rule, and absolutely no security officer would get away with doing it. "How do you pull that off?"

Glen leaned back and put both feet on his desk. "Quietly," he smugly replied.

I shrugged, still frustratingly clueless. "I don't get it."

"Look closer." He shook his foot, knocking one boot against the other. "What do you see?"

Reluctantly I leaned forward, squinting as I studied his boots. Within seconds, the whole puzzle came together. Near the toe of the left sole was a small, perfectly drilled hole.

"You step on it!"

"Line it up, step on it and push it into the boot."

The simplest plans are usually the best, and this was as simple as they come. Raw diamonds aren't glittery and pretty – they're just ordinary looking rocks. Once concealed in the sole of a shoe, they would likely escape the attention of the most fastidious inspector.

"I just walk out the door," he gloated. "Sometimes three or four a night."

"I'm very impressed." It might've been the most honest thing I'd ever said to him, and like Louis Osei a few days earlier, the compliment incited a smug rise in posture.

"Do you still want in?" he asked.

I pushed my chair back and thumped my foot on his desk. "Sign me up."

***

Over the next nine days I singlehandedly stole seventeen high-grade diamonds from the Jorge Creek Mining Company – all via a tiny hole in the sole of my boot. When it came to passing through the three security checkpoints at the end of my shift, the process was always the same. While doing my level best to look innocent, I'd smile and make small talk with the guard on duty.

And it worked every time.

Sometimes my boots weren't even checked, and when they were, the guard paid them very little attention. After walking through the metal detector, I'd collect my phone, boots and belt from the other side and be on my way.

Lifting diamonds was the biggest line I'd ever blurred in my life, but the shot of adrenalin that hit me every time I walked out the front gate left me walking on air.

It was hard to walk without a skip in my step, but my jubilation always dropped a few notches once I got into Glen's car. He was much better at the poker face than I, and it was always business as usual until we pulled up outside the fat cat camp and made the exchange. That's usually when excitement took over.

Today I was especially gleeful. "I got three," I bragged, pulling off my boot.

Glen grabbed a pair of tweezers out of the centre console and plucked the tiny rocks from the rubber sole. "You're amazing," he praised, holding each stone up to the light.

"Amazing but poor," I replied. "When am I going to start seeing some money?"

As exciting as the week had been, it could only go on for so long. I needed to ascertain when the diamonds were leaving town, where they were going, and who he was using as a fence. I continually pushed the issue of money in a bid to find out, but in typical Glen style, he was cagey when it came to answering questions.

"Soon," he replied vaguely. "Very soon."

I slumped back, thumping my head against the headrest. "That's not good enough any more," I complained. "I'm not doing this for free."

I wasn't the only person frustrated by the lack of progress. However shady he might've been, Iron Mike was the only contact I had when it came to relaying intel back to my employer. I'd been keeping him in the loop via text messages sent from the secret phone under the shack.

For the first few days he seemed pleased with the headway I'd made. He'd reply within seconds, using words like "excellent" or "outstanding", but as progress slowed he reverted to his usual round of threats and malice. The last communication I received was less than heart-warming.

- Get the job done. Don't become expendable.

The only hope I had of avoiding that was to keep pushing Tweedledee for payment.

"I want my money, Glen."

"All in good time." He pulled a yellow tobacco tin from his shirt pocket, carefully placed the three small diamonds inside and snapped the lid closed. "There's a charter plane leaving next week," he told me, slipping the tin back into his pocket. "The haul will be delivered to a jeweller in Belgium. Once they're cut and sold, we'll both be paid."

The massive revelation was proof positive that he trusted me implicitly. It also meant that I was closer than ever to wrapping things up and going home.

"Can I see them?" I asked hopefully.

"The rocks?"

"Yeah." I nodded eagerly. "It'd be cool to see them all together before they're gone."

Disclosing the location of a fortune's worth of stolen diamonds wasn't smart, but Glen was no scholar. He was an egomaniac who was keen to impress, which probably explained why he took me to his house to check out the wares.

I was no longer scared of Glen Harris. Over time I had come to realise his foul, crotchety attitude was brought on by stress – an occupational hazard for those who spend most of their time in bed with the devil. In my opinion, he was a lonely, desperate crook who was having a hard time holding it together.

The state of his house did nothing to change my mind. The place was a pigsty. The stench of stale cigarette smoke hit me the second he opened the door, and it wasn't hard to see why. Overflowing ashtrays and empty rum bottles littered every surface. But it wasn't the worst I'd ever seen, and I tried hard not to appear grossed out by it.

"Wait here," he instructed, disappearing into the bedroom.

I stood by the door and waited, my eyes darting across the messy scene. "You know the company provides cleaners, right?" I called.

"I don't want anyone snooping around in here," he replied, returning to the room.

My focus shifted to the yellow tin in his hand. When he gave it a shake, my eyes lit up.

After transferring the gems from the tin in his pocket to the one in his hand, he set it on the bench. "Beautiful, aren't they?" he asked with reverence.

I couldn't decide one way or the other. There was nothing overly pretty about the two hundred or so gems in the tin. They were tiny – some no bigger than the head of a match – but there was no denying their worth. There was hundreds of thousands of dollars in that small tin, and I'd all but sold my soul to help fill it.

"So what happens now?" I asked.

Glen snapped the tin shut. "Be patient and wait for your money," he replied. "A few weeks from now you'll be on easy street."

"I'm looking forward to it." I grinned at him. "More than you'll ever know."

Fool

MITCHELL

Absolutely nothing gets by Mimi. As far as I knew, the only two people who knew about our plans for skipping town were Shiloh and I, but somehow, Mimi was on to us.

Understandably, she was worried about losing her job if I closed the Crown and Pav – so worried that she turned up at the door to discuss it.

"Nothing has been decided yet, Mimi," I told her. "But I'll make sure you're looked after." I just wasn't sure how.

She pressed her hands against my cheeks. "You are a good, dumb boy," she told me through gritted teeth. "Your mother will be proud to have her son home."

"Thank you," I replied.

She dropped her hold and wandered through to the kitchen. "I will make you food," she offered. "Where is the girl?"

I put my fingers to my lips. "Sleeping. She just finished working nightshift."

Ignoring me, she grabbed the only saucepan I owned and slammed it on the stove. "She still needs to eat to keep her mind sharp," she said, tapping the side of her head. "She does very important work."

I frowned. "Since when have you cared about her work?" I asked. "Or the sharpness of her mind?"

Mimi grabbed the basket of vegetables we kept on the counter. "Protecting the diamonds is important work," she replied.

I laughed, but her serious expression remained. "Whatever you say, Mimi."

"Get outside and leave me in peace," she barked, pointing at the door.

"This is my house," I reminded her. "You can't kick me out."

She leaned across the table, jabbing a carrot at me as if it was a dagger. "Today it is my kitchen," she growled. "Now scat."

I knew better than to argue, so I retreated to the front deck, but short of actually stabbing me with the carrot there wasn't anything Mimi could do to sour my mood that day.

Plenty of good things were going on. Shiloh had just finished a nine-day stint at work, which meant she was free and easy for a while. And assuming that the bus from Cape Town didn't break down along the way, the sleek Greeks were due back from holiday within the next day or two. I looked at the shack next door and decided that a bit of housekeeping was in order. The beach had almost claimed their front deck, making it look even more abandoned than usual.

Mimi was obviously watching me. Before I even picked up the broom, she appeared. "You should sweep your own floor," she called. "It's a mess."

I couldn't help smiling. The woman was like an irritating mosquito. "Aren't you supposed to be cooking?"

"A watched pot never boils, dumb boy."

A smart retort was impossible but I was prepared to give it a shot, right up until someone else caught my attention. A man staggered around the corner of my shack, flicking up sand in his wake. Clearly he was drunk, but it wasn't any run-of-the-mill derro. It was Shiloh's idiot boss, Glen.

"What do you want?" I asked.

"Where's Shiloh?" He grabbed onto the railing of the steps to steady himself. "I want to talk to her."

"Well, you can't," I replied. "She's sleeping."

He should've been too. As far as I knew, they worked the same shifts. Levering himself off the railing, Glen staggered a few steps to the side. "She's very good at her job," he slurred. "Crafty and sly. You should be proud."

Today must've been Shiloh Jenson Appreciation Day. Perhaps I'd missed the memo. I looked across at Mimi and frowned. She shrugged her shoulders. "What do you want, drunken fool?" she snapped, sounding far more menacing that I ever could.

Glen pointed a half-empty bottle of rum at her, managing to slosh a good amount on his shirt in the process. "I want to be rich," he yelled. "And I want to be free of this place."

I'd seen enough drunks in my time to know that he was incapable of talking sense, but one thing he was capable of was creating a ruckus. Using the bottle in his hand, he dragged it back and forth along the lattice siding on the shack, singing at the top of his lungs. *Diamonds are a girl's best friend* was the tune of choice – but his plastered, dying-cat version was impossible to listen to.

Not surprisingly, the commotion woke Shiloh. She pushed past Mimi and marched onto the deck. "What are you doing?" she growled.

He raised his bottle. "Celebrating!" he yelled. "Join me."

Shiloh shook her head, looking repulsed. "You're drunk," she said, pointing out the obvious. "Go home and sleep it off."

Glen didn't. He went back to doing his best Marilyn Monroe impression, which was neither authentic nor comical. It was pathetic.

Mimi broke first. In a move I could never have predicted, she reached into a pocket of her dress and pulled out an onion. With the precision of a pro baseball player, she pegged it at Glen. He folded like a cheap suitcase, dropping him to the sand in an instant.

"Mimi!" yelled Shiloh, looking appalled.

I didn't yell anything, but if I had it probably would have been words of praise for such a perfect shot.

Mimi marched to the top of the steps, hands on hips. "Get up, fool."

Glen remained flat out on the sand. For the longest time all I could hear was the sound of breaking waves, and then he finally spoke.

"You spilled my drink, woman," he muttered, disproving my theory that he was dead.

Perhaps the adage about knocking sense into someone is true. After a long moment he sat up and picked his bottle off the sand. "I have to go," he slurred, staggering to his feet. "Things to do, people to see."

None of us tried to stop him as he stumbled away, but Shiloh looked worried.

"We'll check on him later if you want," I offered.

"No." She shook her head. "He's not our problem."

Mimi was in agreement. The only thing she was worried about was whether she could salvage the onion. She puffed her way across the sand, picked it up and brushed it off.

Shiloh threw both arms out. "Did you have to hit him, Mimi?"

"He deserved it," she retorted. "He was making a fool of himself."

Shiloh held her head as if her brain ached. "Jesus Christ," she muttered, pacing the veranda. "This place is Loony Tunes."

Suddenly I was immensely thankful to be out of reach of both of them. I leaned the broom against the shack and leaned over the railing. "Maybe you should go, Mimi," I suggested.

She held up the onion. "But I'm making you soup."

Shiloh spun around. "Not with that, you're not! Take your bloody onion with you!"

***

I swept the sleek Greeks' deck far more thoroughly than I'd ever cleaned my own. Diligence had nothing to do with it – I was in no hurry to deal with Shiloh. I'd dealt with enough pissed-off women in my time to know that giving her some breathing space would be mutually beneficial.

When I did eventually go home, mad Mimi was gone. Her pot of soup took pride of place on the stove, adding another ten degrees to the temperature of the room as it boiled. I turned off the heat and courageously walked into the bedroom.

Somewhere in the bundled-up quilt, Shiloh lay hidden. I could barely see her head poking out, which wasn't one of her brighter moves.

"You're going to get heatstroke," I warned, crawling across the bed.

"We have to get out of here, Mitchell," she mumbled, "or we're going to succumb to far worse than that."

I put my hand on her forehead. "We're leaving," I assured her. "Just as soon as we get through that cauldron of soup."

"She used all the vegies," she pointed out. "We have nothing else to eat until market day."

"Mimi means well, Shiloh." I peeled the quilt off her and dropped it on the floor. "She's just a little heavy-handed."

"She knocked a bloke out with an onion."

It was impossible not to laugh. "It sounds bad when you put it like that."

"It *is* bad, Mitchell," she scolded. "She's a nutter."

I grabbed her, taking her with me as I rolled onto my back. "What about your dickhead boss?" I asked, tucking a loose piece of hair behind her ear. "He turned up here singing show tunes."

"He was drunk."

"He was looking for you."

Shiloh shook her head. "I can't imagine why."

I didn't care why. I just didn't want a repeat performance. "Do I need to have a word with him?" I asked. "Is he bothering you?"

"No." When I tugged at the hem of her shirt, she raised her arms. "I don't know what today's bender was in aid of. Most days he won't even talk to me."

"I don't want to talk to you either," I replied, tossing her shirt across the room.

Finally she smiled. "Did you have something else in mind?"

I trailed my fingertips across her stomach. "All sorts of wicked things, lady."

Shiloh made a grab for the mosquito net that hung from the ceiling, bunching a handful of the sheer fabric against her bare chest.

I put my hands on her hips, holding her right where I wanted her. "You think that will stop me?" I murmured.

"I'm not trying to stop you," she whispered. "I'm just trying to slow you down."

Bin Bin Ruse

SHILOH

After a long spell on the sidelines and a few false starts, Mitchell was finally back to his routine of spending the mornings in the surf. He left the shack just after eight, and I was out the door two minutes later, making a beeline for the fat cat camp.

Glen's drunken antics the day before were unforgivable. If he was having trouble holding it together, I didn't care. If regret or a guilty conscience was driving him to drink, I didn't care. All I cared about was getting him to pull himself together and keep his mouth shut. By the time I got to the top of the hill I had my whole speech worked out: shut your mouth, lay off the drink and stay away from me until the heat dies down.

Mindful of disturbing the neighbours I quietly knocked on Glen's door, but after ten minutes of politely trying to rouse him, patience wore thin. Walking away and letting him sleep it off wasn't an option. For all I knew, Mimi might've caused him some real damage the day before – and death by onion didn't seem like a good way to go.

Kicking the door down obviously wasn't an option, but there was no harm in trying the handle. Much to my surprise, it turned freely, but the biggest shock came when the door swung open.

Twenty-four hours earlier I had stood in exactly the same place, looking at a dishevelled, chaotic scene. Now I was looking at nothing. The living room looked exactly like the house next door – pin neat and beige. Checking out the rest of the house added to my confusion. There was no hint that Glen had ever lived there – even the cigarette stench was gone.

I pulled the door closed and stood on the porch, pulling in as much of the ocean air as I could in a bid to slow my racing thoughts.

It was impossible to think he'd packed up and done a midnight flit, considering the state he was in. It was more plausible that someone else had had a hand in his disappearance, and just thinking about it made my blood run cold. Contacting Mike was all I could think to do. He didn't give a damn about Glen, but he did care about the tin full of diamonds, that had also gone AWOL. Hopefully, a search for one would lead to the other.

***

When I arrived back the shack, I found I had a bit of breathing room when it came to making contact with Mike. I could see Mitchell a long way off shore, so getting back in after was going to take him a while. I wandered around the side of the shack, lifted the lattice siding and ducked under the house.

A well-worn groove in the sand now marked a path to the phone, highlighting exactly how frequently I made the sandy crawl.

My message to Iron Mike was short and almost to the point.

- We need to meet. Rocks are gone.

His reply was almost instant, which grated on me no end. I had to keep my phone hidden under the house, but he probably kept his in his pocket.

-Say nothing. Will meet tonight.

I punched at the letters, annoyed by his vague response.

-Where??
-I will find you.

I had no choice but to leave it at that. Asking for any more information would've been a waste of text.

***

My decision to spend the evening at the Crown and Pav had little to do with hanging out with Mitchell. If Mike was going to come looking for me, I didn't want him anywhere near our home. All I could do was sit at the bar and wait, which I did with the enthusiasm of someone passing time on death row.

"What's going on, lady?" Mitchell asked. "You look like you've got the weight of the world on your shoulders."

He wasn't far wrong, but I could hardly agree with him. I straightened up, trying to look a little livelier. "Just tired, I think."

He smiled, but it was off, and I knew he didn't believe me.

At times it was impossible to know what Mitchell saw in me. Depending on the drama of the day I could be moody, fickle, preoccupied —sometimes simultaneously. It was confusing to both of us, and yet he persevered as if I was worth the effort. When I reached across the bar, he took my hand. "I'm sorry I make you crazy," I said, making him smile.

"Don't worry about it." Mitchell gave my fingers a squeeze. "I like a challenge."

So did Mimi Traore. Whenever she saw us looking cosy, she made it her mission to put a stop to it. "Let's go, dumb girl," she ordered, ambushing me from behind. "Secret business."

"You're not even working tonight," grumbled Mitchell. "What are you doing here?"

Mimi pulled out a handful of beads and leaned across the bar. "Secret business, dumb boy," she hissed, waving them in his face.

The last thing I needed was another string of bin bin beads hitched to my middle, but that wasn't Mimi's objective. It took me two seconds to work out that Mike had sent her to fetch me.

Not even Mitchell was sold on the bin bin ruse. "Don't you have enough beads?" He raised his eyebrows. "You can say no, you know."

Mimi was already dragging me off the stool. "We both know that's not true."

"I'll save your seat for you," he replied.

***

Mimi didn't utter a word until we reached the privacy of the open beach, and then there was no shutting her up. "The bad man came to my house again." Her tone was nervous but strong. "He made me bring you here."

The woman looked terrified, and she wasn't easily rattled. I grabbed her hands and held them tightly, trying to calm her. "Listen, Mimi," I said gently. "You've done nothing wrong. I knew he was going to send for me."

She cocked her head, looking past me. "They're coming," she hissed, handing me a string of beads. "Be careful, dumb girl."

"There's more than one?" I asked, turning to check.

Mimi didn't answer because she was gone, barrelling through the sand as if she was being chased. I turned my attention to the two dark figures approaching along the shoreline. Mike's swagger would've been recognisable a mile away, but I had no idea who the second man was until they were right in front of me.

"Shiloh," greeted Mike with a stiff nod. "You remember my colleague, Reyo."

I cast my mind back to the first time I met Reyo in the Site Services office at the mine. He was friendly, smiley and talkative. The man in front of me was none of these things.

"Of course," I replied. "How are you, Reyo? Still into the Backstreet Boys?" I had learned a long time ago that undercover operatives had no sense of humour. Reyo was clearly no exception. His stony expression didn't waver. I turned to Iron Mike. "Glen Harris has gone missing," I said flatly. "I went to his house today and it's empty."

The coldness of my tone bothered me. Was I was becoming immune to my circumstances? If that were to happen I'd be no better than the vile men in front of me.

"He was picked up last night," said Mike.

I frowned. "By who?"

"Your people."

"*My* people?" I wasn't even sure who my people were anymore. "You mean my aunt?"

Reading their expressions in the dark was difficult, but there was no mistaking the condescending snicker from Reyo.

"Glen Harris is an English citizen," I reminded them. "If he comes to any harm while he's here –"

"My government has no interest in him," Mike cut me off. "*Your* people picked him up." He pointed at me. "They ended the operation based on *your* information."

I shook my head, confused but unwilling to admit it.

"You relayed that he was merely a greedy opportunist," he continued. "No ties to militia groups or any other organisations."

Glen Harris had many grandiose plans, but none that involved *coups d'état* or supplying mercenary groups with weapons. Glen was all about Glen, and judging from what he'd told me, the only plan he had was to cash in his diamond haul and live the life of Riley.

"I stand by that," I replied. "He's just a thief. Nothing more."

Mike spread his arms. "Then your work here is done."

"What?" I choked out the word. "How can that be?"

"The diamonds were recovered in his house. It was a favourable outcome."

There was no way it could've ended that easily. Glen was days away from fencing the gems, which meant a whole new network of crooks was about to surface – and Iron Mike knew it.

"You're closing me out," I accused.

There was no other explanation for it. He'd been relentlessly pushing me for weeks. It made no sense to call it quits just because the diamonds had been found.

Reyo smirked. "You've wanted out for a while now," he reminded me. "Now you have a ticket home."

I should've been jumping for joy. Instead, I felt like I'd been unjustly dismissed without cause. "But … I don't think this is over," I tried to explain.

Mike smiled. "Like I told you before, if you come across intelligence that you deem to be more reliable than mine, run with it." He glanced at Reyo. "But I am telling you your work here is done. It's over, Shiloh."

Airhead

MITCHELL

Although we joked about it, there was nothing funny about living on bread and vegetable soup for days on end. Desperate times call for desperate measures, and I was getting desperate. I woke Shiloh early, keen to get her moving before it got too hot.

"Where are we going?" Her sleepy voice gave no hint that she wanted to hear an answer.

I kissed her cheek. "Fishing. Get up."

She pulled a pillow over her head and groaned. It wasn't the response I was hoping for, but her protest was short-lived. Ten minutes later she stumbled onto the deck and claimed to be good to go.

"Do you know how to fish, Adonis?"

It was a fair question, all things considered. The messy tangle of line at my feet was hardly the look of a professional.

"I do, as it happens." I handed her a reel. "Do you know how to fish, MacGyver?"

"No," she replied, looking a little bewildered. "I've never been fishing in my life."

"No survivalist fishing tips for me then?" She shook her head. "Excellent." I quickly cut the tangled line and kicked it aside. "Maybe I'll get to hang on to my man card for a bit longer."

***

A few hundred metres north of the cardboard village lay a patch of ocean that's always calm. It was a hopeless place to surf, but a decent place to fish.

"Look how still it is," said Shiloh, gazing out to sea. "We should be swimming, not fishing."

"This place is called Deception Pool," I explained, setting the gear on the sand. "Named after suckers like you who think it's a nice place to swim."

"It is," she insisted. "Look at it."

"You should never trust calm water," I replied. "There's a gnarly undercurrent that passes all the way through here. If you went for a dip in that, the coastguard would be picking you up in Brazil in a week or two."

Shiloh's shoulders slumped. "Danger always lurks when things are calm," she muttered.

"Are we still talking about the ocean?" I asked. "Or have we moved on?"

It was hard to tell. The creepy musing seemed to come out of nowhere.

She twisted to look at me. "What scares you, Adonis?" she asked. "*Really* scares you?"

"Besides you?" I teased.

Her lovely brown eyes widened. "*I* scare you?"

Articulating a proper response was damned near impossible. It wasn't virgin territory. I'd been in this predicament a hundred times before where Shiloh was concerned. "Sometimes." Already the conversation was heading in an ugly direction, and I wasn't hopeful of getting it back on track. "Remember how I told you that Charli left here and went to New York?"

She nodded.

"She was chasing a bloke – an American she met at home the year before." I sat on the sand and pulled her down beside me. "They broke up and got back together about three million times," I told her. "It was a train wreck."

Shiloh frowned. "What does this have to do with us?"

I brought her hand to my mouth and kissed her fingers. "Bear with me," I urged. "I'm about to make a spectacular point."

She laughed softly.

"I thought he was a dick," I said with a smile. "He broke her heart over and over, but she just wouldn't let go."

"Why?"

I tilted her face to look at me. "Because she knew he was the one for her," I replied. "No matter how much of a train wreck it was, she never gave up on him."

"Did she wise up in the end?"

"No." I shook my head. "He did. They're married with a kid now."

"I'm glad it worked out," she replied, brushing sand off her hands. "But I'm not sure what your point is."

"The point is, Shiloh, she knew that what she'd found with him was the real deal, and she wasn't afraid of any of the misery that came with it." On the off chance that she was about to jump up and run away, I took her hand. "I feel like you might be the real deal."

"But?"

"But," I grimaced, "unlike Charli, I *am* afraid of the misery that comes with it – and I can't shake the feeling that there's plenty on the way."

Shiloh blew out a long breath that crumpled her posture. "I would never intentionally do anything to hurt you." Her voice was tiny. "You have to believe that."

Using someone else's life story to get my point across proved just how inept I was when it came to explaining how I felt, but Shiloh's words were frustratingly hazy and did nothing to put my mind at ease. At that point, I was certain of only one thing: I was going to get my heart broken.

And because I could see it coming, it was my fault, not hers.

***

Three fish wasn't a bad haul, but by the time we called it quits and headed home neither of us felt like dealing with them. The day had started with a weird vibe and the tension never left, which meant that the damage I'd caused by being honest was probably permanent.

"I won't miss this when we're gone," muttered Shiloh.

"Miss what?" I asked, stepping up onto the veranda.

"Hunting and gathering to get a decent meal."

I looked at the fish in the bucket and agreed. "It does get old quick."

"Might I suggest something more substantial?" asked a booming voice from next door.

I would've welcomed any distraction at that point – even Melito butting in. "Welcome home." I grinned. "What did you have in mind?"

"Spoils fit for a king." He dipped his head at Shiloh. "And a queen, of course."

"You're cooking already?" asked Shiloh. "You just got home."

"It was a long journey," he wearily explained. "Three days of nothing but maafe and rice." He shuddered as if he'd been forced to eat poison. "We're all deserving of a decent meal, don't you think?"

I raised my eyebrows at Shiloh. "Up to you, lady."

She turned to Melito. "We would love to come, thank you."

"Excellent," he beamed, clapping his hands together. "Dress up. It's going to be an extravaganza."

***

Before heading next door for dinner, I decided to take one last shot at making things right between us. The conversation started from opposite sides of the bathroom door. I figured it was safer that way.

"If I hurt you today, I'm sorry," I said. "I never meant to."

"You didn't," she assured me. "But I don't think it's a conversation we should be having here."

"Because you're in the bathroom?"

Her soft chuckle had never sounded sweeter. "No, because we're in Kaimte."

"Oh."

"Everything will be different when we get home, Mitchell. We just need to hold on until then."

I pressed my forehead against the door, feeling confused. "Sometimes I think we speak a different language," I told her. "I'm trying to love you, and you're telling me to wait."

"No, I'm telling you to reserve judgment until we get home."

"What's going to change?"

She didn't answer, which pissed me off. When the bathroom door finally swung open, the urge to argue with her disappeared in an instant. Nothing about her was maddening or frustrating. I couldn't see anything beyond how beautiful she looked.

I'd never seen the short black dress she was wearing before. It was dressy and classy, and perfectly showcased her beautiful legs. Her long dark hair tumbled over her shoulders in big curls – another first.

"What do you think?" she asked, smoothing the fabric along her sides.

"I think you're gorgeous."

"Not too much?"

It was way too much for a shindig with the sleek Greeks, but there was no way I was going to tell her. "You're perfect."

"You asked me what was going to change when we get home."

I nodded, focusing on her lips.

"I'll show you." She turned and grabbed a bag from the bathroom, and then upended it on the bed. "When I packed to come here, I was clueless," she began.

"Everyone is," I replied, looking at the girly junk on the bed.

"I was *extra* clueless." She held up something that looked like a pair of tongs. "I brought a little black dress and a curling iron. I thought I might need them."

"Cool." I grinned at her. "You like ironing."

"It's for hair." When she flicked the end of her brown curls, a picture of Jasmine flashed through my mind.

"Don't ever make that move again," I warned her.

"Airhead, right?"

I nodded. "Total airhead."

"I *felt* like an airhead when I got here – totally unprepared for this place," she explained. "You don't have the full picture of who I am because I can't show you. I am who I am in order to survive my time here."

Unlike me, Shiloh never had a problem when it came to making her point. My push to get to know her better wasn't misguided, just ill-timed.

"I get it," I murmured, slipping an arm around her. "I do."

She flattened both palms on my chest. "Sooner or later you're going to know everything there is to know about me," she said softly. "But it won't happen here."

Options

SHILOH

Melito and Vincent were the rock stars of Kaimte, and tonight I felt like we'd crossed the velvet rope and entered the VIP section of their club.

I hadn't seen a properly set table since I last had dinner with the Kellys in Western Australia, and I had never seen pearl encrusted napkin rings. "Do you think they're real?" I whispered to Mitchell.

"I'm not sure." He motioned to the ceiling with a discreet nod. "Do you think that's real?" When I saw the chandelier hanging from the ceiling, my mouth gaped. This was unfathomable. Our shack was practically falling down around our ears, and the Greeks' home wasn't much better.

"It's Swarovski," claimed Vincent, gazing upward. "Beautiful, isn't it?"

"Lovely," I choked.

"We brought you gifts on our travels," announced Melito, recapturing our attention.

"You didn't have to." I could tell Mitchell felt awkward. I wasn't sure how I felt, mainly because I was hopeful that the presents were food related.

"Nonsense," he replied. "Who can one spoil if not their friends?"

Vincent handed Mitchell a small box. Reluctantly, he stripped the green ribbon off and lifted the lid. "A bottle opener," he said, sounding relieved. "It's great, thanks."

Melito turned and handed me a box. "Your turn, dear Shiloh."

Inside was the ugliest pair of stiletto shoes I'd ever seen in my life.

Disappointment hit me hard, but I hid it well. "Thank you," I crowed. "They're perfect."

Melito flapped his hand at me. "Put them on. Put them on."

Knowing there was no way around it, I slipped off my flip-flops and held on to the back of the dining chair for balance as I stepped into the six-inch heels. "I don't normally wear heels this high."

I didn't normally wear yellow sequins either, and the damned things were covered in them. Unfortunately, the shoes were a perfect fit.

"Of course you don't," said Vincent, clasping his hands. "You're very tall."

Melito grabbed Mitchell's arm and pulled him to his feet. "But not too tall for Adonis," he said, manhandling him into position next to me. "See, darling? He still towers above you. You don't have to miss out on dressing like a goddess." He pointed at Mitchell with both hands. "You've found your perfect match here."

"Like Cinderella," interjected Vincent in a weird dreamy tone.

I wasn't exactly up to speed on fairy tales, but I couldn't remember Cinderella favouring the hoochie look.

"Can we sit now?" asked Mitchell.

"Tell her how lovely she looks first," prompted Melito.

Buying into the theatrics was our only option, and Mitchell realised it too. He dropped to one knee and grabbed my hand. "You, my darling, are a goddess." A bad case of the giggles overtook me, but he pressed on. "Most women would look like a streetwalker in those shoes, but not you." I continued my shameless giggling. "You wear them with class – like a high-priced call girl with a fixed address."

I put my hand to my heart. "My god, that's the most romantic thing I've ever heard."

"It is?" asked Vincent, sounding slightly worried.

I nodded, hoping the giddy call-girl look was believable.

Mitchell stood and flicked the collar of his shirt. "Oh yeah," he quipped. "I'm in."

***

The rest of the night continued on the same strange tangent. The food was wonderful and the company was good, but somehow Mitchell ended up three sheets to the wind.

It wasn't like him to drink too much, but by the end of dessert he was sleepy and dopy, and the only thing propping him up on his chair was me.

"We should go," I suggested. "It's been a long day."

I should've known polite excuses wouldn't work. Vincent leaned across and refilled both our glasses. "The night is young," he said. "Stay for one more drink."

I tilted my head toward Mitchell. "I think some of us have had enough."

Mitchell raised his hand. "Me," he declared. "I've had enough." His head lolled. "You have to take me home," he begged.

I had no idea what was happening, and wasn't sure that Mitchell did either. There were three empty bottles of wine on the table and none had been cleared away. Even if he'd consumed all three himself it wouldn't explain the near-paralytic state he was in.

I kicked off the hoochie heels and slipped my flip-flops on. "I really have to get him to bed," I insisted. "He's beyond sloppy now."

I tried to help Mitchell up, but couldn't move him.

Both men rose and offered to help. "We'll walk you home," said Vincent.

"Thank you," I muttered.

"Don't be too hard on him in the morning." Melito's voice was soft with pity. "Getting a little charged is a sign that a wonderful evening was had."

I forced a smile that probably looked odd.

Vincent got Mitchell to his feet. "Let's go, Adonis. Your bed awaits."

The walk next door was excruciatingly slow. Vincent struggled to get Mitchell to put one foot in front of the other, and Melito did nothing to help. "It's such a lovely night, don't you think?" He looked up at the sky. "Stars for as far as the eye can see."

I wasn't remotely interested in checking it out, and his attitude toward the situation at hand was starting to piss me off. I skipped ahead of him and rushed to unlock the front door.

Vincent manoeuvred Mitchell up the steps. "I'll put him to bed," he offered. "Don't worry about a thing." They disappeared into the shack, leaving me on the deck with Melito. Even though it was the last thing I wanted to do, I felt compelled to make small talk and thank him for the evening.

"It was our pleasure." He leaned both hands on the railing and looked to the sky again. "Look at those jewels in nature's crown," he marvelled. "So brilliantly perfect in every way – like diamonds." Very slowly, he dipped his head to look at me. "I have a thing for diamonds, Shiloh. Do you?"

"No, not really." I always felt a pang of unease whenever an innocent comment hit too close to home, but this felt frighteningly different.

"Shame." He pouted, sticking out his bottom lip. "Up until a few days ago, I had three hundred and thirty of them, but sadly, they're missing. I was told you might know something about their whereabouts."

"No." The word came out in a panicky breath. "Nothing."

The dim porch light flickered a few times, befitting the terrifying scene unfolding before me. Melito wasn't a kind and eccentric neighbour. He was the devil – and I'd been living in his garden the whole time.

Vincent waltzed out. "They're not in there," he said. "I've turned the place upside down."

Mitchell's mystery bender suddenly made a whole lot more sense. He wasn't drunk at all. They'd drugged him to keep him quiet while Vincent tore our house apart.

"I told you," I said weakly. "I don't have them."

A sickening grin crept across Vincent's face. Any hope I had of reasoning with him was lost. He wasn't a softer touch. There were two devils at work – and they were evil in equal measure.

"I have some friends who work at the mine," said Melito. "A couple, actually. Glen Harris – do you know him?"

It was important to give him one-word answers, and less when possible. I nodded but didn't speak.

"He's our courier," said Vincent, interlocking his fingers. "He transports the jewels out of the mine on our behalf."

Melito turned to me. "But you know that already, don't you?"

It was time to change tack. Playing the terrified, doe-eyed innocent was never going to fly. I threw both hands up. "Look, all I wanted was in on a bit of action. There's nothing wrong with making a little money on the side."

"Indeed," he agreed. "But you got greedy. Glen wanted to bring you in. You were our second courier. He assured us you were trustworthy."

"I am!" Telling lies is always easier than admitting the truth, and I'd had lots of practice lately.

"I have another friend at the mine," he explained. "He kept me in the loop while we were on vacation, usually via email."

Melito took his phone from his pocket and swiped the screen. I swallowed hard, anticipating something horrible at any second. He cleared his throat and read out loud. "Glen Harris was arrested at his home last night after a tip-off from Shiloh Jenson. No diamonds were recovered. I believe she is in possession of all stones."

He slowly turned his head. "Well?"

"It's a lie," I snapped. "I wanted a cut, not the whole lot. How would I get them out of the country by myself?" I was rambling now, and couldn't seem to stop. "Who would I get to fence them for me?"

Melito shrugged. "I have no idea, darling." His smooth tone made me want to retch. "But Reyo and I have been friends for many years. He has no reason to lie to me."

My legs were barely functioning, battling to hold the weight of the thoughts now spinning through my head. From what I could ascertain in the seconds I'd had to think about it, there were only two possibilities: either Mike and Reyo were playing both sides, or they'd set me up.

Either way I was screwed.

"What do you want?" I asked, gripping the railing for support.

"It's simple really." Melito rested his back against the balustrade as if we were engaged in casual conversation. "I want my diamonds back. There's a plane leaving here tomorrow afternoon at five. Either my diamonds are on it or…."

"Or what?" I spat, annoyed by the unnecessary dramatic pause.

He leaned so close that I could feel his breath on my face. "Or your boyfriend gets a bullet to the head."

Fear couldn't adequately describe how I felt at that point. Terror didn't cut it either. But I knew if I collapsed in a heap we'd both be dead.

"Collateral damage," I mused, somehow finding the fortitude to call his bluff. "We just might not be that close."

Melito straightened up. "Really?" he asked. "I thought you liked him."

I shrugged – a minor betrayal that caused me actual physical pain. "I like the shoes you gave me too," I lied. "But I had no problem leaving them behind."

The grin that crossed his face could only be described as evil. "I like you, Shiloh. I always have. Now be a good girl and fetch my diamonds."

I straightened in a show of indifference. "I need time to consider my options."

That was a lie too. All I needed time for was to figure out how I was going to get Mitchell and myself out of the country in one piece.

Both men broke into chuckles. "You have until five o'clock tomorrow evening," said Melito. "After that, all bets are off."

***

Our living room looked like a bomb had hit it, and the bedroom was worse. The mattress had been slashed to ribbons, drawers had been upended on the floor, and amidst all the chaos lay Mitchell, zonked out on what was left of the shredded bed. I had no idea what he'd been drugged with. Demanding to know would've shown concern, which could've been costly.

Using the last of my strength, I rolled him onto his side, putting his body in the safest possible position to cope with his stupefied state. For now, there was nothing more I could do. I lay beside him and closed my eyes, concentrating on the sound of his breathing. The lonely wait for morning began, and hour by hour I began to let him go.

***

In a strange twist of fate, the one person I'd been most leery of was now the only person I trusted. It was barely daylight when I called Mimi, but she answered on the third ring.

"Hi Mimi." I rushed out the greeting. "Please, I need you to listen."

"I'm listening," she replied.

At best, the plan I'd concocted during the night was vague, but to her credit Mimi didn't question it. I gave her a short but specific shopping list and told her I'd come to her house to collect it. "In three hours, okay?"

"I can do that," she replied. "Three hours."

Just like that, I'd set the ball rolling.

"Be careful, Mimi," I warned.

"You too." Her voice was quiet but strong. "Dumb girl."

I ended the call not knowing how I'd make it through the day, but the resolve to try was high.

Mitchell hadn't moved all night. I was prepared to let him sleep for as long as I could, because when he woke his whole world would be different. I had no idea how I'd explain that his friendly neighbours were the kingpins of Kaimte's illegal diamond trade – and that was the easy part. Telling him that they were threatening to kill him would be infinitely more difficult.

If luck was on our side, we'd be on our way out of the country by the end of the day. Everything hinged on a clean getaway, which meant tying up as many loose ends as possible – starting with the phone that I kept hidden under the shack.

Like Mitchell, the Greeks were early risers. I was extra vigilant as I crept around the side of the shack, pausing every few steps to listen for any sign of movement next door. For once I was glad the walls were paper-thin. When I heard two different tempos of snoring, I relaxed a little.

I dropped to my knees, pushed the lattice aside and ducked under the house. I'd thought of a hundred ways to smash the phone to smithereens. I expected it to be almost cathartic – a mutinous act that would permanently cut all ties to Iron Mike.

The only way I was going to have control was if I stood my ground and took it. He'd ruled over me for weeks using threats and intimidation, but the days of keeping him in the loop via text messages and mandatory secret meetings were over. Time and time again he'd proven himself to be untrustworthy, and after Reyo's fateful email to the Greeks, I wasn't prepared to chance dealing with either of them again.

I snatched the phone off the cord, and for some unknown reason, switched it on. As soon as the screen lit up, I wished I'd stuck with my original plan. I didn't recognise the number that showed up as a missed call. Sending an enquiring text would've been the smartest move, but I hadn't felt overly bright in days. Instead, I called the number.

Federal Agent Dan Grace is an uppity hard-arse, but when I heard his voice on the other end of the line, it was the sweetest sound on earth.

Despite the fact the he'd uttered nothing beyond hello, I had the whole conversation worked out in my head. He'd tell me that the operation was over and give me instructions pertaining to safe passage out of the country.

Then he spoke again, and got the words all wrong.

"There's a plane heading to a small airport outside of Antwerp," he told me. "That's in Belgium."

"I know where Antwerp is." My voice was quiet out of necessity. If the enemy hadn't been snoring fifteen feet away from me, I might've given a slightly sassier reply.

"We know they're planning to deliver the diamonds to a jeweller at the other end. A meeting has been pre-arranged."

"Peachy," I muttered. "Obviously Tweedledee sang like a bird."

Dan's trademark dark chuckle filtered through the phone. "Yes," he confirmed. "We can barely shut him up."

Now that I had confirmation that the AFP had snatched Glen, every ounce of concern I held for him was gone. Glen Harris was a coward, a thief and a drunk. And I hoped they planned to throw the book at him.

"All's well that ends well, right?" Clearly my brain had stopped working. Nothing was well and nothing had ended.

"Not quite," he replied. "There's a problem."

"Don't tell me. You did something stupid – like jump the gun and confiscate the diamonds when you raided the house."

He didn't reply quickly enough.

"So to get you back in the game, your local contacts falsely informed the key players that I am holding the product. Am I right?"

After a long pause he spoke, but didn't answer my question. "I want you on that plane." His voice was quiet but unapologetic. "By any means necessary."

"If I show up at that airstrip empty-handed, we're dead." I pressed the phone hard to my ear and hissed out the words, trying to whisper and yell at the same time.

"There's no time to organise a replacement product," he informed me. "It would take days to make arrangements with the mine. You're going to have to figure it out on your own."

"And what about my friend?" I asked. "A direct threat was made to his life."

"*Friend?*" The sour edge to his tone infuriated me. "You were never supposed to make friends."

To everyone but me, Mitchell was nothing more than a pawn. He'd been beaten up, tricked, lied to and drugged – and he was still considered disposable.

"I'm not leaving him here to fend for himself." I dropped my head, growling into the phone. "He'll be dead by morning."

Dan managed to sound more inconvenienced that outraged. "I'll organise safe passage for your … colleague," he begrudgingly offered. "Meanwhile, you figure out how you're going to make that flight. As soon as you touch down in Antwerp, a boarding party will pull you clear of trouble."

I didn't have a choice. The only way I could guarantee that Mitchell would get out safely was by agreeing to this absurd plan. I took heart in the fact that it wasn't the first time I'd played the part of a patsy, and considering that I was still in one piece, I might possess just enough talent to pull it off again.

***

The sand under the house felt fifty degrees cooler than the open beach. When I lay down my whole body seemed to melt into it.

In moments of despair, our bodies have a way of shutting down to spare us pain. It wasn't the most opportune time to be making sand angels, but I dragged my arms through the cool sand as if I had nothing but time on my hands. At that moment, I felt nothing – not fear, not worry. It was as if my heart had come up with a way of solving all of our problems, but hadn't told me how.

An immeasurable amount of time passed before footsteps on the wooden floor above jolted me back to reality. Mitchell was awake, which meant I had no choice but to pull myself together and be on my game.

As I dragged my hands through the sand one last time, my left hand hooked something. I had no clue what it was until I raked through the powdery ground again, unearthing a red ribbon.

A few hard tugs were all it took before – like magic – a small calico bag surfaced. In an instant the biggest problem we had was solved. Inside the bag were hundreds of ugly, cloudy diamonds – more than enough to present to the Greeks and get Mitchell out of their line of fire – but even more spectacular than the treasure, was the accompanying handwritten note:

> *Dear Angels,*
>
> *Please protect the dumb boy who lives here, for he is the smartest man I know. Bless him with love and keep him safe.*
>
> *Love,*
> *Charli xx*

"Well, what do you know?" I whispered out loud. "He really does have a thousand angels watching over him."

Dilemma

MITCHELL

I hadn't been hung over for a long time, but it felt like I was doing it wrong. My mouth was dry and my head was foggy, stuffed with cotton wool. When I staggered into the living room, I wondered if I'd been eating the beans out of the beanbags. Judging by the scene in front of me it was entirely possible.

Something had attacked the room. What little furniture we had was upended and strewn everywhere, and I had no idea why. Try as I might, I couldn't remember a thing beyond dessert the night before.

Clearly, Shiloh's memory was as clear as a bell. When she walked through the door a few moments later, she didn't bat an eyelid at the carnage. "How are you feeling?" she asked.

I could barely look at her. I cradled my hazy brain as I paced the messy room. "Did I do this?"

"No," she replied. "You had nothing to do with it." She took a bottle of water from the fridge. "I'll tell you exactly what went on," she said, handing it to me, "but you have to listen with an open mind."

I promised to try. It was the best I could do, considering my brain was mincemeat.

"Vincent tore the house up," she said. "He was looking for a stash of diamonds that were stolen from the mine. They're thieves, Mitchell."

"You're out of your mind," I told her. "I've known them for years. They would never be involved in anything like that."

As I turned, Shiloh stepped in front of me, holding me in place with a firm hand to my chest. "*You're* out of your mind," she corrected. "And that's because your Greek besties drugged you so they could ransack our house without interruption."

It was quite possibly the most ridiculous statement she'd ever made, but I played along. "And why would they think their diamonds were here?"

She dropped her hand, a gesture that perfectly matched her crestfallen expression. "Because they think I have them."

I shook my already foggy head, trying to clear it of nonsense. "Let me get this straight. Melito and Vincent stole the diamonds from the mine, and then you stole them again?"

She was shaking her head before I even got the words out. "It's not that simple."

I leaned down so we were eye to eye. "I'll make it simple," I whispered. "Are you a thief, Shiloh?"

"No," she shakily replied. "But they are, and we're in a whole world of trouble because of it."

I straightened up and folded my arms. "Explain it to me."

My sisters are shameless drama queens, but not even they could've spun the tale she told. It was impossible to believe that my neighbours of seven years were the masterminds behind a million dollar diamond racket, and when she claimed they'd threatened to kill me it was impossible to stay in the room. With an appalled groan, I nudged past her and headed for the bedroom. She followed.

"Stop!" I warned before she spoke again. "I don't want to hear another word."

Hoping to find a shirt, I kicked through the mess on the floor. Shiloh scooped one up and threw it at me. "We have to leave, Mitchell," she said. "If you're not off the grid by five o'clock, they're going to kill you."

As I locked eyes with her, every single day that we'd spent together played through my mind. "What's gotten into you?" I mumbled. I barely recognised the girl in front of me. At some point in the last eight hours, my bright, sweet, level-headed girl had lost her mind.

"Please, Mitchell," she begged. "You have to believe me."

I didn't believe her, and I was angry that she'd gone off on such a farfetched, crazy tangent. I dropped my shirt on the bed. "You're wrecking us," I warned. "Stop it."

She shook her head. "No," she whispered. "I'm trying to save us."

We were getting nowhere fast. "We're done here," I said, heading for the door.

"Where are you going?"

"To roll around in the ocean for a while," I replied, throwing my arms wide. "Far, far away from the crazy."

***

Adding to my pissy mood, the waves that morning were rubbish. It was hardly worth paddling out there but I had a point to make. I had never dealt well with drama, especially drama of this magnitude. For a few short minutes I considered paddling to South America just to be sure I'd escaped it.

Making sure I thrashed every muscle in my body, I lay flat on my board, dragging my arms through the water until they ached. When a cooler head prevailed, I headed back to shore.

I wasn't surprised to see Melito and Vincent sunning themselves on their deck when I arrived home. It was routine and normal, and made Shiloh's crazy accusations seem even more off kilter.

"How are you feeling this morning, Adonis?" asked Melito, waving me over.

"A little rough," I sheepishly replied, slowly wandering toward them. "It was a great night though." At least, I think it was.

Melito threw back his head and laughed. "It's always a wonderful evening when the company is good."

I leaned my board against the railing and stepped onto the deck. "It is," I agreed. "It's nice to have you home."

Vincent stood up and made a rush for the front door. "Don't go anywhere," he ordered. "I have a plate of leftovers for you."

I smiled. This was the Greeks at their best. It was ludicrous to think they were anything other than eccentric, generous souls who relished a quiet life on the beach as much as I did.

With Vincent gone, Melito turned to me. "Did Shiloh enjoy her evening?" he asked. "I haven't seen her today."

Hopefully, the smile I gave looked genuine. "She's a little bit fragile this morning," I said diplomatically.

He nodded sympathetically, but it was Vincent who replied. He handed me a huge platter of pastries. "She's going to need a little bit of extra love and attention this morning," he suggested.

I usually baulked at their misguided relationship advice but I made an exception. Wondering if they might be able to shed some light on her crazy mood, I asked why.

The look Melito flashed me was like nothing I'd ever seen from him before. It was a sinister smirk that cut right through my body. "Because she's trying to decide which is more valuable," he replied. "The three hundred diamonds she stole from us or the life of her oblivious boyfriend."

He said it so casually that I wondered if I'd misheard him.

Then Vincent chimed in. "Poor thing." He chuckled. "I can understand her dilemma. The diamonds are worth a lot of money." He scrunched up his nose as if he smelled something bad and looked me up and down. "You, not so much."

The shift was dizzying, and no amount of thinking time would've helped me make sense of it. Without a word, I dumped the tray of pastries on a deckchair and jumped off the deck. I was almost home when Melito called out to me. "Remind Shiloh that time is of the essence, Mitchell. If she doesn't make her decision by five, we'll decide for her."

Vincent pointed his hand at me, pointing his fingers like a gun. And then, in a blow that I felt, he pulled the invisible trigger.

Juju

SHILOH

The front door slammed so hard that the whole shack shook. A short moment later, Mitchell appeared in the doorway of the bedroom looking nothing short of terrified.

"Pack a bag." The tremble in his voice was one of pure fear. "I don't know what the hell you've gotten us into, but we need to get out of here."

I was way ahead of him. I pointed at the duffle bags on the floor. "I've already done it," I replied. "All you need is your passport."

I was prepared to abandon everything without a second thought, but it would've been remiss of me to expect the same of him. Mitchell stood in the small front room looking lost, which made me wonder if he truly grasped what we were about to do.

"You're not coming back here," I said gently. "You know that, right?"

His eyes darted in every direction but mine. "I don't know anything, Shiloh." When I reached for his hand, he shrugged me away. "What do you know?"

"I'll tell you everything," I promised. "But now's not the time."

"Tell me one thing," he muttered. "Are you a thief?"

"I swear to you, I don't have their diamonds."

The corner of his mouth lifted to form a humourless smile. "You'd never lie to me, right?"

There was no possible way to answer his question without making him hate me, so I ignored it. "We have to go." I thrust his bag against his chest. "I don't know if we're going to get out of this mess, but we have to try."

***

It wasn't the first time I'd switched off all emotion in order to get a job done, but it was a detachment the Mitchell couldn't understand. Apart from asking me where we were going, he didn't say a word on the short journey to Mimi's place, but she was exempt from the silent treatment.

When she met us at the front door and asked if he was alright, he answered. "I'm fine, Mimi," he mumbled, glancing back at me. "All things considered."

Mimi pulled him through the door and turned her attention to me. "Come," she said. "I have something to show you."

"I have something for you too," I replied, following her into the house.

The inside of Mimi's home looked exactly as I thought it would. Brightly coloured cushions were scattered on the floor, heavy woven fabrics covered the windows and posies of bay leaves hung above the doorways. It was basic and homely, and being there felt ten times safer than the shack.

Mitchell seemed to be breathing a little easier too. He sat down on a cushion in the small front room, and when a little boy poked his head around the door, he called him over. "Ronaldo, my man. How are you, mate?"

With a cute bright grin, he ran over and piled onto Mitchell's lap, eager to show off his toy truck.

With Mitchell distracted, I pulled Mimi aside. "I have something to show you." I pulled the calico bag out of my pocket. "I found these under the shack," I murmured. "Charli hid them there before she left."

Mimi snatched the bag. "Trick rocks," she announced. "I told you angels watched over him." She glanced back at Mitchell. "He will be safe now."

I didn't share her optimism, but wasn't game to say so out loud. "Trick rocks, Mimi?" I pointed to the bag. "Please tell me that's a pet name for high grade diamonds. I need them to be real."

She frowned. "No, dumb girl. They're just rocks. The angels fill them with good juju to make them look like diamonds," she explained. "They trick the devil into thinking they're real."

From what I could tell, the angels had made a bloody good show of it. They looked completely authentic, but I wasn't sure that the Greeks would be fooled. "I need to trick two vicious devils," I whispered. "If I can't, Mitchell is going to get hurt."

"The devil's eyes are blinded by greed." Mimi rattled the bag. "These will save my dumb boy." She spoke with absolute certainty. "And now you need to find a way to repay the angels for their good deed. Pass on the good juju."

I shook my head. "I don't have time to deal with angels, Mimi," I replied. "One job at a time, okay?"

Her harsh frown hinted that a nasty lecture was on its way, but she managed to hold back and change the subject. "I got the thing you wanted," she said before throwing her head back and calling out to someone in Afrikaans.

A man came rushing in from the back room. I recognised him instantly. It was the meet-and-greet man from the mine.

"This is Baako," said Mimi. "My cousin."

He vigorously shook my hand. "Whatever you need, Mrs Shiloh," he said. "I will get it for you."

It was the same line he'd greeted me with on the first day I met him – only now, I appreciated it a whole lot more.

"Do you have something for me now?"

Nodding at a rate of knots, he reached into the waistband of his pants and pulled out a gun. "It's a nine millimetre Glock," he announced, haphazardly waving it around.

Keeping a firm grip on Ronaldo, Mitchell jumped to his feet. "Jesus Christ," he snapped. "Are you out of your minds?"

I couldn't blame him for wondering. Baako had no clue what he was doing. I quickly snatched the gun, ejected the clip and hid the magazine in my pocket.

"Do you know how to make it work?" asked Baako, pointing at it. "Pull on the trigger underneath."

Mimi slapped the back of his head. "Stupid boy," she chided.

I racked the slide back and forth, expelling the bullet from the chamber. When it popped out and fell to the floor, Baako scrambled to pick it up.

I tucked the gun into my waistband. "It's empty," I assured Mitchell. "Perfectly safe."

He shook his head at me, appalled. "Who are you?" The bitter question raged out of him.

Before I could speak, Mimi piped up. "She's Good Witch Batman, dumb boy."

Her answer made me cringe, but Mitchell didn't react. He just stared straight at me. And at that moment, I knew I'd probably lost him for good.

***

Mimi's house should've been the end of the line for Mitchell. Her home was safe and isolated. All he had to do was wait for Agent Grace to sort out travel arrangements and get him out of Kaimte. But the best laid plans of mice and men often go awry.

"I'm not staying here," he grumbled. "Wherever you go, I go."

"This is nothing to do with you, Mitchell," I reminded him. "You'll be safe here."

He dangled his keys in front of me. "If you want to leave, I'm driving."

For the briefest of moments, I considered pulling the gun on him, but then considered the reason behind the stubborn stand he was taking. Mitchell was feeling angry, confused and betrayed, but despite all of that, he cared about me – possibly more than I deserved.

"Fine," I yielded, slapping my hands on my sides. "Let's go."

He didn't ask where we were going, for which I was grateful. Easing into the news that I was heading to see Louis Osei would've been impossible, but Mitchell knew Kaimte back to front. As soon as we pulled into the deserted market square, he figured it out.

"Louis is in your posse now?" He sounded disgusted. "You're some piece of work, Shiloh."

Mitchell couldn't speak to me without snapping, which was soul destroying, even though I understood it.

"No," I replied. "I loathe him as much as you do."

He huffed out a sombre laugh. "Could've fooled me."

And therein lies the rub. I *had* fooled him – a million times over. I was not the woman he thought I was. He didn't misjudge me or make a mistake. I'd systematically deceived him day after day for weeks – and I still wasn't able to tell him why.

"Melito and Vincent hired Louis to build an airstrip," I explained as the car rolled to a stop. "That's where I'm supposed to meet them with the diamonds. The problem is, I don't know where it is. I'm hoping Louis will tell me."

It was the most information I'd given him in hours. Mitchell stared through the dirty windscreen, probably trying to process it.

"Why are you doing this?" he finally asked. "There's no need to deliver anything to them – and don't say it's for my benefit. They can't make good on their threat if they can't find me," he reasoned. "All we have to do is leave."

If I were the petty crook that he thought I was, getting out of Dodge would've been the perfect solution. But I had a job to do, and keeping up my end of the bargain with Dan meant that I had no choice but to see it through to the end.

"I promise you." I glanced across at him. "Everything will make sense soon."

His head lolled back. "You keep saying that," he muttered. "Don't promise me anything."

I reached for the door handle. "Are you coming in?"

There was no way I was going to leave him alone in the car, but it seemed polite to ask. He wasn't coping well with being told what to do, and I'd done nothing but make demands since he woke up.

"No," he replied. "Louis is your mate, not mine."

I glanced in every direction, scoping out our surroundings. On market days, it was the most crowded place in town. Today, I hardly recognised it as the same place. With the exception of Louis' Range Rover parked next to us it looked deserted.

"I'm not going to argue with you." I took the gun from my waistband. "Have it your way."

Mitchell leaned to the side, horror-struck. "What are you going to do, lady?" he asked. "Shoot me?"

"No, stupid." I took the clip out of my pocket and jammed it into the gun. "There are seventeen rounds in this gun." I held it to the side and racked the slide. "And now it's loaded."

I tried handing it to him but he refused to take it. "Peace loving beach bum, remember?" He patted his chest. "Total pacifist. I wouldn't know what to do with that thing."

"Well, if someone approaches the car and tries to kill you – let's say, an angry Greek bloke – shoot him."

Still, he refused to take it.

I set it down on the dashboard, reminded him that it was loaded and got out of the car.

"Shiloh," he called.

My heart flipped purely because his tone was gentle. "Yeah?"

"Be careful, okay?"

I gave a tiny smile. "You too."

***

Thankfully, Louis was alone in the shop, sitting with his feet up on the counter while he watched TV. As soon as he saw me, he switched it off. "My beautiful friend," he drawled, throwing his arms wide. "What brings you here today?"

I didn't feel the need to butter him up with small talk so I got straight down to business. The more I talked, the wider his eyes grew, and when I got to the part about needing directions to the airstrip, he nearly exploded.

"I told you not to get involved with the bad men!" He rushed to my side of the counter. "If you go to them, they'll kill you."

"It's not me I'm worried about at this point."

Louis took a step back. "Mitchell?" he asked. "The devil is on *your* back and your concern is for him?"

"Yes," I replied simply.

"Mitchell is as good as dead." His callous words sliced right through me. "You need to get as far away from him as you can."

"Please Louis," I begged. "Just tell me where the airstrip is."

He paced around the cluttered shop, perhaps considering his options. Louis Osei was not renowned for being a generous soul. He gave with one hand while taking with the other, but at least he was upfront about it.

He turned back to me. "What will you give me in return?"

I didn't even need to think about it. "Information."

"I already know plenty, beautiful friend."

I cocked one eyebrow. "You don't know what I know."

It was more intrigue than Louis could handle. He grabbed a pen and some paper off the counter and quickly drew me a map. His demand for information came before he'd even put his pen down.

I snatched the map from his grasp. "There's a GPS fitted to your vehicle," I revealed. "It's hardwired into the wiring of the steering column."

I couldn't work out if the expression on his face was one of betrayal or fury, but when he grabbed a screwdriver from under the counter and marched to the door, I decided it was the latter.

By the time I got outside he'd already begun ripping the car apart. Shards of black plastic littered the ground, and he was still knocking the stuffing out of it with hard jabs of the screwdriver.

If anyone should've enjoyed seeing Louis' prized Range Rover take a thrashing it was Mitchell, but when I looked over at the jeep, he looked as horrified as I was.

"What does the GPS look like?" yelled Louis.

I pointed at the small black box hanging off the now exposed wiring. Louis shoved me aside, leaned into the car and ripped it out.

I had no idea what he was screaming in Afrikaans as he stomped it into the ground, but it didn't sound friendly. "When I find out who did this, he is a dead man!"

"Calm down," I urged. "You're going to blow a gasket."

And if that were to happen, he'd be in the same state as his hundred thousand dollar vehicle.

Louis shrugged and straightened his collar. "You should come back inside."

His voice was calm, but I was still wary. "Why?"

He pointed at the paper in my hand. "So I can draw you an accurate map. That one is a map to my uncle's chicken farm."

Fighting the urge to slap the back of his head, I followed him into the shop. While he redrew the map, I peered through the glass cabinet, checking out the wares. Most of it was junk – paste stones and enamel jewellery, but one piece caught my eye. The black opal pendant was most definitely not junk.

"Do you believe in angels, Louis?" I asked, leaning across the counter.

"Yes."

"And juju?"

He handed me the amended map. "Of course," he replied. "Good juju keeps the angels happy."

"Do you want to score some really good juju points?"

He narrowed his eyes. "How?"

I tapped the glass countertop, pointing at the pendant. "Let me return this to its rightful owner."

"I am the rightful owner."

"Oh, come now, Louis," I crowed. "We both know that's not true. Mitchell paid you fair and square for that necklace years ago."

He glowered. "Prove it."

I turned and headed for the door. "I don't need to prove it," I called over my shoulder. "The angels know the truth. You need to change your ways, Louis Osei – before it's too late."

I had one foot out the door when he called me back. I turned around just in time to catch the pendant as he threw it. "Good luck getting the devil off your back, my beautiful Shiloh."

I slipped it into my pocket and smiled at him. "Same to you, Louis."

Plan

MITCHELL

I lifted the gun off the dashboard twice while Shiloh was gone – and my hand shook both times. The only gun I could ever remember seeing was the ear-piercing gun that my sisters used to use to punch holes in themselves, and I don't think that counted.

Shiloh was obviously well versed in weaponry, and like many other things that had come to light that day it bothered me.

I felt duped on every level. The life I'd built was slipping away with every passing second. I'd had to abandon my house and business, my friends were homicidal diamond thieves and my girlfriend was as shady as heck.

There was nothing naïve or timid about Shiloh Jenson. She was as street-smart and hard as any other gangster in Kaimte, which probably meant she'd been working to an agenda all along. The problem was, I hadn't figured out what it was and she wasn't talking.

When she finally got back into the car, she grabbed the gun and secured it in the glove box. "Louis drew me a map." She spread a piece of paper across her lap. "It's not far from here."

"So what's your plan?" I asked. "I'm assuming you have one."

"Yes." She breathed out the word. "The plan is to stay alive."

***

As far as I knew, Melito and Vincent had never been overly particular when it came to choosing their modes of travel. I expected to drive up on a beaten up old Cessna parked on a gravel track, but the reality was much different. Parked at the end of a short but perfectly serviceable runway was a shiny white leer jet.

"The business of stolen diamonds must be extremely lucrative," I noted, slowing the car to a snail's pace.

"Yeah," mumbled Shiloh. "Stop here."

We were a good few hundred metres from the plane, but there was no hiding. With the exception of the rocky outcrop miles to the west, it was flat terrain for as far as the eye could see.

Once I turned the car off, the droning of the plane's engine was clear. "They're leaving soon, I guess," I suggested.

Shiloh looked at her watch for much too long. "We have until five."

I twisted in my seat, angling my body toward her. "Then what happens?"

She swallowed hard. "I have a confession to make, Mitchell."

Finally, I didn't reply.

"I do have a plan to get you out of this," she began. "But you're not going to like it."

"I haven't enjoyed a single minute of this day, lady. What's your plan?"

She grabbed her bag off the back seat. "I'm going to shoot you."

I literally felt the colour drain from my face. "Sucky plan, Shiloh."

"They're going to kill you whether they get their diamonds back or not," she said matter-of-factly. "You know too much. They can't come back and continue their operation when the bloke next door is on to them. Do you understand?"

"I don't quite understand the part where you kill me," I sarcastically replied.

She stopped rummaging through the bag and gave me her full attention. "You have to listen harder," she urged. "I never said I was going to kill you. I said I was going to shoot you."

She spent the next few minutes laying out her plan – slowly as if I was somehow impaired. The idea was to let the Greeks think I was dead. "When

I get to the plane, I'm going to turn around and shoot at you," she explained. "As soon as I do, I want you to drop to the ground and stay there until the plane leaves."

"You're really going to shoot me?"

Shiloh took my face in her hands. It wasn't a romantic gesture. She was trying to calm me down. "I'm not going to hit you," she said quietly. "I'll shoot to the left of you, but it's only going to work if you hit the deck."

"Are you a good shot?"

She smiled. "I'm a great shot."

I tried to nod but she held me firm. "What's going to happen to you?" I asked.

Worry flashed in her eyes, but she recovered quickly. "I'm going to get on the plane."

I pulled her hands away. "Just tell me," I demanded. "Are you working with them?"

"No." Her voice was barely there. "I swear I'm not."

I was impossible to make sense of the stupid decisions she was making, but when the Jeep's interior clock caught my eye, I realised it didn't matter. It was five minutes to five, and if those were the last five minutes I'd ever have with her it was foolish to spend them trying to get a confession.

I grabbed her hand. "Whatever happens, I hope you never forget me, lady."

"I hope you never regret me." Her voice shook, and for a moment, she was the same gentle girl that I'd spent weeks falling in love with.

I leaned across and lightly kissed her lips, holding her for as long as I could before she pulled away.

"I have something for you." She reached into the bag and pulled out a chunky old mobile phone. "When it's safe to leave, go straight back to Mimi's and stay there. A man called Dan is going to call you on this phone." She forced it into my hand. "He's your ticket home."

I would've asked questions but she threw open the car door. "I have to go."

Real panic finally hit me. Crooked or not, Shiloh had no idea what she was about to walk into. She could've concocted a hundred plans, but none of them would've been better than the one that flashed through my head when I realised I was about to lose her for good.

I jumped out of the car and rushed to her. "Wait," I said, grabbing her around the waist. "Let's just go. We'll go right now."

She shrugged me away. "I have to do this, Mitchell. Just stick to the plan."

When I made another grab for her, she pulled the same move she'd used to drop me on my arse at the beach. I hit the dirt, and in a cruel final blow, the three strings of bin bin beads that I'd accidentally snapped off her waist scattered on the ground beside me.

Greedy Souls

SHILOH

It took every ounce of will I had not to turn back. As I got nearer to the plane, the door opened and Melito strutted down the steps. Even from a distance I could see his evil smirk.

"I see your boyfriend accompanied you," he yelled, fighting to be heard over the engine. "I was rather hoping you would've brought my diamonds instead."

I glanced back at Mitchell. "I thought I'd bring both," I announced. "And then decide which one I want to keep."

Melito threw his head back and roared with laughter. "You've no idea how much I wish you weren't such a greedy soul," he said. "We could've been exceptional business partners."

With just a few metres of distance between us, I stopped. "We still can be," I offered. I took the calico bag out of my pocket and tossed it at him. "There's always room for negotiation."

Melito peered into the bag, and when he called Vincent out of the plane to look, my heart stopped beating. Both men had guns strapped to their sides, and if they caught on that I'd given them nothing more than a bag of white quartz, I was dead.

Vincent finally lifted his head to grin at me – an ugly simper than made my skin crawl. "Beautiful, aren't they, darling?"

I finally released the breath I'd been holding, and felt a little lightheaded because of it. "If you count them, you'll notice that there are three hundred and ninety four gems in there," I stated. "Far more than I took."

Melito handed the bag to Vincent. "A bonus?" he asked.

I shrugged. "I was thinking more of a buy-in fee," I replied. "We could sit down and hatch out a business plan – perhaps during the long flight."

Melito grinned. "The problem I have, dear Shiloh, is that you're not entirely trustworthy."

"I'm loyal." I somehow made the declaration without choking. "You can trust me."

"We'd need a good will gesture of some sort," said Vincent.

"Sixty-four extra diamonds was supposed to be a gesture of goodwill."

"Something more, darling," goaded Melito.

Without saying another word, I turned to face Mitchell who was standing behind the jeep. In a move that the Greeks would never have predicted, I pulled the gun and slyly aimed it at to the left of him.

Not a single force on earth could've stopped the trembling of my hand as I pulled the trigger. A single shot rang out and Mitchell fell to the ground.

Even over the sound of the plane engine, I heard one of the vile men behind me gasp.

"Bravo, Shiloh," praised Vincent.

I turned back to face them. "Loyal enough for you?"

Melito stepped aside and outstretched his hand. "Welcome aboard, darling."

Mistake

MITCHELL

Somewhere along the line, my quiet life on the beach had morphed into a story straight off the pages of a spy novel.

Just a few hours after peeling myself off the hot desert floor, I was picked up at Mimi's house by a bloke called Reyo. I assumed he was one of Shiloh's gangster mates, but didn't care enough to ask.

"Dan sent me," he vaguely explained.

Getting into cars with strangers has never rated highly on my list of things to do, but I was downtrodden and off my game. Reyo wasn't the chattiest bloke I'd ever met, but nothing about him seemed threatening. The one time he did speak was to tell me that I looked unwell. "You should drink Kaimte tea," he said, glancing across at me. "The sweeter the better."

"Thanks," I muttered. "But I'm not a fan of sweet things."

"Not even sweet women?" he asked.

"I wouldn't know," I replied. "I don't know any."

***

The plane that had been sent to pick me up looked nothing like the Greek's fancy leer jet. The little twin-engine prop plane looked barely capable of taking off, but I climbed aboard as if I had no choice, and perhaps I didn't.

Reyo handed me some papers. "These are your connecting tickets," he explained. "All the way through to Hobart."

"Where is this plane going?" I asked as he clambered through the open door.

"Johannesburg." He turned back and grinned. "Safe travels, my friend."

He then forced the door shut, effectively closing the book on my Kaimte life. I had mixed feelings about the finality of it. Through no fault of my own I'd somehow lost the lot.

***

The person who arranged my flights back to Australia must've been a sadist. Thanks to three unnecessary layovers, it took me four days to get there. By the time I arrived in Melbourne, I'd all but lost the will to live.

The queue at customs was brutally long, and even after lining up for half an hour, I still didn't get through. As the customs officer scanned my passport, a burly AFP officer appeared at my side and demanded that I follow him.

I didn't ask where we were going as he led me out of the crowd. I was travelling from Africa. For that reason alone, I'd probably been flagged for interrogation.

I was shown through to a small windowless office. Without being asked, I sat down at the empty desk. "If you want to search my luggage, you'll have to find it first," I told him. "I haven't collected it yet."

"I'll find it for you," he offered, one hand on the door handle. "Just wait here. Someone will be in shortly."

As soon as the door shut, I put my elbows on the desk and rested my head. I was probably close to sleep when it opened again, but pepping myself up took no effort at all.

Shiloh was standing there, looking nothing like the girl I'd let go of just days earlier. She'd always been straight-laced and neat, but now she looked even more rigid. Her long hair was pulled back into a tight ponytail, and the black skirt suit she wore was prim and formal. She looked like a schoolteacher or a librarian…. or a police officer.

The light bulb in my head went off with a bang.

"You're a cop," I choked out the words as if they were hard to pronounce.

295

Shiloh closed the door. "I wanted to tell you a hundred times."

"Just once would've been enough."

Looking totally dejected, she pulled out a chair and sat down. "I couldn't tell you, Mitchell."

"You could explain it to me now, Shiloh." I spread my arms. "The floor is yours."

"I still can't tell you much," she quietly replied. "The investigation is ongoing, but the Greeks were taken into custody as soon as the plane landed in Belgium. Glen is locked up too so they're all out of action."

"Congratulations," I replied, cocking my head to the side. "A job well done."

There was no mistaking the hurt in her eyes, or the wretched feeling that came with knowing that I was the cause. Being angry and sarcastic wasn't the fairest approach, but I couldn't change how I felt.

"You lied to me, Shiloh," I told her, drumming my finger on the desk. "Every single day."

"Never about the important stuff."

"How do I know that?" I snapped out the bitter question. "For all I know, you could've been using me from the start to get close to the Greeks."

Moving in next door to Melito and Vincent would've been a great way to scope them out on a daily basis. That made me the perfect mark. Just thinking about it made me feel stupid.

"You give me too much credit, Mitchell. I'm not the ace federal agent you think I am." She sounded totally beaten down and defeated. Wickedly, I felt relieved that the damage was mutual. "I am a small town police constable," she said, staring straight at me. "I had no idea what I was doing in Kaimte, and I had no clue who the bad guys were until they revealed themselves."

The desk between us might as well have been a brick wall. She felt miles away from me, and I wasn't hopeful of closing the distance. I was furious and hurt and she was defensive and hurt. There was no room in that mix for reason and understanding.

"What are we even doing here?" My eyes darted around the small room. "What were you hoping for, Shiloh?"

She kept her eyes low. "I just wanted a chance to make things right."

The tough conversation was halted by a knock at the door. To me, it felt like a reprieve.

Shiloh cleared her throat, pulling herself together. "Come in," she called.

The same bloke who'd picked me out of the custom's line poked his head around the door. "Your luggage is here when you're ready," he said.

I nodded. "Thanks."

He turned his attention to Shiloh. "Will there be anything else, Agent Brannan?"

Fatigue was getting the better of me. For a moment, I wondered who he was talking to. Then my brain snapped into gear leaving me to wonder who *I* was talking to.

"No," she replied. "Thank you."

With a nod of his head, he pulled the door closed and disappeared. The tension that filled the room had now become palpable.

"Brannan?" I spat out the word. "That's your name?"

"Yes," she whispered. "Shiloh Brannan."

There weren't words to describe the frustration I felt. I pushed my chair back. "We're done here."

"Mitchell, wait." In total contrast to anything I'd shown her, her brown eyes were soft and so was her voice. "Just so you know, I never lied about how I felt. I treasure every moment I spent with you."

"We have a problem then." I reached for my phone, swiped the screen and set it down on the desk. Shiloh looked down, studying the picture of herself that I'd taken just a few days earlier.

"Because I'm in love with this girl." I pointed at the screen. "I don't even know who you are."

My hand was on the doorhandle by the time she spoke again. "I'm sorry," she said gently. "Truly."

I turned back to face her for the very last time. "Don't be sorry, lady," I replied, shaking my head. "It was my mistake, not yours."

***

My plan of having my mother collect me from the airport in Hobart quickly fell by the wayside. When I called her from Melbourne, she and my father were in Singapore, two weeks into a three-month cruise.

"We had no idea you were coming home," she wailed. "We've been planning this trip for months in celebration of your father's retirement."

I was so far out of the loop that I didn't even know Dad had retired.

"Don't worry about it," I replied. "The girls can pick me up."

"Will we see you when we get home, Mitchell?" Her voice was packed with hope, and setting her mind at ease felt good.

"I'll be here, Mum," I promised. "I'm here to stay."

That ended the call on a high, but I still had to deal with my sisters. Lily is the calmer of the two so I opted to call her. The problem was, they were always together, which meant Jasmine was within earshot when she answered.

The news that I was an hour's flight from home incited shrill screams that nearly made me drop my phone – and that wasn't the worst that I had to deal with.

When I finally walked through the arrival gate, I was met by both sisters, a bunch of unruly kids, and a bloke holding a 'welcome home Mitchy' sign and a bunch of balloons.

Jasmine started crying and fanning her face. "Oh my God," she screamed, throwing her arms around me. "You're finally home."

She hadn't changed one bit. Her blonde hair was still dodgy – so dodgy that half of it looked glued on. Maybe her kids had styled it. The little girl bouncing around with a toy bucket wedged on her head didn't look like the sharpest tool in the shed, but her brother looked shifty enough to handle a glue stick.

Rounding off the trio was baby Lachlan, a stocky little bloke who was the spitting image of his father, minus the balloons.

"I can't believe you're finally home," beamed Wade, pulling me into a crushing hug. It was the most bizarre gesture I'd ever seen a grown man make, especially considering we were meeting for the first time.

"This is Wade," announced Jasmine, pulling him off me. "My husband."

"And your brother-in-law," added Wade with a wink.

Desperate for an escape, I turned my attention to Lily. "How are you, Lil?"

She playfully punched my upper arm. "You look really tired."

"It's been a long few days." I smiled at her. "You look good, though."

I meant it. Unlike Jasmine, she'd managed to tone herself down over the years. Her hair was darker and no part of her sparkled.

She hugged me tightly. "I'm glad you're home," she whispered. "It's been lonely here without you."

***

The car ride from Hobart to Pipers Cove was reminiscent of the bus journey from Kaimte to Cape Town. The only thing missing was the caged chickens.

Jasmine and Wade drove a minivan, and if that wasn't horrific enough, I was forced to sit between the twins on the very back seat.

"You can get to know Linc and Cheynie a little better," suggested Wade, eyeing me through the rear vision mirror. "But watch out for Cheynie. She gets carsick."

I quickly snatched the toy bucket from Lincoln and returned it to his sister. "Chunder in the bucket," I instructed, pointing at it.

Lincoln let out the shiftiest laugh I'd ever heard a little kid make. "It's not her mouth that gets sick," he informed me.

Mercifully, the kid held it together and after a while, not even the noise bothered me. I concentrated only on the scenic view that whizzed by much too fast.

The April weather was much colder than anything I was used to lately, but the white-capped ocean and sweeping cliffs reminded me that above all else, I was home and I was safe.

Despite the relief that brought, there was a tinge of sadness wedged in my chest that I just couldn't shift. Coming home was meant to be a new beginning, but the girl I was supposed to be sharing it with was long gone.

Beyond Repair

SHILOH

I felt as if I'd been away for a hundred years. In truth, I'd been gone for little more than two months. Not surprisingly, the town of Lawler seemed to have coped without me.

With the exception of the Easter decorations adorning the shop windows on the high street, nothing had changed. I even spotted Gladys in the playground as I drove past, sipping from a bottle concealed in a brown paper bag. I considered waving as I passed but didn't want to startle her. The last thing I felt like doing that day was untangling her from the play equipment.

The only stop I made on the way home was at the Sergeant's cottage. Allan was nowhere to be seen, but Lynette was hotfooting it around the garden, most likely chasing something fluffy or furry. She was so preoccupied that she didn't even see me pull up.

As I wandered up the path to the house, she struck. "Gotcha!" she yelled, scooping a white rabbit off the ground. "Thought you could outrun me, did you?" Predictably, the rabbit didn't answer, but I swear I saw it smile. "Touch my broccoli again and I'll bloody have you," she warned, lowering him to the ground.

Finally she spotted me. "Shiloh Brannan," she crooned in her lovely Irish brogue. "You're a sight for sore eyes."

"Did you miss me?"

She shrugged. "We made do."

When I grinned at her, she rushed over and threw her arms around me. "Of course we bloody missed you." She grabbed my hands and took a step back, holding my arms out while she surveyed for damage.

"I'm good, Netty," I assured her.

"Well, you look to be in one piece."

If she'd had the power to see beyond my eyes, she would've noticed that I was busted beyond repair, but that was a revelation for another day.

"Come inside," she said, hooking her arm through mine. "You can tell me all about it."

My whole body seized at the prospect, a reaction that Lynette picked up on immediately. "Or you can tell me nothing," she amended, giving my arm a squeeze. "And that would be fine by me."

Hospitality

MITCHELL

Jasmine and Wade lived right in the centre of town. In keeping with the rest of the street, the modest brick home was neat and tidy. The well kept lawn was obviously Wade's pride and joy. He explained his weekly fertilising routine to me three times before we reached the front door.

"It's all about contingency," he said, confusing the hell out of me. "You have to be contingent."

The man was so stupid that I couldn't even listen to him without squinting. I glanced back at Lily who was trailing behind with Lachlan in her arms. She rolled her eyes. "I think you mean consistent, Wade," she corrected.

"Pretty sure that's what I said, Lil," he replied, bobbing his head from side to side.

I had to make other sleeping arrangements. There was no way I was going to survive more than a night of Davis hospitality, and when I walked into their house, I realised even one night might be pushing it.

My eyes darted in every direction, trying desperately hard to take it all in. The walls were a vile shade of lime green that made me queasy.

"Home sweet home," quipped Jasmine, doing her best *Sound Of Music* twirl. "What do you think?"

"It's…. bright." If I'd had an hour to think about it, that's still the kindest reply I could've come up with.

"Calming, right?" asked the muscly fool standing next to her. "Like a nature scene straight out of Africa." He pointed at the leopard print cushions on the couch. "You should feel right at home."

"It's like I never left."

Jasmine grabbed my hand. "I'll show you your room."

The excitement in her voice made me feel like a jerk. She was trying so hard to make me feel welcome, and all I could think of doing was getting the hell out of there. For that reason alone, I did my best to ooh and ahh in all the right places as she threw open the door of the guestroom and gave me the grand tour.

"I want you to stay as long as you like."

I wasn't sure how long I could stay in a room with red floral wallpaper.

"Thanks," I replied. "I'll be happy in here."

Whether it made sense or not, Jasmine had a knack of seeing through me. It was a twin thing that I'd been trying to shake since birth. She slumped down on the edge of the bed and heaved out a long sigh. "I don't think you're happy at all," she accused. "I could tell there was something wrong as soon as I saw you."

I sat beside her. "I'm just tired."

"It's more than that." She shook her head. "You don't have to tell me."

Even if I had been willing to confide in her, I had no idea how to explain the events of the past few months. I'd seen and done things that would never be believed. Even I had trouble wrapping my head around it – and I was there at the time.

"All you need to know is that I'm home and I'm here to stay," I told her. "I'm going to get to know my niece and nephews and hang out with my sisters."

She glanced across at me and smiled. "I know we're not close, Mitchy." I didn't even cringe when she shortened my name. "But you've got plenty of friends here. You should probably know that Charli's back in town."

I got the impression that she didn't necessarily want to share that information, but I was thrilled that she had. A bit of Charli Blake counsel was exactly what I needed to drag me out of the doldrums.

"You two are friends now?"

As far as I was aware, hell hadn't frozen over.

Jasmine shrugged. "Occasionally - when Adam holds her back."

My laugh was cut short when Lincoln stormed the room. "Mummy," he called desperately. "Cheynie was carsick in the garden."

Jasmine let out a despondent sigh. "I'll be there in a minute, baby."

"Do you need a hand hosing her down or something?"

"Why?" she asked. "Are you offering?"

"Hell no." I threw both hands up. "I'm her uncle not a zookeeper."

Distraction

SHILOH

Every minute that I spent thinking about Mitchell caused me intolerable pain. The only cure I could think of was to keep busy and throw myself back into my job.

Allan tried to talk me into taking a few extra days off, but didn't push for a reason when I declined. "You do what you need to do," he told me. "Besides, it'll be nice to have someone around to make me coffee." He wiggled his eyebrows at me. "Netty gets really annoyed when I call her over from next door to do it."

It felt good to laugh, which meant the best place to be was wherever Allan Kelly was. "It's good to be home," I said randomly.

He winked at me. "It's good to have you back."

Despite his penchant for kidding around, when I bared my soul and told him the whole story, Sergeant Kelly didn't downplay the ordeal I'd endured in Kaimte.

"Don't let it change who you are." He put his hand to his heart. "The only things with the power to change us are whiskey and lovers," he said, sounding more Irish than usual. "And even then they need to be bloody good to do it."

"Stellar advice as always, Sergeant." I could barely speak for laughing. "I'll keep it in mind."

***

Gladys Evans was shaping up to be another good distraction. Just two hours into my shift, I took a call from the manager of the local car dealership.

"She's locked herself in one of the vehicles," he reported. "You need to get down here and pull her out."

I ended the call with a heavy sigh, grabbed the keys to the patrol car and called out to Allan. He wandered out of his office with a cup of tea in one hand and a chocolate biscuit in the other.

"It's Gladys," I told him. "She's raising hell at the car yard."

He bit into his biscuit. "Welcome home, Constable Brannan," he replied, charging his cup of tea.

For the first time, I realised I was actually happy to be here. I'd tasted life on the wild side, and was safe in the knowledge that it wasn't for me.

"There's nothing wrong with life in the slow lane," I told him.

He grinned. "Keep your seatbelt on, just in case."

***

I heard Gladys long before I saw her, yahooing through the driver's side window as if the stationary car was moving a hundred miles an hour. When she saw us walking toward her, she frantically flapped her hands. "Get out of the way, coppers!"

Allan approached as if he was on a routine traffic stop. "Where are you headed, Gladys?" he calmly asked.

"The city," she barked. "I've got tickets for dinner and a show."

"Well, dinner at the station will be pretty decent tonight," he told her. "Maybe you'd like to go there instead."

Gladys gripped the steering wheel and gazed through the windscreen. "What about a show?" she asked.

"You're in luck." Allan opened the car door and gently helped her out of the car. "Young Shiloh's just spent two months in France," he told her. "She's been training at the Moulin Rouge."

The tanked old lady beamed at me. "Bloody marvellous!" she shrieked. "Count me in."

***

The cells at the Lawler lockup were Gladys' second home. I'd given up feeling bad for her. After spending time in a place where people suffered true hardship, it was hard to be sympathetic. She always got a warm bed and a hot meal, but the one thing she didn't get that day was a burlesque performance.

"I don't mind," she said. "I've never been a fan of musical theatre."

After giving her a few hours to sleep off the effects of her bender, I returned to the cell with coffee and a handful of the sergeant's chocolate biscuits. "Don't tell him," I said, handing them to her.

"I wouldn't tell an Irish copper anything," she replied, bringing her cup to her lips. "You can't trust 'em. They're nothing but a nation of drunks."

We weren't exactly run off our feet so when Gladys asked me to stay and chat for a while, I agreed.

"Tell me about your holiday," she demanded.

There really wasn't much that I could tell her, so I shared the parts that made me smile. "I saw fireworks in the desert at midnight and I saw the Atlantic ocean at dawn," I said wistfully.

The cup shook as she brought it to her lips. "Where did you stay?" she asked.

"In a grotty little shack on the beach. It was bliss."

Gladys dropped the biscuits on her lap and pinched her own cheeks. "You have colour in your face now," she said.

"A tan, you mean?"

She shook her head, making her frizzy grey hair even wilder. "No, Shiloh," she replied. "A flush of pink. It's very telling."

I shouldn't have been paying the silly old woman a skerrick of attention, but I couldn't help asking what she meant.

"Pink in the cheeks means warmth in the heart," she replied. "I can tell you've spent time kissing the sun."

I headed toward the door. "I have to get back to work."

"Tell me one more thing before you go."

I slowly turned around. "What would you like to know, Mrs Evans?"

"Was he handsome?"

"Who?"

Gladys chuckled so hard that her dentures began to slip out of her mouth. "The sun," she replied, still cackling as she shoved her teeth back into position. "No point kissing the sun unless he's handsome."

A picture of Mitchell flooded my mind. "He was perfect." I smiled brightly. "Handsome and sweet and strong and kind."

"But it didn't last?"

I felt my smile fade. "No."

"That's the problem with kissing the sun." She slapped her hand down on her knee. "It's just too darn hot to last forever."

"We gave it a good crack," I replied. "He loved me until he couldn't. That's all I asked for."

Two-Can Fran

MITCHELL

The first thing I missed about Kaimte was breakfast on the deck. I couldn't see the ocean from Jasmine and Wade's back veranda, but it was relatively peaceful until the happy couple decided to join me.

"What are you doing out here?" asked Jasmine.

I held up my mug. "Just enjoying a quiet cup of coffee."

She pointed to the stack of gym equipment to the right of me. I hadn't even noticed it before then, but obviously it bothered her. "It'd be better out here without all this junk."

Wade gasped. "This is not junk, Jas," he scolded. "It's very important equipment."

When he rushed over and wrapped his arm around the cross trainer, I wondered if he was about to kiss it.

"If you were married to a fisherman, there would be crab pots and fishing line everywhere," he told her. "You wouldn't stop him fishing."

Jasmine frowned. "Of course not."

"And if you were married to Mitchell, you wouldn't stop him surfing."

A strangled groan escaped me. The conversation was wrong to begin with, but now it was getting creepy.

"And if your husband was an artist," he continued, "You wouldn't stop him artist-ing, would you?"

I'd had all I could take. I handed my cup to my sister. "I'm out of here, Jasmine," I told her.

"Where are you going?"

"I'm not sure," I called without looking back. "I'll let you know when I get there."

***

The second thing I missed about Kaimte was my car. There's no bigger reminder that you've lost everything in the world than an aimless wander around town on foot.

Getting to the beach from Jasmine's house meant trekking down the main street. Floss Davis must've spotted me through her shop window as I passed. She came barrelling outside and pulled me into a tight hug. "It's good to have you back, lovie."

"Thanks, Floss."

She took a step back and looked me up and down. "How are you holding up?"

"What do you mean?" I had to ask. The pitying look on her face was awful. Perhaps I looked down and out.

Her hearty chuckle threw me straight back to my childhood. "I heard you were shacking up with Jasmine and Wade. That house is like a circus."

I grinned. "I'm hoping to make other arrangements soon."

I didn't sound anywhere near as desperate as I was.

"I might have an idea," she replied.

Floss turned around, and nearly ran into the bloke who was heading out the door. Far from apologetic, she collared him. "Adam, you remember Mitchell Tate?"

"Long time no see," he replied, extending his hand.

The gesture of shaking hands with Adam Décarie felt odd. It was fair to assume that we'd both done some serious growing up over the years, but the pointless juvenile tension was still there.

"Mitchell is looking for somewhere new to lay his hat," announced Floss. "I thought you might to be able to help him out."

Floss Davis had always been a little on the eccentric side, but if she was suggesting that I shack up with Adam and Charli, she was certifiably insane.

"It's fine," I quickly replied. "I've got it sorted."

I doubt she believed me, but she moved on. "Did you get your paint, Adam?"

"Norm is mixing it for me now."

"I'd better go and check on him," she said, shuffling toward the door. "He's a menace with a colour chart."

With Floss gone, the awkwardness intensified. I had no idea what to say, but Adam was a little more sociable. "If you are looking for somewhere to stay, I do have a place," he offered. "I'm renovating the shop next door to the old bank into a flat. It's not finished, but it's liveable."

The place he was talking about was just a few hundred metres further down the road. I didn't know if it would be suitable, but beggars can't be choosers. I thanked him and asked if I could check it out.

"Sure," he replied. "I was heading there anyway."

***

It didn't take me long to realise that the preconceived opinion I had of Adam was wrong. He wasn't arrogant like I expected him to be, and he wasn't stuck-up. He probably felt just as uncomfortable as I did, but he was the one who kept the conversation alive until we reached the shop.

"Charli is expecting you," he said. "Jasmine called her last night to let her know you were back in town."

"I can't wait to catch up. I've really missed her." The thoughtless comment was cringeworthy. "That didn't sound right at all, did it?"

"Relax, Mitchell." Adam laughed. "We're good."

"That's a relief." I looked at him and grinned. "I was worried you might think I'd come home to make a play for your wife."

"You'd be brave to try," he replied. "She's seven months pregnant. My house is a whole world of crazy at the moment."

I directed my laugh at the pavement. "Charli's always been crazy."

"I know," he agreed, jamming the key into the lock. "Luckily for me, I've always had a thing for crazy."

***

From the outside the old stone building was fairly non-descript, but the inside was a different story. The oak floor was polished, a brand new kitchen was in the process of being built, and the addition of a bedroom and bathroom had transformed an abandoned old shopfront into a neat little flat.

"You did this?" I asked, genuinely impressed.

Adam ran his hand down the nearest unpainted wall. "Yeah," he casually replied. "I'm halfway through restoring a boat, but took a break to work on this."

Construction wasn't Adam's trained profession. I was curious to know how a lawyer from New York had come to make such a wild career change.

He shrugged. "Sometimes you've just got to change course and choose the things that make you happy."

I wasn't in the right company to be having such a deep conversation, and Adam seemed to pick up on the fact that he'd touched on a raw nerve. He walked to the centre of the room. "It should be ready in a week or two if you're interested in renting it."

I glanced around the unfinished space, settling my attention on the half built kitchen. "That soon?" I asked.

"I'm keen to get it done and move on," he replied.

"To what?"

He picked up a broom off the floor and leaned it against the wall. "I'll probably finish the boat, but what I'd really like to get my hands on is the old brewery."

The brewery was a majestic old building located on the outskirts of town. After being vacant for more than fifty years, it cut an imposing figure. As a kid, I was terrified of the place, but I'd spent many Friday nights there as a teen getting smashed on cheap booze and partying with my mates.

"You can see the whole cove from the second floor of that joint," I remembered.

"I wouldn't know," he replied. "I haven't been able to get in there."

"I have." I grinned at him. "I lost my virginity on the second floor balcony."

He smirked. "Classy."

"Trust me, there was nothing classy about two-can Fran."

Adam punched out a hard laugh. "Well, it'd make a fantastic restaurant or bar, but so far it's a no-go," he explained. "Your dad refuses to sell it to me."

"That's because he doesn't own it."

My father owned a lot of real estate in Pipers Cove, but the Brewery wasn't part of his portfolio.

"But I did a title search," he said. "It's definitely Tate property."

I swept a sheet of plastic aside and peered out the window. "But you've been schmoozing the wrong Tate," I replied. "I own the brewery."

When my grandfather passed, he generously willed my sisters and I property. The girls got vacant farmland and I inherited a creepy old building.

"No kidding," he drawled in a serious New York twang. "I don't suppose you want to sell it to me?"

I might've been down on my luck and desperate, but I wasn't broke and desperate. "No," I replied. "But I also think it'd make a great pub. If you're interested in renovating it, I'd consider a joint venture."

It wasn't the sort of deal that could be brokered on the spot, but for the first time in days I felt a glimmer of hope that I could make things work if I stayed.

"Let me think about it and get back to you," Adam suggested. "In the mean time, maybe you should give two-can Fran a call and let her know you're back in town."

***

When it came to piecing my life back together, I was on a roll. I spent the rest of the day with Lily, who graciously offered to drive me to Hobart so I could buy a car. I settled on a red jeep, just like the one I'd recently gifted to

Mimi – except this one was twenty years younger and nowhere near as lethal when the windows were wound up.

"Are you sure you can afford it?" asked Lily, shamelessly kicking the front tyre. "It's a lot of money."

I was by no means rich, but I'd saved a decent nest egg over the years. It was hard to waste money in Kaimte because there was nothing there to spend it on. Most of the time we couldn't even buy decent food.

"I've got it covered, Lil," I assured her. "It's all about contingency."

She broke into a fit of giggles. "Yeah, you've got to be contingent."

***

By the time I finally made it to Charli's place, I'd been in town for three days. I wasn't expecting a hostile reception but the little girl who greeted me at the front step did her best to menace me. "Hark!" She threw out her hand, stopping me in my tracks. "Who goes there?"

"I'm Mitchell," I replied, pointing at the door. "Are you going to let me past?"

"Not yet." She wildly shook her head. "I have some questions for you."

I had some questions for her too. First, I wanted to know what hark meant.

"It means lovely things," she replied. "Are you ready for the other questions?"

"Go for it."

"Do you like golf?"

I shrugged. "I've never played golf."

Bridget clearly had. When Adam strolled out of the shed with a club in each hand, she leapt off the step and ran to him.

The club he gave her was almost taller than she was, but the little girl had no problem swinging it through the air like a baton.

"Lower your weapon, Bridget Décarie," her father ordered. "No swinging it around."

"I might not swing it," she replied.

Her ambiguous answer didn't cut it with Adam. "You raise that club above your head one more time and we're not going anywhere."

The kid must've really enjoyed golf. She lowered it to the ground in an instant. "But golf is lovely, Daddy. Sometimes you need to swing it."

With the exception of her blonde hair, Bridget looked like a mini version of Adam, but there was no mistaking who her mum was. She was still arguing the point as he strapped her into the car.

Adam might've had his work cut out for him, but when Charli came to the door, I knew I did too. "Three days," she grumbled. "You've been home three days and you're only just visiting me now?"

"Look at you," I crooned, cocking my head to the side. "Huffing and puffing like you're five-feet-six."

After a stiff slap on the arm, she grabbed my shirt and pulled me into a hug. "God, it's good to see you."

"You too, crazy weirdo." I took a step back, looking her up and down. "And there's plenty of you to see these days."

It wasn't a fair jibe. As little as Charli was, I might not have noticed the baby in her belly if I hadn't already been told about it.

She rubbed her hand across her stomach. "Massive, aren't I?"

I grinned at her. "The only thing massive about you is your mouth."

***

The cottage was supremely quiet, and I got the impression that was a rarity. We sat at the small dining room table sharing a pot of tea that I had no interest in drinking. What did interest me was talking. Over the next hour, I laid out the whole sorry saga, beginning with Shiloh and ending with Shiloh.

Understandably, most of Charli's curiosity centred on the diamond drama. She knew Melito and Vincent long before the mine was even open. "Do you think they were always crooked?" she asked.

I shrugged. "Who knows?"

"I'm sorry you went through that, Mitchell."

When I told her I'd been through worse, I was telling the absolute truth. And when a tight frown crossed her forehead, I knew she understood exactly where I was coming from.

"So what's your plan?" she asked. "How are you going to fix it?"

I almost smiled. "It's fixable?"

"It is if you want it to be."

"No, craziness, Charli," I mumbled. "Just tell me how to get through it."

She leaned across and flattened her palm against my chest. "You know that crushing feeling you have?"

"Yeah."

"And the ache in your bones?"

"Yes," I replied. "It's constant."

She pulled her hand away and straightened up. "Your brain thinks you're in actual pain," she said. "Only love can hurt like that."

It wasn't the deep and meaningful chat I was hoping for. As far as advice goes, she'd given me none – and her diagnosis sucked.

"You love her, Mitchell," she added. "And I can guarantee it's not because of any lie she told you. You weren't duped into feeling that way."

"Of course I was," I complained. "Everything she ever told me was a lie – even her name."

She reached for the teapot and refilled her cup. "So let me understand," she replied. "You love her because she spun a good story?"

Heartbreak wasn't the only pain I had going on at that moment. Frustration was rising. "No," I grumbled. "I love her because she smells like the ocean, and she's unbelievably sweet."

Charli smiled. "Those are good reasons."

"She stayed awake all night when I was hurt, just to keep an eye on me," I added. "And she encouraged me to come home and reconnect with my family. That's why I love her."

Ramble over, Charli stood up and carried the teapot to the sink. "No one is perfect, Mitchell," she said gently. "And when you stop expecting them to be, love is a much easier game to play."

"I wanted her to be perfect," I muttered. "I thought she was the one."

She leaned forward, resting her elbows on the counter as she asked a random question. "Do you know why your pub was called the Crown and Pav?"

I had no clue. I'd never even wondered.

She slipped her wedding ring off and held it to the light. "It's short for Crown and Pavilion – the angles of a cut diamond," she explained. "The crown is the top part." Charli put the ring back on and held out her hand. "The pavilion is the pointy lower half."

"Make your point, Blake."

"Raw diamonds are nothing special. They're just ugly rocks," she replied. "But once they're cut, they become interesting and lovely." The visual prop on her finger shimmered as she rolled her wrist. "People are the same, Mitchell. Perfection doesn't exist. We need the angles."

Charli's take on the world was so left of centre that only she understood it. Fortunately her brilliant storytelling made it possible for idiots like me to learn a thing or two.

"Thank you for dazzling me with magic." I dipped my head at her. "I needed it today."

"That wasn't magic," she replied, smiling. "That was me being scientific and logical."

"Well, it was perfect."

"So you're going to go and find her?" she asked hopefully.

"I don't even know where she lives," I replied. "I barely know her name."

"I know where she is." Charli walked to the couch and rifled through her handbag. "I got a parcel in the mail yesterday." She dropped an envelope down in front of me.

"What is it?"

She nudged my arm. "Have a look, stupid."

When I upended it, Charli's black opal necklace tumbled onto the table. I blinked a hundred times, stunned. "I haven't seen this in years."

"Me neither," she replied, nudging me again. "Read the letter."

A one-line note could hardly be called a letter. In true Shiloh style, it was short and to the point:

Paying forward the good juju.
Shiloh

My eyes drifted to the pendant on the table. "I'm glad you got it back, Charli."

"Me too." She slapped my shoulder. "And you can thank Shiloh for me when you go and get her."

"I told you, I don't know where she is."

She had the nerve to slap me again, harder this time. I whipped my head around to look at her. "You're very violent when you're knocked up," I complained. "Stop hitting me."

"And you're an idiot when you're sad and heartbroken," she replied. "Stop being an idiot."

Charli turned the envelope over and thumped it down on the table. "Look at the postmark. She's in a place called Lawler. Google it, find out where it is and go there."

I deliberated for too long, which pissed Charli off. "You're still looking for a reason to go?" she asked incredulously.

"Maybe."

I wasn't sure why I was dragging my feet. The fear of the unknown is a powerful beast.

"Let's go," she ordered. "Logic didn't work, I'm going to give you magic."

I was almost scared of her by that point. Without a single word of protest I followed the grumpy pregnant woman out to her car.

***

When we were kids, the brewery wasn't the scariest place in town. It was trumped by a derelict little cottage that stood four doors down from the supermarket. When Charli pulled up in front of it, I was convinced she'd lost her mind.

"Crazy Edna's house?" I choked. "You're off your rocker if you think I'm going in there."

She undid her seatbelt and then made a grab for mine. "I can do it," I snapped.

She pulled a face. "So do it."

I leaned closer to her and put on my best creepy voice. "I hope she cuts off your hair and boils your bones, Charlotte."

"She won't," she insisted. "Edna's retiring. That's why we're here."

"You can't retire crazy."

"She's not crazy, Mitchell," she replied. "She's magic. I've seen it firsthand."

As antsy as Charli was to get out of the car, I managed to hold her back until she told me the reason for our impromptu visit, and it had nothing to do with magic. "She's having a garage sale," she explained. "Poor Edna can't live in this shabby old house any more. Her sons have arranged for her to move into a nursing home."

I shrugged. "What does that have to do with us?"

"Well, you're moving into your own place soon."

I could feel the frown creeping across my face. Something awful was on the way.

"You need furniture." She threw open her door. "And Edna's selling everything."

There was nothing appealing about furnishing a house with a creepy old lady's hand-me-downs, but Charli didn't see a problem with it.

"We're not buying a thing," I warned, trailing behind her. When we stepped onto the porch, I repeated the declaration. "Nothing, Charli."

She lifted the brass knocker and rapped on the door. "Okay," she finally agreed. "We're just window shopping."

I'd dealt with Mimi's witchy nonsense for years, but she'd never instilled the same level of fear that Edna Wilson did. Even as a grown man, my heart was thumping when she opened the door.

"Hi, Mrs Wilson." Charli's sickly sweet tone didn't suit her one bit. "We're here for the garage sale."

"It doesn't start until tomorrow, dear." Edna's voice was shaky, but very kind for someone who'd made a career of eating small children. "Come in, anyway," she added.

Edna showed us through to the front room. "Everything has to go," she said, waving a shaky hand through the air. "Pick what you like. I'll leave you alone to browse."

As soon as she was out of earshot, Charli pounced. "So what do you reckon?" she asked excitedly. "See anything you like?"

I pointed at a crystal ball on the table. "How about that?"

Charli picked it up and turned it over. "Put that down," I hissed. "That's got to be bad juju."

Cackling like a true witch, she did as she was told. "Come on, Mitchell. There must be something you like."

I saw nothing but the ancient props of an old charlatan who'd spent her lifetime conning money from people.

Charli pointed to the wall behind me. "Dried starfish?"

I screwed up my nose. "No."

She laughed, and when I caved in and turned around to check out the dead starfish, she laughed harder.

"Aw, look," she drawled. "I'm pretty sure this bloke is one of Adam's relatives."

I turned around to see an ugly little black dog standing in the doorway. Nothing made me want to go near it. Even from a distance I could tell that it stunk. "It's a French Bulldog," I told her.

Making allowance for her baby belly, Charli crouched down as best she could. "That's what I said," she replied, patting its head. "One of Adam's distant rellies."

I couldn't focus on Charli's nonsense. I was too busy focusing on my own. "Shiloh wants a French bulldog," I remembered. "She's going to call it Peppermint."

I cringed as I said it but Charli wasn't fazed by the strange name choice.

"To each her own," she replied. "My kid has a doll called Treasure."

I reached for Charli's hand and helped her to her feet.

"This is a sign, Mitchell," she said, pointing at the dog as if she was casting a spell. "You wanted magic. There he is."

"I never said I wanted magic," I argued. "And I'm sure he's not for sale."

"He is a she," announced Edna, returning to the room. "And everything is for sale. I can't look after her any more." She smiled, though it had a rueful tinge. "We're both getting too old."

"What's her name?" I asked.

"Patricia," she announced grandly. "Derived from the Latin word *Patrician*."

Charli chimed in. "What does it mean?"

"Noble." Edna tapped the side of her nose and leaned in close. "But your wordsmith husband could have told you that."

Charli smiled but I missed the joke.

Edna turned to me, terrorising me with her intense stare. "I want to show you something."

When the old lady turned around and grabbed a jar of sand of a shelf, Charli intervened. Perhaps she knew what was coming. "Mitchell's not interested in a reading, Mrs Wilson."

Edna carried on as if she hadn't spoken, dumping the jar on the table and spreading the sand with her hands. "If the winds prevail from the east, the dunes will run north to south." Her eyes never left mine as she dragged her fingers through the sand. "Tell me why."

When I opened my mouth to speak, no sound followed. I cleared my throat and tried again. "Because sand dunes form at ninety degrees to the prevailing wind."

The old lady smiled brightly, looking far friendlier than before.

"That's very impressive, Mitchell," praised Charli. "How do you know that?"

"Because Shiloh told me," I replied, bewildered. "And as far as I know, Mrs Wilson wasn't there at the time."

Charli gripped my arm just as hard as she'd slapped me. "I told you," she whispered. "It's magic."

I expected a moment of magic to be serene and tranquil, but the stinky bulldog killed that notion by wandering over and sniffing my leg.

Edna clicked her fingers and called her back. "Patty, come here."

Charli lost the plot. "You have to take her now," she insisted, nearly pulling my arm out of the socket.

I grabbed her hand, trying to keep her still. "Why?"

Charli flashed me the biggest grin I'd ever seen her make. "Because she belongs to Shiloh." She pointed to the dog at my feet. "It's Peppermint Patty."

***

After sitting on a plane for four hours, hiring a car and driving south for another five, I came to the conclusion that Lawler might as well have been on a different planet. On the plus side, if I turned up at Shiloh's door and she told me to take a hike, the chances of running into her again were nil.

It took me two months to work up the courage to track her down, but when a sign on the roadside alerted me that I was only ten kilometres out of town, fear reared its ugly head.

I knew I was stalling when I pulled into the fuel station, and the act of filling the car with petrol it didn't need was as cowardly as they come, but I did it.

Part of me was ready to call the whole thing off and skulk home, but as I stood at the bowser and mindlessly watched the numbers tick over, I realised a different part was winning.

I loved Shiloh, and that trumped fear.

Just as I hung the pump up, a small white car pulled up on the other side of the bowser.

And that's where my journey ended.

Shiloh didn't even notice me. She got out, lifted the pump and got on with the job of filling her car.

My position didn't change, mainly because I was unable to move. Seconds passed like hours and it was becoming impossible to believe she couldn't see me standing there.

Trying to catch her attention, I moved closer.

Nothing.

When I waved and still got no response, I knew she was intentionally blanking me.

"I thought police officers were supposed to be observant," I called.

"They are." I almost jumped at the sound of her voice. "I see you, Mitchell."

I walked over to her. "And you're just going to ignore me?"

"Our last meeting didn't go so well," she replied. "I figured it might be best to let sleeping dogs lie."

Feigning indifference, I folded my arms and shrugged. "Makes sense, I guess."

She turned around and hung the pump up. "But now that you've spoken to me, it's an awkward chance meeting that's likely to cause us both damage."

"Shiloh, how can it possibly be a chance meeting?" I dropped my hands to my sides. "I'm four thousand kilometres from home."

Finally she looked at me – and I saw nothing but hurt. "You should've stayed home," she told me. "There's nothing here for you."

"You're here."

"I got over you, Mitchell," she growled. "Why would you come here and dredge it all up again?"

I wasn't convinced that Shiloh was over anything. There was too much venom in her tone.

"I have no plans of dredging up a single day of the past," I assured her. "I'm only interested in going forward."

"There's no point then," she replied. "Because I happen to like our past."

"All of it?"

"Even the bad days." She stepped closer and lowered her voice. "And trust me, my bad days were entirely different to yours."

I had to concede that there was some serious backtracking to be done. To this day I had no idea what her job in Kaimte had entailed, and the reason why was simple. She'd protected me from it.

"Giving you a hard time for lying to me wasn't fair," I told her. "I should never have done that."

Finally, I seemed to have touched on the right words to say. Her stance relaxed as if a tonne weight had been lifted off her.

"You want to know the worst part?" she asked.

I nodded but didn't mean it. I was trying to bring love and roses back, not doom and gloom.

"I knew it was going to end badly," she said. "Right from the start."

I took her hand – and she let me. "It should never have ended at all," I told her. "We should've come home and picked up where we left off."

"But we didn't."

"And that's my fault, Shiloh." I gave her hand a squeeze. "I own that one."

"I couldn't go through it again, Mitchell." Her voice was so quiet that I struggled to hear her. "It's too much to cope with."

I took a step back. "I understand," I said sadly. "But it's not the outcome I was hoping for. I've no idea how I'm going to break the news to Patty."

"Who's Patty?"

"My French bulldog," I replied. "She was looking forward to meeting you."

Shiloh smiled for the first time. "You're lying."

I grabbed my wallet from my pocket and pulled out a picture. "This is one of the better shots of her," I explained. "You can't see her underbite."

The photo shook in her hand as she burst into a fit of giggles.

"I miss your laugh," I told her.

Her eyes drifted upward, locking my gaze in hers. "I'm leaving," she told me. "You literally caught me on the way out of town."

I looked across at her car. The back seat was packed to the hilt with luggage. "Where are you going?"

She shrugged. "I have a plane ticket to Melbourne. Beyond that, I'm not sure."

"You quit your job?"

"Not exactly," she replied. "I'm owed a lot of time off so I thought it might be a good time to get away for a while."

"Well, I know of the perfect place." Playing it cool was impossible, but I tried. "It's a little town on the east coast of Tassie."

"Sounds lovely."

"I could take you there," I offered. "Show you the sights, introduce you to a few people, that kind of thing."

"Do you think we could be happy there, Mitchell?" she asked. "In a little Tassie town?"

"I guarantee it." I took her face in my hands and gently kissed her. "We're going to fall hopelessly in love, and then things are really going to get good."

THE END